~~ A prelude to ~~

Off The Moon

The book called Powerful, Raw, Compelling, Visceral,
Romantic, Intelligent, Intriguing...

Nearly a decade before Ryan and Kaitlyn
came
Daws and Deanna
in a clash and blend of spirits.

There is no greater love...

"Die when I may, I want it said by those who knew me best
that I always plucked a thistle and planted a flower
where I thought a flower would grow."
Abraham Lincoln

Also by LK Hunsaker

Finishing Touches (2003)

Rehearsal: A Different Drummer (2006)

Rehearsal: The Highest Aim (2008)

Off The Moon (2009)

Protect The Heart (2010)

Stanley: A Raindrop's Story (2010)

Dedication

To the Shepherds...

Acknowledgements

First, to those who read *Off The Moon* and asked for more of Daws.
This is for you.

With thanks to the following for assistance with military research:
Jack & Annette McRoberts, Carrie & Sean O'Kelley, Paul Phipps,
and especially
my own Sergeant First Class (Ret.), Rulon Hunsaker.

Also, many thanks to my beta readers and editors who made this book
better than it would have been otherwise: Liz Hunsaker, Maureen
Schneider, Carrie O'Kelley, Annette McRoberts, and Dorothy Murphy.

Thanks to Eric Hunsaker for being the head and shoulder model, and for
knowing right off what the buildings were; to Kelli Eyer for providing
that bit of football knowledge I didn't have, and to Kathi Hawkins for beta
reading and website management.

Finally, to all of our Armed Forces, past and present.
Hooah!

Moondrops & Thistles

A Novel

LK Hunsaker

ISBN 978-0-9825299-6-6

Cover art: LK Hunsaker

elucidate publishing
staff@elucidatepublishing.net
PO Box 1262, Hermitage PA 16137

United States of America

This novel is also available in electronic format, in both full version and shorter and spicer version.

PART 1

"The good shepherd lays down his life for the sheep."
John 10:11

=== January 1991 ===

A downpour either way he turned. Opting for the lesser storm, Daws walked away from the television and toward the one small window in the sparse room. Lightning flashed thin streaks in the distance. He was drawn to it the way he was drawn to artillery fire in the night. He always enjoyed night training, the way the howitzers shot their rounds high up into nothingness and left a trail of smoke, now and then with a burst of flame. He especially enjoyed the rare bursts of flame. After tonight, he wasn't sure that enjoyment would last. The call would come. He could do nothing but wait for it.

Thoughts of home surfaced, but he couldn't go. He had leave time saved. It wouldn't matter. They were on stand-by. All leave was cancelled.

Not that he had any particular reason to be home. No one was there to worry if he was there or anywhere else, but it was still home. He'd found that thought increasingly important over his ten years of service. After seven years of moving at the whims of the Army, he'd put in for his current duty station as a condition of reenlistment. He was now at least close enough to get back to the city with an easy five and a half hour drive. Daws had a fleeting thought that he should have gone drill and requested Fort Dix. Would've been closer. Maybe he still would.

"The liberation of Kuwait has begun."

At Fitzwater's voice, Daws yanked his eyes back to the screen. Apache helicopters had struck Baghdad and Kuwait. A shiver crawled through his body into his soul. He was prepared, as well as a man could be prepared for the journey into something unknown. His mind was set for it to happen. Still, he wasn't gung ho waiting and hoping, as a few he knew. Very few. Most were resolved, aware it was their job, what they'd signed up to do if ever necessary, what they'd trained to do. They would happily go on about their business if the call didn't come, however.

It would.

He turned from the dull light of the room to the barely dark outside the window, to raindrops reflecting the building's security light as they fell, to tree branches whipped by rushing wind. Thunder rumbled louder, announcing the storm's advance. Appropriate.

A sharp ring startled him, even though he was waiting for it.

As he turned the television down and grabbed the receiver, he managed to pull his well-taught military bearing into his voice, as well as his stance. "Dawson."

"Sergeant. I assume you're watching the news."

"Yes, Major."

"I wanted to be the first to let you know, although your lieutenant will send out the formal announcement within the hour. We leave tomorrow."

Tomorrow. He'd hoped for a couple of days. Still, they'd been warned. "My men will be ready."

"I have no doubt." The major's voice was calm, light. As always. "At ease, Sergeant. I can feel you at attention even through the phone."

"Yes, Sir."

A light chuckle preceded a pause. "Fred, it'll be good to have you at my back."

He faltered at the use of his first name. Only for a second. "I will be proud to be there, Sir. And I intend for every one of my men to come home."

"God willing."

Daws tried not to hear the doubt in his major's voice. "Sir?"

"Yes?"

"Your family knows?"

"Yes. Just now. They'll be fine. Marianne is a strong woman. If not for the boys, she'd likely re-up and go with. Will is here to help. I only hope he doesn't go off and get married while I'm away."

Images of things to come flashed on the silent television screen as Daws made himself listen enough to hear without allowing it to sink in too far. "I have no doubt he'll wait for your return."

"I imagine so, even if it has to be during leave. I do hope for a short deployment as they predict, for all of us. Now go out and enjoy your last night of freedom for some time to come."

"Have to call my men."

"Yes. After your lieutenant calls, and don't let on you already know. No point him getting his nose out of joint because I broke protocol."

"Wouldn't dream of it, Sir."

"You're a good man, Sergeant. Never thought I'd see war again before I retired, but since it's in the cards, I'm more at ease knowing you and your men are on my team." He waited only a moment when Daws didn't answer. "Go out and enjoy yourself tonight. This storm should blow by fast with as fast as it came in."

"God willing." Daws knew Major Reynauld meant the lightning storm. He also knew the major would realize he didn't.

Hanging up, he returned his attention to the silent television and some guy in a suit and tie trying to look appropriately concerned as he relayed whatever they decided the public should know. Daws walked over, clicked it off, and went to the window. The lightning was right on top of them now. He'd heard the crackle over the line when it struck. He hoped it wouldn't turn into an ice storm, since the temperature was hovering barely high enough to keep it liquid.

Tomorrow. Most of his men had young wives or girlfriends, some with children. Daws was thankful he didn't have a spouse and child to leave behind. He would be better able to assist his men without his attention distracted.

He did need to call Sonya, although he wasn't convinced what they had was enough to label her a girlfriend. She had to know he was leaving. He would do that first. It would be easier than calling his men.

Waiting through several rings, Daws nearly hung up before he heard the breathless greeting. "Did I call at a bad time?" He lowered onto his couch.

"No worse than your usual timing. What's up? I was on the treadmill."

"Sorry."

"Can I call you back?"

"Quick question and I'll let you go. Have plans tonight?"

"Not really, only ... wait, it's a weekday. You have to be up at o-dark-thirty, right? You want to go out tonight?"

"Maybe I'll just drop by for a quick dinner. I'll bring it. Sound okay? Won't stay long." He got up again, walked around behind the couch, and checked on the storm. It was lessening, the rumbles quieter, more distant.

"Well, how about I call delivery and let them run around in the rain to save you getting soaked?"

He considered changing his mind and asking her to go out, somewhere around others. Somewhere not too quiet. But he wasn't sure how she'd react when he told her. "I'll be wet anyway. No need to pull them out."

"So this way you'll be less wet, and I'll tip them for it. Come on over. What time?"

Giving himself an hour, he was barely off the phone when it rang again. His lieutenant. Daws did his best to act unaware. Seemed to work.

Two of his men were out and he left messages for them to return the call as soon as possible. As he waited, he ran through the shower. Jumping back out again at another ring, he wrapped himself in a towel and went to break it to the next to last. Corporal Jenkins, with a six month old daughter he never stopped talking about. And he tried the last one again. No answer. He went to get dressed and tried once more just before he left. He'd call from Sonya's place if needed. Luckily, the private picked up. He didn't take it well. He had a new girlfriend; he needed a few days for her to let it settle in. When his rambling went on too long, Daws called him to attention and told him he'd been warned, that if she was still around when he got back, he'd know she thought he was worth the wait. If not, she wasn't worth the worry.

Daws didn't have much confidence Sonya would think he was worth the wait, but he supposed he could be wrong.

=======

"*Moron.*" Deanna swiveled back toward her desk and half wished the man would have heard her. She supposed that would be grounds to get fired, though. Maybe she didn't care.

Of course she cared.

At twenty-seven, she expected to be more than just assistant to a production manager. She did more of his work for him than she was paid for, or that was ever acknowledged. She'd been at the top of her classes, even while supporting herself with the waitress job that quickly led to the hostess job – she had great people skills. Her mother used to say it would be her saving grace, if she could rein it in and throw it the right direction. Deanna long ago decided marketing was the right direction. She could talk her way out of, or into, most anything. She critiqued every commercial and every advertisement, seeing things she'd do differently. Maybe she wasn't always right, but she could always convince someone she was. She had her hard-earned business associates, strong in English, along with her graphic art certificate. And she had six years with the same company. Whatever the socio-political scene these days said, advertising was still a man's business and harder for her to be granted the respect she'd earned.

But that was the game and Deanna would keep playing it while she worked her way up. Not the way he wanted her to do it, either, the slime ball. So she wore her skirts fitted instead of baggy and droopy. She wasn't droopy. There was nothing at all droopy about her and she wouldn't pretend otherwise. All those mornings at the gym weren't for nothing. It didn't mean he had the right to assume she was what she wasn't.

Moron. All men were nothing but morons. A shame she still needed, wanted, one of them. Not *that* one, though. Not if her boss was the last man on earth. Well, maybe then. After all, he did have the right parts. At least she assumed he did.

Allowing herself a chuckle and hoping if it ever came to getting stuck with the last man on earth that his parts would be worthy of the task, Deanna dropped the folder holding next week's potential schedule onto her desk and checked the time. Ten more minutes. Then she could walk out of the metal and glass excuse for a building and find somewhere more quaint. There were still a few quaint bars in Manhattan. Some still had pretty brick or stone fronts instead of metal and glass. Of course, they all held the same scum-bag mentality men: looking for one thing and pretending otherwise. Such a difference from her little hometown. Kentucky didn't have much to offer as far as the kind of job she wanted, but it did have real men who weren't afraid to get their hands dirty or open a door for a lady. Men who still said ma'am and please and thank you. She had no doubt they were looking for the same thing, but at least they were more often polite while doing it.

If only she had a good reason to go back and visit. Maybe she could find one of those willing to move to New York with her. She chuckled again. Not likely. And not in the time she'd be able to afford to take off from work.

When the phone rang, she glared at it. Five minutes till quitting time. Did she have to answer? With a sigh, she figured she did.

"McCallister and Sons. This is Deanna. How can I help you?"

"Have I told you recently how much I love your sexy voice over the phone?"

She controlled a grin and glanced over to find him behind the glass in the next office. "Have I told you recently you shouldn't call me here? You'll get me fired."

"Of course I won't. I would never do anything to hurt such a sexy, incredible woman."

"Yeah, okay. I'm old enough to know a line when I hear it. And it's time to get out of here, so you'll have to find a better line tomorrow." She reached down in her drawer to claim her little black handbag.

"Deanna, don't hang up."

"Why shouldn't I?"

"I'll be at Verlaine's just down the street for an hour or so after work. I hope I might run into you there."

Verlaine's. The fancy French-style bar-lounge. She'd been there once, not for long. "Can't do it, Todd."

"Big plans tonight?"

"Oh, yes. I have a big night planned: a private spa and a bottle of Italian wine, a dozen roses, and the most gorgeous hunk I've ever laid eyes on."

Silence came from the other end. "Oh. Well."

"I'm teasing." Deanna played with the file on her desk as though she was working, but she was tempted to look over to get his reaction. "Turn the spa into a skinny shower stall and the wine into a hard lemonade, the roses into a half-dead houseplant, and you'll be closer."

"And the hunk?"

"Patrick Duffy. I taped Dallas the other night and have a date with my television."

He laughed. "Well, maybe I can do better than a night of lemonade and television."

"Hard lemonade, and you can't. I'll get fired."

"No, you won't. Promise."

"How can you promise that? I don't work for you."

"Let's just say I know things about that boss of yours he doesn't want anyone else to know, including the way he keeps trying to grope you."

"How do you know that?" She looked over at him.

"I pay attention. And I'll put an end to it. Meet me tonight. Let's talk."

Everything inside Deanna told her to turn him down. Dangerous territory. Way too dangerous. But, he was close enough to a hunk. He was cute as heck; she couldn't deny that. And he was smart. Classy. He even held the elevator for her once by pressing a finger against the 'open door' button. It wasn't quite the same as a strong arm reaching around to pull a heavy door open, but it was more than many did these days.

"I'll meet you in the lounge area. Look forward to it." Todd hung up, the air of victory hanging in the tone of his voice.

She should have refused. She still could. Her lemonade and VCR were waiting for her. The mostly dead plant. The skinny shower she bumped her elbows on.

Maybe it wouldn't hurt to accidentally run into him, only for an hour or so, to enjoy some good conversation and a glass of wine before she went home alone.

========

The rain was only sputtering by the time Daws got to Sonya's apartment. As soon as his coat was off, she greeted him with a kiss and pulled him in toward the couch. "Food's here. Smells incredible, nearly started without you." She plopped down and grabbed one of the dishes.

Sonya talked about her day as they ate Thai food on paper plates with plastic forks. He liked Thai; he liked most anything, but he would have preferred an actual plate and fork. He wouldn't insult her by suggesting the idea.

"So." She dropped her empty plate on the coffee table and turned to him, pulling a socked foot up on the couch between them, her arms around the bent leg. "What brought you over tonight? You usually insist we wait for a weekend. Miss me? Or just looking to get lucky?"

"Last chance for a while. To come over."

"Why?"

Using the Guinness she'd brought him as an excuse to stall, he grabbed a quick swallow. "Heading overseas in the morning."

"What?" She dropped the foot back to the floor. "How long have you known? And you didn't tell me?"

"Sonya, I just got the call. We're heading to Kuwait."

She stared as though he told her she had to go with him. Then she bolted up from the couch and turned to stare again. "No, you're not. You tell them you won't go."

"You know I can't do that."

"Of course you can. We have no business there, anyway. For what? Stupid oil? Tell them no."

Daws grabbed a deep breath and stood to meet her. "That's not what it's about, and I have orders. I leave tomorrow."

"No. Fred, you tell them you won't go."

"Sonya, this is what I am. You knew that when we met." He grasped her hands, hoping for at least a somewhat peaceful send-off, if not more than that.

"I didn't expect you to actually ... fight. You know I don't believe in it."

"And yet you're dating a soldier. Not the first time, either."

She balked a bit at his reference to the two she'd mentioned having dated before him, more than once. "Well, playing around on post with guns is one thing. It's target practice. No harm in that."

"What do you think we're practicing for?"

"But I didn't think you'd ever ... it's like grown up Boy Scouts. Camping. Fishing. Shooting targets. Macho stuff that's really sexy, but..."

"You know it's not the same."

"I know we shouldn't be there. We have no right."

Daws nearly backed off. There was never much point in arguing the issue. This time, he couldn't. "If someone invaded your house, you wouldn't fight them off?"

"That's different. And no one invaded our house. It's someone else's house, not our problem."

"Isn't it? What if our policemen felt that way?"

"That's different."

He moved closer and caught her eyes. "Have any idea what's going on over there? How they've invaded people's homes and are murdering them by the hundreds? There's not one woman or child safe..."

"Their own government should stop it. Or someone over there. Not us. Not you. Why should I risk losing you for someone I don't know?"

"It's the *government* doing it, a strong country against a smaller one. How do they fight against that? And do you think it'll stop there? With Kuwait? It won't. It'll keep spreading like it did when Hitler took Czechoslovakia and everyone ignored it, until he then took Poland and joined forces with Mussolini and ... it'll keep going until we're not safe here, either. There's more behind it than you realize..."

"It's not Hitler. It's just a little country. They're not bothering us. We don't have the right to interfere."

Daws dropped his eyes and bit his tongue. "All right, I can't argue with you tonight. I wanted to tell you in person..."

She pulled her hands from his. "If you do this, you do it without my blessing, and don't ask me to feel sorry for you or..."

"I have *never* asked anyone to feel sorry for me." Daws held his position and her eyes until she turned away. With a deep breath, he nodded. "I think there's nothing more to say." He went to put his coat on and paused at the door. "Take care, Sonya. I wish you well."

She looked at him but did nothing to stop him.

He walked out. There was so much he wanted to say to her but he didn't have the energy. There would be enough fighting to come. He didn't need it on his last night of freedom, freedom he would have to give up temporarily in order to help secure Kuwait's freedom. He couldn't help wonder how she would feel if a stronger nation ever tried to annex the U.S. Would she still think everyone else should stay out of it because it wasn't their problem? Daws sure as hell hoped they wouldn't. He also wouldn't stand by and watch his neighbor's house get invaded and do nothing. It wasn't different. Invaders never stopped until someone stopped them. History had proven that throughout the centuries, both small and large scale. Success made victors stronger. That couldn't happen with this regime. It was far too dangerous. Large scale dangerous.

Trying to put the thought aside, Daws considered heading to the NCO club for more pleasant company. Stepping outside changed his mind; the rain had turned into sleet. It pelted the back of his neck and he turned his collar up. He'd rather be home alone the rest of the night than risk driving on freezing roads. If he had his druthers, he'd spend the night in his actual home, but New York City was too far a drive for only one short night, even in good weather. And he wasn't allowed that far away.

========

As she stepped inside Verlaine, Deanna pulled out of her coat and wrapped it in on itself in order to keep the wet outer layer from brushing against anyone. At least the place was warm. She expected the rain might turn into snow overnight, or worse, ice. She shivered thinking of it.

"How 'bout I buy you a drink to help you warm up?"

She turned her eyes to a man at her side. Way too much hair. It was in his eyes and along his chin, to the extent she could hardly see anything else. And he was short, too short for her five feet and seven inches, plus three inch heels. "Thanks. I'm meeting someone." Deanna hadn't yet decided whether or not to act like she was there specifically to hang out with Todd. Maybe she'd act uninterested and keep some distance while she viewed this bit of his personal life. You couldn't tell personality well enough at work; in order to know them, you had to see them outside the office. She'd learned that lesson.

Verlaine was made for socializing, not for privacy. Even on a work night in the cold rain, the long bar and row of tables for two placed side-by-side were relatively full. Candles added light to the dim modern interior. The tall ceilings helped minimize the crowded feel and muffle the voices. Not that she minded crowds. Or noise. And she enjoyed the eclectic music selection. Jazz at the moment. It was nice. She hoped they'd avoid techno, though. She could happily live without that.

"Looking for someone in particular, or will I do?"

She tried hard not to roll her eyes and instead brushed the stranger off gently without more than a glance, then remembered Todd said he'd be in the lounge area. Of course. Sitting at the bar wouldn't look elegant enough for him. He'd be on the couch, likely in one corner.

It didn't take long to find him there, and to find she was right. A redhead was flirting with him, drink in hand, legs crossed so her short dress fell well off her legs toward her thighs. Deanna held back and ordered Ginger Sake from a passing waiter. She'd have only one to help get warm and to help convince herself she belonged in Todd's crowd. She didn't, of course, but she'd learned well how to act like she belonged wherever she was.

He only somewhat flirted with the girl in return, and pulled back when she tried to move in against him. Whatever he said appeared to appease her well enough. She didn't quite stop flirting.

With drink in hand, Deanna ambled toward him. She spoke to a woman briefly who complimented her hair, assuring her the color and curl were natural so she didn't have a hairdresser name to share, and gave the man beside her a very quick casual grin at his smile. Then she moved along.

Todd rose when he spotted her and beckoned her over; at the same time, he crowded the flirting girl farther away until she moved. Very slick. And effective. He touched Deanna's arm, barely, professionally. "Imagine running into you here. Will you join us?" He gave a nod toward a few others, from the office. His coworkers.

"I suppose I can for a few minutes. I thought I was meeting someone, but I must have been mistaken." Accepting the space next to him, Deanna had to wonder if he didn't realize they would be there, or if he knew very well they would.

"We've ordered several tapas. Spring rolls, portabellas, calamari. Any of it sound all right or should I add to the order?"

"No need. If my friend arrives, we'll have the shrimp tempura. If not, I won't stay long enough to matter." She sipped her drink with a quick catch of his eyes and skim of his body. The jacket he had on at work earlier was gone, as was the tie. His shirt was unbuttoned nearly as low as the V of her blouse. His build was decent, although she figured he could stand to step away from the desk now and then and pump up the muscles. Still, he was worth a look. Or two.

Todd caught her perusing him as he stopped a waitress and added shrimp tempura to the order. "This way you'll have them already if he does show, or if he doesn't. My treat."

"Did I say it was a he?"

"I suppose I assumed."

"Never a good idea." Suddenly, Deanna wished she'd gone on home alone for her date with Patrick Duffy and her big comfy robe, plus a large plate of leftover spaghetti.

"I don't think I've seen you here before." Lenny, from Todd's creative team, eyed her over his Bloody Mary.

"Unlikely you would have." Deanna crossed her legs, noting Todd's careful glance at them as she did. "I've only been once."

"Yeah? Funny you happened to hit our monthly after-work wind down."

"Is that what this is? Guess it is funny. It wasn't intentional; I try hard to leave work behind at night. No offense."

Todd interrupted Lenny's response. "Is it a date you're meeting?" He shifted closer. "Since you didn't say and I shouldn't assume."

"No." She touched his eyes. "Only an acquaintance."

"Is that so? And yet you agreed to meet at a place you don't generally come and you don't seem awfully fond of. Interesting."

Deanna took a sip of her Sake and shrugged. "Not so interesting. I'm open to new experiences. At least once. Sometimes even twice." She relished how hard Todd had to try not to react.

"Twice would mean it isn't a new experience, though." Lenny didn't bother to hide how he admired her legs.

She waited to answer until he finished and remembered where her face was. "Not necessarily true."

"How isn't it?" He leaned in, his elbows propped on his legs, his eyes on her.

"Well, the same act, done differently, or doing something different in the same place, makes the experience new, doesn't it? For instance, if the first time you're here, you sit and talk business and go home alone, but the next time you decide to walk around and find someone separate from business, maybe someone you want to take home when you go, that's a whole new experience. Is it not?"

Lenny rubbed his lips together, staring. Todd nearly choked on his martini. Deanna pretended not to notice he did as Lenny kept her gaze.

"Maybe. Although either way, there's a chance you'll get screwed."

Deanna grinned and raised her glass to him. "Touché. And on that note, I should get out of your way." She let her glance flow around the small group. "I didn't mean to interfere and it looks like my acquaintance isn't going to show..."

Todd touched her arm. "You're not interfering."

"Not at all." Lenny jumped in, with apparent refusal to allow Todd to grab her attention. "You're in admin, right?"

Deanna sipped the Sake and noted Todd move again; this time his lower leg pressed into hers, under the table enough the coworkers wouldn't see. "I'm lead assistant to the production manager. At the moment."

"At the moment? You plan to move elsewhere?"

Todd cleared his throat. "No work talk tonight. That's the rule, if you'll remember." He threw a pointed stare at his colleague.

It worked well enough and Deanna was glad to have the focus off her. She listened to the two men and three women banter about sports and families and such. The flirting girl continued her attention toward Todd and snagged her favorite snacks as soon as the dishes were set on the table. Including the shrimp.

Deanna did enjoy one, until the girl made a production of sucking the shrimp out of the tail. That was all she could take. "Well, I think I've waited long enough. Nice to see everyone. Good night." She swallowed the last of her drink and stood, straightening her skirt. Lenny tried to object. She brushed him off and headed toward the bar to pay her tab.

"Can you call me a taxi, also?"

The bartender gave her a nod and went to grab her tab and ID as he stuck the phone between his shoulder and ear. Deanna always enjoyed watching them as they did so many things at once: kept orders straight, made change while taking orders, grabbed the phone to take calls and make them, and in between joked with patrons to make them comfortable. Maybe she'd missed her calling. She could do that. Although she didn't figure that was what her mother meant by throwing her people skills in the right direction. Still, it could be fun.

"I'll get that." Todd pushed up beside her and handed the bartender a ten dollar bill. "Keep the change."

Deanna accepted her ID but turned to Todd. "That's not necessary."

"I insist."

She raised her eyebrows.

He shrugged. "Least I can do after dragging you out to a place you apparently don't enjoy."

"It's fine. As I said, a new experience."

"And you enjoy new experiences."

"Depends. Sometimes I do."

He grinned and edged closer. "I'd love to find out which you do and which you don't."

"Would you?"

"How about you wait here until I get my coat and I'll see you home?"

A little too pointed for her taste. And much too soon. "Get your coat if you're ready to leave." When he grinned again and walked away, back to his colleagues, Deanna headed to the door, found her taxi, and went home. She figured she'd hear about it at work the next day, but the guy wasn't about to get away with that kind of assumption. And things too often came easily for him. She wouldn't be one of them.

========

"Three sixty-four S3." Daws raised his voice only enough to be sure his squad heard him over the farewells. He didn't let himself linger on any of his men's last moments with wives, kids, or girlfriends. He didn't want to see it. They shouldn't have been allowed on base. This kind of goodbye would have been better done at home. *"Fall in."*

He gave them more time than he normally would to assemble into formation. Other squads were still hanging on their loved ones. His was the first to order semblance. Daws supposed it was due to the other squad leaders having their own families there. He didn't mind being first. And it was time.

As others followed suit, Corporal Jenkins took a step forward. "Sergeant?"

"Corporal?"

"I think our families would appreciate a word from you."

"Why?" When his men exchanged glances, he looked over at the small group standing as close to their soldiers as they dared. Young women. Little kids: the oldest four, the youngest ... the six month old Corporal Jenkins doted on, in his mother's arms. The mother was just a girl, her face barely more than a baby itself, her long hair pulled back in a barrette.

Talk to them? And say what? He gave his corporal a 'thanks a lot' glance and searched for something to say that might be encouraging but without false promise. Their tour could be as short as a few weeks or as long as ... years. There were no promises given.

With a deep breath, he strode closer to the families, within hearing distance of his men in formation. They wouldn't break it without his order.

"The men seem to think you want a word from me." He avoided their eyes, although he felt them. "I have no words of comfort to offer. You can be assured our mission will come first, whatever the cost." With the mistake of looking over at Private Butler's new wife as she wiped tears, Daws dropped part of his bearing and softened his voice. "However, you can also be assured each one of them is well trained and I have full confidence in them. I'm proud to have them at my side. And I intend to bring them all home. We leave as a full squad; we'll return as a full squad. I'll do anything in my power to make that happen. In the meantime, be strong for them and make them proud."

As he nodded his own farewell and began to turn, a soft "Hooah," echoed by the other women, made him pause. His lips curled up slightly, and he took his place in front of his men.

========

"Ms. Meyers."

Deanna nodded at Todd as they passed each other and continued to the break room. Glad no one was there, she allowed herself a deep, refreshing breath as she refilled her coffee and stirred in too much creamer. It was strong, though, with a bitterness that said it had been sitting too long.

"Ah, I hoped you were alone."

She turned at Todd's voice. "Just getting coffee. Have to get back."

He blocked her path. "You walked out on me last night."

"You assumed too much last night. Excuse me." She tried to pivot around him.

"Deanna. I was only offering to accompany you home and talk about that little issue I mentioned over the phone. The one I said I would take care of."

"And I should believe that, based on the conversation?"

Todd grinned. "I believe the slant of the conversation was more your doing than mine."

"All right, I'll give you that, but I was annoyed."

"About?"

"The work crew? You could have warned me."

"Would you have come?"

"No. You still should have warned me."

"Okay, you're right. I apologize. How about I make it up to you over dinner tonight?"

"I don't think so." She again tried to move around him.

He took her arm. "Please. Have dinner with me."

"It's a work night and I've already done that once this week."

"Friday, then?"

"I'll think about it." Deanna pulled from his grasp and went back to her desk.

========

Daws checked the depth of the trench alongside the tent and the sturdiness of the wall of sandbags.

"All good, Sergeant? Or do you want another four foot so we can bury ourselves standing up?"

He looked down into the hole at the man covered nearly head-to-toe in sandy dirt, as they all were. "Keep it up, Kefner. I'm sure someone on latrine duty wouldn't mind being relieved."

The private laughed. "*Relieved*. Hell, Sarge, my bet is anyone on latrine duty has no problem with *relieving*."

"Want to find out?"

"No, Sergeant." He snickered again. "I'll keep digging this hole as deep as you want. Just tell me when."

"Looks like you could use a couple more inches." Daws nodded toward a spot in front of the private, his gaze daring Kefner to make another comment. He didn't. Daws was almost disappointed.

"Looks like you're already deeper than the rest, S3." Major Reynauld came up from behind Daws and peered down into the trench with a quick return salute to the men. "Carry on. I'm interested in knowing just how far your Sergeant thinks you should dig."

"Till we get back to the other side of the world. Or farther into hell, if that's possible."

Daws didn't bother to answer Butler's comment. "All right. Dismissed. Go get as clean as you can. Kefner, finish your two inches first. With that big head of yours, you'll need it."

"Yes, Sergeant. Damn sure true but it oughtta be wider, not deeper, in that case." The private snickered while the rest of the squad jumped all over his claim, then pushed his shovel deep into the dirt, threw it over the side, and pulled himself out of the hole.

Daws took another walk around the edge of the trench, pushing at the sandbags.

"Might as well release yourself, since you've released your men, Sergeant."

"Yes, Sir. Just double checking."

"For the fourth time, I would guess." The major moved up to him and set a hand on his shoulder. "Relax, Fred. It's late and you're off duty, by my orders. Go get some rest. Or go grab a phone and give your girl a call. We have a few minutes of phone time tonight. Might be the last chance for a while."

"Have no need for a call." He shifted one of the bags.

"Even if you don't, she'd appreciate it."

"Don't think she would." Daws scratched the back of his head. He needed a shower, a full shower, not a cold field shower. "Broke it off."

"Ah, I didn't know. Since when?"

"Day before we deployed."

The major propped himself on the sandbag wall and gave him a thoughtful nod. "Kind of figured she might be one of those. You need to find yourself a real woman, one worthy of settling with: hardy, intelligent, open-minded with good common sense. And energetic is always good."

Daws pretended not to see the sly grin. "I don't seem to be too appealing to that type. They take one look and hurry the other direction."

"You need to learn to let your hair down. That's your problem. Laugh now and then, Sergeant. You're allowed. The right kind of woman will appreciate that sense of humor of yours once you let it out."

"Talk to your family tonight, Sir?"

"You're changing the subject."

"Yes, Sir."

He laughed. "All right, Sergeant. I'll let it go again. I'd like to see you with a healthy, hardy, sweet girl, though. One who'll both stand up to you and stand with you. I'd worry about you less."

"Worry? For what reason?"

"You won't always be in the Army, Fred. You're going to need something to go home to one of these years. And it sure makes you look forward to the end of all this when you know you'll be in your own bed every night, cuddled in to warm, soft arms."

"Suppose it would." Daws looked over to where four of his men were playing horseshoes. It had amused him to watch them melt down AK 47 barrels just enough to wrap into semi-circles. Another unit had confiscated the weapons from the enemy and destroyed a huge cache. He didn't want to know why his men had a few of the barrels. Didn't bother to ask. Neither did anyone else. Fewer weapons to be used against them was something to celebrate.

He put himself back in the conversation. "Have no plans to get out for some time to come. I'm happy enough with what I'm doing."

"Well, something tells me that'll change. Twenty-eight years of this have taken a toll. Not sure I should have pushed it quite that far, and I'm not sure I'd recommend it. Which reminds me, once I retire, I intend for you to come over and get to know my boys. See what you're missing."

"They're doing all right?"

"Yes." The major shook his head. "Although my little hothead is starting to worry Marianne. She didn't appreciate that I laughed when she told me, but they've had some protestors at the gates and I guess some of the kids around town have said some things to Ryan. What does he do? Cuts his hair off military style, which Marianne is just livid about since he has beautiful hair, and claims one of my BDU shirts. He took the rank off and he's wearing it as a jacket, just to throw it in their faces." The major chuckled. "Scares her to death, and I have to say it worries me some since he's only fourteen and no bigger than I was at that age, but you have to admire his spirit."

Daws could see the pride shine strongly. He could also see the worry, and the way Major Reynauld wished he was home with his boys and his wife. That was something he didn't figure he needed. It would only make the job harder.

When the major wound down and told him again to get some rest, Daws pushed through the tent flaps. With a quick scan to be sure all was as it should be – only his soldiers were there, playing cards, reading, or resting, on olive drab cots lined up along each side, their belongings

stacked neatly against the head of the cots and the sides of the tent –
Daws grabbed his soap and a pair of sweats and went to clean as well as
he could. The way he saw it, the lure of a hot, private shower at the end of
each day was as inviting a thought as having some woman's arms
waiting. Well, maybe close, anyway, and depending on the woman.

=======

Deanna couldn't quite refuse to let Todd walk her up to her
apartment. He'd behaved well on their first date. The conversation was
interesting enough to hold her attention. He'd promised her boss would
not bother her again. He'd taken care of it. Quietly.

She had a fleeting thought that he'd done it more to mark his
territory than for her dignity. Either way, it would be nice to go to work
without being constantly on guard and looking for a ditch to avoid the
tornado.

Todd followed her in and scanned the place. It wasn't much to see –
secondhand furniture in unmatched patterns, an old desk that held her
small television and collected her important papers, a little stereo on a
bookshelf that held more music than books. From the door, he could see
the whole place, except into the one bedroom.

"You're happy living here?"

She took his coat and hung it on the rack. "It works. Want coffee?"

"No, thank you." He wandered over to the one valued piece of
furniture: her art table.

Deanna wished she'd thought to put her sketches away.

He picked one up, a pen and ink study of the Manhattan skyline at
night. "What is this for?"

"Nothing. Playing with the medium. I haven't done much with it but I
like the contrast of the dark sky and bright lights every time I see them
from a distance. I can never help staring."

"And this?" He traded the city sketch for another.

"Oh. Just a few thoughts and sketches. Again, nothing to look at.
Keeps my hands busy."

Todd set it down and looked over at her. "I heard you had art
training of some sort. It shows."

"I have a design certificate, plus extra art classes."

"Then why are you working admin?"

"My full degree is in business. That's what was available. Sure you
don't want coffee? Or I have iced tea."

"How about wine? Or something stronger?"

"Hard lemonade. Best I can do."

Todd threw a surprised look and came to her. "And I thought that
was a joke. The hard lemonade, half dead houseplant, and your hunk."

"Not a joke." She nodded toward the plant. "All true."

One side of his mouth curled. "Maybe I should have taken you to my place. I have a nice Cabernet I've been saving for something special. Would have been glad to open it."

"I had enough for dinner. Sorry I can't offer you better, though."

He touched her arm. "It's fine. Next time I'll be more of a gentleman and bring something with me."

Deanna had to wonder if he was still talking about drinks. If he meant the "something" that came to her mind and he didn't bring it, it didn't matter. He wouldn't need it.

Not nearly so fast.

He kissed her. Quickly, before she had time to draw back or consider whether she wanted to kiss him, Todd took her arms and leaned in. It was nice enough. Not great, but not bad. Firm but not aggressive. Enjoyable but not terribly sensual.

Maybe it wasn't a good sign that she was analyzing the kiss as he was kissing her. She usually did that afterward.

"I suppose I should go." Todd studied her as though waiting for her to argue, to ask him to stay.

"It is getting late. Thank you for dinner. I had a nice time."

"Deanna." He ran his hands up and down her arms. "I could find an excuse to stay, if I had a hint you might want the company."

She wasn't sure she'd heard that line before, and she'd heard plenty. "You're moving too fast for me, Romeo. What would our parents say?"

"Our parents?"

"It was a joke. You know, the Montagues and Capulets and ... never mind. I did have a nice time. How about we leave it at that for now?"

He released her and stepped back. "All right. For now. How about dinner tomorrow night?"

"Too soon."

"Next weekend?"

"Maybe."

He smiled, a disconcerting smile. "Playing hard to get. I like that. Love a good chase." Stepping back toward the door, he gave her a bow. "Good night, fair lady. Until we meet again."

Deanna sighed as he closed the door. He wasn't exactly Prince Charming. Charming maybe, but not a prince. He might do, though, for a while. She had no plans of settling too fast. She had a career to build, things to achieve. A man too tied to her would only be a distraction. For now, company at night, even someone who would do his own thing in the same room, would be good enough. Todd was independent. She didn't see him as ever clinging. It could work. For a while.

Daws felt his squad's apprehension as he watched Major Reynauld. Finally, the major lowered his head from where it had been tilted up toward the sky, and cast his eyes on his group of officers and NCOs. "Let's do this. And do it as you've been trained: *straight forward, no holds barred*. We all came together; we all leave together. You and the mission are one and the same. Neither will fail."

Neither will fail. Daws felt the strength swell inside that always came when their major addressed them. A gentle man, he was also one of the strongest Daws had known in his lifetime. Maybe *the* strongest. When he gave orders, he did it with full conviction that they would be followed, not with self-importance or with even a hint of rudeness, but with rightful authority. Daws had never, in the three years he'd served under the man, seen him disparage anyone. He'd rarely seen anyone bother to argue with the major. Anyone who knew him knew it would be pointless. He would listen, yes, but he never made decisions without first backing them up with knowledge. Once decided and presented, the course was set.

Still, on occasion, he joked with some of his most trusted men, both officer and NCO, about his past and how much trouble he got into as a child. He gave his wife, who he met when they were both military and stationed together, full credit for moving him past his youthful stubbornness and into responsible adulthood, such as it was. And he adored his children.

That was enough to endear him to Daws. Not that he wanted children of his own, but to be adored by a parent, even only one of them, was something he would like to have known.

Not that it mattered anymore. They were both gone and he had his Army family: his major and his men. It was the only family he planned to have.

At the burst of icy wind mixed with blowing sand, he clenched his body to prevent a shiver and his eyes to prevent irritation. He refused to look as cold as he was. Daws had always thought New York winters were harsh, but at least they didn't have the infernal sand. Even with thick wool socks, the wool sweater under his uniform, and his winter coat with thick leather boots, the cold penetrated. If he had the luxury of a washing machine and dryer, he would layer two pairs of socks. His toes were cold. But he supposed that would be the least of his worries soon.

=======

Deanna turned away. Such a stupid move. She knew better. She never should have stayed with him.

Parts weren't all that mattered. You had to know how to use them.

She sighed and pulled the blanket up around her shoulders. Maybe it was first time nerves. Far from the first time for either of them, it was at least their first time together. It took time to learn each other. He was at least attentive. She could teach him to be more than that, give him tips he apparently had never been taught. Anyway, she supposed he had a chance of improving.

Unable to sleep, she got up slowly and slipped his shirt over her shoulders, fastening one button in the center. She didn't want to turn lights on until far enough away they wouldn't bother him, so she stumbled through the living room, her feet icy against the hard floor, and to the kitchen. It didn't take long to peruse the pantry; there wasn't much in it. She always had snack bars in hers, as she so often needed to grab something quick before bed to hold her until morning.

Giving up, Deanna went back to the living room and stood beside the big window. City lights glowed through the dark. She couldn't see the stars. Too cloudy. More snow tomorrow, they said. She'd have to get up and out early to make it back home before it got too deep.

=======

A piercing blast jerked him out of a restless sleep. Alarms. Shouting.

Daws jumped from his cot, pulled into his boots, frag jacket, and helmet while yelling at his men, grabbed his mask, and ran across the compound toward the smoke. Half-dressed soldiers were running the opposite direction.

"A *SCUD*." A passing voice mixed with yelling and gunfire and alarms … and unmoving bodies carried out of the barracks.

Daws knew his men were right behind him and didn't bother to check before yelling over top of the commotion. "Let's *go*. Search for the injured first. Get 'em *out*."

There were warnings to stay out of the building, of instability, of more attacks. If it was a SCUD, there was low possibility it would hit the same target. He urged his men on. A dangerous tactic, one he could very well be reprimanded for. Still, there were men inside, a few still straggling out. He would hope, if it had been his barracks instead, someone would go through hell or high water to find them. And his unit wasn't the only one going in.

Smoke was heavy. He pulled his gas mask on, checked his men for theirs, and sent the ones out who didn't have them. They could help as they could outside. After it all settled, he would pull them aside for an off-the-record reprimand. This wasn't training. It was war. He was taking them all back home.

He spied motion in a corner, under a pile of wreckage, and signaled to a couple of his men to follow. They moved pieces of cots and clothing and wood and metal to clear a path. A young soldier looked up, his eyes dazed.

"Can you move?"

The boy stared. He couldn't have been over nineteen. Daws nodded toward Jenkins to help lift the kid. There was no time to bother with a neck splint. The building, what was left of it, shivered and creaked. With Jenkins holding the boy's legs, Daws at his shoulders and back, they kept him as close to the same position as they found him, eased him out to the open night air, and left him in care of a medic.

He was stopped as he tried to return. "All are out, Sergeant."

Daws turned to find his men and yelled their unit name, taking count as they appeared. "Where's Andrews?"

"Think he's still inside, Sergeant. Didn't see him come out."

"Do what you can out here. *Go.*" He dismissed them and headed back to a huge gap in what used to be a wall.

"Can't let you go in." A hand grabbed his arm. "Building's starting to collapse."

"Have a man inside."

"Then he better get out. You can't go back in."

"The hell I can't." He pushed past the man, no idea of his rank since he hadn't put enough of his uniform on. And he brushed the arm away as it tried to stop him.

Yelling Andrews's name as he pulled the mask from his face, Daws watched anything that moved, dodging as much of the worst of it as he could.

"Back here, Sergeant. Kinda stuck." A cough followed.

Daws followed it, ducked falling debris, and found his specialist attempting to free his ankle from a piece of large metal. Support beam.

"Was about to cut it off." Andrews coughed again, trying to grasp at whatever air was still left. "Think I could crawl out of here before I'd bleed to death? Trying to decide which would be worse. That or suffocation."

Daws glanced at the knife in his soldier's hand. "Not finding out today. Put that away. It'd be damn hard to go back to climbing scaffolds with one foot."

"I could do it." His voice shook between coughing.

"Yeah, I bet you could. Don't need to prove it. Where's your mask?"

"Gave it..." the cough interrupted. "Gave it to a kid having a hard time breathing."

Daws pulled his own off and strapped it around Andrews's mouth, despite his protest.

"Let's get this off, and fast. Building's about to tumble." Timing it, they pushed together, and Daws covered Andrews's head when it shifted more debris. "Gotta do it this time. Give me all you got. One, two..." On three, he shoved his back into the beam and lifted with his arms.

"I'm out."

Dropping the thing, he grabbed Andrews around the back and yanked him away from more debris, larger debris.

"Thanks." He coughed through the mask.

"Don't thank me yet. Let's go." He slid an arm around his back, gripping him underneath the other arm, and helped support Andrews as he hopped beside him. The foot was useless. And they were moving too slow. Hard enough getting over the mess without hopping through it. "Stop." He moved directly in front of his specialist, back to front. "Give me your arms."

"I'm too damn big..."

"*Give* me your arms." With some struggle, he raised Andrews over his back and gripped his legs. His chest burned. And his legs. The man was a good three inches taller, even with his own six feet and an inch or so, and not slight. He ducked a falling piece of something and kept his mind focused on the exit, the open air, on getting them all home. Andrews slid the mask back over his mouth. He didn't argue. He needed to be able to breathe long enough to get them both out.

"*Dawson.*"

He was barely aware they were outside again when his major was in his face, and the weight lifted from his back. He bent forward and steadied himself with hands on his knees. Throwing the mask out of his way, he gasped for whatever fresh air he could find.

"You have to get farther away. Keep moving."

He followed his major's orders without hesitation, as always. Until he was beckoned to stop and sit. Through his burning lungs, a rough cough tried to clear his air passage.

"That was a fool-hardy thing you did." Major Reynauld crouched in front of him.

"Yes, Sir."

"You were told not to go back in."

"Yes, Sir." Daws coughed harder and tried to catch his breath.

"Are you aware it was a colonel you disobeyed?"

"No, Sir. He wasn't wearing rank that I could see."

A smirk brushed over his commander's face. "Would it have mattered if you had known?"

Daws hesitated. Career-wise, he should say it would. Truthfully, he couldn't do it. "No, Sir. My man was inside. We all came together. We all leave together." A cough nearly doubled him over. Damn, his chest hurt.

"Breathe easy, Soldier." The major set a hand on his arm.

"I suppose this means an official reprimand."

"It should." He waited while a medic put a respirator over Daws's mouth.

The oxygen soothed him, enough to pull it away again to ask the medic about Andrews's foot.

"No idea. Got at least twenty dead; trying not to lose more. The foot has to wait." He hurried off.

"Sergeant Dawson." Major Reynauld pushed the respirator back to his face. "I want you to report to the E6 board as soon as we're stateside again. I'm putting you in for a commendation."

"Sir." Daws moved the thing so he could talk. "With all due respect, it's not necessary. I was just doing my job, no more."

"Sergeant, you *just do* your job more willingly and more professionally and more selflessly than any other NCO I've seen, and better than many officers. No argument. It's an order."

"Yes, Sir."

=======

Deanna sifted through a pile of old notes Phillips dropped in her inbox – how many times did she have to tell him that wasn't what her inbox was for? Most of it was shredded or tossed or filed.... She stopped just as she was about to drop one in the trash and looked at it closer. Brand manager needed, for a little coffee shop just opening. Leaving the rest be for the moment, she took the note and tapped on her boss's door.

"Busy."

"As always." She went in anyway, hoping her sarcasm didn't shine through too much. "Quick question about this note."

"If I gave it to you, file it wherever it belongs. What's the question about that?" The jerk didn't even bother to look over.

"About the brand manager job. Have you given it to anyone?"

He raised his eyebrows as he peered over his glasses. "Why is that your concern?"

"Because I can do it."

Now, he swiveled his chair to gaze at her directly. "You."

"Yes. I can do it."

"You have a job."

"A job that was supposed to be temporary as I worked up. You know I have the qualifications. I'd like you to assign me." She saw him about to argue. "If I move up, they may give you an assistant more amenable to what you want. Don't think of it as helping me…"

"I have no need or desire to help you."

"Obviously. Thank you for being so honest." She pulled her shoulders back and held his gaze. "So give me this job you know I can do and get me out of your way."

"If you do it right. If not, I look like the idiot for suggesting you. Why should I take that chance?"

"To get an assistant you like better."

"Hm." He turned back to his scribbling. "Brand manager is for creatives. You're business."

"My degree says I'm both. I can do it."

"Too late. Already shifted it over to Bodin to assign. Think he took it himself. The idiot. It's a pissant job, should've gone to one of the newer crew."

Todd. He'd handed it over to Todd. Maybe she still had a chance, if Todd hadn't assigned it.

=== March ===

Daws settled onto his cot and tried to ignore how cold he was, how his skin burned from the mix of frigid air and blowing sand. He tried to forget the visions of the day, the charred bodies along the roadsides and the billowing dark smoke in the too-close distance. The frightened, wide-eyed, skinny children orphaned by enemies of their parents who ran toward Daws and his men as they'd gone through the village to be sure no invaders were left. The cease fire had been called three days before. Their task now was to be sure it was upheld.

They'd given the kids all of the food they had on them, mainly MREs which were largely tasteless but accepted with humbling gratitude and words he didn't understand. Some of his men had candy in their pockets from boxes their families sent. They started carrying it instead of eating it themselves after seeing so many children who hoped for any kind of handout.

His stomach growled and he ignored that, also. He'd given away everything he'd had for the night's meal. The little girl's big brown eyes were too hard to refuse. Daws had carried her to the medics where they were treating dozens of children. He barely felt her weight. There was little possibility she'd be able to use that leg again.

He clenched his burning eyes and tried to push the God-forsaken place from his thoughts. It felt truly forsaken, with too many nights since he'd been able to see the stars. Dust and clouds and smoke mixed to conceal anything above. He wished it could conceal the sights on the ground instead.

Sleep. He had to sleep. They had to be up and moving before daylight.

=======

She shouldn't give in. It would make her look too easy. Although she supposed maybe she was. Their late nights of working on the project Deanna could have done by herself led to too many nights spent together, and far too many implications. He couldn't just give it to her, he said. He'd already met with the clients and they expected him to follow through.

She wasn't horribly sure that was true, any more than it was true that Phillips had already turned it over to Todd when she asked about it.

Maybe it was true. Why would he ask her to move in with him, despite the flak he would get at work, if he didn't care enough about her to be honest, to want to help her get ahead?

Todd swirled his champagne glass and Deanna watched the bubbles stream to the top. He reached across the table, beside the burning candle in a crystal vase, and waited for her hand. "Are you going to answer me sometime tonight?" He grinned, like the Cheshire cat, as though she couldn't possibly refuse.

Maybe she couldn't. What would it hurt to try? Deanna hadn't actually moved in with a man before, although she'd been close a couple of times and they may as well have been living together. At least this one was taking that step.

"Deanna, my flower, live with me. Come and share my empty apartment."

"It's hardly empty." She thought of his white leather couch with red suede throw pillows, his massive entertainment unit in gray and red, the fully stocked kitchen and bar, ceramic floors with white and gray area rugs. The apartment was well-furnished, immaculate, if a bit cold.

"It feels empty without you in it." He caressed her fingers.

"I don't know, Todd. I like having my own space."

"That little tin can with no view?"

"It's not much, but it's mine. I found it on my own and rented it on my own, and it's mine. What happens if I give it up to move in with you and then you change your mind?"

He gave her a placating grin. "Okay, so let's take it slower. Move in with me and keep your apartment. There's no risk that way. I'll even cover your rent until you decide you don't need it."

"No, you don't need to..."

"I want to. I want to show you how much I think this will work, how much I want you to be with me."

Deanna sipped her own champagne. She hated champagne but he insisted it was a special occasion. She avoided him by turning her eyes around Aureole. It was much like Todd: elegant, smart, expensive, showy, and yet professional. She loved the large glass windows where she could nearly feel as though she was outside if she tried hard enough. The brown theme helped to counter the modern silvery crisp look. The service was excellent. They spoke English unlike the last one he took her to, with the snooty waiter who scanned her once and refused to look at her again. She'd requested Todd choose something more casual this time. And she meant casual as in jeans and a sweater, not dress and heels. Maybe he didn't get less casual.

Still, her veal was perfect and she lingered with her dark chocolate torte to offset the champagne.

Todd was uptight constantly, even relaxed. He said she brought out the other side of him he had a hard time showing: the light-hearted, easy-going side. Deanna struggled with that image. The most easy-going he ever got was to not insist on putting his pants back on after sex while they were just hanging around the apartment chatting. She suggested once he might as well not bother to get dressed again. While he teased in return, he still covered himself with his briefs and a robe.

"Deanna?"

She'd never been intimate with any of her native Kentucky blue collar boyfriends. At times, when she was with Todd, she wondered how someone more used to physical activity would be in...

"Deanna?"

"Sorry." She shoved the thought from her head and grabbed a bite of chocolate.

"You need to think about it?"

She nearly asked about what. Until his question came back to mind. Living together. Time to think. "Yes, I need time to think about it."

He nodded and signaled the waiter for the check. She decided not to mention she hadn't finished her dessert. Just as well. Less time in the gym.

He was silent while flagging a taxi, but he did at least hold the door for her. He didn't, however, speak on the way back to his place. And he didn't bother to ask if she wanted to go back to his place. Maybe she didn't. Maybe she wanted to go home to think about it.

Still silent, he unlocked his door and went in, leaving her to follow. She considered not following.

"Cabernet?" He held up a bottle.

She closed the door behind her and agreed. At least she liked Cabernet. Pulling her coat from her shoulders, she placed it on the coat rack and slipped out of her shoes. He constantly told her not to bother; he'd have the floor and rugs cleaned whenever needed, but she couldn't do it. The floor was cold, though, and she hurried to his bedroom to pull out the slippers she kept there. She also had a change of clothes or two, her hairbrush and a blow dryer, and some basic cosmetics, plus the requisite toothbrush. One drawer in his bathroom belonged to her. Most were empty. He at least wasn't a bathroom hog.

Or a closet hog. Few suits hung in his closet and few underclothes were in his dresser. He said he tended to leave too many at the cleaners and picked them up as needed.

She slipped in to brush her teeth and check her hair, pulled off her hose that she hated, stuffing them into the back of her drawer. When she returned, he was sitting on one edge of the white couch, his glass on a coaster on the side table, as always, hers on the glass coffee table.

"You didn't ask if I wanted to come over tonight."

He looked up from his paper. "I suppose I expected you would."

"Maybe I don't want you to just expect." She stood on the other side of the table.

Todd refolded the paper, set it aside neatly, and came to her, grasping her hands. "If you drop that word from your vocabulary, darling, it would better show how intelligent you are."

Deanna tilted her head. "Maybe I like to *just* say what I think."

He sighed. "Very well. We're alone anyway." He gave her a light kiss. "And I am sorry. I suppose I hoped enough you would want to come I let that interfere with asking. Do you mind? I can call a taxi if you'd rather, but this would be so much easier if you lived here. Then there would be no asking or expecting to worry us. I would know you wanted to be here." Todd kissed her neck and slid his hands behind her waist, down to her rear, her thighs.

"I suppose I do." He smelled of Jovan White Musk, his favorite scent and the only one in the apartment. She'd told him once he should try something a touch more masculine, more gritty, even regular musk without the citrus. He'd asked if she didn't think he was masculine enough and then attempted to prove otherwise. Deanna wondered if he would repeat the attempt if she gave him the suggestion again. It had been one of their better nights.

"Move in with me, my flower. I want you here every night instead of only when I can get off early enough to drive out to your place and bring you back. There is no sense in this being so complicated. Unless there is someone else you need to save time to see."

"Of course there isn't." She closed her eyes and concentrated on his touch.

"Then..."

"Okay. But I'm keeping my apartment for at least the rest of the month, and we'll see how it goes from there."

He moved to see her face. "Of course. Let me take care of the rent..."

"No. If I hold it after this month, I'll pay it. I won't feel kept."

A sly grin crept across his face. "That's one thing I admire about you, Deanna. You have an incredible amount of spunk."

"It's called self-preservation."

"Hm." He moved back to her neck. "Whatever it's called, it keeps me on my toes."

"That's good. You better stay on them. I won't be easy to hold onto."

"No?" A grin accompanied his fingers unhooking her bra. "I think you're quite easy to hold, and I always enjoy the holding."

=======

Daws dropped his ruck on the floor and himself on his bed. Alone again, after the past two months of living in a tent on a cot breathing smoke from oil fires and sand and the lingering stench of gunpowder and illness and blood. Only two months. He felt, while out there, as though it was two years. Now, in his nearly bare one bedroom apartment, he had to tell himself it was real, not a nightmare. His mind had to accept the reality; he would not let it turn into a perpetual nightmare. It was part of him, a part he would accept and control.

The images of the motor pool parking area as their convoy pulled in was, in some aspects, harder to accept. The flood of spouses, girlfriends, children, parents.... They held large signs and grabbed up their soldiers as soon as they could possibly get close enough.

Daws brought all of his men back. Andrews was on crutches but was sure he would be able to climb scaffolds again once he went back to civilian life. A couple of others had minor injuries. Most were unscathed physically, other than the smoke in their lungs and the drugs they had to take. They could do nothing about either except hope for the best, that there wouldn't be long term effects. Daws still felt some chest congestion, although he refused to mention it. It would work itself out in time.

He'd watched the major greet his family, his wife and two sons and the girl Daws expected was the eldest's girlfriend, but he kept distance. He kept distance from all of the families, instead making sure everything got where it needed to go before he could dismiss them for a few days off. When they returned, equipment would need to be well cleaned to remove sand and dirt and all would need to be put back in order.

Until then, he had three days.

What to do with those three days was beyond his fatigued brain's comprehension. It wasn't enough time to make the drive to New York City from Fort Drum. Not worth the energy he didn't have.

========

Lowering into the too-stiff arm chair, Deanna took a sip of her Cabernet. The apartment was quiet, far too quiet. Funny how her own "tin can" never felt as empty as Todd's penthouse suite. There was certainly a difference between being alone when expected and being alone by abandonment.

With a larger swallow, she berated herself for the thought. He hadn't abandoned her. It was a business trip. Again. Funny how they were only on weekends. After work on Friday. Between those and working out of the New Rochelle branch and bunking with a friend instead of making the commute back and forth to Manhattan, Deanna had to wonder why it mattered to him that she move in. She was sure she had seen him more often when she had her own place. Which she didn't have anymore. Things were going well. She saw a possible real future with Todd, at least for a while, even if he wasn't quite her prince. Maybe he could be. Maybe she'd take him down to Kentucky and see if he would get on the back of a horse. Then she would know.

She sighed, nearly laughing at the thought of her Manhattan businessman on a horse in the middle of a muddy field. But, he was closer to being a possibility than any of the other jerks she'd dated. Definitely more possible than the first one.

Trying to wipe away that memory, Deanna took another swallow. Then she frowned at the glass. She didn't want Cabernet.

Going to the sink, she dumped it, corked the bottle and put it back in the refrigerator, and went to find her shoes and a jacket. Todd had nothing but fancy wine and a few bottles of hard liquor to mix with this or that. Too fancy. Not that she minded at times, but sometimes she just wanted to unwind and let her roots show.

He could deal with the fact that she littered his refrigerator with a six pack of hard lemonade.

"Tell him to return to base."

"Sergeant..."

"That's an order." Daws stood at the radioman's side and peered out at the approaching storm, the lightning in the distance. Fog was rolling in. Thin dark clouds nearly flew across the three quarter moon that provided some light as it could manage. Clouds rolling in front of the moon at night always sent an eerie shock through his gut. Rain, he didn't mind. Thunder and lightning, he didn't mind. Usually. He did when they had people up in the air. Those evil-dark cloud wisps, he always minded.

The helicopters didn't need to be out any longer, whether or not flight training would be completed on the timeline expected. The Flight Op NCOIC had left him in charge for the week. It was his job to ensure safety. Since the major started pulling him toward Flight Operations, Daws had studied the protocol, read the manuals, paid more attention to weather patterns. He had no interest in flying. He wanted his feet on the ground. He was only there because Major Reynauld insisted. Technically, the major suggested Daws consider the move, said promotions would be faster. Not much difference between the major's suggestion and insistence, as far as he was concerned. Hard to deny the compliment in it, as they worked more closely now than before. The major wanted him at his back, as close to his right hand as Daws could get as an enlisted.

He listened to the reply over the radio. Both helicopters were turning around, the lead chopper piloted by one of the new second lieutenants and the control chopper by Major Reynauld, working as a guide, as morale assistance, so the new guy didn't feel alone up there. Accidents for beginners most often happened when they felt alone, the major said.

It wasn't necessary for the major to still train recruits since he was nearing retirement. But he loved it; it was his favorite part of the job, working with young men and women to guide them into their careers. His calm, firm voice helped them relax. His optimism fueled them. So whenever he could grab the chance, he took them up.

A deep breath encompassed Daws when he heard blades cut through the air. Lightning grew closer. Thunder rumbled wider. The choppers grew from light specks in the growing dark to great metal birds, their approach making them louder, larger. The second held back to allow the first an easy landing, without interference. The new pilot was doing well; the landing was smooth and on target. Daws told the radioman to bring the second one in.

Sudden silence drew his eyes back up. The motor stalled. The blades slowed. Daws started walking out toward it. "Come on, get it going."

Another pilot followed on his heels as he moved into a jog. "Don't get too close. It could go down."

"No, it's not. Come on, Major, get the damn thing going."

Nothing. No sound. If thunder still echoed across the sky, he didn't hear it. And then a blast and the bird dropped. He ran, got yanked by a hand behind him, saw the crash, felt the heat of the explosion, and he shoved the hand away and ran full speed toward the flames. He had to get out. Before the thing exploded again, the major had to get free from it.

Daws covered his mouth with his arm, reminded of the burning oil stench and his aching lungs, but he pressed forward until he saw the slumped figure. *"Major."* No movement. Blood gushed from beneath the helmet, his face, the plastic shattered. He called him again. No response. Daws yanked the seat belt off, pushed his arms beneath the still body, and pulled it out, toward open air. He didn't stop until someone told him to stop, to put him down, medics were on the way.

"Major." Daws pulled the plastic away as much as he could without risking worse damage. He left the helmet in place in case of neck injury. With a glance down his commander's body, he cringed. A large gash ran from hip to rib cage. Flying metal. Nothing else would have done that much damage.

A larger explosion rocked the chopper, sent debris flying. He sheltered the major's body as well as he could. A flashback took him to the barracks in the Gulf: the smoke, the stench, the blood. Too much blood.

"Dawson."

He found the voice, his major's eyes on him. "Sir, hold still. Medics are on the way. Nearly here."

"It's funny." His voice was strained. "My father ... he flew a P-51, the Mustang ... during Korea, a dog fighter. Lots of missions. Came home."

"Sir, tell me later. Save your strength." He glanced up as two young pilots took the major's other side.

"Died of a heart attack in his sleep. Didn't see it coming." He coughed trying to catch breath. "Rather do it this way."

"Agreed, but give it another thirty years or so before you do."

The major's lips curled up, only for a moment. Then he grabbed Daws's arm. "Do something for me."

"Of course. What do you need?" He felt the beginning of soft raindrops on the back of his neck and leaned farther over his friend.

"My family. Especially ... my Ryan. He's ... just a boy. Not fifteen yet."

"Sir..."

"Watch over him. He's ... so like me. Long road ahead. He'll need..." His eyes closed; pain permeated his expression.

"He'll be fine. Stop talking. Medics are here."

"Dawson." He coughed more. Barely. Struggling. "Watch over him. Tell me."

"Major..."

"Tell me."

"Yes, Sir. I will, whenever you need."

"You're a good man, Fred. Proud to have served with you." His body went limp.

"Major." Daws heard the medics jogging their direction and saw the pilots move out of the way to allow them space. It was too late, and he didn't figure it would have mattered even if they were there the second it happened. Too much damage. Too much blood lost. Eyes open, but empty, his chest not rising, the major had released his arm at some point, the arm limp, fingers open.

The medics checked his pulse, felt for breath. Told Daws to move aside.

He ignored them, sitting still, holding his commander's head in his arm. The rain increased, brushed down the back of his neck into his collar, mixed with the blood soaking his sleeve. One of them pulled a plastic sheet over the body, kept the rain off.

"Sergeant?"

Daws looked at him.

"I'm sorry." He pulled the major's helmet off and moved the sheet up over his face.

=======

Deanna unlocked the door and shifted the grocery bag to the other arm. She rarely enjoyed cooking, at least she didn't for herself, but she looked forward to making full use of the kitchen luxuries and then letting the dish simmer in the oven while she soaked herself in a steamy bubble bath and waited for Todd. No business trip this weekend. No New Rochelle. Just the two of them for two and a half days.

As she opened the door, she frowned at the living room light burning. Had she forgotten it when she left this morning?

"Oh." Todd stepped out from around the corner and stopped. His hands paused from where they'd been tying a shiny red tie, atop a white shirt, and black tux. "You're home early."

"Pulled strings." She moved into the room and set the bag on the table. "You look very sexy tonight. Did I forget something we're supposed to do?"

"Oh. Um." He dropped the tie to unravel around his neck and took a few trepid steps closer. "No."

"No? Then you're dressing up for me? Because I'd planned to dress down for you, after a nice meal and...." The look on his face turned a pitchfork in her stomach. "Where are you going?"

"It's ... only a little business thing. Nothing major."

"Business? Funny, I didn't hear about anything going on."

"No, it's ... departmental. Sorry I forgot to mention it."

"You mean you hoped to get out before I got home so you wouldn't have to invite me?"

"Deanna, you know how awkward it would be. Someone from another department as my date?"

"How about your live-in girlfriend as your date?"

He closed the distance between them and stroked her hair. "You know I would want you there if I could, but this is ... well, a big deal could hinge from it and I can't afford to go with someone else's secretary..."

"I'm *not* a secretary." She backed away from him. "I'm the lead assistant to the main production manager who could easily be a brand manager if anyone would give me the chance..."

"Yes, but..."

"But what? You're the one who said it was okay for us to date, to live together, that being lead assistant was high enough up it was fine, particularly being in a different department. Why isn't it tonight?"

"Deanna, it's only a business thing. It's not worth all this." He moved in again. "Tell you what. I'll try to be early tonight, and tomorrow I'll make it up to you. How about we leave the city, get away?"

He was avoiding the issue, hiding. She watched him continue to fix his tie. He always had such issues with his tie. Out of either habit or an instinct to help she had trouble controlling, Deanna moved up and took over. The slick fabric slid through her fingers. The heat from his body seeped into her hands. His cologne drifted into her senses. *Go away.* Would she let that appease her? Maybe. "You mean overnight and through Sunday?"

"I'm afraid I can't do that." Todd ran a hand along her arm. "I'll have to get back to the other office tomorrow night, but..."

"Why? You said you were here all weekend."

"Yes, but things changed. You know how it is..."

She backed up.

"Deanna, my flower, don't be mad. Order out for something incredibly luscious, indulge yourself with a long hot bath, and I'll try to be back early."

"Don't bother." She grabbed the grocery bag and took it to the kitchen, stuffed the perishables in the refrigerator, and left the rest on the counter. He could put it away or overlook it.

"Deanna."

She brushed back past him and headed to their room. He followed but she pretended he wasn't there, as though he ever really was, and found her old jeans she hadn't worn in forever and a comfortable sweater.

"Wouldn't your lounge clothes be nicer around the house?" He stood in the doorway, arms crossed.

"I'm going out."

He straightened. "Where?"

"Oh, I don't know. Somewhere there are other people. Someone to talk to. Wherever I decide looks interesting."

"Not by yourself. Wait until tomorrow and I'll..."

"You're going by yourself. Don't tell me I can't."

"It's different."

Pulling out of her work blouse and dropping it on the bed, she eyed him. "Yes. You're right, Todd. It is different. Because I'd take you with me tonight if you were willing. I would love to take you to one of my places, to anywhere I like to go or have to go, if you only would. You, on the other hand, want me not to go."

"It's not that I don't want you to go..."

"Of course it is. Don't lie to me and say otherwise or I won't be back."

"Really?" He crossed his arms again. "Just where would you go? You let your apartment lease expire. Where would you go?"

"Think I don't have friends?"

"Do you?"

Her stomach tightened. She tried to argue. But he was right. "Well, you know, maybe I'll find some friends tonight instead of sitting here alone waiting for you again." She pulled the sweater over her head, switched the skirt and hose for jeans, shoved a belt through the loops, checked the mirror, and decided she hadn't felt so much herself in ... since she could remember.

"I'm sorry." Todd crept closer and wrapped his arms around from behind. "You're right. I've been unfair. I'll cancel New Rochelle this weekend and stay right here with you. Okay? Or you can take me to one of your places, anywhere you want to go. I look forward to it, and to meeting any friends you make." He kissed the side of her head.

"You're not changing my mind. I'm going out. Unless you decide not to go out."

"I can't. I have to go, and I need to run. Just be careful." He moved around to face her. "No dark sidewalks alone. No seedy bars where I'll have to worry..."

"I can take care of myself. I always have."

He gave her a light kiss. "I know. I only think you shouldn't have to now. Try not to be out late and I'll do the same. Have fun. I have to go." With another kiss, he walked out.

She was nearly asleep when the phone rang and she grabbed it, checking the time. One o'clock. "Yes?"

"Deanna."

"Todd, are you okay? Where are you?"

"I'm fine. And I'm sorry, but I can't get back tonight. I'll be there in the morning and we'll have all day."

"Why can't you?"

"The thing lasted too long. Client talked forever. Wants to meet first thing for breakfast and it's too far to run back and forth, but I'll be back late morning, maybe early afternoon. I am sorry. Did I wake you?"

"No. I was waiting for you, or trying to wait for you." She rubbed her eyes.

"I am sorry. Go to sleep. I'll see you later. Have to go, exhausted. Night."

She didn't have a chance to answer before the phone clicked. His voice lowered at the end, nearly a whisper. With a deep breath, she tried hard not to believe what her brain kept telling her.

=======

Daws carried the right front edge of the casket to the waiting spot in the cemetery. The major's wife wanted him buried at home, in Vermont, where they both grew up, where she planned to return as soon as she arranged their belongings and cleared their quarters. So he was in Vermont, carrying his major to his final resting place. Full military honors. There were assigned pall bearers for funeral details, but Daws insisted on being one of them this time. He didn't want his major to be carried by soldiers he didn't even know. There should be at least one he did. As it turned out, they all were. Every pall bearer was one of the major's men, and many others attended the funeral. There would have been more if they could have been granted the leave for it.

On signal, they set the casket on the waiting frame. He stood at attention during the prayer, during taps, and during the three-volley salute. The major's youngest son jumped at each shot from the seven M-1 rifles. *Take care of my Ryan. Tell me.* How did he expect Daws to take care of a teenager in Vermont when he was stationed two hundred miles away? Even if he lived in the same neighborhood, what did Daws know about teenagers? He'd barely been one himself, other than technically.

The boy stared at the casket. His mother was on one side of him, his brother on the other, an arm draped over Ryan's shoulder. The brother would look after him. Daws could see that in the way he already did. Mrs.

Reynauld was a strong woman, indeed. Other than a few light tears, she held her bearing with grace and looked after her sons. When presented with the flag, she nodded a thank you to the soldier.

The boy ran off as soon as services ended. Literally. He ran. His brother followed.

Daws stood back as family and friends filed past Mrs. Reynauld with condolences and hugs, the oldest son's girlfriend at her side. When much of the crowd had cleared away and Mrs. Reynauld started toward where her boys had stopped running and sat together in the distance, Daws interrupted her path. "Ma'am."

"Sergeant Dawson. Thank you. And please extend my thanks to all of the men today. I would like to do it myself, but I need to check on my sons."

"No thanks necessary. The major was highly respected by his troops. We all mourn his loss with you."

She gave him a light smile, again glancing over toward Ryan and Will. "Tracy." She set a hand on the girl's arm, the one still attached to her side. "Go on over with them. I'll be right there."

"I don't mean to hold you up..." Daws took a step backward.

"No, please." Mrs. Reynauld gave Tracy a nod and waited until the girl walked away. "Edward talked about you often. About your service during Desert Storm, your bravery, as well as how he could ask anything of you and not worry how it would be done. He was quite impressed, and he wasn't an easy man to impress. I was glad to see you at his side again today. I know it would mean a lot to him."

He hesitated at her words and moved his eyes away from where she dabbed her own with tissue. "Thank you, ma'am. He knew well how to inspire us. The credit is his. It was an honor to serve with him. And to be here today." Daws clenched his insides, pulling every bit of his trained bearing he could muster. "I would like to offer you my service in any way I can." He handed her a card. "This goes to my unit. They can always reach me. If you need anything, please call."

She hugged him.

Daws wasn't sure how to respond to a hug. Tears he could handle. Yelling he could handle. Even his drill sergeant screaming in his face and shoving him in the mud, he handled fine. He wasn't prepared for a hug.

Luckily, it was short and she traded for his hand instead. "You take care of yourself. Build a good life. He would want to know you did. And thank you again. I do have to go check on Ryan. He's taking this so hard. His father's son..." She forced back emotion and gave him another nod before moving away.

=======

Deanna picked the shirt up off the closet floor. Why the man was so neat in every other aspect and such a slob about throwing clothes inside the closet instead of in the laundry bag, she didn't understand. Taking it over where it belonged, she started to put it inside and stopped. A red mark caught her eye and she opened the shirt farther to inspect. No. It was ... food. What food was red? Bright red. And oily. Her fingers rubbed against it. It smeared. And there was a scent.

She raised the material to her face. Perfume. Not hers. Not a scent she would ever wear.

She lowered to the bed, staring at it. Not again. Why? Why did she always fall into the same trap? The cheaters? The low-down scumbag cheating jackasses. Why hadn't she learned to avoid them yet? How did she learn that?

"Deanna?"

She looked at him. In the bedroom doorway, perfect as always. Well groomed. Smiling. Together. And such a scumbag liar.

"What's wrong?" His eyes fell to the shirt as she raised it, the stain bunched between her fingers. "Oh. No, Deanna, it's not..."

"Don't talk."

He crept forward. "It's nothing."

"*Don't* talk. You *liar*. You filthy scumbag *liar*."

"Deanna, I can explain that."

"I bet you can. They *all* can. You're all the same. I *asked* you. The late hours. The overnights. The weekend business trips. I *asked* you. And you *lied* to me."

"It's only ... a complication. No more."

"Complication? What, that I found out? Yeah, I bet that is a *complication* for you, you *scumbag*." She got up and threw the shirt at his face. And she went to her dresser and started pulling things out.

"Come on. Stop this and talk to me." He took her arms.

"Talk? About what, Todd? How long has it been going on? Since I moved in? Did I get boring to you when I became so available? Or did you wait just until I let my apartment lease expire so you'd figure I have nowhere to go and would have to stay with your cheating, lying ass? If so, you figured wrong. I'd rather sleep in the alley than stay here and let you prowl around..."

"I'm not prowling around. There's only one. And..."

"Oh, well that makes it okay. That makes it just fine and dandy, right? Only one, Deanna. You're still number two and that's not so bad, right? Is that what you expect me to believe?"

He pulled her in closer. "Deanna, I'm sorry. But listen to me for one minute, would you?"

She felt her breath try to strangle her. "Fine. One minute. And then I'm leaving."

"Don't leave. It's you I want."

"Oh please..."

"My minute's not up." He leaned closer. "It *is* you I want. I'm only ... well, I'm stuck and getting out of it would be complicated, but it's you I want to be with."

"Complicated? Is it? How long have you been seeing her?"

"Deanna, it's..."

"How *long*?"

He ducked his head with a sigh. "Five years."

"*What?*"

"She's my wife. I have to be there enough to keep her from walking and taking everything..."

Deanna shoved his chest, hard enough he nearly fell. She wished he had.

"I haven't wanted to be with her in years. It's for the kids..."

"*Kids*? You have not only a wife but *kids*? And you ... you brought me into this not even *telling* me? How *could* you?"

"Deanna..."

"*Don't* talk to me. You not only *cheated* on me and *lied* to me but you made me the *mistress*. What made you think I would be okay with that, with being a *mistress* for some other woman's husband?"

He shrugged. "I didn't think you were all that particular."

She felt her fist balling up. She felt the anger rage. And she felt the thud against her fingers when they connected to his jaw. She didn't feel remorse. She didn't feel anything close to caring or respect or ... or anything toward him except fury. Wasn't particular. She *wasn't particular.*

"Okay." He fingered his jaw from a safe distance. "Maybe I deserved that. Is it out of your system now? Can we talk about this? You're the one I want."

With a shake of her head, she hurried from the room, threw her shoes on, and bolted out the door and down the hall to the stairwell. She wasn't waiting on the elevator. Wasn't *particular.* She was a heaped bushel more particular than that. He had no idea who she was. He had no idea....

Forced leave.

Daws threw a few things in his ruck and locked the door behind him. The captain insisted he take leave to regroup. Too much too soon, he said. He needed a break.

What his captain didn't understand was he had nothing to give him a break, other than the empty New York apartment that was an inheritance from his parents. Not empty. It was furnished, still with their furnishings. He used it now and then when he was in the city, which wasn't often, but the will asked him not to sell it. So it sat there. And he paid someone to check on it out of the money they left him. The only time he touched it. He lived fine off his military pay. What did he have to spend it on? His album collection was his only item of value. The music knowledge it gave him sat in his brain as unused as the apartment. The old guitar that sat in the corner, its case collecting dust because he couldn't get it right enough not to irritate himself, had some value. Not much to him. It was another failed attempt. The only thing he'd found in the world he was good at was the Army. Leading men. Protecting them. Learning how to do whatever needed to be done to make sure the mission, whichever mission it was at whatever time, was successful. What he would ever do with all of those learned bits of information, he couldn't fathom. Not anywhere else.

The major told him once he was amazed at how Daws could be thrown head first into any task and come out as though he had been specifically trained for just that task. Common sense. Figure it out. Think it over. Not amazing. Necessity. Self-preservation.

As he reached for his car door, Daws saw an image of the boy again, standing at the funeral, clenching and unclenching his fingers. The major's Ryan was small, scrawny, with long thin fingers. The kind that could play a guitar. Daws couldn't play the thing because his hands were too bulky, too thick, his fingers too wide and not long enough. Maybe the boy could do better with it. Maybe it would give the boy something else to think about.

They hadn't left base yet. If he remembered, the Reynaulds were leaving the next day.

He threw his ruck in the car and went back up to his apartment to grab the instrument. Setting it on the back seat, he drove to the motor pool and left instructions that it be taken to the major's house. A quick scribbled note to go with it said only that it was to Ryan from a friend. They were not to say who the friend was.

And then he headed toward New York.

=======

Deanna called in sick from within the cheap hotel room. She'd barely slept, in her clothes, no less, since she hadn't taken anything with her when she stormed out. He would be at work by now.

Pulling herself together as much as was possible without even a hairbrush ... or the toothbrush which had been the first thing she left at Todd's ... she took a deep breath, pulled the door shut, kept an eye out for odd characters hanging out in the hallways, dropped the room key at the front desk, and started the long walk back to his place. At least she'd put her sneakers on as she left instead of her nicer, less comfortable shoes. The walk would do her good, if the weather held out.

Mist dampened her face as dark clouds sifted along the city sky in between the sun trying to hold its own. Appropriate, really. A downpour would be more appropriate. Maybe it would help wash him off her. All of him, including every memory of every second they were together. She supposed it was good he'd been away so often: fewer memories to wash off.

So many of her past friends had given her so much credit for being so together. Smart, energetic, capable in whichever job she had at whatever time, and her looks weren't all that bad. She kept herself in shape and had enough curve to pull plenty of male attention. Of course she worked hard to keep it that way. Those girls who were so "jealous" as to be bitchy about it could do the same instead. Sitting on the sidelines eating hot dogs while cheering on their favorite boys was all well and fine, but they would be more energetic and in better shape if they got off the bleachers and did something of their own. Anything. Even if they walked around while their boys were playing or practicing, at least it would be something.

But she supposed they didn't have to. Their parents gave them what they wanted: name brand clothes, cars, money to hang out. Of course she was capable. What choice did she have? She was given nothing she didn't earn. Ever. Well, maybe when she was very young, beyond the age she could remember. Since then, she often didn't even get as much as she earned.

As she didn't now, in the stupid assistant position where she was treated more as a gopher than as a creative talent. No wonder Todd didn't want to take her to his functions.

Time for some changes. Apartment. Job. Maybe a different city. New York hadn't become what she hoped. Just finding a place to live would be a huge challenge, something nice and safe that she could afford on her pay. She felt her eyes roll. Stupid. It was so stupid to let her apartment go. Maybe it was still open. With a snicker, she shook her head. Not at that rent, it wouldn't be. And probably the rent had been raised since it could be after she let her lease expire. Someone else was probably paying twice as much now and still happy to have it at that price.

Where would she go? Marketing was her one true love. Eventually, she wouldn't be an assistant. But she did have to stay where a good job in her field would be possible. She didn't want to do advertisements for a little hometown department store. She wanted more than that. She wanted to help market something in which she truly believed. The only problem was that she hadn't found that thing yet.

It would come.

And she couldn't leave New York until she found it. The answer was there. She knew it was. Why else would she have been drawn to the city instead of Boston or Chicago or Los Angeles? She couldn't leave, not until she lost all chance at it, until she could no longer survive there.

She rested on a bench at the edge of Central Park when her thighs began to protest. Wishing she had a piece of bread to draw the pigeons closer, Deanna sat very still and watched them. They fluttered away a foot or two when a jogger went by and then settled right back in. Strong birds, pigeons were. Survivors. Grabbing any opportunity of possible food wherever they could get it, acknowledging they had to move over at times to let something bigger and stronger pass by, but then going right back to where they were, unruffled, so to speak.

New Yorkers didn't like them much, even though the birds were such a perfect metaphor for most New Yorkers. Not friendly. Not unfriendly. Simply strong and independent. Survivors.

Deanna couldn't leave New York. She'd become too much one of them.

========

Daws pulled his Chevy into the building's garage and handed the parking pass to the attendant.

"Well, hello Mr. Dawson. Nice to have you back again. Here to stay this time?"

Mr. Dawson. The phrase threw him. "*Sergeant* Dawson."

The skinny boy with longish red hair stared. "Oh, I didn't know. You weren't part of that conflict over there in the Gulf, were you?"

He felt himself bristle more than he should have. "War. That was no conflict. Conflict was those having to put up with peacenik protestors who don't know their asses from a bomb hole in the ground and don't have a damn idea what was really going on. It was a war, no matter how short it was. And yes, I was there." Before the kid had a chance to answer, Daws pulled off toward his space.

Conflict. Nice way to describe what he'd seen. Too nice, and there was nothing nice about it, other than how careful they tried to be not to take civilian lives. No matter what the damned papers said. He knew. He'd seen it. The "civilians" with dog tags and machine guns. The kids with bombs strapped to them being pushed along in front of "soldiers" as safety nets since they knew American soldiers would never risk the children. They would stand back and be shot first. They often were. He heard the radio calls, the back and forth verifying civilians had been evacuated, which also gave the insurgents time to evacuate, or prepare. Heard his CO.... Didn't matter. People would think what they wanted. They always did.

Whenever the major had the chance to call home, he always asked his wife how they were being treated. She brushed it off, saying yes she saw protests and a lot of them stood along the road leading into the base with hateful sayings on signs. Will, her oldest, got out and backed one of them away when the guy blocked their car. Ryan jumped out after him. Luckily the MPs were right there and it didn't go farther. From what the major said, his family mainly stayed on base during the worst of it. His wife wasn't bothered by them, but Ryan was. He was too likely to attack, too constantly afraid for his father not to take the protests personally. And he was young, and scrawny.

Like him. The major said his youngest son was too like him and had a hard road ahead.

Pulling his ruck from the back seat and making his way to his door, Daws wondered again just what he was supposed to do about it.

The apartment felt empty. Hollow. The first thing he did, as always when he came back, was walk around the whole place, checking. Opening every door. Watching for anything that had been moved. Satisfied it was as it should be, he went out to the balcony and stared over the city. Clouds covered it. The streets were damp from drizzling rain. He figured it would get worse before it cleared.

Nothing surprising about that.

And it did. As he stood out there, his hands gripping the iron rail, the rain strengthened.

He no longer saw the city. He saw the chopper going down, his major, his friend, lying on the grass with rain spattering the plastic cloth. He saw the three quarter moon with those damned evil-dark clouds rushing across it.

It was dusk now. The moon was hard to see, and it was only a sliver, meshing with the gray buildings with lights burning and gray sky with lighter gray highlights. Lighter gray on gray, like the drops pelting the city. He focused on individual drops, how each one reflected a touch of lighter gray within the gray outline. Reflecting the moon, his grandpa had said. Daws barely remembered him, his mother's father he rarely saw and lost early. The strongest memory he had was of his grandpa talking about moondrops, the little bits of nature that held more than a soul could imagine.

"Do you realize, Fred, that the same drop of water that just wetted my palm may came back and wet yours in another fifty years? Not the whole thing, of course, but a tiny little part of it. Think of how each tiny drop of water has touched so many people from so many places throughout the centuries, and not just people, but animals, and trees, and lakes, and mountains. And all of that touching is forever embedded in each moondrop." Grandpa clasped his rain-spattered, work-roughened palm over Fred's smooth little boy palm, and then opened both to show the shared dampness. *"So you think now, when a moondrop lands in your palm, you're holding part of eternity and something connected to everything else in the world."*

He called them moondrops, because the moon oversees it all, through centuries, through its eternity. And he swore if you looked closely enough at a raindrop as it fell, the moon's soul was reflected back at you.

His mother called the old man crazy. Maybe he was. But there was a part of Daws that wanted to believe the rain wetting his palm as he stuck his hand out as far as he could reach had also once touched his grandfather's, the only relative who ever bothered to talk with him about anything not absolutely pertinent.

=======

She should wait until morning. It was starting to rain again. But he could be back after work. She didn't want to see him. The flowers and note Todd left on the table in his penthouse did nothing but infuriate her more. How stupid did he think she was? Maybe some women would believe he planned to leave his wife for her. She wasn't some women. She knew better.

And if he would, she didn't want him. What made women think if a man cheated on his wife, he wouldn't cheat on his girlfriend? Did they truly not care? Were they that desperate? Deanna may have let herself be taken in too easily, but she was far from desperate. She'd live alone forever first. Or she'd have short flings as she needed. But at her place, where *they* had to leave when it didn't work.

Grabbing her bags, she set them at the door and slid her coat over her shoulders. The one he'd bought for her because her older coat didn't look nice enough when they were out together. She was stupid enough to let him get rid of the old one.

She'd been far too stupid too often. But no more. At least ... well, she'd try, anyway. There had to be someone out there still worth a try.

Deciding to splurge, she flagged a taxi and gave the driver a hotel address. The guy called her ma'am. Apparently she still looked the part of Todd's ... well, of whatever part he had wanted her to play. The nausea crept back in as she considered the thought. So she shoved it away again.

The hotel doorman opened her door and helped with her bags, carrying them to the front desk where they called for a bellhop. Deanna was splurging fully tonight.

In the room that matched the exquisite decor of Todd's apartment except with more warmth, she slipped out of her shoes, dropped the coat to the floor, and flopped into one of the big arm chairs. She was suddenly starving. Getting up again, she found the hotel menu and cringed. For what she would get for those prices, she might as well go to a regular restaurant and get four whole meals to take out. But did she want to go out?

No. The rain grew harder, the sky darker. She wanted to relax in the shower and lounge on the bed and watch television until she was too tired to think.

Maybe she did. Maybe she wanted to go out, to find some kind of connection with another human soul. Or maybe she'd give up on that and get goldfish. She heard they were soothing. And they were quiet. Colorful. Settling in a little apartment with quiet fish could work. Until then, she wanted company, noise, action of some kind. But she would eat first. The heck with the price.

=======

Daws left the kitchen where he'd stood against the counter to eat a heated can of soup, and returned to the window. The rain spattered against the glass and rolled down.

If he hadn't called the helicopters back so soon or had called them back sooner, maybe it would have happened differently. Maybe the major's chopper wouldn't have stalled. Mechanical error, they said. No one's fault. Weather's effect, possibly, but just a freak accident. Maybe. Maybe in another ten minutes or so, the chopper would have worked the bug out on the way back to the landing strip and it wouldn't have stalled. Or if he'd called them back sooner, they could have both landed before the thing stalled. Maybe. An investigation said otherwise. Said he'd done nothing in error, and neither had the major. Not that it changed anything.

Two months of active war zone and the major comes out unscathed. One stupid training flight and he was gone. A flight Daws was in charge of.

No longer. He'd moved back out of Flight Ops, back to headquarters.

His men were glad to have him; Daws was glad they allowed him back, had moved his replacement elsewhere. His men would all move on eventually, but for the time being, the small connection he had with them was all he had.

He turned, surveyed the apartment. And then he went out on the balcony beyond the ceiling to floor windows. Rain brushed against his hands and arms and head. Cars sloshed through the wet streets below. Horns hollered and doors slammed. It was all so distant, so far down, away from where Daws stood, alone. He wanted to be closer.

Making sure the balcony door was locked, he found his coat and his keys and headed toward the street. Which direction? It didn't matter much. Either way there would be normal city life: cars splashing, horns blaring, doors slamming, people dashing to and from cabs and buildings, holding umbrellas or newspapers over their heads. Normal life. A group of three women who saw him heading in their direction, although he was only walking down the sidewalk, veered widely and kept eyes on him. He tried not to see them, or to at least look like he didn't. Their umbrellas matched their coats which matched their shoes. Their salon hairdos stayed in place. Perfect makeup didn't run in the misty air.

Normal city women. If not horribly real.

He walked farther down the sidewalk than he remembered going before on foot. Not that walking just to walk was normal for him. He got quite enough of it in the Army. He didn't need the exercise, and it wasn't much. He was in no hurry, took his time.

At a bus stop across from a bar, he lowered onto the metal bench. A good place to watch the life around him, people coming and going. Talking outside under the canopy. He wasn't close enough to look like a stalker. Still, he got a couple of wary glances.

His build, his height. And his military hair cut. It often got attention outside the base. He didn't often bother to go far outside the base. Especially since returning from Kuwait. One of his men told him it showed on him too much, made him look far too serious, on top of the way he'd always looked too serious. Daws supposed that could be true. He supposed, once he decided to look for someone not to be alone with, which he didn't see happening in the foreseeable future, he might have to try to look less serious. It could, he thought, be too late at that point to turn himself around.

Didn't matter. Whatever happened, happened. He had his military family.

And he had a fourteen year old kid to try to figure out how to help look after.

Eyes clenched, he tilted his face up to the rain as it grew harder, more insistent. Listening to the rain hit the metal and cement, and tires throwing water that didn't quite reach his feet, he thought of the boy.

What was he supposed to do about him?

"The bus isn't running any longer tonight."

Daws swiveled toward the voice. A woman with an expensive-looking dark trench coat and a pastel-swirl umbrella gave him a curious stare.

"If that's what you're waiting for..." She took a step forward. "Are you all right?"

"Fine. I'm not waiting for the bus." He stood automatically. Then he wondered if he shouldn't have, if it would look threatening.

"No?" Another step forward allowed the street light to highlight dark hair, dark with a touch of red, and touches of makeup that looked uncared-for, half worn off through the day. "What are you waiting for?"

"Nothing."

"Nothing? You're sitting in the rain getting soaked to the skin at a bus stop not waiting for anything?"

He saw amusement spread over her face. "I'm not crazy, if that's what you're thinking. But thank you for checking."

She grinned. "No, you don't look crazy, although you do look in need of company. Mind if I sit with you?"

Maybe she was crazy. "Why?" He studied her eyes as she took a couple more steps closer. She didn't look crazy. She looked ... beautiful, shining, very much alive.

"Maybe I'm in need of company."

Daws took a step backward. "Thank you, but as I said, I'm not looking for ... anything."

She laughed. "Don't worry. I'm not hitting on you. And I'm not a hooker. Do I look like one?"

"Hard to tell these days. Didn't mean to offend you."

"I'm Deanna. And I'm not. A hooker or offended. I am amused, and I'm maybe a little more naive than I should be, and I'm greatly intrigued as to why you're out here in the rain after midnight. So what do you say? Can I sit down? My feet are killing me. I wore the wrong shoes. I tend to do that."

Daws glanced down at her feet. The heels were at least two inches. "At least they match each other."

She laughed again. "Well, I am just a little more together than that. Maybe not much, but a little." She took another step closer. "Are you going to ask a lady to sit?"

"Depends. Why are you out here alone in the rain after midnight?"

A deep sigh raised her shoulders and lowered them again. "Didn't want to be inside alone again. You're safe, right? You look safe enough."

"Do I? You're one of the first to think so."

She moved in close enough he could see a hint of green in her eyes. Her gaze held his, then fell along the rest of him, and back up again. "I can see why. But they apparently don't know what to look for. I feel safe enough. And honestly, I feel safer standing here talking to you than I have with any of the jerks I've ever dated. Maybe I'm the one who's crazy. Am I?"

"I haven't met the jerks you've dated."

Another grin. "That's not what I meant."

"I won't bother you."

She nodded. "Yes. I thought you wouldn't. You don't look at me like I'm prey."

Prey. Daws could see why men would. She was so full of life, so open. Vivacious. Charming. He dropped his gaze and motioned toward the bench, then did what he could to wipe the rain off.

"Oh, don't bother. Nothing will go through this coat." She stopped him and lowered, crossing one leg over another and motioning for him to join her.

When he did, she scooted closer and put half her umbrella over his head.

"You don't need to do that."

"You're getting wet."

"I'm aware of that fact."

"You want to get wet?"

He shrugged. "I've been worse than wet." Actually, he'd been much worse than wet. He'd been covered in thick mud, sprayed with CS gas yearly in training to be sure he could handle it if it was ever real, marched through sleet and snow drifts, was nearly frozen more than once, and he'd been shot at. Someone worrying about him getting wet was almost laughable.

"Well." She turned enough to see him better. "I'll feel better if I share this with you, so you can just put up with it."

Stalled by her statement, he forced his mind elsewhere. "You'll ruin that coat sitting here on this dirty wet bench."

She shrugged. "Doesn't matter. Hate the thing, anyway."

"Then why do you have it?"

"It's a gift from an ex user, translated live in boyfriend who didn't bother to tell me that not only was he cheating on me, but he was cheating on me with a wife I didn't know he had. Yeah, maybe I should have guessed, but I don't seem to do that well. You'd think I'd learn, right? Never got fooled by a married one before, though. Guess my judgment's getting worse instead of better. Not a good thing, trust me."

"Some people are harder to judge than others. Wouldn't blame yourself."

"No? Ever been so duped by a live in?"

"Never had a live in."

"You're kidding, right?" She tilted her head and again ran her eyes down his frame and back up. "You're kind of nice looking to not have had a live in. And old enough. Thirty-two, three?"

"Twenty-eight."

"No, you're not. No way you're that young." She raised a hand to his face and turned his head more directly to hers. "You're serious."

"So I've heard."

"I mean...." She dropped her hand, but kept staring. "You're old for your age. Why?"

Daws felt his eyebrows rise.

"Sorry. I'm being pushy, and you haven't even told me your name yet."

"You haven't asked."

"I'm asking now, and apologizing for my rudeness."

"No need. I'm Daws."

"Daws? That's a first name?"

"Fred Dawson. I don't much like my first name and don't tend to use it."

"Fred. I like it. It's not a lying user's name."

He raised his eyebrows again. "I suppose it is for some."

"Not for you."

"No."

She graced him with a light grin. "So Fred Dawson, what are you doing out here in the rain after midnight?"

He hesitated, thinking of the warmth of her fingers as they'd touched his face, so briefly, unafraid. "Looking for life."

Deanna looked as though she might cry, for only a second. "Is it that hard to find?"

"At times. Not tonight."

She turned her head and stared out at the street where rainwater rushed along the edges looking for an open drain.

"Can I walk you somewhere?"

She looked back at him. "Am I bothering you? Interrupting your search?"

"Not at all. It's late. You're cold."

"How do you know I am?"

"I can see it."

She grinned. "You're not?"

Was he cold? In more ways than she could imagine.

She took his hand. "I think you are. What direction are you heading?"

He nodded down the sidewalk.

"Oh, well, I'm opposite. You don't have to wait, you know. If you want to leave, don't let me stop you."

"I'm not in a hurry."

"No? Good. It's been a long time since I was in the company of a real man. You know, one who will sit on a metal bench in the cold while it's raining and not worry about his hair getting messed or his coat and shoes getting ruined."

"Including the ones you date?"

"Unfortunately."

She was incredible. Beautiful. Caring. Aware of her faults and yet confident. And she wanted a real man? Maybe he would lead her a little farther down that road. "Where are you finding these pansies?"

She laughed. "Generally at work since that's about all I do. Now and then I stop at a bar but I find pretty much the same there, or else the ones looking for a quick one-nighter before they go home and sleep it off. I'm not too horribly particular, but that, I don't do. A girl has to have some standards. Even a girl who has been too horribly naive. But you know, I keep thinking that prince might still be out there somewhere and I'll find him faster if I try more often. Guess that doesn't make much sense."

And she was a risk taker. Daws shrugged. "I couldn't say. More likely not to take much of a chance, and don't too often."

"No?" She pushed hair back from her face and eyed him. "You look to me like you're one to push limits, to take chances."

"Do I?"

She raised his hand and turned it over, running fingers along his, over calluses and healed scars. Daws watched her face as she did. She wasn't turned off by it. With a sigh, she lowered their hands again and found his eyes. "Yes. I think you are. Maybe not with relationships, but otherwise."

He dipped his head. "Guess I can't argue that."

"So what makes you so willing to take chances physically, but not with your heart?"

He'd never thought about it. And he'd never been asked. "Haven't found anyone worth taking that chance."

Her eyes held him, peered in too deeply, searching. And then she shifted and returned to a grin. "Ever been on a horse?"

"A horse?"

"Yeah, you know, the big brown animals with pointed ears and long swishy tails." Her eyes sparkled.

"I've seen them. From a distance."

"Wow. You are a city boy, aren't you? Been here all your life?"

"No. And I know you haven't been."

"Do you? Does it still show? I try not to let it."

"Why?"

She shrugged. "Have to fit the image, you know, to get where you want to get. Not that I'm trying to be what I'm not or anything, just … trying to survive."

"Understood." Daws noticed her shoulder getting wet and pushed the umbrella farther over her. He didn't care if he got soaked. He'd sit out there all night uncovered in the pouring rain just to keep talking to her.

"So where else have you been?" She moved closer yet, putting him more under the umbrella.

"Here and there. Are you from the south?"

She chuckled. "And I thought I hid it better than that. Yes. But I'll only tell you if you keep it to yourself."

"Who would I tell?"

She grinned. "Okay. I'll take that as your word. I'm from Kentucky. The bluegrass state, birthplace of President Lincoln although Illinois likes to claim him. Hillbilly central. But I'm not one. Quite. Even though I do hate to wear shoes and I go barefoot at home whenever it's warm enough."

Daws couldn't help an image of her bare feet and legs walking around his apartment.

"Did I just turn you off?"

He raised his eyebrows. "I'm not bothered by feet."

She laughed. "No, I imagine you're not easily bothered. At least I'm hoping you aren't."

"Why's that?"

"Oh." She pulled her eyes away and looked out over the road, at a car driving by, its driver casting a curious glance. "I guess it's just nice to think not all men are so particular these days, that it's still possible to just be myself without always putting on airs, that I could lounge around the house with a man and wear old jeans and kick my bare feet up on the couch without..." She shrugged.

"A man who'd be bothered by that isn't worth your time."

Deanna met his gaze. "Maybe not, but someone has to be, right? Not that I'm desperate. I'm not. I do okay on my own. It just gets too quiet at night and someone to talk to...." She sighed and looked away. "Just someone to talk to about my day would be nice."

Yes. Daws understood that completely. He considered giving her his number, but he was afraid she'd misunderstand. Could he say he'd be willing to listen without scaring her? Would she believe that was all he was offering? He wasn't sure it was, or that he might want...

"I should get back, I guess." Her gaze remained across the road, where bar patrons went in and out, laughing, talking. "I'm supposed to work in the morning. I think I won't, though."

"Where do you work?"

"An office uptown. I'm lead assistant to the main production manager of a huge marketing firm. Supposedly. Mainly, I fetch coffee and manage paperwork and avoid groping hands from the guy who keeps me in a job. But someday, I'll be more than that. Creative director, maybe. And you? What's your story? I've told you nearly all of mine. I'd love to hear more about you."

"Not much to tell."

"Oh, I don't believe that one." She pressed in closer and covered him better again. "But if you don't want to say, I won't push." She switched her crossed legs, letting her foot rub lightly against his leg. "So tell me this, where do I go to find a real man instead of a pansy? Smart and hardworking, loyal, honest, a gentleman, but not afraid to get his hands dirty?"

Daws considered the way she emphasized loyal and honest as he peered into her green-flecked eyes. She'd been hurt too often. And still, there was such a spark. "Fort Drum."

"Where?"

"Army base. West side of the state across the lake from Canada."

"You're a soldier."

"Yes."

"Explains the haircut. I don't see a lot of those in Manhattan."

"I don't imagine."

"So what are you doing in the city?"

"R & R, as ordered."

"R & R?"

"Rest and Relaxation. Forced leave."

"Forced? Why? Did you go commando on some jerk who deserved it?"

He couldn't help a light grin. "Not yet. Guess I was getting too close. Just came off a funeral detail."

"For someone you knew?"

"My CO. Commanding Officer. Good man, one of the best."

"I'm sorry."

Daws nodded, staring out at the bits of flickering water dropping through the dark sky. He ignored the buildings across the street, focused only on the rain, and the dark.

"Have a girlfriend in the city? Or a wife, maybe, and a kid or two?"

"No current girlfriend and I've never been married."

"You didn't deny the kid thing."

He grabbed a breath and dropped his eyes to the gutter, the rushing water along the street. "None of my own. One I have to look after. Have no idea how. I was sitting here trying to figure that out."

"So you're here to check on him? Or her? A relative?"

"My CO's kid, in Vermont."

"Oh. So, you're from Vermont and this is just ... an escape? Did you just pick a place and go?"

Daws studied her face. Wife? Girlfriend? And she wanted to know how long he would be there? Did he dare tell her?

"I'm being nosy again. You can tell me to stop."

She still held his hand. Daws stroked a thumb along her fingers. "Why do you ask?"

A deep breath raised her chest. A shift of her body said the simple touch affected her. "Oh. I ... you have somewhere to go, right? You didn't get out here and get stuck not finding a room?"

"If I did?"

"Well, I ... I can't offer an actual room since I don't have one anymore, but I do have a hotel. There's a couch. You did say you were safe. You can't stay out here all night..."

"I live here. That is, I have an apartment here and I come back now and then on leave."

"Oh." She grabbed another breath. "Good."

"You live out of a hotel?"

"No. I ... I was not only idiot enough to move in with a married man, even though I didn't know he was married because I would never do that, but I'm a double idiot, because when I left this morning, I dropped the key in an envelope and mailed it to the office, so I can't get back in if I don't find something else. I'm in a hotel for now, but I can't stay there long. I'll call in sick again tomorrow and go hunting." She shivered.

"Can I walk you to your hotel?" He stood, her fingers still in his.

She stood beside him. "I'm in the other direction."

"That's all right."

"I couldn't ask that. It's so late already and..."

"And either I walk you back or try to stop a cab for you."

"I walked alone to get here."

He nodded. "Don't mean to be insulting, but I wouldn't feel right to let a lady walk down a dark city street on her own if I have any means to prevent that. It's not in my nature."

She started to speak, then closed her mouth again and took his arm instead of his hand.

As they headed toward her hotel, Daws moved to her other side – the side next to the street, where the man belonged.

Deanna couldn't help squeezing his arm to feel how solid it was. Even beneath the thick jacket sleeve, she could tell it was rock-firm, and her hand only wrapped part way around. Maybe half, or just over, including the stretch of her thumb.

She must have squeezed too hard, though, since he looked over at her, with a glance at her hand. "You work out a lot? Or is all this natural?"

"Comes from tensing it so often to keep from going commando on some jerk who needs it."

She caught a grin. So, there was a lighter side to him, a teasing side. "Hm. Is that so? Ever let yourself just do it?"

"Against orders. Not worth the mark on my record. But generally, you don't need to do it as long as they know you could."

"I suppose that's true. Kind of a shame, though, to have something you can't use."

He stopped walking and turned to her. "Some things are more worth having when you don't use them."

Deanna felt tension in her body drain, tension she hadn't realized was still there. More worth having. Part of her felt it might be a dig, since she'd made it so obvious how much she'd been used. That maybe he thought she was at fault for allowing it.

She supposed she was. "You know, not everything is so easy."

"Easy?"

"It's not like I knew they were lying users when I started dating them. I don't do it to myself on purpose. Some of us apparently just..."

"Deanna." He stepped closer. "That wasn't necessarily what I meant. And it wasn't an insult, not to you. A man who would use such a beautiful, charming, intelligent woman instead of honoring her, respecting her, is nothing but a fool. It's his loss much more than yours."

She loved the way he said her name. She loved that he said her name, as he held her eyes. She loved the honesty she saw in his. "I've always wondered why women have such a thing for men in uniform." She ran fingers along his stubbled neck, down the front edge of his unzipped jacket. "It's not the uniform. It's what's inside. Are all soldiers so honest and..."

"No."

Taken aback at the abruptness, she waited for more response.

"There is no group in the world that is all anything. We are trained to be respectful and in control of our actions, to be courteous to all civilians, but there's only so much you can do to train someone who doesn't have it inside. There are plenty of soldiers I know who I wouldn't want walking you home at night, or any lady. Most, however, and any of my men, I would trust to at least do that."

"Any of your men?"

"My squad. Under my command."

"So you're ... kind of high up. An officer?"

"No. Enlisted. Sergeant, which makes me an NCO. Non-commissioned officer."

"Non-commissioned?"

"A leadership position without the title or officer pay."

"Oh, then why don't you just be an officer instead?"

He frowned a moment. "Same reason you're more comfortable in jeans and bare feet, I suppose."

Same reason? Deanna pondered that. Maybe he wasn't quite as self-assured as he appeared. Maybe he was more comfortable down in the mud with the cowhands than behind the fence supervising. She had no trouble picturing him that way, on his knees in the dirt checking a horse's shoe or rubbing its leg to be sure it wasn't injured. He wasn't the type to be afraid to get his hands dirty.

She had to push that thought from her mind. "So you trust your men more because you're better at training them?"

"No. Because I won't have them in my unit if I can't trust them. They get transferred or kicked out, depending."

"Oh. But ... if you have them kicked out and then no one wants to bother to train them, to teach them better...?"

"Not my problem."

She drew back.

"Don't misunderstand. I give them a chance. They are always welcome to discuss anything with me. They are given time to get themselves together and become trustworthy. If they don't do it, that's on their heads, not on mine. My job is to train soldiers who can support the mission. My main duty is to my country. If they can't hack it under my demands, they need to be elsewhere, doing something far less demanding. I will not take anyone into battle if I don't believe he has a good chance of returning safely, not only physically, but mentally. Some of them don't need to be there, and I try to make sure they aren't."

Deanna nodded and began walking again, her fingers still around his arm. She'd never given any thought to the matter, to the military at all, really. She'd followed the recent conflict and empathized with those who had loved ones over there, but it didn't affect her daily life. She didn't see any daily life that seemed interrupted. She'd been asked her opinion once. She hadn't bothered to give it, because she couldn't say she had one, one way or the other.

It was a whole different thing to be confronted by it smack in the face.

When they approached the hotel, to where she could see its blue canopy reaching over the sidewalk, she stopped. "I'm just up there."

He glanced at it and gave her a quizzical look. "The Marriott Marquis? That's where you're living while you search for a place?"

"First night there, and I can't really afford it, but it'll push me harder to get out and move on. Besides, I felt like splurging, since whatever I find will be much less than what I've had. Not that I'm one of those spoiled have-everything types. I'm not. I had a low rent nice place and I was stupid enough to let it go. That's what I have to find again, if it's possible. Not that you wanted to know all that."

He nodded.

"Well, I should let you get back. You'll freeze." She released his arm.

"Doubtful. It's well above freezing."

Not far enough above for her, but she supposed with that build, he stayed warm easily. "Thank you for walking me back."

"My pleasure."

She grabbed a deep breath and tried to figure out what he was thinking. He'd grown quieter, looked more distant again.

"Good night, Deanna. I wish you well in your quests."

"Thank you. And you, too."

He took a step back and started to turn.

"Fred?" She moved up in front of him again. "How often do you get back to the city?"

"Not often."

"Is that ... weeks? Or..."

"Months, generally." He tilted his head. "Good to meet you." He started away again.

"Have I said something wrong?"

Turning back, he raised his eyebrows. "Why do you ask?"

"You're ... I was enjoying the conversation..."

"And I appreciate that you're trying not to be rude, but I've seen that expression before. I understand you don't approve of my career or the way I do it, and I respect your right to feel that way."

"No." She moved closer again. "I didn't say that."

"It shows."

"No, I ... it's just that I had no idea; I've never thought about it. I don't disapprove. I only don't quite understand. Maybe ... are you going to be here a few days? We could ... well, I would like to try to understand."

"No need. I'm very well used to it."

Deanna pressed closer and dropped the umbrella to her side. The rain tickled her face, dripped through her hair onto her scalp. "I haven't enjoyed a conversation like this in ... so long I can't remember. So if you have free time, I would truly like to spend some of it with you."

His face lowered toward hers. "Deanna, I'm not here often. My career is what I am. I don't know how long I plan to stay in or what I'll do if I get out. I think you're looking for something different, something more normal, for someone who's home at night. There is nothing normal about my life, and as much as I'd love to spend my leave in your company, as much as you have time for, I think it wouldn't accomplish anything except..."

She reached up and pressed her lips to his. He was startled, but he didn't back away. As she persisted in the kiss, he accepted. Softly. Tenderly. Without moving in or placing a hand on her, anywhere. And she found his eyes when she broke off the kiss. "I'm stronger than you think I am, Fred Dawson. And I have no idea what normal is. I'm not sure I care to know. I do know that every thought in my head right now says to take time off work for as long as you're in the city, even if it risks my job, just to be able to spend time with you. I've never done that. I've never wanted to do that. But I do. And if your career is what you are, then I have tremendous respect for it."

Daws had no idea how to answer. He'd tried to put off talking about his work, since he figured she would back away as soon as he did. It happened. Often. Or if they didn't right away, they became demanding of his time, time he didn't have when he was in the field or away at training or spending from five in the morning to seven at night at work because he had to be there. He knew how high the divorce rate was within the military, and how many found their spouses or girlfriends cheating because the alone time became too overwhelming. As well as how many soldiers had flings while they were away on training missions and their wives found out. No matter how often he warned his men, both ways, it still happened. He supposed it was largely inevitable.

"So?" She peered into his eyes.

"You don't understand how hard it can be to even hold a friendship together, much less anything else..."

"You think I don't?" She touched his neck, let her eyes follow her fingers. "Try being a woman becoming a professional in New York where men are in charge and intend to stay that way. They want you to bring their coffee and warm their beds. They don't want you to be competition. And there's more of them. How many friendships do you think I have under the circumstances? Most of the women I know are the wives and girlfriends and mistresses and receptionists. The ones who are professionals or trying to become that see me as competition. They don't want that, either. I know how hard it is to hold a relationship together. Trust me; that I know. I've yet been able to do it. But I keep trying. Does that make me naive?" She shrugged. "Maybe. But it also means I'm strong enough to keep trying. It means I want it enough to keep trying. I'm not a quitter. And I'm not afraid to be on my own."

The fire Daws saw inside her drew him in, despite how hard he tried not to be drawn in. The warmth, the energy, was hard to resist. He raised his hand to push wet strands of hair from her face. "What would you say to breakfast before you start apartment hunting?"

Her expression was half amused, half wary. "You expect me to ask you up tonight?"

"No." He lowered his hand. "I meant I'll come back in the morning. There's a little place I always go for pancakes when I'm here. Wouldn't mind company."

"You are an actual gentleman. What do you know? I didn't realize there were any left."

"Don't jump to conclusions. You don't know what's going through my head right now."

Deanna laughed. "Well, Fred Dawson, at least it's not coming out through your fingers. That's close enough." She touched his hand but didn't quite grasp it. "I would love to meet you for breakfast. But I don't plan to be up early. I plan to linger and lounge and make full use of this too-extravagant room while I have it."

"What time?"

"Eleven too late? That's check out time."

"Only staying one night?"

"Guess I better. Might take me a while to find what I need. Usually does." She winked.

"I'll be here at eleven."

With a grin, she tilted her face up to the dark sky. "The rain stopped."

"It'll start again."

Deanna met his gaze. "We can only hope. Maybe it'll wash away past sins."

Unable to resist, Daws let his fingers slide down her face and under her chin. "If tonight had been my only night of leave, it would have been worth the drive." Before he couldn't control himself enough, he moved back. "Let me walk you to the door."

She didn't argue. She folded the umbrella away and ambled along at his side until the doorman hurried to open it for them. For her. He wasn't going inside.

"Good night, Deanna."

She set a hand on his chest, over his coat. "Would you like to come up? Just long enough to get warm?"

"No."

"No? You look like you would."

"Maybe. But I won't. Not tonight."

"I don't mean for it to be ... sordid, or anything." She lowered her eyes a moment and returned them. "I never do things so fast, despite what you may be thinking."

"I didn't expect you did."

"No? Maybe since you won't be here long, though..."

"I can't tonight. My head is in Vermont and I need to keep it there for now."

She nodded. "You had a lot of respect for your CO."

"More than anyone else in the world."

"I'm so very sorry you lost him." Deanna touched his face. "Okay. Tomorrow, then. I look forward to it. Good night, Fred Dawson."

He stopped her when she started to turn, and leaned in to claim her lips. Her warmth spread through him, the willingness mixed with hesitation, the way she slid her arms up around his shoulders and set a palm against the back of his head, the way she caught his eyes when they parted and threw an expression of hope for things to come.

Daws noted the doorman trying hard not to pay attention or comment when Deanna finally walked away, into the hotel, up to her room. As he headed back the way he'd come, he thought of her eyes, her lips, her smile. Her laugh. The walk seemed short, despite how far he had gone away from his apartment. Before he let himself into his own building, he looked up as the rain grew harder, parted his lips, and let the moisture in.

Early morning rain gave way to moist-aired sunshine. Daws stepped out on the sidewalk and pushed his sunglasses over his eyes. He couldn't remember the last time he'd allowed himself the luxury of sleeping past sunrise. Or when he'd felt better rested. Still two hours before he could go meet Deanna, he decided to stretch his legs in the other direction before he returned for a shower.

The sidewalk bustled with city dwellers on their way to work, or to grab coffee before work. He didn't understand the recent penchant for going out to get coffee instead of simply throwing grounds and water in a machine and waiting the two minutes until it was done. He much preferred drinking from his own cup, a real cup of ceramic, substantial enough not to bend under his fingers, than from a flimsy throw-away thing that who-knows-how-many hands had been on. Not that he was all that wary of germs; in his line of work, that would be impossible. Still, the disposable feel of coffee on the go didn't sit well with him.

He'd savored his first two cups of the day as he always did, propped on the couch watching the news. Even when he recognized the rhetoric for what it was, it at least kept him in touch with what was said, with what was believed by the general masses. And current events were part of the upcoming E6 board. He had to stay in touch.

Part of him resisted going to the board, now that Major Reynauld wouldn't be the one to oversee it. He would go. It was an order. The order still stood although the major was no longer around to enforce it. He'd learned that lesson years ago, as a child. The one to have to enforce something got done wasn't, or shouldn't be, the one who gave the order. It was the one given the order who was responsible for enforcing it. That concept too often went over his unit's heads. Some picked it up. Many didn't.

Thoughts of his major took his mind back to Vermont, to the Reynauld family. He'd left his number with his unit with instructions to notify him immediately if the major's wife called with any need, any request. His lieutenant had suggested they could take care of whatever needed to be done, there was no reason Daws should take personal charge of seeing to them. *A jerk who deserved it*, as Deanna would say. And Daws wished he could deck him. Instead, he'd repeated his major's request for him to personally look after his family. The lieutenant, as much as he disliked Daws, would never counter that.

Maybe he would swing up by Vermont on his way back to Drum. It would add time to the trip, but he liked to drive. He would like to drive even more when he finally found the car he wanted. His old Chevy was all right for the moment. Since it had to sit so often while he was away, it would do. He didn't want anything he was too particular about until he would be around enough to care for it the way it needed, or until someone was.

Deanna rolled over and checked the alarm clock. "*Oh.*" Ten-fifteen. Had she really slept that long? She never slept that long.

Fred would be there at eleven, and she had to be not only ready and put together enough she wouldn't turn him away, with any hope, but packed and checked out. Unless she stayed another day. No. That was too much luxury, too much expense.

She hurried in and out of the shower, hanging one of her blouses in the bathroom so the steam could help straighten the wrinkles from her suitcase, and then wondered if it was still raining. Pulling the curtains back, she squinted at the bright sunlight. A beautiful spring day. Perfect. It would be nice for apartment hunting, nice for looking better than she had the night before in the rain when she'd felt so fatigued and lost.

With a quick blow dry to give her hair a head start before she left it to dry on its own, Deanna added gel to control the frizz. She was so often jealous of women with silky sleek hair that looked full of moisture and easy to care for, when hers was like a straw mop unless she added stuff and was careful not to over dry. Sometimes it still looked like a mop. She could only hope it wouldn't today.

Adding a touch of color to her face, Deanna was careful not to overdo that, either. She used less than she would for work, since at work, they would complain if she didn't look professional enough with eye liner and color and mascara and lip liner and.... It was too much. She hated messing with it every morning. And something told her Fred Dawson wouldn't appreciate that much fuss. A touch of blush, some soft lipstick, and a light brush of mascara. Enough.

Her hair cooperated nicely, a surprise as unexpected and as welcome as the bright sunshine, and she pulled into her jeans and casual blouse. Unsure of the temperature, she kept her light sweater out, grabbed her bags, took a glance around to be sure she didn't forget anything, and headed down to meet him.

She didn't find him in the lobby, and he hadn't said whether he would come in. Hoping he hadn't changed his mind, Deanna went to return her key card. "Can I store these here for a few hours?" She glanced at her bags, the two on the floor and the one over her shoulder.

"Store them? Are you coming back tonight?" The hotel attendant barely moved his eyes from the computer.

"Why would I check out if I was?"

"Well, we do store luggage for those who come in early and are staying that night. However, since you're on your way elsewhere, perhaps they could store them for you?"

"I'm not sure where that elsewhere is going to be and I'm meeting a friend for breakfast before I find that elsewhere. Is it a problem to have them sit in your back room with other guests' luggage? I am a paying guest, as well. I'm not looking for a handout, you know."

"I did not mean to imply you were."

"Then it's not a problem? You could have simply said 'of course we can'."

"Ah, Mrs..." He looked down at her registration paperwork.

"*Ms.* My marital status has no bearing here."

"Of course not. And what time would you be back to claim your luggage?"

"I'm not sure."

He gave her one of those 'why is this my problem' looks.

"If I was one of your regular customers, you would have no problem with it. I'm paying the same rate they are, at least. Is this really a problem for you?"

"You can put them in my car."

She turned. Fred was behind her. "Well, good morning." She couldn't help a smile. He looked incredible dry and clean-shaven, his substantial chest well featured beneath a plain navy tee.

"Good morning. Let me take this." He reached for the bag that was over her shoulder.

"You don't need to."

Her protest didn't stop him and he threw it over his own. "Are you checked out?"

"Yes. I was just..."

"I heard." He threw the attendant a rather unfriendly look. "No need to bother. We'll put them in the car until you decide where you'll be tonight."

"Oh, well thank you, but after breakfast I have to..."

"Apartment hunt. I remember. Thought it might be easier with wheels. If you want company, that is."

His company, she definitely wanted. "You don't have other plans or something you should be doing?"

"No. It would keep me from having nothing to do. That's not a feeling I'm comfortable with, and why I don't take leave often."

She grinned. "I can just imagine you aren't. Thank you, I'll accept, if you're sure."

By way of answer, he grabbed both suitcases, stepped back, and nodded for her to lead. He refused to let her carry even one of them.

As he loaded them into the trunk of a brown Chevy Malibu, Deanna couldn't help notice how clean it was. There was a first aid kit and what she guessed were flairs, both in a side pocket. Otherwise, there was nothing in it. Not even dirt or paperwork. She looked in through the back windows when he moved to open her door.

"It's not much, but it runs well."

"Oh." He'd caught her studying it. "Did you clean it out for me?"

He frowned and glanced inside. "Why?"

"There's nothing in it, no empty cups, no papers, no ... anything."

"There generally isn't."

"No?" Deanna stood beside the open car door, next to his arm holding it for her. "Are you this meticulous about every aspect of your life, Fred Dawson?"

He leaned in, only a touch, and held her gaze. "About anything that matters."

"Is that so?" She wanted to run a hand down his chest and press her lips into his again. "Should I wipe my shoes before I get in? And if I set paperwork in the back, will you kick me out?"

"I'll let you slide today." He stepped forward and nearly brushed his body against hers. His eyes showed the start of a grin. "Getting in or have you changed your mind?"

He smelled of ... something fully masculine. Woody and sensual. Light enough she had to be close to smell it. It wasn't overdone. Or understated. It was just enough. "I haven't changed my mind. I'm going to have a wonderful time trying to get to know you. Fair warning." Deanna brushed a shoulder against him as she lowered into his car, not accidentally.

She sighed as he again opened her door and held it until she got into his car. Six strikes in one day. Too expensive, too noisy, too far from work, or too creepy. None of them could possibly do.

He got in on the driver's side and looked over at her. "Where to next?"

"I can't do this anymore today." Deanna tossed her list in the back seat. "Guess I should find a place to land for the next few nights. Any thoughts on a hotel that's not horribly pricey but either near a bus stop or close enough it won't be a fortune in cab fairs to lower Manhattan?"

"Yes, I have thoughts on that. Are you hungry? How about dinner?"

"I'm famished, never mind I ate too much this morning. But it's my treat since you paid for breakfast and you've been carting me all over the city. I should find a hotel first, though, and maybe freshen up."

"You look fine, and we'll talk about the night's arrangements as we eat. Choose the restaurant."

Deanna nearly argued, afraid she'd get stuck at some seedy little motel if she didn't reserve soon enough, but she was famished, and if she looked good enough for him, that was good enough. "You want close by or farther out?"

"Either."

"Not tired of driving?"

"No, I don't get to often. Doesn't matter. Just tell me where."

She led him out of Manhattan and into Yonkers to a place one of her early dates had taken her. The food was luscious with large helpings, the atmosphere nice and casual and not too loud, and it wasn't priced horribly high. Not too high she couldn't afford to treat him as a thank you.

He'd been such an incredible gentleman all day, opening every door, assisting with questions as she needed but not so far as to be imposing, patiently following her directions to each address she found in the listings she thought might work, and he didn't even complain when they backtracked because she skipped one. She wondered if he was only on his best behavior since they'd just met. It would hardly be the first time. They had a tendency to show their best face for the first couple of weeks before it dissolved to show their actual structure.

Somehow, she couldn't imagine Fred Dawson faking anything.

He did answer questions about his job when she asked. He didn't volunteer extra information. That was all right. He said he had another six days of leave. She would have time yet.

They both ordered tea and she alternated her gaze between the menu and the man sitting across from her. She wouldn't call him gorgeous; his face was more square than classic and his features were nice but not stand out. He was attractive, though, and she couldn't help wonder what he'd look like with more hair.

When he looked over his own menu and caught her eyes, she knew she'd been caught.

"Sorry."

"For what?" He looked at least a touch amused.

"For staring. You know I was."

A light grin skimmed his mouth. "Yes. And what did you decide?"

"About what?"

"Whether or not you'd be embarrassed to be seen with me around your friends."

"Oh. No. I wasn't ... why would you think that?"

He shrugged. "Would you be?"

"Embarrassed to be seen with you? Obviously not. And I can't imagine any reason I would be."

"Can't you?" He lowered his menu.

"No."

He kept her eyes as he reached across the table to touch the side of her face. "You are a truly beautiful woman."

Deanna's first instinct was to treat it as a line, a come on. But she couldn't believe it was. She'd already asked him up, the night before. He wouldn't have had to try so hard. Before she could figure out how to answer, he pulled his hand away and gave her a soft grin. Then he returned his attention to the menu. She did her best to do the same.

"You're asking me to move in with you?" Deanna pulled back against her chair.

"I think you misunderstand." Daws leaned forward. "You need a place to stay. I'm rarely here. Instead of paying someone to take care of the place, I'm offering you the second room."

"You mean you want me to stay after you leave."

"Yes."

"Oh." She took another bite of her brownie, with a touch of ice cream, balancing them as she ate.

He wasn't sure whether she was relieved or insulted. He was sure he'd handled it wrong. "Only if you have interest, not if you don't. It's an offer, not a request. It sits empty much of the time..."

"And you would trust me there? You hardly know me."

"You've trusted me all day long. The way I see it, you had more to lose than I do. It's only an apartment. Furniture. Nothing more than that. How did you know it was safe to offer the couch in your hotel room last night, or to get in my car today?"

"I don't know. Something told me I could." She played with the fudge along the edge of her dessert plate, making a design with the tip of the spoon.

He took a sip of his coffee, watching her. "I suppose I hear the same voice."

She raised her eyes. "So ... if I accept, what does it entail? I mean, do I take over the rent and utilities? How much is that? Because...."

"No. There's no rent. Utilities are paid. I mean only opening windows, keeping the cobwebs out, running the water. General use."

"No rent?" Deanna sucked another bite of brownie and ice cream off her spoon as she eyed him. "It's ... in a decent part of town? Because, well, not to be too awfully particular but you saw some of those places today and I'm okay at self-defense but I don't want to push that too far."

"I wouldn't ask you if it wasn't safe, and decent. And again, it's only an offer. I can keep things the way they are." He set the cup down. "Think about it. I'll show it to you if you want. Tonight, or tomorrow."

"Okay. You show me and I'll think about it."

"Tonight or tomorrow?"

"I don't have plans tonight, well, other than finding a hotel. You said you had thoughts about that..."

"Yes. Are you ready? No rush if you want to finish."

"No, I've had too much. Sure you don't want to try it? Even a bite? If you're worried about my germs, hand me your spoon."

"Worried about your germs? After that kiss last night?"

She grinned and scooped up a large piece of the brownie, topped it with ice cream, and held it out. Tempting him. Testing. Daws gripped both the spoon and her hand and leaned in to accept. He didn't rush. He held her eyes as he closed his lips firmly around the dessert.

"Oh, Fred Dawson." Deanna grabbed another quick bite of ice cream and turned the spoon upside down to lick it clean. "You, I think, could be horribly, horribly dangerous."

Funny. Daws had the same thought about her. He washed the rich chocolate down with a long swallow of now lukewarm coffee. "Ready?"

"I'll try to be."

Pulling her chair out, he enjoyed the way she automatically took his arm, and the way she again squeezed his bicep. Testing its hardness. Or enjoying its hardness. Its girth. She liked sturdy. That much, he knew about her without doubt. And she was sturdy. Daws heard the major's voice echo through his head about finding a sturdy, caring, energetic girl. He would like Deanna. Daws also had no doubt about that.

She was silent on the way to his place after the day full of conversation. He supposed she might be nervous. It was one thing to ask a man into your own place and another entirely to go to his. Like a fly into a spider's web, one girl had told him. He would do what he could to put her at ease.

When he led her into the apartment, her jaw nearly dropped. Daws left the door open for the time being, to leave her an easy escape route if she felt she needed it. "Not what you expected?"

"No." She went in farther, straight to the ceiling to floor windows with the balcony on the other side. "This is incredible. Look at this view."

He shut the door and joined her, not too close. "Want to step outside? It's better from there." With her nod, he led her to the balcony.

She gripped the metal railing as she looked out over New York in the dark, lit up with a million tiny sparkling lights. "The Army must pay well."

He laughed. "No. Not at my rank, it doesn't."

"Then how do you afford this?" She swiveled to face him. "You're not into anything ... on the side, are you? Because no matter how attracted I am to you, I won't have anything to do with anything shady."

Attracted to him. Daws moved closer. "You are an amazing woman, Deanna." He touched her face. "I'm into nothing shady. This belonged to my parents. No rent; I own it. Never liked it much before, but it's growing on me."

"Didn't like it? How could you not like this? It's stunning." She looked back in through the windows. "So much space and so open and ... and it sits empty?"

"Keep thinking I should rent it but I like to have it when I am here, instead of worrying with a hotel."

"I can imagine."

"If you agree to move in, I would still expect to stay when I'm in the city. But I'm not here much and there are two rooms. Let me show you the rest." He took her hand and led her to the kitchen first. Judging from her response, he figured she thought it was adequate enough. Then the guest room. The main bath. And the master suite.

Deanna turned a circle in the middle of the room. "This is bigger than my last apartment all smooshed together. Is that a walk-in?" She looked at the mirror-covered closet doors.

He went over and opened them to show off the large walk-in closet, complete with a wall of shelves for sweaters and small niches for shoes. His mother was addicted to shoes. He wasn't sure she had ever worn any one pair more than a few times a year. But she'd kept them all. He gave them all to Goodwill.

"It's every woman's dream." Deanna pulled down the built in ironing board and pushed it back up again. "I can't believe you don't have one already."

"Have what?"

"A woman." She moved in front of him, very close in front of him. "Why don't you?"

"Hard lifestyle. Not many are willing, or stay willing. My job comes first; I have no choice on that. We're called GI for a reason. Government Issue. We belong to the Army."

"But most soldiers are married, aren't they?"

"They are. Often doesn't last. Or if they last, it's by a thread. Not sure I want to put someone through that."

She dropped her eyes and set a hand on his chest. "I have every feeling in the world it would be worth it."

"Because of the closet?" Maybe he should have waited longer to show his apartment, to give her a hint about what he had beyond his military pay.

"No. Because of you."

"Deanna..."

"So." She retreated and ambled back into the center of the master suite. "You haven't told me yet what you want in exchange for letting me stay here, other than that you'd be here when you're in town. Would you want me to leave then?"

"No. As I said, there are two rooms. This one would be yours."

"Oh. No. I couldn't let you do that. This ... this is yours."

"I don't stay in here. I use the other."

"Are you kidding? Why?"

"This was my parents' room. It's all still their furniture. I do use the master bath. But I wouldn't if you agree to stay. It would be yours." He nodded to the corner where the door was half open and followed her when she went to look. "Nice for long hot baths when you're wet and cold from talking to a stranger after midnight."

"A Jacuzzi tub." She walked up to it and ran her fingers along the edge. "Big enough for two." She turned back to where he waited at the door. "Even when one of you is on the larger side."

Daws tensed when she touched his shoulder, caressing him with both fingers and eyes. He had to distract his thoughts. "Think you might be interested?" He moved back out into the suite.

"Oh, I'm far more than simply interested. If you're sure." She closed the distance and returned her hand to where it had been.

"I've never been more unsure of anything, if you want the truth."

She smiled. "That makes two of us. Should be fun, huh?"

He leaned in and let his hand slide around the back of her head as he kissed her. He shouldn't have done it there, in the master suite, so close beside the bed, but he'd never in his life been as comfortable in that room as he was at this moment. No matter how unsure he was.

"Deanna." His forehead met hers, hands resting on her waist. "Stay here. I'll be glad to know you are."

"I'll be glad to be here. And I'll take very good care of it for you."

He followed when she walked back out to the living room, slipped out of her shoes, and lowered onto the couch. "So none of this furniture was your idea?"

"No." He walked most of the way over, but stayed on his feet. "It's been this way since I can remember. I keep thinking I'll update, make it more..."

"More you?"

He tilted his head in acknowledgement.

"So maybe we could go shopping tomorrow and you can show me what you would pick out if you had all the money to choose anything you wanted for your place."

"Tomorrow? You're not working?"

"No. I'm taking the week off while you're here. Unless you get sick of me."

"Can you afford that?"

"Depends. How much are you charging me for rent? Because you know I can't do what it's worth."

"No rent." He lowered onto a chair facing her. "I don't want anything, except maybe to be able to call you now and then. The phone's hooked up. I'll leave the number for you."

"Fred, I can't do that. At least let me pay you something."

"I won't have to pay someone to come by and care for it. Fair enough for me."

"Are you sure?"

"If I am, you can afford to take the whole week off?"

"Yes."

"Then I'm positive."

She grinned. "So, shopping tomorrow? I'll be easy on you. I promise. Just window shopping. I do that a lot."

"Know much about decorating?"

"I do okay."

"Maybe we'll do more than window shop, then." He started away from her. "How about coffee? Or wine?"

"Either sounds good. But, a question. How soon did you want me to move in? When you leave?"

"Tonight. That way I'm here as you get used to it, if you have questions. I'll put coffee on and go grab your bags." He didn't let her argue and didn't let her walk out to the garage with him. Setting her suitcases and shoulder bag in her room, he had to wonder if that was all she had. By the time he returned to the living room, she'd found cups and had two sitting side by side on the coffee table.

He sat next to her and sipped it carefully. "Do you have more things somewhere we should pick up tomorrow?"

"I rented a little storage space. Todd didn't want all my stuff at his place so it's tucked away. It can stay there."

"Nothing you want? Then why are you keeping it?"

"Oh, I do want it. A lot of personal stuff, books, music – I'd especially want my music, memorabilia. Things like that. They'll wait. Maybe I'll grab at least some of my albums, though, one of these days. If you don't mind."

"Bring what you like. If it'll fit in your room, no discussion needed. Anything bigger we might talk about."

"Everything I have would fit in the suite, with room to spare, but you're sure?"

He kissed her. Light. Quick. Just to touch her lips. "It's your room. Other than taking walls down, decorate as you wish."

"I still think you should take the suite. The small room is fine. It's as much as I had at my own place."

"You can't enjoy the closet that way." He grinned and sipped more coffee. "And I won't be here enough to warrant all that space."

She dropped her eyes. "Well, when you want it back, say so. I don't have a lot. It won't be hard to move." Crossing her legs, she leaned back against the couch. "So what happened to your parents?"

Daws grabbed a swallow of his coffee. He'd expected her to ask eventually.

"You don't talk about them?"

"Not generally. They're more a distant thought than anything else by now."

"They've been gone a long time?"

"No. A few years. I was already out and gone. Didn't affect much."

She shifted, facing him more directly, and set a hand on his leg. "Still ... it was hard, I'm sure, even if they weren't supporting you anymore."

He couldn't help a snicker. "They're supporting me now about as much as they ever did. As I said, this was theirs. Everything came to me." After he said it, Daws wondered if he should have. He never told anyone. He was military. He lived on his military pay. This was all separate. He didn't want her to think otherwise.

"You're an only child?"

He met her gaze.

"Sorry, I'm being snoopy again. I'll stop." Deanna pulled back, uncrossing her legs and bending them up beside her. Making herself at home. In her nearly bare feet.

"Have an older sister somewhere." Daws held his position, maintaining the distance. At least physically. "Half sister. Haven't seen her since the funeral. Hardly did for several years before. She refused to take anything, said it was mine." He shrugged and took another swallow, with the thought that he should have opted for wine instead. "Not that she needs it."

"You weren't close to any of your family?"

"No. I was taught to take care of myself early on, and I did that. They fought to have custody of her over the summer, only to have someone here when I was out of school since they couldn't leave me alone legally. As soon as she turned eighteen, she didn't come back. Don't blame her." He stood and took her empty coffee cup. "How about we switch to wine? Or I have a few other choices. Have a favorite drink I should know about?"

Deanna smiled. "I don't know. Should I tell you or make you guess? My guess is you don't have it."

"You're very well right. Don't have a lot here. Coffee's always stocked. It's in the freezer to stay fresh. Move it out if you want since you'll be using it."

"Whatever you have is fine. I'm not horribly particular." She stood next to him, took the cups, and set them on the table. "Well." Moving in close, she slid her hands over his shoulders. "I am about some things."

"Yes, I can imagine you are. Are you going to tell me what you like best?"

She chuckled and ran fingers along his neck.

"I meant as far as a drink."

"Did you?" She slid them into his hair, or at least over his hair. "Going to let this grow out once you can?"

"Maybe. To an extent. It was never much longer before." He allowed his hands to lower from her waist to her hips.

"So what happened to them? You didn't say."

He felt his chest expand and nearly pulled back, but her eyes held him in. "They were … adventurous. Always out running somewhere, including places most people would never go. Never found out exactly what happened, but they were where they shouldn't have been, in the middle of something they shouldn't have been in, and they were shipped back to the States in body bags. That's about all I know, and all I care to know. Whatever it was, it kept me from getting the assignment I wanted."

"In the Army? Why?"

"Needs a high security clearance. They checked my family history. Whatever they were doing down there screwed my chances. Not that I even knew what they were doing."

"That's not fair."

He shrugged. "Security is more important than personal gain. It's as fair as it can be."

"You don't resent it?"

"I don't resent the Army. They have to put the mission and the country first. I do resent my parents since they didn't give a second thought to what it would do to me. It was always them first. Yes, I resent that. I resent that some of my superiors look down on me because of it. They know more than I do, I suppose. I've had to work harder to get where I am. There are still some who don't trust me."

"I'm sorry."

"No reason to be. What you want to overcome, you can, if you're willing. I'm still rising fast enough, heading to the E6 board by order of the major, as soon as I'm back. I'll have to spend time studying while I'm here."

"E6 board?"

"For a promotion from Sergeant to Staff Sergeant. Senior NCO. It'll look good on job applications when I decide to do something else, if I do."

"And what else are you thinking about doing, if you do?"

"Haven't decided yet."

"Well, Sergeant Dawson." She kissed his neck; her arms tightened around his shoulders. "Whatever it is you decide to do, I'll bet anything you'll be darn good at it." Her lips moved up to his jaw, swirled in front of his face, teasing. Offering.

Daws had the implicit feeling she'd moved the conversation away from careers and into something much more personal. Or he hoped she had. When he had all the teasing he could take, he claimed her mouth, pulled her in. He wondered if she had any idea what she was doing, how hot the fire was she'd started to kindle. Sonya had been his last. Four months ago. Before war. Before losing the major. And she was never much of a spark. Barely that.

He'd never told anyone what he just told Deanna, never wanted to tell anyone. There was always the fear they'd back away, believe the worst, that he could turn out like his parents, that it would come back at him somehow. He supposed it could. The thought was always in his mind. Always. After finding what information he could, he'd picked up the self-defense training he'd started years before. He was well trained, well beyond what the military taught him. He was an expert marksman and had some basic training in marshal arts. He put himself through a defensive driver course. Everywhere he was, he watched everything going on around him, and he'd learned how to do it without anyone knowing he was.

Security would be his best option, he supposed. But he didn't want to be a night guard or anything nearly that understated. He couldn't imagine walking around a building all night. Secret Service was out, because of his family history. There had to be something similar, though.

Or he would be a lifer with the Army. He had no plans to settle too much, to marry, or have kids. He could very well stay in and go wherever they sent him.

Although he could see himself, at this moment with Deanna in his arms, with full knowledge she wouldn't turn him down, not the way she was pushing for more, at least part settled. The thought disturbed him. He couldn't let her think it would be more than occasional get-togethers, maybe some talking over the phone.

He pulled back.

She didn't allow the retreat. The hand behind his head held firm, and she kissed him again. The woman knew how to kiss, how to intoxicate him, stun him into allowing her to have her way. But only so far. He would never be that fully controlled.

He grasped her hands and forced space. "How about that drink?"

"If I didn't know better, I'd think you were afraid of me, Sergeant."

Maybe he was. He didn't answer.

"Don't worry. I'm a big girl. I take care of myself well. I'm not needy. I'm not asking you for anything."

"Aren't you? It tends to feel that way."

She grinned and leaned in to kiss his neck. "Well, maybe I'm asking for a little something. I love how this feels. I love the way you feel, the way you smell. The way you want to give in but won't. Hard to find a man with that much control. It's nice. It feels safe. Not something I'm very used to feeling. And I really enjoy kissing you. You kiss nice. I'd sure like to enjoy it for the next few days while I can."

Daws took her head gently in his hands, gazed into her eyes. "You know I don't have any expectations only because you're staying here."

"What if I have expectations?"

He felt himself exhale too sharply at her lips against his neck, the curve of his shoulder, behind his ear, her hands sliding down to his hips.

Clenching his eyes, he grasped for the control she thought he had that she admired. It was too soon. He was there only a few days. "I tell you what. If, after I've been away for however long I'll be away this time, you still have interest..." He moved back to see her face, to raise her chin. "If you still have expectations by then, I'll do my best to fulfill them. While I'm here. But realize I have two years left on my enlistment, and I may very well stay in for twenty or more. It could be I'll never be able to give you more than a week or two at a time every few months."

"I do realize that. And yet, I can't imagine not having those weeks, or at least giving this a chance." She ran fingers along his arm. "Okay. We'll take it slow. But in the meantime, we can still enjoy this, right?" Her lips pressed back in.

Yes, she was going to be very dangerous.

=== June ===

"Get lost." Deanna swerved around Todd and continued toward the copier.

"Deanna, come on. I've apologized how often already? We're separated. I told you, it's you I want. I even left her for you. I'm at the penthouse full time now. Come back home."

"I'm at work. Keep it up and I'll file sexual harassment."

"No, you won't."

She swiveled to face him. "Be glad I haven't already. I said no. I mean no. I want nothing more to do with you."

He stepped closer. "You're still angry. I understand."

She nearly laughed. "Todd, I'm over being angry. To be honest, I was over being angry the night I left, or at least by the next night." Thoughts of the *next night* swirled through her head: walking in the rain, sitting with Fred on the metal bench, his lips touching hers. "Honestly, I don't care enough to be angry. I just don't care that much about you." She ran the two papers through the copier and returned to her desk. He wouldn't follow her. Too obvious.

A folder sat on top of what she was working on, another stupid note from her boss clipped to it. Skimming, she rolled her eyes. Did he think he had to spell everything out? Might as well be written in crayon, the moron. She flipped through the contents. There was no need for the note; it was all self-explanatory, nothing she hadn't done at least twenty times before.

"Understand my instructions? Wasn't sure how long you'd be and I have to leave for my meeting."

Deanna forced herself not to roll her eyes at him. "I'm not five and my English comprehension is very good. Got it the first time you told me the first time I did this."

"You might want to watch that attitude, Miss Meyers, if you're trying to work your way up in this company. Or if you want to keep the job you do have."

She didn't answer. Her work was too good to get fired. She knew how far she could push. She knew he didn't want her to go anywhere considering how she lightened his work load. And he knew she knew. He could screw his attitude warning.

Twenty minutes and she could go home, to Fred's apartment. She wasn't sure he'd call tonight. It had been several days since he was in the field doing some kind of training he wouldn't specify. He did tell her enough to know he was in a tent on a cot with only nightly field tent showers and an occasional "whore's bath" as he'd called them, when he scooped water into his helmet, used it to clean what had to be cleaned, dumped it, and put it back on his head. She could see him sweaty from June's heat, dirty from working outside all day, and sleeping near naked beneath the scratchy wool olive drab Army-issue blanket. Deanna envisioned it every night as she got into the king sized bed and wished she could be out there with him. She'd told him that the first night he mentioned it. He said it was his least favorite part of the job and she'd change her mind if she actually tried. Maybe. But his dirty sweaty nearly naked body was so much more a turn on than the office morons in their pressed, starched, and perfect suits and ties.

"Something funny?"

Deanna glanced at Gail, collected herself, and tried to finish what she could before five o'clock came. The rest would wait until nine the next morning. Nothing like his six a.m. to seven p.m. days in the field, or o-six-hundred to nineteen-hundred, as he called it. He had to have incredible stamina to be able to do that several days in a row, or several weeks. She supposed she shouldn't be considering his stamina, either.

"Share the joke in your head with the rest of us, why don't you?"

Deanna didn't bother to look over. "No joke, and it's nothing to share."

"She's got a new bed warmer. Don't you? Fess up."

"Grow up, Margie. We're not seventeen." Deanna crumpled the stupid note and tossed it in the trash.

"You mean eighteen, right? Because seventeen would be illegal." Margie glanced at her gossip buddy. "Or maybe that means she was still illegal when she had her first bedmate. What do you want to bet?"

Deanna rolled her eyes. "Legal depends where you are. Some places it's fifteen, actually. And why don't you just admit you're only mad at me because you wanted Todd? I know you are, and he's free again, or as free as he'll ever be, if you want to go for it." She shoved the folder in her file cabinet and grabbed her handbag from the drawer. "I'm out of here for today."

Margie's mouth gaped. "It's ten till. And I don't want your seconds."

"Okay. I don't believe you, but if it feels better to tell yourself that instead of admitting he wants nothing to do with you, go ahead. And I can tell time. Boss left early; it's fair game. Have a nice night." Deanna used her too-sweet voice and sauntered past them to the elevator.

===

Daws pushed out of his boots and stripped off the BDU shirt that could nearly stand by itself at this point, with the sweat and dirt caked together and dried. He dropped it on the tile floor and headed toward the shower. But there was one thing more urgent: he went back to grab the phone and dialed New York. It rang four times, five. Maybe she was out. It was after seven; she'd had plenty of time to get home from work.

About to give up and try later, he heard her voice. "Thought I'd missed you."

"*Fred*. Hey, you're back in from the field?"

"Just now. And I need to shower, but thought I'd check in first since it's been a few days. How are you? Were you heading out?"

"No, I...." She chuckled. "Just got out of the shower. Had to throw the towel around real fast to catch the phone without soaking the floor. Hoped it might be you."

Just out of the shower. Only a towel around her. He should have waited and showered himself first.

"Still there?"

"Yes. Sorry, tired. Didn't sleep much out there."

"You sound it. But I hoped you were tongue-tied at the thought of me standing here wet and nearly naked."

"Hm. Trying not to think of it. Can I call back in about ten minutes? I'm not even clean enough to talk to you over the phone."

"Of course, but I don't mind, you know. I wouldn't even mind if it was in person."

"I think you might. I can't even stand myself."

"Okay, go shower and I'll get dressed. Good to hear your voice. I've been wondering if you were okay."

"Were you?"

"More than I should be. Making it hard to work." She paused. "Anyway, go get clean. I'll be here."

With his agreement and the click from the other end, Deanna clenched her eyes a moment. She couldn't do that again. She had to be sure he knew she could handle the separations, that she would be fine. And she would be. She was. She only ... she missed touching him.

Crazy woman. One week with the guy she hardly knew didn't give her any right to miss him.

She did, though.

She was barely in her pajamas with a thin, thigh-length robe wrapped around when the phone rang. Quick shower. The man didn't mess around. With a grin, she grabbed the cordless and went to pour herself a glass of wine. As they chatted, she settled into the big armchair he always used, the one she had so often joined him in, her legs over his, her body cuddled against his chest and stomach, wrapped in his arms. He made her feel small, physically, not something she had ever felt before. Mentally, she felt larger around him than she ever had.

They talked for nearly two hours, both grabbing something to eat as though they were together. He told her about Todd's come on, about her boss talking down to her again, and about jealous Margie. She didn't mention the bedmate age conversation. He might pry too much if she did. That was too much information too soon. Eventually, if they had an eventually, she would tell him.

"I've been talking too much. It's your turn. Tell me about the field."

Daws stretched his legs out in front of him. "Nothing more to say. Heat, dirt, noise, tiny-ass cots, scratchy blankets, mosquitoes. About covers it."

She chuckled. "Sounds fun, but what were you doing exactly?"

He didn't want to tell her he couldn't tell her. It would sound more mysterious than it was, more secretive, but still, there were things he did not say over the phone. Some soldiers said far more than they should. Papers often said far more than they should. Still, he didn't.

"Okay, I get it. You can't say or you don't want to."

"Tell you what." He pulled his legs back in and leaned forward. "When I get back to the city, I'll tell you anything you want to know, within regs."

"Will you?"

"If you're interested."

"I'm interested, Fred."

Those three words made him want to jump in the car and drive to the city. Couldn't do it. He had to be at the motor pool at o-eight-hundred. "I can tell you my promotion's going through. Points dropped just enough. I get pinned next month." And he wanted to invite her, to have her there since his major wouldn't be.

"Yeah? Wonderful! I'm not surprised you're moving up, but I'm happy for you. Is it a big ceremony thing?"

"Not big, no. Walking across the stage of our theater with a handful of half-interested spectators. My men will be there. And wives or girlfriends of whoever else is getting promoted."

"Oh. They can go? I mean, wives, of course, but..."

"I can invite who I wish." He tried to decide how to ask without asking.

"Have anyone to invite?" She sounded cautious.

"You. If you were close enough."

"No one else?"

"No."

"What if I could get there? Would you actually want me or would I be intruding? And be honest. I know you barely know me and I'd understand…"

"Would you want to come?"

"If you'd want me there, not otherwise."

Daws stood and paced. Yes. Maybe he did.

"Well, anyway." Deanna's voice lightened, shifted. "What does this mean for you? Does it change your job?"

"It means I'll get charge of a platoon instead of only a squad, from the eight men I have now to around twenty-five or so, depending. I could also go drill, which I'm thinking about. Could have already. Didn't because the major wanted me here. No real reason not to now."

"Okay, not to sound like a moron, but I don't know what you mean."

He grinned and stood looking out the small window to the near-empty street. "You're not. Sorry, I tend to forget not to use Army language with civilians. A squad, which I have now, is part of a platoon. They're generally run by junior NCOs: E4 & E5. Four squads fall into one platoon. E6 and E7s are platoon sergeants who work with the platoon leader, a lieutenant. They guide him but still have to answer to him. A platoon is part of a company; a company is part of a division." He paused to give her time for it to sink in. "It's like a large office where your general employees work under assistant managers, who are the squad leaders. The assistants answer to the managers, who are the senior NCO's, or platoon sergeants. And of course there are different levels of managers, which take you to First Sergeant and Sergeant Major and so on. The officers are the bosses. Your direct boss would be the platoon leader who works for the company commander – whoever is just above him. The owner would be the division commander. Make any sense?"

"So that means I'm like a squad leader as you are now, but with a smaller squad."

"Yes." Daws wandered back to the couch and perched on the edge of it. He hadn't thought of their 'ranks' being the same, but he was glad she made the connection and put herself on the same level.

"Okay, but, going drill means what?"

"Drill sergeant. The one who turns civilians into soldiers." At her silence, he got up again and paced the small apartment.

"Like the guy in *An Officer and A Gentleman* who was so nasty?"

Nasty. Daws grinned. "Yes, like him."

"So your men would hate you and you'd yell in their faces and make them do pushups in the mud and…"

"If they need it."

"That wouldn't bother you?"

"No."

"Why? How could you yell and inflict so much ... hardship on them and have it not bother you?"

"Because I know if they can't deal with me, they need to go home. A good drill sergeant saves a lot of lives, physically and mentally. It's the most important job an enlisted man can get, at least one of the most important." He waited through her silence. "Deanna, it's not much different than being a parent. A parent who doesn't discipline his kid and make sure he learns how to be an adult once he becomes one has failed as a parent, and that kid will fail. They discipline because they care how they will turn out. If they can't do that, they shouldn't be parents. If they do it well, they end up with responsible adults who succeed. Same thing with the Army."

Again, silence. He went back to the window. "You're bothered."

"No, I ... does it change you? To become a drill sergeant. Will it change you?"

Daws frowned and tried to consider how to answer. "I would suppose, to an extent, but not who I am. People change when they become parents, I've heard, but still, they are who they are."

"Okay."

"You don't have to worry. I would never act that way to you, if that's what you're wondering."

"How do you know you wouldn't? If you got too used to yelling and expecting orders to be followed. How do you know it wouldn't carry over?"

"I already expect my orders to be followed, and they are. I'm not above yelling at my squad and having them do pushups in the mud or rain or snow. I've done it. Will again, I imagine. But I'm in charge of them. I would never be in charge of you. Whole different thing."

"Well, I guess I'm glad to hear you realize that. Because I'm not one who will let someone take charge of me."

Daws felt himself relax. "I know. I admire that. And I have no interest in being in charge of ... anyone outside work. I get enough of that. So unless you join the Army and are unlucky enough to get me as your drill sergeant, my going drill wouldn't affect you."

She chuckled. "Well, that's a thought. At least I'd get to see you every day, right? I'm not a big fan of mud, though, so I'd rather do pushups somewhere cleaner."

"Hm. Think I'd have to insist you be reassigned to someone else. Can't have you hate me like *the nasty guy* in the movie."

"I thought you didn't care."

"I don't. Not with anyone else." He grabbed a deep breath. "Deanna, if you can get the time from work, and if you're interested, I'd love you to come next month. Might be nice to have someone besides my men there, and only because they have to be."

"You want me to come?"

"I would love for you to come, if you can. I understand if you can't."

"I'll be there. Just let me know when exactly, as far in advance as possible, and tell me how to find you when I get close."

"I'll come meet you. I look forward to it." Daws hated just how much he looked forward to it, to seeing her again.

=== July ===

Daws paced on the station platform. Her bus was due ten minutes ago. He'd rushed from work to be there in time, although she said it was okay if she had to wait for him. He didn't want her there alone waiting. And he didn't want to waste the time, the little time she was able to wrestle from work.

He approached the ticket counter and waited while someone tried to make up their mind about whether to accept the bus travel or leave from Syracuse and take the train. He wished the train ran into Watertown. He hated that she had to take the bus all the way, either that or switch from train to bus at Syracuse. Too much messing around, she said. Maybe he'd take the hour-long drive to the train station to send her back home. If she didn't refuse again.

Finally, he got up to the window and asked about the delay.

"Had a hold-up last station, but she's on her way. Should be any minute."

"Hold up? Is there a problem with it?"

"No, Sergeant. All's okay. Someone didn't show for work, is all. Only a few more minutes. Sorry about the wait."

Daws nodded and continued pacing, until he heard a heavy vehicle grow closer and watched it head his direction. He started toward where it was coming in but realized it was going too fast to stop that far back and halted, trying to look calmer than he felt. If any of his men saw him, he'd never hear the end of it.

It seemed forever before the doors finally opened and passengers poured out. He wasn't the only soldier waiting. Relatives often came in to visit over long weekends. He'd arranged, by pulling a few favors, to have the ceremony on a Friday. She only had three days off from work. Plugging them on each side of the weekend gave them five days, or three plus parts of Thursday and Monday. Not enough. But they'd make do.

He saw her before she saw him. Studying her, the auburn hair waving as she searched the crowd, his nerves dissipated. She looked at him, past him, and returned the surprised gaze. And she headed for him.

Daws met her part way and had to brace himself when she all but jumped into his arms. Much warmer greeting than he expected.

"I nearly didn't recognize you." Deanna stepped back and eyed him head to toe. "Look at you all dressed up like a real soldier."

"Didn't have time to change. How was your trip?"

"Incredibly inept. Doesn't anyone know how to do their job anymore?" She touched his face. "You could have taken the hat off. It wouldn't have taken me so long to know you."

"Can't. I'm outside. Let's find your bag."

"Oh." She stopped him with a hand on his chest. "Am I allowed? Or will you get in trouble if I touch you in public?"

He grinned. She was so charming. "Not as long as you don't take me out of uniform."

She caught his eyes. "I wouldn't do that. At least not in public. In private, I can't promise anything."

His stomach twinged and he backed up to offer his arm. He didn't dare say anything else at the moment. She was too good at turning it around on him.

Deanna kept an arm around his waist as they waited for the luggage. She told him about the woman beside her who hardly took a breath in between her chatter and a kid playing music so loud through his headphones she could hear the thump, thump of every song. Until she recognized one and started to sing with it. He stared at her and turned it down. A woman across the aisle told her she had a nice voice and Deanna laughed at herself while relaying the compliment, said she absolutely did not, but she could hold a tune. And she mentioned sitting at the bus station waiting for the driver to get there so they could leave, how she checked in at the window every two minutes until the man was sick of her but she was impatient.... "I'm sorry. I'm talking as bad as that woman I complained about."

Daws raised a hand to her face and brushed at the hair in front of her ear. "Don't be. I'm enjoying every word. Nice to talk in person instead of over the phone."

Deanna hugged him. "Yes, it is. Nice to be able to touch you, too. You'll have to tell me to back off if you get sick of it."

He answered with a grin and nodded toward the bags sitting beside the bus. When she found hers, he took it and led her to the car. She continued her chatter. He stayed quiet and listened. So much life, so much optimism. It was in every word she said, every different tone of her voice. At the car, he put her bag in the trunk and opened her door.

She kissed him. Not a quick kiss, but a long, deep, needy kiss. Then she laid her head against his shoulder. "Remember what you said about those expectations?"

He stroked her back. "I remember very well."

"Does it only apply to when you're in the city? Or does it apply here, too?"

Daws grabbed a deep breath and held her close. "I should warn you, we have plans tonight, on base."

"For what? And you didn't answer me."

He couldn't possibly answer at the moment. He had to keep his head on the task at hand. "I mentioned I had to go pick someone up today, since I had to be out of the office early. Raised their dander and they had to know who. Several of them insisted on meeting you tonight. Nothing fancy, just the NCO Club. If you're okay with it."

"Your men?"

"Mainly. A couple of other squad leaders may be there."

"I'd love to meet them. And you still haven't answered."

"I suppose I'm not sure how to answer."

She chuckled. "Well, I guess we'll figure it out as we go."

He beckoned her into the car. Getting in behind the wheel, he started the engine and grasped her hand. "We'll go to my place first so you can freshen up and I can get out of this. Will it rush you too much to leave then for dinner?"

"No, I'm starving." Deanna ran her other hand down from his shoulder to his forearm. "This is nice, though. I never realized how good such ugly colors could look. But it is nice. Very sexy, really."

"Never thought of it that way. You'll see it again tomorrow. And Monday. And I should let you know ... not that I minded, but when I'm in uniform, we'll have to be more ... discreet."

"What did I do? I didn't take you out of uniform."

He checked to be sure no one was close enough to the car to see in, and returned the kiss. "That. It'll have to wait till I'm out of uniform, or at least in the apartment."

"Oh. Sorry..."

"Don't be." Daws brushed the side of her face.

"I'm so glad to be here."

He couldn't do more than nod, and take off toward his apartment.

Pulling in to the building's parking lot, Daws saw her look around, confused. "It's not much; mainly single soldiers live here, and a few young families."

"Is this base?"

"No. I haven't lived on base for some time. Privilege of making rank. You can move off, and sometimes you get kicked off when space is a problem."

"Is it?"

"Barracks get crowded. The new ones coming in need them. Those of us who can live off-base get kicked out."

"Why don't they add more?"

"Not enough funding for that. They pay us extra for living off base. It doesn't cover it all unless we share, but it's quieter out here and I'd rather have my own place than deal with a roommate bringing girls over all the time. Did that often enough." He opened the door and went around to open hers, then grabbed her suitcase.

"And you didn't have girls over all the time? Because I know it would be easy enough for you to find them."

He closed the trunk and caught her eyes. "Glad you think so. But as I said, I haven't tried too often."

She smiled and held his free arm as they walked toward the building and up the stairs.

"Speaking of, is Todd still harassing you?"

Deanna gave him a soft shrug. "Not too much. Nothing I can't handle."

"Tell him you're involved."

"I did. He doesn't believe me. Said I should bring you to Verlaine's some night and prove it. I didn't tell him why I couldn't. It's not his business and I don't want him to know..." She stopped.

"That I'm not around." Daws unlocked his door and let her in first, closing it and setting his cap on the hook where he always kept that and his keys. "If you ever think he needs a stronger voice to tell him to back off, let me know."

"What are you going to do, come back to the city just to talk to him?"

"If I need to."

Deanna studied his face and set her hands on his stomach. "Sergeant Dawson, you're starting to sound possessive."

"Am I?" He set her suitcase down and wrapped his arms around her waist. "Should I back off?"

"No. I've been hoping you might be, at least enough to know it matters. I'm also wondering how you explained who I was to your men. It would be nice to know what to expect."

"I told them you were someone important to me and they'd all have extra duty for three weeks if they aren't on their best behavior."

She laughed. "Well then, I suppose I better be on my best behavior tonight, too, so I don't get extra duty. Of course, it might depend what that duty is."

Daws rubbed a thumb against her lower back. "Why is it I feel like I'm playing chicken with a howitzer whenever you're around?"

"Do you? What's a howitzer?"

"A very large gun." He raised a hand to her hair, stroked it from behind her ear down to her shoulder. "Very dangerous, and very effective."

"Yeah? Good. Because you are." Deanna met his lips, and pulled back. "Where do I go to freshen up?"

He gave her the quick tour of the apartment, not that there was anything to see, and set her suitcase in his room. "I'll take the couch. I don't generally have company so the one room is sufficient."

With a slight hesitation, she said she would freshen quickly and disappeared into the bathroom with a small bag. He took the opportunity to grab clothes and went back to the living area to pull out of his uniform and into a pair of jeans and a non-Army T-shirt.

"That was a nice view." She returned as he pulled the shirt over his head. "Too fast, but nice. Do you work out every day?" Deanna glanced toward his weight set at one end of the room.

"Depends on the day's events and how tired I am. You freshened fast. Figured I'd be done before you were."

"If I'd known you were changing out here, I would have been faster." With a wink, she wandered over to inspect his set. "Can I use it while I'm here?"

"Use anything you like, Deanna. You don't have to ask."

She turned back, started to say something, paused, and changed tracks. "I think you better take me to dinner, because it's been a long time since I've seen you and that view you just gave me ... well, it was really nice and I'm trying very hard to be a lady for you, since I do think that's what you want."

Maybe not as much as she thought he did. Daws forced control as he moved in front of her. "I never want you to try to be anything. For me or for anyone else. Don't. You're plenty enough lady for me." He fingered a strand of her hair, her naturally wavy uncontrolled hair that echoed who she was inside, and met her lips in a deep kiss.

Her fingers slid barely underneath his shirt, and she pulled back. "Let's go eat. I don't want to be out late."

Deanna handed Fred her state identification card when he asked for her license, to show the MP at the gate along with his military ID. The gun on the man's hip made her nervous, but he was friendly and told them both to have a nice night. Even knowing it was nervy, she asked to see Fred's card before he returned it to his wallet. With a curious expression, he handed it to her as he pulled through the gate. It was like a driver's license except with a green background and no address. It showed his height as six feet, his weight as 215. His birthday December tenth. Five inches taller than she was, and nearly 80 pounds heavier. It was all muscle. She knew without a doubt, after seeing the flash of his bare chest and abdomen, that he had no extra fat. She couldn't say the same. Not that she had a lot extra, she kept in shape, but she was built round. Hereditary. Nothing much she could do about it. He was built like a Mack truck. An extremely sexy Mack truck.

Trying not to think of that glimpse, she held the card in her hand and focused on the brick buildings all in a row, marked with numbers on their fronts and signs telling what was inside, she supposed, along with directional markers pointing here and there. She had no idea what some of it meant. Class VI. Mess hall she knew was the dining area. JAG? Commissary he'd mentioned – a grocery store. Shoppette? It had to be a mini shop of some kind. LSO. 10th Sustainment. Garrison Command. She felt as though she'd just landed in a foreign country.

"That's our motor pool."

Deanna looked over to where he pointed. A tall chain link fence was topped with barbed wire. Inside she saw … tanks? And big truck-like vehicles that looked like they were meant to carry something. A helicopter.

Helicopter. He'd said his major died in a chopper crash. "Do you fly those?"

"No. I stay on the ground."

"Don't like to fly?"

"Not particularly. I do as I need to. And I can fix the things if they need it, minor fixes. I'm more an organizer. I make sure we have what we need to have when we need to have it, and then make sure it all goes back where it belongs."

She nodded, too overwhelmed to ask about the many things she saw since she didn't know where to start asking. Soon, he pulled into the parking lot of a pretty brick building with a lot of windows and neat shrubbery. It even boasted flowers and colorful plants along the sidewalk. Everything she'd seen was perfectly cared for, neat, and pretty. Not what she would have expected.

"This is it." He put the Chevy in park, turned off the engine, and grasped her hand. "Relax."

"Who says I'm not?"

"I see it on your face."

"Is there anything I should know to say or not say? How do I greet them? They won't be in uniform, right? So I won't know their rank..."

He squeezed her fingers. "Don't worry about it. I'll introduce you and they won't expect you to remember all their names. They also won't hesitate to remind you of them. It'll be fine, Deanna. No different than meeting people at a regular bar."

She rather doubted that was true. Especially since she'd never had to show her ID to get into an area and then drive past barbed wire and guns.

Taking his offered arm, she focused on smooth breaths. She didn't do this anymore. She didn't get nervous in public anymore. She'd worked too hard to convince herself not to. And she didn't.

But she was. She was as nervous as she could ever remember being.

Fred greeted a few men by rank and stopped for quick introductions to a couple: the woman a soldier, her husband civilian. Did he know everyone?

They entered a large room where men and women stood around chatting or sat at tables eating, some in uniform, some not. A buffet ran along one wall. It smelled incredible. She made out the greasy, overpowering smell of fried chicken and hoped there were mashed potatoes. Anything at this point.

"Sergeant Dawson, we figured you'd bailed on us tonight."

She turned with Fred as he faced the voice. There were three of them, young men, one so young she had a hard time believing he was legal to be military. They noticed Fred set a hand on her back and exchanged glances while giving her their greetings and saying how nice it was to meet her.

"You're not what we expected." The one he called Private Anderson studied her.

"No?" She glanced at Fred but he didn't seem to mind, though it was hard to tell. He was in full business mode. "And what did you expect?"

The kid shrugged. "Someone more ... well, tough. You know, in order to deal with him."

Fred rubbed his chin but didn't interfere.

She took it as a sign to answer as she wished. "How do you know I'm not?"

"No offense, ma'am, but I mean, you know, burly and harder. For lack of better way to put it."

She couldn't help an amused smile. "You apparently haven't learned yet just how much a woman's softness can put her in control. You will."

One of them snickered. Private Anderson glanced at his sergeant and pulled back at whatever he was going to say. "Yes, ma'am. I suppose that's true."

"Do they have to call me ma'am? It makes me sound old."

"Yes. They do." Fred moved his gaze from them to her. "It has nothing to do with age, only with respect." He excused himself from his soldiers and said they were going to eat and would be over later.

"Over?"

Taking her to the buffet, he grabbed a plate and handed it to her. "The next room has a bar and music. You'll meet the rest there. They were just the scouting party."

"Oh. Was the way I answered all right? I don't want to embarrass you."

"You're fine, Deanna." His voice softened. "As I said, don't worry."

Daws slid a hand around her back as she talked to the squad leader he spent the most off-hours with. Not often, as he generally went back to the apartment and stayed in after work, but on an occasional weekend, Zakowsky would talk him into catching a movie or hanging out somewhere. He was single, divorced, five years older than Daws, and interesting enough for decent conversation.

Deanna seemed to think so, as well, or she was being polite. She wouldn't have had to worry at all. Socializing for her was as natural as leading men was for him. She'd charmed his men already. He had no doubt she would, but it was nice to watch, and nice to see her grow comfortable in his world. Of course, the Enlisted Club was only on the edge of his world, a place to unwind. The next morning, when they were all back in uniform and respecting the tradition of the ceremony, she would see a different side.

Zakowsky asked her where they'd met. She answered New York and tried to leave it at that. The sergeant pushed for more, for how, when he knew Daws kept to himself so well.

"We were both out walking at the same time." He answered for her. "Ran into each other."

"That's it? Just met on the street?"

"That's it."

Zakowsky shook his head with a grin. "Daws, only you would meet a girl that way, and one so perfectly fit to your temperament. Or so it seems. I think she'll do okay keeping you in line."

He didn't bother to comment. Instead, he excused them, citing her long bus ride, and gave their quick farewells.

When he slid behind the wheel again, he pulled her fingers to his lips for a light kiss. "What do you think? Could you do this again?"

"With you? Of course. And I see why you love your job. They all have such an incredible amount of respect for you. That was so nice to see, and it would be nice to have. Maybe I should go to work with you and see how you do it."

"Deanna, if anyone at your job doesn't have an incredible amount of respect for you, it's because they don't know who you are. Because they should have."

"How do you know? You've never seen me at work."

"Because I know you aren't one who would do things half-assed. You put your whole heart into everything you do."

"Not that it gets me anywhere."

"One of these days, it will. And if it matters, I would be glad to work with you any day, in any job."

She gave him a grin and leaned over to cup his cheek with her palm. "Let's go be alone a while."

They didn't talk on the way. She looked out at the darkened base, its lights highlighting what needed to be highlighted, then at the town as they approached his apartment. The way her eyes scoured him when he had his shirt off flashed in his mind and he shoved it out. She was a lady. He would treat her as such. Never mind the hinted expectations.

Before he had the engine off, with the car barely stopped, she leaned over, set a hand aside his face, and met his lips. Then she pulled back and opened her door. So much for letting him be a gentleman. He turned the key, unlatched his seatbelt and looked up, amused, as she waited in front of his car. She tilted her head and motioned with a wiggling finger. Daws made her wait a few seconds, watching her through the front window, and stepped out. "I would have come around to get your door."

"No need. I'm a big girl. I've been opening my own doors for a long time."

"You'd rather I didn't?"

"No. I'd rather you did, as you do, at the right time. But don't think I always expect it."

He remained beside his door. The building light gave her hair a glow from behind, outlined her curvy figure. Shadowed her face.

"Are we going in?" She held her ground, also.

"Beautiful night. Feel like a walk?"

"Okay." It sounded like a question and yet not quite.

Daws went to her and offered his arm. He wanted to talk. And he wasn't sure she would if he took her behind closed doors. He guided her along the sidewalk, the only interruptions the song of crickets or an occasional dog bark, a car rolling past with its lights adding to the soft street light glow for a moment. Her fingers squeezed softly into his arm. Soft fingers. Long nails, but not too long, real, painted a soft mauve. "What's been going on at work that you haven't told me yet?"

"Oh, nothing unusual."

"No?"

She shrugged. "Well, the head moron and I came to an understanding."

"Did you? About?"

"I told him I understood I would never go farther up in the company and he told me he understood that I still wanted my job anyway. Not helpful, but I guess it's out in the open and I gave him a chance to counter that. He didn't, so I don't have to wonder about his intentions any longer. What I don't know for sure is how much power he really has, if he can hold me back."

"You should look for something better."

"Yes. Maybe. It's not easy to find, and I have time in, a higher pay grade because of my time. It shows longevity. That has to count for something."

"But it's not what you want."

"It's ... at least in the same field as what I want. As close as I've been."

He listened to her relate other jobs she held while she'd worked her way up. To him, her willingness to do all the shit jobs on her way to where she wanted to be meant much more than longevity at some stagnant position. He would, if she was working under him, recognize the determination, the patience, the ability, the stamina. She had incredible stamina.

And then she mentioned the other girls giving her a hard time, how they guessed she had another bedmate.

"She said that to you in the office? You can't have her reprimanded?"

"Hm. I'm afraid city offices don't have the same standards you apparently have. It would come back at me if I tried. I'd be the one in the wrong for my inability to 'get along' with my peers. Of course, they aren't my peers. They're secretaries, new, with no training beyond that. I'm technically in charge of them, but ... well, with the way they throw themselves at the moron, they can easily bypass me and go straight to him. He loves their submissive 'do anything for you' attitude even if they don't mean it. No way in the world will I play up to the jerk that way."

"I wouldn't think so."

"I'd get higher faster if I did. I don't play the game right."

"No, you do. They don't. But it's much harder to win when you play by the rules, particularly against an opponent who doesn't. It can happen, but it's harder."

"Maybe it can."

He felt her sigh and let it go. They walked another couple of blocks and he turned them back, used the different direction as a conversational shift. "You still have family? Your parents? You haven't said anything about them."

"Nothing much to tell."

"What do they do?"

She sighed again. "Mom is the typical homemaker who doesn't do anything but that. I used to try to get her to do anything else, pick up a craft, play cards with the girls, something. She would never do it. I think because Dad doesn't want her to do anything else. Can't tell you how much I resented that she'd let him run her life that way."

Daws nodded to himself. Made sense. Explained her insistence about being independent, not allowing him to "take charge" as though he might want to. "What does he do?"

"Oh. He lays floors. Or used to. He's retired now. He also did some cement work. Things like that. And he took care of animals now and then. That changed with the year. We had chickens for a while, goats, turkeys, peacocks that made the most dreadful noise, a couple of horses he tried to breed but they didn't seem to like each other much."

He chuckled. "Man of many interests."

"Man who couldn't commit to one thing. Drove Mom crazy."

"And you."

She looked up at him, questioning.

"That why you're determined to stick this job out, like it or not?"

"No." She turned her eyes forward again, down at the sidewalk. "I'm sticking it out because it's the one thing I've wanted more than anything in the world and I'm not willing to let go of the chance only because a few morons try to stop me."

By the tone of her voice, Daws decided it was again time to route around. "Have siblings?"

"A few. And I don't want to try to explain them so how about we let that go?"

"Okay."

"You're offended now."

"Not at all."

"You sound like you are." She stopped and faced him. "I left all that behind on purpose. It's no longer part of me. Of my life. Any more than yours seems to be."

He studied her eyes. So firm, resolved. Of course she had to know better. Your family roots weren't ever fully left behind. His weren't, regardless of how he tried. They never would be. Not enough. "I'm sorry you felt you had to put it behind you."

"Yeah. Well, it happens."

Daws raised a hand to her face. "If you ever decide you want to talk about it more, I'm always willing to listen. But I'll understand if you don't."

"Will you talk more about yours?"

"Nothing much more to say about mine."

"I don't think I believe that, but I'll give you the same offer." Deanna brushed his lips, hinting. "Ready to go in yet or are you still afraid of me?"

"Yes."

"To which?"

"Both." With a quick grin, he led her to his building and walked her up the stairs.

As she settled in, he pulled out two hard lemonades and took them to the couch where she sat with bare feet pulled to her side. Deanna accepted one of the bottles, looked at it quizzically, and peered into his eyes.

"Am I right?"

"How did you know? Did I slip up and tell you?"

He gave her another grin, took a long swallow, and rubbed a hand over her shoulder with a light massage.

"Guess it's true." She returned the favor by caressing his leg.

"What's true?"

"You're not bothered by feet. At least by my bare feet on your couch."

He caught her eyes as he took another swallow, and set the drink out of his way. "Are you ticklish?" At her raised eyebrows, he clarified. "Your feet."

"No."

Daws slid his hands around the leg she had resting atop the other and coerced it gently around until her knee bent upward and her foot rested against his leg. "You have beautiful feet. Can't imagine anyone bothered by them."

"Well, it's not very classy, I guess, to run around the house with bare feet. Not sure why it isn't since they are clean..." She broke off as he began to massage her foot.

He watched her face to be sure it didn't tickle and he wasn't too rough. Her eyes closed, her head dropped back, and her expression ... made his body tense. It took little encouragement to get her to shift to the end of the couch, allowing access to both feet. And she pried her lemonade between her thighs for security, to prevent spilling it as her body loosened, relaxed.

"That feels incredible."

"Does it?" He pressed his thumbs up the middle of her feet, watched her body rise in response.

Suddenly, she pulled away, put her bottle on the table, and pressed in against him, her mouth to his, arms around his neck. He tasted the lemonade, felt her body surge with her breaths, circled her small waist and encouraged her closer. It took little encouragement. She was fire. Bright. Hot. Piercing his armor of what he thought was thick as Kevlar. She was proving how wrong he was. It wasn't Kevlar. It was aluminum. Durable. Versatile. But not unbendable.

She found his eyes, her mouth still close to his, her body supported by his. "She was wrong."

Daws searched his thoughts for what he'd missed. "Who?"

"Margie. At work." Deanna skimmed fingers over his hair, avoided his eyes.

Wrong. What had she said that he should have remembered? "About what?" He saw her hesitate, meet his gaze as though he should know. "Sorry, my mind is fully elsewhere. You'll have to..."

"I wasn't seventeen."

Seventeen. The bedmate comment. "No?" He slipped his fingers beneath her fitted blouse, nudged it out of his way.

"Would you think less of me if I had been?"

"No." Her skin was incredibly soft. Warm.

"Seriously?"

He stopped and met her eyes. "Deanna, past is past. I enjoy you for who you are. Whatever happened to bring you to this point had some purpose."

"Think so? Or maybe I just royally screwed up and I could be farther than I am if I hadn't."

"I suppose we can all say that about something."

"Can you?"

"Of course."

"About what?"

Images of the chopper crash flashed through his head. He wouldn't say yet. It was too soon. "Several things. But like I said, it's in the past. I moved on. Kept going. What more can you do?"

She studied his face. "I was sixteen." Deanna dropped her eyes, lowered her head. "And stupid. Naive. I believed him when he said I was the only one for him and would always be the only one and … I was a kid from nowhere trying to go somewhere and he said he could help me get there. He was much too old for me. It … just happened, although I never meant for it to happen, but he said I was so old for my age and I would go far and…. He was nothing but a lying user. My first one. Took me a long time to recover from that. Years. Maybe I haven't yet."

Daws moved his hand back over her blouse, caressed her back. She needed to talk tonight. To let herself open up, to learn to trust him. "I'm sorry your first experience was with such a stupid ass. He ought to be locked up."

"It was my fault just as much, for trusting someone I shouldn't have."

He pulled her face up to see her eyes. "You should be able to trust others, Deanna, especially when you're still so young. It's not your fault you can't. It's his, and everyone like him. The fact that you keep trying means more than how many mistakes you've made. That's what I see, the way you keep trying."

A touch of moisture gathered at the corners of her eyes and he leaned in to kiss them, then her face, her forehead, her nose, her lips. She pressed closer, met his lips.

He eased back and encouraged her to sit up again, retrieved their drinks.

They talked until she appeared far too tired and he realized it was nearly midnight. "You should get some sleep. We have to be up early."

She caught his hand. "Fred. I've never told anyone that. Ever. I wasn't sure I should tell you, since we hardly know each other and I don't want you to have the wrong impression. Though maybe it's too late for that."

Daws stood and helped pull her up with him. He led her back to his room, stroked the side of her face, and gave her a light kiss. "Having you here for my promotion is not a small thing. I wouldn't invite just anyone. I've never wanted to invite anyone on base, much less to something that matters to me this much. And I'm glad you're here." He gave her another kiss and backed away. "Good night, Deanna."

She changed into her night shirt and slid under the blankets of his bed. She was the first, his first, at least in a way. The first he wanted to invite on base, to allow in his professional life. With as much respect as she had for him, she couldn't take it any other way than an honor.

A few tears fell as she thought of it. She couldn't remember the last time anyone had treated her with such respect. Maybe no one ever had.

How anyone could turn him away only because of his lifestyle, she didn't understand. Being treated like this, even if only for a few weeks a year, was more than worth giving up the constancy of being used on a daily basis, of being lied to, disrespected, wanted only for her physical attributes. She would take this any day.

Startled by a sudden presence in the near dark, Deanna pulled back. "Sorry to wake you."

Fred. She looked over at the red numbers on the alarm clock. Four-seventeen. "What's wrong?" She sat up, pulling the blanket around her.

"I have to go out. Didn't want you to wake up and wonder where I was."

"Out? At this time?"

"Problem with one of my men. I have to take care of it."

"At four in the morning? He can't wait?"

"Part of the job." Fred sat beside her and stroked her hair. "I should be back soon. You have the alarm set for the time you need to be ready?"

"Yes, but..."

"Okay, go back to sleep." He started to get up.

"Fred? You'll be careful?"

He gave her a light grin and returned long enough to kiss her head. "It's fine. Sleep, Deanna. I'll be back."

"You better be." She watched him leave the room, heard the apartment door close. He was in uniform, his BDUs. Part of the job? She knew from their phone calls he'd had to go collect one of his men from a bar before because of a scrape of some kind, but would he dress in full gear for that? Maybe.

At the alarm, she pushed it to stop the noise and forced herself up. The apartment was quiet. Seven o'clock. Maybe he was back and asleep.

Deanna pulled into her robe and went out to the living area – she wouldn't call it a room since it was joined with the same space as the little dining table and the kitchenette. He wasn't there. Nearly three hours, and he wasn't home yet. With a frown, she realized she had no way to check on him, no phone number, couldn't get on base without him, and had no knowledge of even how to ask someone who would know.

He said it was fine. She'd do her best to believe it.

She started a whole pot of coffee. He would need it when he got home since he'd been up so early. Could she have gone with him? She supposed not.

Pacing the small apartment with a pause now and then to look out the window at the vivid Western New York sunshine, Deanna heard the pot sputter as it finished brewing and went to find the coffee mugs. She had to chuckle at how the mugs were all the same in his little apartment as they were in his city apartment. So were the plates, the glasses ... everything was perfectly in order and perfectly matched. She wondered what he would have thought about her place. She didn't have one mug the same as another. They were from wherever she saw one she liked, in all sizes and colors and sayings from cutesy to so serious as to be funny. She also had mixed dishes and glasses she'd picked up here and there, mainly from department store clearance sales. What would he say if she grabbed them from storage and added them to his apartment?

She was tempted to find out. After all, he hadn't kicked her out when she threw paperwork in the back of his car.

Deanna figured she should run through the shower and pull herself together to be ready when he was. Surely, he would be back in time to get to his own promotion.

As she was drying off, the phone rang, and she pulled her robe over still-tacky skin. She went over to it but wasn't sure if she should pick it up. Would he want anyone to know she was there? Did they already? Supposing she could claim it was the wrong number, she answered with a simple hello.

"Deanna, I'm glad you answered. Wasn't sure you would."

"Fred, where are you? Are you okay?"

"Yes, but I can't get back in time to get you here."

She cringed. All that way to see his promotion and she couldn't go? "Okay."

"I'm sending Private Anderson to pick you up. He should be there in half an hour."

"Oh."

"That all right? If things change, I'll get there instead, but it doesn't look like I will. I'll be lucky to get to the theater in time. If I'm not, don't worry. He'll stay with you until I can meet you." His voice sounded odd.

"But you're all right?"

"Yes. I have to go. I am sorry about this."

"No, it's okay. I'll see you soon." She hung up with a frown. She'd heard commotion in the background, voices, talking over a speaker system of some kind. Paging ... doctor someone. A hospital. It sounded like a hospital. But he said he was fine. Maybe the soldier he checked on was there. She should have asked if he was all right, also.

In twenty minutes, as she was adding the final touches to her hair, which looked like a straw mop since she'd had to blow it part of the way dry, a knock made her jump. Despite knowing who it had to be, Deanna left the chain in place while she opened the door enough to see a uniform on the other side.

"Ma'am, I'm Private Anderson. We met last night."

"Good morning. Just a second." She closed the door enough to unchain it and opened it for him.

"I'm here to escort you to the theater. The sergeant called you, I think."

"Yes. I need only two minutes. Come on in."

"Oh, no ma'am. I'll wait here, and I'm early so don't rush."

"You can come in."

"No, ma'am, not without the sergeant at home, but thank you." He stepped back and waited for her to close the door.

Regardless of his request not to rush, she did, and Deanna hoped she looked good enough for the ceremony, in case he would still be there for it. Would they reschedule if he wasn't? She'd miss it, then, since she had to be back in the city by Monday night.

Deanna grabbed her handbag, stepped out, and pulled the door closed. "You'll have to forgive me, but this is all new to me, so how do I address you?"

He smiled. "You can call me Charlie. Civilians don't have to follow our formalities."

"Then can you call me Deanna instead of ma'am? At least when we're not in public?"

"No, ma'am. Sergeant Dawson would have me against the wall if I did." He waved a hand toward the stairs. "After you." Charlie followed a couple of steps behind, out to Fred's car, and opened the door for her.

She looked over at the young man curiously.

"I don't have wheels of my own. Must be doing something right if the sergeant not only allowed me to escort you, but also drive his car. Highlight of my career so far. He's not easy to earn respect from."

Deanna studied the young man's face. There was nothing derisive or sarcastic in the comment or in his attitude. Only pride. "He seems well respected by his squad."

"Oh, yes ma'am, and a lot farther out than that. Has the attention of a lot of higher ups, as well. We figure he'll make First Sergeant before too much longer, earlier than most."

Deanna tried to remember Fred's quick lesson on military rank, but her mind shifted to his phone call. "Is he all right? He sounded ... rushed, on the phone. Or..."

"He'll be fine, ma'am. Just a scratch. And I better get you there on time or he'll have my hide."

She wanted to ask more, but he nodded for her to get in and she didn't dare argue and risk him getting in trouble. A scratch. At the hospital. Her stomach turned.

Charlie slowed in front of a large red brick building and waited for pedestrians to cross in front. He turned into the parking area, stopped at the edge next to the grass, came around to open her door, and accompanied her to the main sidewalk. "I'll go find somewhere to park and meet you in a minute."

Deanna considered saying she could walk from the parking lot as well as he could, but she was too far out of her element to argue. Men and women in uniform swarmed around the place and gave her a nod or quick smile as they passed. They didn't know who she was. Why did they bother? Or maybe they knew Fred's car and saw her get out of it?

Part of her wished to be back in the city where she blended in with everyone else instead of sticking out in her "civilian" clothes among all of the uniforms. There were a few others not in uniform and she studied them as they talked with soldiers, apparently completely at ease. Many of them knew each other, or at least acted as though they did. That also made her uncomfortable. She was used to not being known and no one else being known as they all hid in their public anonymity.

"Hello."

Deanna turned toward the voice, a well-dressed woman with a friendly smile, and returned the greeting.

"Are you here for the promotion ceremony? You look lost."

"Oh, yes, I am. Both, I suppose."

The woman smiled again and took her hand. "New to military life?"

"I'm only visiting. Yes, I'm very new to this."

"Welcome to Fort Drum. I'm Mandy Hodgkins; my husband is Captain Shel Hodgkins. Come on in. You can sit with us if you're alone. You have a friend or family member being promoted today?"

"I'm Deanna Meyers. I'm here with Sergeant Fred Dawson."

Recognition lit her eyes. "Daws? I didn't realize he had anyone coming for this. It's lovely to meet you. From what we all know, he doesn't ever have visitors. Such a quiet man. Now and then he'll say two or three words to me if I try hard enough. Are you a relative?"

"No, I'm...." Deanna hesitated. How much should she say?

The woman grinned again. "Ah. Please come sit with us. It'll be nice to get to know you."

"I'm ... I'm sorry, but Private Anderson escorted me and he should be here in a minute. He's parking."

"Oh? Where is Daws, then? He brought you to visit and dumped you off on one of his men? I'll have to speak to him."

"Ma'am." Charlie took Deanna's side but addressed Mandy Hodgkins. "He had an incident with Barney this morning."

"Not again." The captain's wife rolled her eyes. "What did he do this time? And did he have to do it on promotion day?"

"I'm not sure of the situation, ma'am, but the sergeant is meeting us here. Any time, I hope."

Deanna hoped so, also, as she obeyed and followed the friendly woman inside, with Charlie close behind. She felt like turning back as they entered the theater. There were even more uniforms inside, talking, laughing, standing around the aisles or sitting in the movie theater-like chairs. Several eyed her, not unfriendly, only curious. She figured she looked as nervous as she felt. Or maybe they all knew each other and knew she was an outsider.

Charlie stopped someone, another uniform, and asked if he'd heard from the sergeant.

"He's trying to get the hospital to release him."

"Release?" The private lowered his voice. "He said it was a scratch."

The other one, whose name tag read Butler, shrugged with his head. "You know the Sarge. Something he'd make the rest of us take a week off for he'd call just a scratch on himself. My guess is he'll wrangle himself out of there soon, whether or not he should."

Charlie cleared his throat and glanced at Deanna, then introduced her as the sergeant's friend. Butler gave her an embarrassed greeting and assured her Sergeant Dawson would be fine. And he walked away.

"Would you like to sit with Mrs. Hodgkins?" Charlie looked bothered. And he looked like he was trying to cover.

"Can you take me to Fred?"

His eyes widened. "I'm afraid I can't do that. Not without his say so."

"He's hurt."

"He'll be fine, ma'am. They'll take care of him, and if I know him at all, he'll be here any minute."

She had no way to argue or to go find him herself, so she let him lead her to Mandy. Charlie waited for her to sit, then stood at the end of the aisle, surveying the crowd.

"Excuse me. I'll be back." He gave her a nod and hurried away.

Deanna watched him as well as she could, but he disappeared into the midst of a sea of green and brown. They all looked the same at a distance, other than different builds and skin tones. And many builds were nearly the same. She tried to be polite and follow the conversation beside her, but her eyes were out in the sea, looking for his face.

The ceremony started. She stood and set her hand across her heart for the National Anthem played by a few soldiers with shining instruments, and she sat again when everyone else did. Still, she didn't see him.

Three soldiers were promoted, pinned, and handed a black folder, which Mandy said were their promotion certificates. And his name was called.

She waited as nothing happened, looked around the room, and heard murmurs. Then a few more uniforms entered the theater from a side door up front and one separated from the others. He walked up the steps. Fred. He'd made it. Deanna breathed easier. He was there. Walking. He seemed all right. The officer giving out the awards looked down at his uniform, said something privately. Fred nodded in return. And the ceremony continued.

Deanna felt her eyes get misty as he stood at attention while they spoke of his recommendations, specifically the words from his major who had insisted he go to the board. Fred's face remained even, unemotional. He didn't even shift his weight or turn his head. Until after he was pinned with his new rank and he accepted the folder, gave the man a quick, sharp salute and walked down the other side of the stage. Deanna found where Private Anderson had gone; he was at his sergeant's side as soon as Fred reached the bottom of the steps.

It seemed an interminable amount of time before it was over and everyone got up to wander, grasping the hands of the newly promoted.

Charlie took her side again. "He'll meet you down front if you'll come with me."

If? She only wished he would walk faster, push through the crowd with less tact, less patience.

Fred's serious demeanor lightened when he caught her face. She made her way through those congratulating him and gave him a hug. Other women were hugging some of the soldiers. Deanna figured it must be okay. He flinched as her arm went around his sides. She drew back and looked down at him. The side of his shirt was slashed, and stained a deep reddish brown. A large stain. Not only a scratch.

"It's all right, Deanna."

Her eyes met his. She refused to speak. There were too many people around, too many to notice if she became emotional. He didn't. Neither would she. She would show him she could be strong enough to deal with his career, even if she didn't feel it at the moment. Instead, she gave him a light kiss on the cheek and congratulated him.

The thankful expression in his eyes told her she'd reacted well, had made him proud. And she wondered if her face echoed the private's face earlier as he relayed how the sergeant must be proud of him.

Deanna maintained her composure throughout introductions, congratulations, and teasing from Mandy Hodgkins that Daws hadn't told anyone about her beforehand. When she tried once to ask him what happened, he said only that things got out of control and he'd tell her more later.

Only when she was alone in the bathroom at the reception following the ceremony did she allow a few quick tears. He was in pain. She could see he was. She could see how hard he tried to hide it. There was a lot of dried blood on his shirt. How much more had there been?

Another woman was there when she stepped out of the stall blotting the corner of an eye. She gave Deanna a sympathetic grin and waited until she'd washed and dried her hands and checked to see that her mascara didn't run. The woman with a young face but touches of gray streaked along the temples studied her. "You did well today. He's proud to have you here. You'll be a good Army wife."

"Oh, I'm not ... we're not..."

"I know, but I won't be surprised if you are soon. I've known Daws for some time. And I've been an Army wife for seventeen years. You'll get used to those private tears you'll hide from the rest of the world. It's part of the job, but you'll be fine." The woman gave her a soft hug and left her alone.

Part of the job. Was it still a job she wanted if this was a regular part of it? She had enough issues with her own job. Did she need them from his, too?

Yanking herself back together, Deanna took a deep breath, checked the mirror again, and went to find him. He was sitting, talking with two other men, older men. The rank on their collars looked impressive although she wasn't sure what they meant.

Fred saw her and beckoned her over, standing. When he grimaced, one of the men set a hand on his shoulder and told him to sit. He obeyed and introduced her. A captain and a major. She bit her tongue until they excused themselves and she finally had them alone. "No one's close now. What happened?"

He set a hand on her forearm. "Had to put one of my men in lock up." Pain radiated over his face. "I've seen it coming. Kept trying to reach out to him. Thought he had a chance to straighten up. Not a bad kid, only misguided." He clenched his eyes, only for a second.

"Fred, I mean ... and I'm sorry about him, but, did he do this to you? How bad is it?"

"No, he didn't. I got in the way to save his scrawny ass. Not that he didn't deserve it, but I doubt he'd've come out as well."

"As well? That's a lot of blood. How bad is it?"

"No PT for at least a couple of weeks. Limited duty."

She frowned. Did he think that answered her question?

He took her hand. "I have a few stitches. Fine otherwise. Don't worry."

Mandy Hodgkins came over, stood in front of them, and studied Fred. "Just heard what you did. You should have let him take his own medicine. He had it coming."

Fred stood. "My job to look after my men. No offense, ma'am, but there wasn't much choice."

She smiled at him and gave him a careful half hug. "Go home, Soldier. You've done your duty for today."

"Suppose I have to, ma'am, since the captain just gave me the same orders."

"Of course he did. I insisted." With a grin, Mandy turned to Deanna. "Make sure he follows orders and rests. That may be hard to do, but something tells me you can. I hope we'll run into each other again."

Deanna was surprised when she also got a hug. "Thank you. So do I." She started to assist Fred however he'd allow, but one of his men was there, one from the night before. Jenkins, his name tag stated.

"Need a ride back, Sergeant, or are you okay to drive?"

"Is my car here?"

Jenkins cast a glance behind Deanna to Charlie. "It is. And I can follow while he drives you and bring him back."

"Get back to work. You don't have the day off because I do. You're in charge today, Corporal."

"You're not driving." Deanna interrupted. "You might pull the stitches. You're too…"

"It's not a race car. We'll take it slow. Unless you want to drive."

Her eyes widened. "I don't drive."

"Not at all?"

"Why drive in New York when it's faster and cheaper to take the bus?"

He nodded and asked Anderson for his keys.

"You're not driving." She took the offered keys before he could reach them.

"Deanna…"

"Don't argue with me, Sergeant Dawson. I'm too stubborn to let you win this one." She heard a snicker before Mandy told Anderson and Jenkins to take the sergeant home and see that he got up the stairs all right.

===

Daws had barely kicked his men back out of the apartment when Deanna started to unbutton his shirt. She started at his stomach. Carefully. Her body close to his, her face turned down to the dried blood at his side. He brushed hair from her neck, tried to bring her attention to his face instead. "It's bandaged well. You can't see it."

"Not with this T-shirt covering it." She finished unbuttoning and pulled the slashed side out of her way. "Isn't it too hot to wear this heavy thing over another shirt?" She gripped the tee and started to pull it from where it was tucked in his pants.

"It's not as heavy as it looks. This is a summer uniform. Not bad with the sleeves rolled." He caught her hands. "It's all right. Relax, Deanna."

She raised her eyes to his. "In other words, you don't want me to see how bad it is."

"It's not bad. Nothing important was in the way."

"I think your skin and your blood are both rather important, Staff Sergeant Dawson."

"Also easy enough to mend or replace." He pulled her hand to his lips. "I'm sorry. Didn't mean to worry you. Tried to get them to let me go sooner."

"You should sleep. You were up so early and this ... you have to be exhausted."

Daws saw the worry in her eyes, the way she tried to cover how upset she was. "Deanna, relax."

"Relax? You're stabbed in the gut and I should relax? I couldn't even call and check on you. I didn't know where you were or who to call to find out..."

"I'm sorry. I didn't plan to be long. I'll leave you a number if I have to go out again. But I have Monday off, so..."

"If you go out again, I go with you."

"Well, since I won't be working, I guess that's safe enough to agree to." He brushed hair away from her face. "This isn't how I planned to introduce you to Army life. And this isn't a common occurrence. I ought to add to his charges for doing this now, while you're here."

"What happened exactly?"

Daws took a deep breath, cringed at the pain in his side, and went to start coffee as he explained as much as he could, about Barney's trouble with his girlfriend that led to too much drinking that led to violent eruptions that led to more trouble with his girlfriend. He'd been trying to work with him for two months, ever since the kid joined his squad. He had him talking to a counselor, working on his drinking, pulling extra duty whenever the kid lost too much control. Nothing worked. There was still something he wasn't doing well enough. And now, chances were good he'd be chaptered out. Barney's road would, in all likelihood, go downhill from there.

It felt like a failure, although the other squad leaders and his captain assured Daws he was doing all he could and should take no fault in it.

Deanna agreed with them, tried to reassure him. She shifted closer, careful of his side, and ran a hand along his face. "You're tired. Why don't you lie down and I'll make something for lunch? Is there anything here to cook with?"

"Basics, but I'll take you out for lunch. You don't need to..."

"I don't want to go out. I want to stay right here with you. Alone. Besides, I have orders to make you rest."

Leaned back against the counter for support, he fought to keep his eyes open. They'd given him pain medication. Too much. It was hard to fight off. "Alone sounds good, but don't bother..."

"I want to bother." She gave him a light kiss. "And I want you to lie down while I make lunch."

"Can't."

"And why can't you?"

"Don't want to miss any of the little time you're here." He ducked his face in next to her head. "You smell incredible. What is it?"

"Rose and jasmine. Glad you like it. I picked it out for you."

"Hm." He found her lips, teased them. "Always know so well what a man will like?" Daws told himself to stop talking. The meds were kicking in too strong.

She chuckled. "You'll have to wait and find out. Now lie down. And don't argue with me, soldier." Deanna backed away and took his hands, led him to the couch. "Let's get you cleaned up first, though. Where do I find another shirt?"

In pain enough, and with the strong medication he was under, Daws didn't argue. As she went to his room, he pulled the BDU shirt from his arms, glad she couldn't see the struggle it was to move that much. The thing was beyond repair. He'd have to replace it, take it in to have his patches sewn onto the new one. And it was faded just enough, he'd have to get new pants, also. They wouldn't match enough otherwise. He couldn't stand for his shirt and pants to be different shades. At all. They had to match.

Deanna returned, set the clean tee on the arm of the couch, and sat next to him. She gripped the bottom of his brown T-shirt and tugged the edges out of his pants. "This, too."

"I'll do it." He set his hands over hers.

Her eyes flashed amusement. "I've already seen you, you know. Not like you have anything to hide."

Except the bandage, which was bigger than he'd let her think, and bloody. He knew it had bled more during the ceremony.

"Fred?"

"How squeamish are you?" He watched her eyes.

"I'm not. And it's worse than you told me, isn't it?"

"I'll need to change the gauze. They sent more; it's in the front pocket." He nodded toward his discarded shirt and waited until she found it. "I'll take care of it. If you want to see what's here to cook, I'll come help in a minute."

"No, you won't. And I'll do this for you."

"Deanna..."

"I'm not squeamish. I had to take care of my little brothers and they were always getting themselves hurt. I've helped birth a horse. Even put one down when it was too hurt to save. That was hard, but I did it, and I didn't even cry over it because I was told not to. I can do this."

Daws raised a hand to her face and slid it back to cup the side of her head. "I don't want to make things harder for you."

She shook her head. "I'm not afraid of this being hard. I'm used to hard. It builds character, right? And I have to tell you, soldier, I'm thinking you're worth it. So if you're not, tell me now."

He knew without a doubt he wouldn't want to let her leave Monday. "I can't promise I'm worth it, but I can promise I'll try to be. And part of that, the way I see it, is not making things harder for you."

She ran fingers down his shoulder, over his chest, to his stomach. "I know you're no more used to asking for help than I am, and you think it's okay to keep giving of yourself to everyone who needs it, without getting anything back. But as tough as you are, you're still human, and I can see it's high time someone started giving to you, want it or not. So let me tell you something right now, Fred Dawson. Don't play Superman with me. I've done it enough to see through it. And if this thing is going to work at all, you'll have to let me help you when you need it. I want to be the one who gives to you, because someone should. And because ... I'm really getting kind of hooked to you and you matter to me."

Her claim on him, already, when they still barely knew each other, stunned him. Other than his major, and Captain Hodgkins to some extent, he couldn't recall one person who cared enough to make that kind of claim, to care whether or not he was being looked after. "I'll be glad for the help." Daws felt relief surge through his body as he said it. He would have had to go use the bathroom mirror to change it himself, to put the cream on it, over the stitches. He wasn't sure he could stand that long while the pain reliever was still taking effect, on top of getting up at four a.m., on top of the blood he'd lost. He'd pressed his arm against his side afterward, to prevent as much blood loss as possible. Still, it had flowed well.

"Let's get this off, then." Deanna again gripped his T-shirt and he leaned up enough to allow her to pull it off. Her eyes dropped to the bandage.

He looked down at it. Saturated. It had even started to soak his shirt she still held. He took it from her and dropped it to the floor.

"You might need to go back in."

"No. It's from being on my feet. It'll slow down now. Sure you can do this?"

"Lie down."

He obeyed and watched her face for indications he should make her stop. She carefully pulled the bandage off, winced at the sight of the wound, and went to get water and a cloth. Deanna barely touched him as she cleaned off the excess blood, applied the ointment, and rebandaged him. If she was going to be sick, she didn't show it.

"Want this on or are you warm enough without it?" She held the clean shirt.

"I'm all right for now." He didn't want to sit up even long enough to pull the thing over his head. "I am sorry." He reached up to touch her face. "Didn't plan to spend the weekend this way."

"Glad I'm here to take care of you. Would you have come back here alone?"

"They would have made me stay on base. They tried as it was. Don't be surprised if they call and check in."

"Should I answer if you're asleep?"

"Don't plan to be asleep."

"But if you are?"

"Yes. You should answer. Otherwise, they'll be at the door." He felt his eyes try to close. Damn drugs.

"Go to sleep, Freddy. You'll heal better." Deanna stroked his forehead, down his face, around his ear.

The touch relaxed him too far. Soothed him. His eyes refused to stay open. "Half hour, maybe. Then wake me up."

She gave him a soft kiss. Her fingers slid down his bare shoulder, his arm, to his fingertips. Then to his chest, where they stilled, rested. "The view's even nicer up close." She kissed him again, on the lips, then quickly on the chest, and she got up.

As his body grew heavier, his breath slower, Daws wished she'd come back and touch him again....

Deanna set a hand against his forehead just long enough to be sure he didn't have a fever. He was warm but no more than normal, and the July heat kept him warm enough she didn't bother to cover him. The bandage had a couple of fresh blots of red already, but they were small. If he remained still, she expected it would stop.

To keep herself occupied, she went to the kitchen and rifled through his few cupboards. He had more than the basics. She could make him a nice lunch, and then supper. He could try to refuse. She wouldn't let him.

It was too early to start cooking, so she wandered the apartment and stopped at the little window. Deanna couldn't help wonder if he ever looked out at the non-view of grass and sidewalk and small houses and miss the view from his balcony. And why did he give up his New York apartment and the freedom to go anywhere he wanted for pressed uniforms, four a.m. duty calls, stiff regulations, and knowing they could send him anywhere they decided, even back into a war zone? His apartment was owned, no rent. That in itself gave him the ability to pick up a job that would cover food and utilities and he'd still be okay. Why did he do this?

She went back over and carefully checked his head. No change that she noticed. His chest rose and fell easily, normal.

Suddenly overwhelmed, Deanna rushed to the bathroom, closed the door, and sat at the edge of the bathtub. She shoved her palms against her eyes, trying to block out the sight of the wound, his blood soaking through to his shirt.

But the tears persisted. It was okay. He wouldn't know.

After she calmed again, she washed her face with plenty of cold water, pressed a dry washcloth over it, and went to be sure he was still asleep and comfortable. The bandage was only slightly more stained.

With a deep breath, she went to fix her face. Her eyes were red. She didn't have Visine with her. Maybe he did.

Rifling through his medicine cabinet felt too much an intrusion but Deanna wasn't sure they'd settle fast enough without help. She wouldn't snoop; she'd look only for what she needed and ignore the rest.

It didn't take long. Not much of anything was in there. No Visine, but what looked like it. Deanna picked it up. It said eye redness/pain reliever. Exchange brand. An orange price tag that said AAFES. Like one of the brown signs she'd seen on a building.

The expiration date said it was safe, so she grabbed a tissue and put two drops in each eye, felt the immediate refreshment. She returned it to the shelf and writing on a brown prescription bottle jumped out at her: *as needed to sleep*. Deanna couldn't resist. She grabbed it to look closer. The familiar name of a strong nerve pill made her cringe. Prescribed to Fred.

The label said there were thirty. No refills. Two months old.

Although she knew she should put it back and forget she saw it, Deanna opened the bottle, spilled them into her hand, and counted them. Twenty-six. He'd used only four.

Putting it back, she quickly replaced her makeup and noted her eyes were nearly back to normal.

Would she admit what she'd done? How could she without admitting what she was looking for and why she needed it?

He'd only taken four. When? Two months ago ... May. The month they met, when he was on forced leave. For nerves? Bad enough to keep him from sleeping? And he'd spent his time helping her.

Deanna fought the emotions try to well up again and went back out to check on him. Still asleep. No new blood she could see. With another deep breath, she went to start lunch.

Daws cringed at the pain and opened his eyes. He smelled ... food. Tomato. Beef. Trying to pull himself up, he stopped and grabbed quick breaths. The pill had worn off. He felt every bit of the wound. He moved slower, used his arms...

"Hey. Let me help." Deanna came to his side and wrapped an arm under his arm, around his shoulder. When he was upright enough, she sat next to him and set a hand against his forehead. "You need another pain pill. Let me get it."

"No." He grabbed her hand.

"No? It's all over your face that you do."

"Makes me too tired. What time is it?"

"Doesn't matter. Lunch is ready. Hope you like burritos. They're still warm."

"Deanna." He looked around her over to the clock. Nearly two hours. "You were supposed to wake me."

"You needed sleep."

"Wanted the time with you." He clenched his eyes when he turned too far and a pain shot through his side.

She rubbed his back. "I was here. And you were right. Corporal Jenkins called to check in. So did Captain Hodgkins."

Called? "Didn't hear the phone."

"I grabbed it quick. As hard as you were sleeping, though, it could have kept ringing and I doubt you would have heard it. I probably could have taken advantage of you, too." Her eyes teased.

"Hm. Maybe. If you decide to try, at least wait till I'm awake. Wouldn't want to miss it."

"Is that an invitation, soldier?" She slid her hand up the center of his back to his nape, caressed the indentation with one finger. Soft. Sensual.

Daws pulled her in and claimed her mouth. Not as long as he wanted. Damn his side hurt. Damn bad timing.

"I'm taking that as a yes." Her breath whispered against his lips. "But don't worry. I'll let you heal first. Don't want to hurt you." With a wink, she got up. "Let me bring you a plate."

"Getting up anyway."

"Sit still. I'll get it."

"I'm not refusing your help, but some things you can't do."

"Oh. Well, I can bring you a plastic bottle. I'll look the other way."

"Not going to happen." He gave her a grin and accepted her help to get up. She was stronger than he expected, more help than he expected.

Walking made the pain worse, as did pulling his clean shirt over his head, and he was just as glad she already had the plates on the table. He didn't complain when she pulled out his chair. It looked as incredible as it smelled. He did take the time to thank her before he dug in. Within a couple of minutes, he propped his free arm against the table to help support his weight.

"Will you take your medicine if I get it for you?"

"No."

"Freddy…"

"Tonight. Before bed. I want to be awake before then."

Deanna was horribly grateful to Shel and Mandy Hodgkins. They'd brought dinner, which prevented Fred from complaining about her cooking again, or from trying to take her out. His captain forbade it, and they stayed to visit, to help be sure he remained relatively still. Mandy pulled Deanna aside once and asked how she was holding up. In full honesty, Deanna told her she couldn't stand the thought of leaving him Monday. Mandy assured her the sergeant would be well cared for.

Still, she wouldn't want to go. Not only because he was injured.

He did give in and take the pain pill before bed, when she again cleaned his wound and replaced the bandage. And he agreed to move back to his bed, only after she said she'd sleep by his side, on his uninjured side.

Daws was relieved to feel much better in the morning. The pain was still there, still throbbing, but less sharp. Getting up carefully so he wouldn't wake her, he went to check it in the mirror. He hoped to hell Barney was happy with himself. And he hoped the private was doing all right. As soon as he could move better, Daws would go check on him personally. Until then, Jenkins could keep track. Or until Monday. Tomorrow. She had to leave tomorrow.

He had to be awake today, so he opted for ibuprofen instead of the prescribed pills with codeine. Grabbing them from the cabinet, he popped three in his mouth and turned on the sink to cup enough water to swallow them. As he returned the bottle, he noticed his sleeping pills had been moved. He always kept them label out. Precise.

With a frown, he spilled them into his hand and counted. All there but the three he'd taken and the one he'd dropped down the sink. The eye drops were moved, also. He straightened both and closed the cabinet. Should he ask her? She'd only been curious since none were missing. If he asked, she'd want to know why he had them. Daws wasn't sure he wanted to discuss it.

He returned to the bedroom long enough to see she was still asleep and went to make breakfast. Nothing fancy. Eggs and French toast. Quick and easy.

She came out as he was about to go wake her. "You shouldn't be cooking. Why didn't you get me up?" Deanna ran a hand through unbrushed hair.

"Good morning." Daws ran his eyes down her deep red night shirt to her bare legs and feet. And back to her lusciously messy auburn hair.

"Oh, don't look at me. I haven't even..."

"You're beautiful." He moved up close and kissed her, a soft bare touch of her lips.

"I'm not. I'm a mess." She set a hand on his stomach. "You look like you feel better. How is it?"

"Fine. And I do. What do you want to do today?"

Deanna frowned and raised his shirt to check the bandage. "Still clean. Or did you change it already?"

"I did, but it's fine."

"Not bleeding?"

"No." He subtracted the distance she'd added, slid his hands around her waist, felt the curves of her body underneath the barely there fabric. "Sleep all right?"

"Hm. Yes and no." Deanna caught his eyes and rested her arms over his shoulders. "Yes when I was enjoying being beside you and no when I kept waking up to check for a fever or anything. You had me worried, Sergeant Dawson. Glad you look better today."

"Didn't need to worry."

"Right. And you wouldn't have if it was me instead?"

His back stiffened. "Don't let it be you instead." The thought hurt his stomach more than the knife had hurt his side. "Come sit down. Breakfast is ready."

She couldn't talk him into staying in all day and resting, so Deanna showered after she helped with breakfast dishes. By the time she was done, he'd arranged for Zakowsky and his current girlfriend to go on a day trip with them: a short drive up to Alexandria Bay and a boat tour around the Thousand Islands area.

Zakowsky insisted on driving, on Fred taking it easy if he was crazy enough to run around.

Although Deanna agreed he was crazy, she couldn't remember having a nicer day. With the drive each way nearly an hour, and Fred in the back of the SUV with her, plus the long boat ride where they sat up front overlooking the lower deck while the other couple wandered, they had plenty of time to talk. And to cuddle. She took advantage of it and he didn't object. In between her teasing, caressing what bare skin she could see or easily find, planting quick kisses here and there, he pointed out landmarks along the way. Fred offered to take her into Boldt Castle at some point, when he was better up to walking, but Deanna wasn't entirely sure she wanted to see it. The story was too sad: losing his beloved wife only four years after having the thing built for her. It reminded her of the Taj Majal story, although she did want to see that some day. For artistic reasons.

They all stopped for a nice dinner on the way back home and Zakowsky didn't linger when he dropped them off.

Deanna rubbed Fred's arm as he closed and locked the door. "Sit down; I'll make coffee."

He grabbed her hand. "That should be my line."

"Why?"

"You're visiting."

"But I'm not the one who's injured."

"Deanna, it's fine."

"Hm." She raised his shirt, as she had several times during the day, to check it. Clean. "Good. Let's keep it that way." She tried again to head to the kitchen but he didn't release her. He pulled her closer and brushed a hand through her hair. Easing in, he teased her lips, kissed her nose, her forehead, brushed his cheek against hers, and found her mouth, took her in.

Deanna felt her body trying to mesh with his. He didn't rush the kiss. He lingered, fueling her desire for him, tantalizing her with what felt like a promise. At least she took it that way, as a promise of more to come. When he could. When it wouldn't hurt him.

"Freddy?" Her lips nearly brushed his as she spoke.

He took her bottom lip gently between his teeth, only for a second.

Her knees nearly gave out. She felt his hands slide down her hips. "This is unfair, you know."

"Why?" He kissed her jaw and her neck.

Her eyes clenched. "Because I want you. I already want you so badly I can hardly stand to keep my hands where they belong, and..."

He pulled back.

Deanna met his gaze; his brown eyes sparkled, peered deeply into her. "You have to know I do."

"Hoped you did. Said earlier you were taking it as an invitation."

"Oh. But you're..." She glanced at his side. "You can't..."

"Hell I can't." Closing the small distance, he took her in again, then led her back to his room.

She watched as he removed his shirt, and when he started to unbutton hers, she let him. Deanna had never allowed it before, had always insisted she undress herself, keeping at least that much control. But she did. She stood and allowed him to take charge, reveled in how gentle he was, how he took his time, how he kissed her in between. And she helped him with his jeans, to keep him from straining his side, she said.

Not bothering to hide the fact she was studying him, all of him, Deanna finally met his eyes.

They looked amused. "Meet your approval?"

"Oh yes, Fred Dawson." She ran a hand down his bare hip. "Very much so. So far."

His eyebrows rose slightly. "Well, as I said, I'll try hard to meet your every expectation."

"Gotta tell you." Deanna closed the distance; her skin met his. "You've already surpassed any expectations I used to have. So it's looking good."

He met her lips and held them as he moved to the bed. Again, he took his time, planting kisses, caressing her skin, giving them both time to ease into comfort with each other.

"Deanna, tell me you can handle this lifestyle." He kissed her forehead. "The separations." Her nose. "The long hours." Her chin. "Possible moves." Her lips. "Things I can't tell you or you can't repeat." He set his face alongside hers and spoke into her ear. "Distance from people who won't understand, who'll try to make you think I'm some kind of … villain. Or worse." He returned to her eyes. "Before I let myself depend on you, before I want more than I should. Even though I can't promise you much of anything, tell me you can handle this, all of it."

The occasional debate in Deanna's mind as to whether or not she wanted the job, the one with private tears, dissipated with his gaze. His vulnerability. Yes, she wanted it. She wanted to be the one at his back, the one who was there for him the way he was there for everyone else.

"Yes." She slid both hands to the sides of his head. "And I only need one promise."

"Anything I can."

"Be faithful to me."

"Completely. And I expect the same."

"Yes. Completely. And yes, I can do this with you. I want this." She reached up to brush his lips. "But your side. Are you sure it won't hurt you?"

"No. And I couldn't care less."

Daws cuddled in behind her. He'd have to take her to the bus station in a couple of hours. Too soon. And then he'd have to go to the clinic. Hoping he could hide the pulled stitches from her, the blood that filled the bandage again, he'd changed it, added an extra layer of gauze, and had been lying still with his hand pressed against it. But she stirred. His hand was still clean; so far, so good. He carressed her hip, her leg, and he kissed her shoulder.

She turned and met his lips. "Mm. I don't want to leave you today."

"Come back when you can, and I'll take leave when I can."

"What if I just call and quit and stay here with you?"

"You don't want to quit."

"Don't I?"

He stroked her hair, forcing himself to argue. "Maybe at the moment, but you've worked too hard. You can't give up now." He stopped a coming protest with a kiss. "You'll get there. I have faith in you. I know you will."

===

Deanna saw her bus start to board and touched his face. She was glad he hadn't worn his uniform so she wouldn't have to keep too much distance. "You be careful. Don't overdo it. Go get that fixed up again and let yourself heal."

"You be careful, too." He ran fingers through her hair. "Don't let that jerk get too close. Let him know I'm not far away if you need to. If you ever want, I'll call him myself and tell him."

She met his lips and gave him a careful hug, took in his scent, gritty but sensual, barely there aftershave. "Before I go, there's something I have to tell you." Checking to be sure no one was close by, she leaned in beside his ear. "You know those expectations you were worried about? Yeah well, far more than fulfilled. You are better in *every* way than anyone I've ever known."

A teasing glint met her eyes. "Wait until I don't have stitches to work around." The arm around her waist pulled her closer.

She chuckled. "Something to look forward to?"

"Hope so." With a glance toward the bus, he took her hand and walked with her to the door. "Call when you get in."

"I will. Take care of yourself, Fred Dawson." She gave him a light kiss, quick, since she wasn't sure how much public affection he'd appreciate even out of uniform, but he made it deeper. And touched her eyes.

"Never had this much trouble letting someone leave."

"Oh." She threw her arms around his neck, despite the driver beckoning the doors were about to close, and hugged him. "And I can't tell you how much I'm glad you invited me to breakfast that next morning." Her emotions threatened to overtake her control and she gave him a light peck on the side of his face and slid away, up into the bus.

Deanna grabbed a seat on the side she could see him. As it began to move, he walked with it a few steps, then stopped. She held onto the sight of him as long as she could, and held her breath to force back the tears she wouldn't allow.

Quarters.

Daws tried to argue. The doctor, a colonel this time, head of the clinic, backed him down. Ordered him to three days of quarters and then limited desk duty for the following month, with a threat that it would be longer if he pulled any more stitches. He hadn't quite admitted how he pulled them, but even with his assurance it wouldn't happen again, the colonel sent him back home. For three days. And he wasn't to leave the apartment.

He wouldn't even let him drive home again. Daws told him he had no one available to pick him up. The colonel gave his P.A. instructions to see to it one of the sergeant's men was called.

Damned frustrating. He could drive. And what was he supposed to do with three days alone? He should have asked Deanna to stay the week. But then, if he pulled stitches again, they'd probably confine him to post. Without her.

Deanna stepped off the bus at her stop and pushed the umbrella open.

"*Hey*. Couldja wait till you're farther out? Nearly poked my eye out with that thing."

She turned at the raucous, scratchy voice to find an unkempt scraggly beard and bloodshot eyes from the man getting out behind her. "Back away from me more, and then your beady little eyes will be quite safe from my deadly umbrella."

"Aren't you the funny one. Fraid you're gonna melt if ya get wet? I doubt ya will since ya ain't that sweet, *sugar*." His eyes dropped down her frame.

"Not to the likes of you, I'm not. And keep your beady eyes where they belong or I'll poke them out on purpose. Go find a sleazy little hole in the wall to crawl into, slime ball." She pivoted and stalked toward the apartment, Freddy's apartment, wishing with everything she was he'd be there. She too often entertained herself by thinking one night when she got home, he would just be there, as a surprise. And every time he wasn't, she told herself to stop being so foolish.

The rain spattered from the sidewalk onto her feet and ankles and she wished she'd worn her uglier shoes. And maybe her stuffier outfit. Maybe Mr. Full-of-himself wouldn't have bothered her today if she had. She'd wear it tomorrow. See if it made a difference.

Freddy wouldn't even call tonight; they were in the field. For several days. How he got around his doctor's orders to be out there with his men, she wasn't sure, but selfishly, she wished he hadn't.

Thinking of him, she didn't pay enough attention and had to catch herself when a couple of guys in suits with their huge black umbrellas nearly ran her off the sidewalk. "Excuse you. Wanna watch where you're going?"

One of them half-turned and threw a dismissive glance as he kept walking.

She grabbed a deep breath. Most often, she loved the city. She loved the energy and the vibrance and the lights at night and that anything you could want to do was right there a cab ride away and most people left you alone. It was comfortable. On days, though, such as this one, when the slime balls got to her, she wondered why she was still there. Her job was going nowhere. Every day, she was more annoyed to be in the office. Todd wouldn't stop with his suggestions about what she should be doing to get ahead, what it would take for him to help her get there. And her boss was more insufferable by the hour.

She could quit. Move. Just hop a bus with a suitcase and ... and go wait at Freddy's door until he came home. He'd let her stay. She had little doubt he would. But there was that touch of doubt. Maybe he'd let her stay a while, but then what? When he got to know her better? When he saw her every morning before she had a chance to pull herself together, brush and tame her hair, add some pink to her cheeks and lips. Except he had seen her that way. He didn't appear put off, or turned off.

Such a gentleman. A strong, self-assured, self-reliant, unassuming, sweet, gentle gentleman. Oh, how she adored him. Would he want her there? If she asked? But what would she do? Deanna didn't expect there was much call for a marketing expert on the military base or the little town around it. She could scour the little stores, she supposed, to see if they needed promotional help, but she doubt they'd pay close to what they did in New York. Of course, if she didn't have rent, which she didn't, she wouldn't need to be paid much. She had plans, though. Her plans needed funds.

Besides, it was bad enough she stayed in his apartment without paying rent, even if she did the cleaning and such on her own to save him that expense. She couldn't ask him to pay it again so she could go live with him there. She'd never be that selfish. And he had faith in her to make it to where she wanted to be in her career.

But she wanted to be. Part of her wanted to be that selfish. And she wanted to see him again. Five weeks since she visited. He wouldn't have leave for some time yet. Maybe not until Christmas. Three months.

She could call in sick for a few days and go see him. She had sick time coming.

Under the canopy covering the entrance to his building, her building, she lowered the umbrella and shook it out, then started to pull the door open. She jerked back when it came at her quick, shoved from the inside. The guy glanced at her and let it go instead of even holding it for the two seconds it would have taken her to walk through. Were there no gentlemen left in the city? She hardly noticed before. She did now.

With a sigh, Deanna made her way to the elevator, waited impatiently to get to her floor, and hurried to get in and chain the door behind her. Kicking her shoes off, she set her handbag and umbrella in the holder and went to check the machine, as she always did first thing.

Two messages. The first was another telemarketer and she hit delete before she could find out what he was selling. The second...

"Deanna, sorry I missed you. I stole a couple of minutes to find a phone. Have to head out again. Have a nice night and be sure to use that tub to warm yourself up well after today's rain. Will call again when I can."

She hit save, just to save it, and slumped down into a chair. She'd missed him, because she agreed to work an hour late to cover for the lazy jerk again, because Freddy said he'd be out and couldn't call. And she missed him.

Daws shoved the mix of rain and sweat from his face and helped his men store the rest of the equipment for the night. He wished she'd picked up earlier. Now he'd have to wonder if she only worked late or if something was wrong.

"Sergeant, what do we do with this?"

Pulling himself back to where he was, he surveyed the box of ammo, still sealed, and went to try to find a dry place for it.

He also wondered about Barney. The stupid kid had gone AWOL instead of owning up to his pending charges. There was nothing more Daws could do for him. It was out of his hands. When they found him, and they would find him eventually if he was still in the States, he'd be court marshaled. Daws figured he was in Canada by now. Despite himself, he couldn't help think Barney should stay there. Maybe the flight would convince him he better straighten himself up.

Barney's girlfriend, though, was beside herself. She'd spent twenty minutes with Daws trying to make him go search personally, yelling it was his fault he was too hard on him when he was already having so much trouble. Daws stood and let her yell. She only needed to yell. He wanted to tell her she was half of Barney's problem, but he couldn't. Against protocol. Maybe the boy would be better off away from the screaming banshee.

His side pulled at him and he changed positions as much as possible while moving the box up into shelter. He'd been warned it would take some time to heal completely. The scar would remain. Didn't matter to him, though he couldn't help but wonder if it would continually bother Deanna.

He wished she'd picked up earlier.

========

Fred brushed off her questions about his side. Deanna knew what it meant: it was worse than he wanted her to know. She'd tried to tell him he shouldn't be out in the field already, not until it was fully healed. But Fred Dawson was not one to shirk duty, even when he should.

At least she could start talking to him at night again since he was back on regular days.

As tired as he was, she couldn't hold him on the line. "You should get to bed. I'm going to let you go so you can."

"Tired of talking to me already?"

She heard the tease in his voice and wanted to throw her arms around him. "You know I'm not. I ... have some work to do anyway. And you should rest. Take care of that side."

"It's fine."

"I know better."

"Do you?"

She grabbed a slow deep breath. "Just take care of yourself, okay?"

"Tell me what's wrong."

"Nothing."

"I know better."

She couldn't help a light grin. "Nothing more than normal. Mostly...." Deanna stopped. She wasn't about to add pressure on him.

"What?"

"Nothing."

"I'm not letting you go until you tell me."

"No? What if I hang up?" She wanted to set a hand against his chest, run it down to his side to check it herself.

"You won't. Tell me. Mostly what?"

"I miss you." She clenched her eyes and bit her lip. She shouldn't have said it...

"I miss you, too."

Shivers began in her chest and spread through her body. "Do you?"

"You doubt that?"

"Oh. Well, you know, you're ... kind of a strong, silent, stalwart type, you know, and ... I wasn't sure..."

"Not when it comes to you. I do miss you. Every day, Anna."

She bit her lip again, unable to answer.

"Are you still doing okay with this? You haven't changed your mind?"

"Oh. About us? Of course I haven't, and yes. I'm a strong, stalwart type, too, you know. At least enough. Yes, I'm okay. Yes, I still want this. Yes, I'm waiting for you."

"Good to hear. What work do you have to do tonight?"

Changing the subject. She was glad he did, and briefly mentioned a couple of ideas she had for a current campaign she thought she'd develop and see if someone would actually look at them. A long shot, maybe for nothing, but she wasn't giving up yet on getting where she wanted to be.

"Go get 'em. I know you will. If not there, then somewhere." His voice sounded suddenly ten times more tired.

"Thank you, but go to bed. You need sleep."

"Might have to do that. Longer tomorrow, okay?"

"I'll be here. Good night, Freddy." She waited for his return and set the receiver down. He was so tired. She wished she could be there to be sure he ate well and slept.

Too restless to work on the campaign that would likely be pointless, she decided to write home first. The letter she'd received two days before had been rattling her brain every minute since. Should Deanna suggest her mom just leave him? She wouldn't do it. And maybe she would stop writing about it. Not tell anyone.

Deanna was the only one her mom really talked to. The other kids weren't "strong enough." In all honesty, they were too self-absorbed to consider anything but how it would affect them. They were all right there, all still going to her for everything. But then, they didn't know. They'd been told their mom was away visiting relatives. She knew better.

The letter, still on the coffee table taunting her, made Deanna wonder if another "visit the relatives" spell was soon to come.

=======

"Harding." Daws caught up with the specialist when he paused at his name.

"Sergeant?"

"You're a friend of Specialist Andrews from 3/64th?"

The stocky blonde kid frowned. "Yes, Sergeant. Something happen?"

"No, nothing like that. He said you're from southern Vermont."

"Yes, Sergeant."

"Anywhere around Bennington?"

"Not far from there. I'm up in Manchester: twenty, thirty minutes away."

"Headed back on leave soon, he said."

"Labor day weekend plus a few days."

Daws nodded. "Have a favor to ask. Our major was lost in an accident a few months ago."

"Major Reynauld. I remember, Staff Sergeant. Andrews was upset by the loss. A good officer, he said."

"His family is in Bennington. Mind checking on them while you're back? Just say the 3/64th S3 is still around for assistance if needed. See that they're all right."

"Of course, Sergeant. Happy to. If his wife won't mind the intrusion?"

"Don't imagine she will. Told her we'd be available."

The specialist gave him a curious look, but said nothing and waited for further instruction.

"Go in uniform if you're taking it."

"Always do. Mom insists I wear it to church when I'm home. Likes to show me off." Harding rolled his eyes with a light grin.

"Enjoy that. Nice that she does." Daws handed him the address and thanked him.

As the specialist went on about his task, Daws headed back to his own. Labor Day weekend. Nothing much would be happening around base, essential personnel only. Of course, his men might take their extra time off too much to heart. If they did, Jenkins could handle it. He was in line for the E5 board. It would be good training.

Of course, if Daws was going to take a couple of extra days over the holiday, he could swing by Bennington himself. It wouldn't be too far out of the way. That could look too obvious, though. Harding driving the twenty miles since he was right there would look like no more than an off-hand detour to check in. And Daws wasn't sure he was ready to see the boy again, the one taking it so hard, the one so like his father.

It would also give him less time with Deanna. He was all right with their nightly phone calls, but something was bothering her and she wouldn't tell him. Being together only the one night before nearly two months' separation wasn't a good idea, and he hadn't planned on sharing the bed with her when she visited. He'd planned to wait to see if she could handle the long-distance relationship. He wasn't sure yet, based on her calls. She was holding too much back.

=======

Deanna checked the time as she considered the invitation. Movies with the girls. It sounded like fun; she hadn't been part of a group of girlfriends since ... forever ago. The three girls she'd met the night she went out on her own to spite Todd were her crowd. Easy-going, chatty, spontaneous...

"So? Are you coming with?" Cat's voice came over the line.

"I don't know." She needed to be off the phone. He hadn't called yet. "Can I let you know in about a half hour or so?"

"Deanna, we have to be there by then. Get your shoes on and go outside. We'll pick you up."

"Sorry. I can't leave now."

"Why? Big date?"

No, but a phone call she didn't want to miss. "Maybe next time, okay?"

"Aw, but it's Michael J. and the last night *Doc Hollywood* is playing. You know you want to come."

She did. "Sorry, and thanks for asking. Wish I could. Next time." With a sigh, she hung up and returned to her warmed up meat loaf. It was only a movie. She'd catch it when it came out on video. Deanna hoped they'd call again. It was the third time she turned them down. When phone calls were the only time she had with Fred, she wasn't about to miss them.

===

Twenty-one-hundred already. He hadn't had time to pick up the phone other than for duty. And he couldn't use the duty phone to call long distance. "Cowan." Daws caught his E-4 as he came back from his break. "I'm out for a while."

" 'Kay, Sergeant. 'Bout time."

"Yeah, it is." He grabbed his hat and strode out the door before anything could stop him. Glad it was busy rather than slow, to make the night go faster, Daws wished he'd thought to warn Deanna. She'd be worried by now, he supposed. Although, with as erratic as his schedule had been, maybe she wouldn't.

He didn't have time to go back to his apartment for a call and still grab something to eat, so he drove the couple of blocks to the PX food court and pulled out his calling card. There should still be fifteen or twenty minutes on it, if he remembered well enough. He couldn't stay on that long, anyway.

Since they were about to close, Daws went to grab a meal from Burger King first. They didn't much appreciate him ordering so late when they were trying to clean for the night, but it was that or skip the phone call to leave enough time to drive off-base to the twenty-four hour chain he didn't like much.

Her voice was sleepy when she answered.

"Hey, Anna. Did I wake you?"

"Freddy. Everything okay? It's late. You just got off?"

"I'm on Staff Duty tonight; won't be off till morning."

"What does that mean?"

"Guard dog duty."

"What?"

"Sorry, a joke. Making checks, keeping an eye on the store, handling calls. A necessary evil."

"And you have to be up all night?"

"All night. I'll be off tomorrow so I can call after I wake up."

"Oh."

"Meant to warn you." He turned as the PX manager closed the mesh wire security door over the entrance and locked it. "Can't stay on long. They're about to kick me out. Thought I'd be on break earlier."

"That's okay. Glad you let me know."

"Go back to sleep. Sorry I woke you."

"No, you didn't. I'm watching a movie."

"In that case, sorry I interrupted."

"I'm not. Have a good night, Freddy."

He nodded at the woman who said they were closing. "You too, Deanna. Talk to you tomorrow." At her okay, he hung up, apologized to the woman for holding her there, and grabbed his late dinner to take back to work.

Deanna kept her hand on the receiver for some time. He hadn't even asked what she was watching. Or how her day went. She wouldn't have told him she gave up plans with her friends waiting for his call, but he could have warned her. She could have gone and been back already.

He was calling during the day tomorrow. He didn't say what time. Now she had to decide whether to cancel the next day's plans, also. Or call him back afterward. She should have told him of her plans. But he hadn't given her time. He needed to get an answering machine for his small apartment, even if he didn't like them. At least he could call and leave her a message. She couldn't even do that.

Too annoyed to watch the comedy that wasn't working, anyway, Deanna turned it off and replaced it with the stereo. Bryan Adams came over the airwaves. Great. The last thing she needed was the song that reminded her of him. They listened to it together that night, their one night together. He'd told her when she heard it to know everything it said applied to how he felt about her. All of it. She'd answered it would be okay to fight for her, but absolutely not okay to die for her. He hadn't answered.

When the song ended, Deanna turned the radio off, and the lights, and went to bed. She didn't even want to go out tomorrow. Not without him.

=== September ===

A gust of chilly air yanked at her jacket and Deanna gripped its edges as she strode away from the noisy bus stop. It was too early to be so cold, but then, in New York it was hard to tell what each day would bring once September hit. Another few days, and she'd likely be shucking off her blazer as soon as she stepped out of the office building. She hoped. She liked cold okay and dealt with it fine for the most part, but she wasn't ready for it yet.

She'd like it better with a warm body to cuddle against. Since the body she wanted was across the state, she'd make do with a hot bath and a hot cocoa, plus the super sized candy bar she'd been hoarding for the right time.

Her girlfriends hadn't given up yet. They invited her to one of the clubs they hung out at a lot. It was Friday, and a long weekend, Cat argued: time to dust off the same ole work week dust and hit the town. Maybe she would, after Freddy called, and depending how late they talked. The past couple of days had been long for him, so he called late and didn't talk much. He nearly fell asleep on her at least once and she had to raise her voice and beckon to him before he apologized and said he better get to bed.

If he called that late again, she'd be in her pajamas already and unwilling to go anywhere.

She tried to talk herself into stopping at the little market on her way to her building, but it would wait. She could make do with a sandwich and soup again. At least until she went out. Then she'd allow herself to splurge. It was Friday, after all. Time to brush off the dust.

A couple leaving her building, hand in hand, said hello and Deanna returned it through her surprise. In the few months she'd been there, her hellos had been promptly ignored, and she'd quit bothering.

Maybe they were starting to accept her.

With a sigh, she figured it didn't matter if they did or not. She was beginning to wonder if she'd be there much longer.

Freddy seemed too disinterested in talking recently. He hardly said much about what he was doing, even when he wasn't tired. He listened and consoled as needed … was she complaining too much? He could be tired of hearing it, she supposed. After all, he had the tied hands of a relationship without any of the benefits. So did she, except even just talking over the phone with him was more a real relationship than any she'd ever had before.

Sad commentary on her dating life, she supposed.

The elevator stopped in between the ground floor and where she wanted to be, and she didn't bother with more than a nod at the couple and their young children as they stepped in. Why were they heading up? Maybe they had friends in the same building. A novel thought. Making friends in the same building. It would sure make it easier to get together regardless of rain, wind, or the coming snow. Deanna wondered if there was a couple right there she and Freddy would both get along with.

If he was ever there enough to find out. And if he was interested in doing "couple" things. Like going out with her to her places and meeting her friends. Would he? If not, she supposed it didn't matter. She was used to doing things on her own.

Finally at the right floor, she ambled down the hall and fumbled for her keys. As she opened the door, she stopped. Did she have the wrong place? No. The key opened it. His furniture was there. But she smelled something lusciously enticing and the lights were on and … music. Soft music filled the air. Richie Sambora. *Ballad of Youth.* A CD Deanna introduced to him.

He was home.

After all the times she'd wished he would just be there, he was there. She'd given up thinking it would happen...

"Deanna." He stepped out from the kitchen. And he looked incredible, in black trousers and a soft gray shirt, the sleeves rolled to his forearms. "Hope I didn't scare you."

She shook her head, dumped her handbag and jacket on the floor, and ran into his arms. He nudged only a touch at the impact and enclosed her within his strong grip, but gentle. Always so gentle, which always surprised her.

"Now that's worth coming home for." His face nuzzled against the side of her head.

"You have no idea how glad I am to see you." Holding tight, she escaped into his warmth, his firmness, his sturdiness. Never had she been so glad simply to have her arms around a man, around anyone. Ever.

"What's wrong?" He pulled back enough to see her face.

"Oh. Nothing now."

He studied her a moment, then took her hands. "Dinner's ready. Do you want to freshen up first?"

"No. I just want to hold onto you." She wrapped back into him.

He chuckled. "You have four full days and then some to do that."

"Yeah? Not long, but I'll take it." She found his mouth, gently, then possessively. His hands ran down her back, to her hips.

"Hm." He kissed the side of her face as he broke from her lips. "We better eat while it's warm, because it won't be if..."

"We can reheat it." She ducked into his neck and felt the stubble growing in, smelled his hugely masculine cologne...

"It'll be better now than warmed. Not that I'm not tempted, but I hoped you wouldn't be late tonight. Thought about calling your office."

"You can, you know." She planted another light kiss on his lips. "Let me go wash the city off real quick." Backing up a couple of steps, gripping his fingers, she scanned him again. "I really can't tell you how glad I am that you're home."

"Are you all right?"

"Yes." A light nod reaffirmed her word. All the stuff that had nagged at her near constantly now faded. It didn't matter. She knew it would matter again once he went back to work, but for now, she couldn't be bothered with it, or by it. She held him again before she went to clean up.

Deanna left her nice clothes on, except for the hose she was glad to be free of, washed her face, and reapplied a touch of basic makeup. The man looked too good to go back out to him too natural.

Dinner was exquisite: baked chicken with a luscious crème sauce, barely steamed broccoli, new potatoes, and a sweet German wine. They talked while sitting across from each other, and she leaned in to caress the exotic flowers on the side of the table. Canna lilies, he said when she asked, coral. She was more touched by the way he chose them because they reminded him of her than she'd been by Todd's full dozen red rose bouquets. More casual than elegant. More personal. Romantic but not overdone. Not pushy.

He'd made the dinner himself, after driving the five and a half hours from base and stopping at a store to pick up what he needed. He'd learned to cook from his family's housekeeper who had doubled as his caregiver. The woman had made him cook with her to keep him out of trouble and prevent him making messes while she was busy.

Deanna admitted she did cook more than burritos, and fairly well, but nothing fancy. She was a vegetable freak, into whole grains and lean meats and ... considering his planned menu, she wondered if he hadn't figured that out already. His grin said he had, and he admitted he'd watched what she ordered at restaurants and noted the groceries in the apartment.

"Regular Sherlock Holmes, aren't you?" She took a sip of the wine and breathed it in before swallowing. "Is there anything you can't do, Fred Dawson?"

"A lot of things I can't do."

"Yeah? Like what?"

He shrugged. "Can't play the guitar worth anything."

She laughed. "Oh? You've tried?"

"Tried for a while. Had to give it up. Annoyed the hell out of me."

"So should I tell you I play a mean Chopsticks on the piano?"

He raised his glass as in a salute, then took a swallow. "You'll have to show me. Do you play?"

"Not other than that. I have no rhythm. Mother used to tell me so all the time. Tried dance class once, too. Ended up spraining my ankle."

"I'm surprised." He eyed her.

"Why's that?"

"The way you move, I figured you for a hell of a dancer."

"Have you fooled, don't I?" She grinned. "Well, I do okay on a club dance floor. My hips swivel well." She paused to enjoy his expression. "As long as I don't try to overdo the feet, I'm all right. And I've found no one cares about the feet if the hips work well." Deanna threw him a wink.

"I imagine that's true." He got up and grabbed his empty plate and hers. And she joined him in clearing the table, in washing and drying the dishes, putting away leftovers.

"Should have asked if you have plans tonight, or this weekend." He pulled her closer to him. "Am I interrupting anything?"

"If you were, I'd cancel it." She pressed her lips against his neck.

"Deanna, honestly. If you have plans..."

"No." He was so warm and he smelled of something so masculine and strong and...

"You're sure? Nothing?"

"Hm. A few friends asked me to meet them at this little club I like. But I can do that any weekend."

"Friends? Ones I've heard of?"

She pulled back. "Female friends." Her tone was sharper than she meant.

"I didn't ask."

"And you didn't plan to ask?"

He rubbed a thumb along her face. "Hadn't even crossed my mind."

"Honestly? Because..."

"I won't ever accuse you of anything. And if I was afraid of what you were doing, I wouldn't be..."

"What? You wouldn't be what?"

"I wouldn't have let anything start between us." He met her lips, only for a moment. "You mentioned a couple of women you went out with a while back. Wondered if they were the same ones. Trina and..."

"Cat. You remember that?"

"Nearly anyway. Knew it was a C name."

"I'm sorry. I just ... I'm used to..."

He pulled her back in, gave her a deeper, longer kiss. She felt herself draining, unwinding, melting into him. She kept a good grip on his arms when he released her, for the support.

"Do you want to go meet them as you planned?"

"No." She slid a hand to his chest. "I want every minute with you I can get. Unless you want to go. But you had a long drive, and it's no problem..."

"I'd be glad to escort you, if you want me there."

"Yes." She stared at him, waiting for the punch line.

With a nod, he released her and suggested she do whatever she needed to do and he was ready whenever she was.

Daws sat at the table sipping cola next to the one other male who was part of the group and watched Deanna swivel her hips out on the dance floor with her girlfriends. She was right. She swiveled well. And she nearly glowed there, in her element, among a few friends and a mixed crowd of friendly acquaintances and strangers.

She caught him staring and gave him a teasing smile.

"Want to dance?"

He looked up at the woman, barely a woman, more a girl. "Thank you, no. I'm here with my girlfriend."

The girl rolled her eyes and walked away. His *girlfriend*. It was the first time he'd called her that. He hadn't had one of those since high school. It was always 'the woman he was dating' if he mentioned her at all, and that was good enough. Deanna was too much more than that.

As the music changed to a slow sensual beat, her eyes touched his and she came to him. "Hey sexy." Deanna leaned down from behind, her arms over his shoulders. "Would you like to dance? I know you turned that other girl away, but thought I'd give it a try."

"Might just have to accept this time." He grasped the fingers in front of his chest.

"Yeah? After saying no to her? She was kind of hot, don't you think?"

"Didn't notice."

She pressed in closer as her friends took their seats. "I find that hard to believe."

"Noticed she was young."

"Hm, not sure how I should take that."

He turned his head up enough to catch her eyes. "Considering I look four years older than I am, according to who you ask..." Daws waited to be sure she remembered judging his age at thirty-two. Apparently, she did.

"Okay. Never mind the age thing. Why else would you say yes to me and no to her?" She rubbed fingers along his neck. A soft, light touch.

"You're more convincing."

"Think so? Just wait till later."

He heard the chuckles from her friends and pulled her in close as he stood. "Taking that as a promise."

"You should." With a grin, Deanna took him out to the floor.

Daws stopped keeping track of everyone around them, stopped watching for unexpected surprises he wanted to see coming, and held her in, absorbed himself in her warmth, her curves, her trace of perfume. He recognized the singer's voice but couldn't place her so he asked.

"Whitney Houston, love this song. And wow, you move nice." She tilted her head down toward his body. "Didn't expect that since you're built like a Mack truck."

"A Mack truck?"

"You know, one of those big sturdy wide work trucks that can do anything you need them to do."

The hint was well taken. The teasing was unmistakable. He enjoyed the fire in her eyes, the open dare, and he was more than willing to feed it. "I'm sure there are things they can't do."

She grinned. "Like play guitar? Well, I can let that slide since they weren't made for that. Why do you think it's usually the little skinny boys who end up guitar icons? They can't keep up with the trucks. What else are they going to do to catch a girl's attention?"

"You're not into the skinny types?"

She scanned him again. "Apparently not. I've dated a few. Never did it for me like you do, I have to admit." Her eyes peered into his. They looked more brown than green tonight. He'd noticed they had a tendency to shift with her moods. Brown was a good sign.

"Deanna, if you're not careful, we're not staying here long."

Her lips curled up slowly. She pressed closer. "Didn't plan to stay long, Sergeant Dawson. Just wanted to see how you'd do at one of my places with my friends, since you offered and all."

"Did I pass muster?"

"So far." A glint in her eye told him she wasn't quite done with the test. It made him want to grab her and take her home.

Deanna managed to wait until they were in his apartment before she began to unbutton his shirt, at his stomach.

"Are we going to do this right here beside the door?"

She let her fingers brush against his bare skin as she moved them up to the next button. "Mm, would that turn you on?"

He brushed a strand of hair from her face. "Too late for that. Bed might be more comfortable, though, or at least the couch."

She chuckled and paused to set a palm on his cheek. "In a hurry, Sergeant?"

"Am *I* in a hurry?" He raised his eyebrows and looked down at his shirt.

"Oh. Well, I'm checking your side. You keep telling me it's fine over the phone, but every day I wish I could check it myself. So I am." She released the rest of the buttons she could see, never mind they wouldn't all need to be undone in order to check his side, then tugged the shirt tails out of his pants to finish the job. Deanna ran fingers over the wound, softly, carefully. It was still pink and bumpy. "Does it still hurt at all?"

"No." When she raised her eyes to his in a question, he shrugged. "I feel it at times, but it doesn't hurt. Would you like more wine?"

She shook her head and let his shirt fall back in place. "You never told me what they said when you had those stitches fixed."

"To follow orders this time and not do anything strenuous. I did tell you that."

"Yes, but ... that was it?"

"Doctor didn't say more than that. A couple of my men who knew you were there made comments, only for about three seconds."

"Now that, you didn't tell me." A grin skirted her face.

"Didn't last long."

"No, I imagine it didn't." She set her hand back over the scar. "No stitches to pull tonight."

"In a hurry, Ms. Meyers?"

"Yes. I've missed you."

=======

"Am I interrupting?"

Looking up toward the familiar voice, Deanna closed her sketchbook. "Oh. Hi Trina. Have a seat. Are you alone? I've just ordered..."

"No, I can't stay. Heller's outside having a cigarette. I'm grabbing coffee." She sat, half perched in the cafe's chair opposite the table, and leaned in. "I've been hoping to catch you, though."

"Have you?" Deanna glanced out the window where Trina's fiancé talked with some girl. "We're still meeting for the movies tomorrow, right?"

"Well." Trina shifted in her chair; her gaze flicked between the dessert menu and the counter. "See, that depends. I'm not sure I can go. Is your boyfriend still in town?"

"Why?"

"Well." Trina picked up the menu and set it down again. "Heller doesn't want me there if you're bringing him."

Trying to register what she meant, Deanna looked back out at the man. He had a hand on the girl in a way that would irritate her if it was Freddy. And he was keeping watch on Trina.

"Don't misunderstand. I think he was wrong to say such a thing to your date, whatever his opinion, and I told him he shouldn't have, but..."

"Wait." Deanna gave her new friend full attention. "He said what to Fred?"

"He didn't tell you?"

"No. What did he say?"

"Well, then, maybe it doesn't matter. I don't want you to be mad. We all enjoy your company. Even Heller has nothing against you, but..."

"What did he say?"

"I..." Trina looked up at the counter when they called out an order. "That's mine." She got up. "I only need to know if he'll be with you. Heller won't go if he is and he won't want me to go."

Deanna stood. Leaving her sketchbook on the table so her waitress would know she'd return, she waited until Trina picked up the coffees and walked out with her, against the girl's objection. She held the door and walked up to Heller. "What did you say to Fred at the club?"

He looked at Trina, who informed him Fred hadn't repeated it, luckily. With a shrug, he dropped the cigarette butt and smashed it into the sidewalk. "Told him he seemed like too nice a guy to be stuck killing innocent people in other countries and I could help him find a better job." He took one of the cups from Trina and complained to her about the lid he didn't want.

"You actually said that to him?" Deanna took a step closer and nearly gagged on the old tobacco stench.

"Hell, they were all thinking the same. Your gal pals. If you can get him out of the evil empire, I can see him being okay to hang with."

Deanna looked over at Trina. "You all think that?" She felt herself shake; she was furious. Thoughts of clocking him the way she had Todd came to mind. Or harder. Much harder.

"He shouldn't have said it." Trina touched her arm. "It's not our business."

"Do you all feel that way?"

"Well. Not all. And it doesn't matter. You're one of us and we want you around..."

"No, I'm not." Deanna faced Heller. "You're a complete moron and you don't know what you're talking about. You weren't there. You don't know. And you don't have to worry. Neither of us will be there tomorrow or any other day. If you happen to see me, or us together, move to the other side of the street. Maybe he can't do anything about your stupidity and your rudeness, but I can. And I have a good right hook." Without allowing time for his shock to turn into a comment, she whirled and went back inside to where her lunch was waiting.

Fred hadn't told her. He hadn't even reacted that Deanna had seen. He was friendly to her group all night. She'd noticed he ignored Heller as they were leaving but he returned Trina's goodbye.

Deanna tried to focus on her sketches as she ate, on ideas for a current campaign, on quick still lifes of objects around her that she could use later. But her anger grew. Not only toward the moron, but also toward Fred. He should have told her.

Turning to a clean page, Deanna sketched a characterized jackass, and added Heller's face to it. What kind of parents named a kid Heller, anyway? Did they not like him, either? *One of them.* No, she wasn't. Even before she met Fred, she wasn't. What gave them the right to have such a negative opinion of something when they didn't know? When they had no experience and hadn't even bothered to try to find the truth?

Maybe she was guilty of plenty of anti-violence thoughts herself. She didn't understand why people had to constantly fight each other. It was always something: land, money, religion, love. It never ended. She didn't believe it ever would, no matter how often or how well you fought.

Still, she had much more admiration for someone who would stand up and fight for what he thought was right than she did for cowards who didn't believe anything was worth fighting for. How sad would that be?

And how could she fault soldiers for their willingness to fight for other people, for those who couldn't, or wouldn't, fight for themselves, for their liberty, for their right to survive, when she'd just balled her fist wanting to deck Heller just because of a simple insult? People like Heller backstabbed each other in business all the time. How did he think that was better than fighting *for* someone or something? He was one of the worst, from what Deanna had heard so far. Trina bragged about how he rose so fast in his company by turning against his coworkers, by stomping on those who had helped him. And he had any right to judge Fred?

Maybe she should go tomorrow and tell them what Freddy had told her. How the children lived in fear. How the women were little more than slaves to their arranged husbands. How they weren't even allowed to learn to read. How some of the soldiers spent time reading to the children and teaching them words, giving them food, notebooks, pencils. How some of the soldiers who served in Desert Storm got out of the military and had returned to continue to help them, educate them.

Deanna supposed it wouldn't matter. They were too secure in their own comfort to worry about someone else's, beyond judging what they didn't understand and didn't really want to know.

The rest of the afternoon, she pondered whether to ask Fred about it when he called. Finally, she decided not to. It was his business to handle it the way he wanted.

And yet, once on the phone and conversation lulled, she told him about running into Trina and asked why he didn't tell her.

"He has a right to his opinion, Anna."

"But it was so rude. And I had no idea they felt that way..."

"Then it doesn't matter."

"It does matter. How can I hang out with them now? Knowing what they think?"

"Forget it. Go have fun with your girlfriends and don't talk politics."

"I can't do that." She lowered onto the big chair. "Even if I don't talk about it, I'll think about it."

"Which is why I didn't say anything. Let it go. It doesn't matter to me in the slightest, as long as they don't harass you."

"It matters to me. He didn't have any right..."

"Yes, he does. He does have the right to express his opinion. That's one of the big things we fight for every day – to protect our rights by making sure no one comes in to take over and take them away. This would be meaningless otherwise."

Deanna stood again and paced around the room, stared out the big window at the city. "I suppose. But you're a better person than I am, Fred Dawson, since I still want to deck him good."

"Never said I didn't want to. I did tell him I had no interest in any job he had in mind since I need to do something that actually matters. That worked well enough. Interrupted his thoughts of self-importance. Hard for that type to realize not everyone thinks they are as important as they think they are."

Maybe it was good enough. And she was glad Freddy wasn't bothered. Still, she wished she'd decked the moron.

Daws looked up from his desk at the knock and beckoned Andrews in. His specialist brought his friend in with him – Harding, the one sent to check on Mrs. Reynauld.

"How was your trip home?" Daws motioned for him to sit as Andrews left again.

"It was good, Sergeant. Thank you." Harding sat at the edge of the metal chair. "Stopped by the major's place, as you asked. His wife insisted I come in for coffee and a doughnut. Nice lady."

Daws nodded. "She's doing well, then."

"Yes, Sergeant. Seemed fine."

"How are the boys?"

"Will, the oldest, seems fine also. Shook my hand and sat to talk with us a while. I didn't go into the house until I saw he was there. He insisted."

Daws leaned back in the chair. "And the youngest?"

"Ryan." Harding bounced his heel, shaking his leg. "Heard his name over and over but didn't see him. There was a squealing guitar overhead, though. Mrs. Reynauld apologized and offered to go stop it. I told her it was alright, I was plenty used to loud music."

"Heard his name, why?"

"He's a rebellious thing, from what they said. The brother thinks they'll have to push him into the military when he turns eighteen to give him a place to put his ... uh, frustration and energy."

Daws tried not to sigh. His frustration. Maybe the Army would help him, if he was as much like his father as the major said he was. But for now, he was barely fifteen. "Is he getting in trouble?"

Harding hesitated. "Sergeant, can I ask why we're doing all this? Why the big interest? From what I've seen, there are dozens of kids right here on base dealing with a lot of things, and families that need more help."

"That may be." Daws sat up again and crossed his arms on the desk. "However, the major asked me to watch out for him and I owe him the respect to do as he asked. Every family on base has a chain of command if they're willing to use it. So again, is he getting in trouble?"

Harding fidgeted. "From what they said, he's holding on okay, no big trouble, skips class every now and then but grades are still good. He's hanging with guys they're not sure about because they're playing together. Seems to be the worst he's doing."

"In a band?"

"Sounds like it. But from the squealing I heard, he needs a ton more practice. Just switched from acoustic to electric and getting used to it, so they said. I can't see he'll ever do much with it, though. From what I heard, anyway."

Daws stood. "Thank you, Private." As Harding stood, he took his hand.

"Want me to let you know next time I go home?"

"If you don't mind. This isn't part of your official duty, so you can refuse."

Harding shrugged. "Andrews respected the major a lot and there aren't many he has that much respect for. Glad to help if I can, Sergeant, on duty or off."

Daws paced his office after he closed the door. Rebellious. Skipping classes. And just what was he supposed to do about it? If the boy wouldn't even go downstairs to greet the soldier, he sure wouldn't take advice from Daws, particularly if he knew who he was, or that he'd been there when his father died. Maybe he'd have to figure a way to keep an eye on the boy without letting on who he was. Could work.

A band. The guitar Daws left him apparently did give him an outlet. He was using it, squealing not withstanding. Could be a good sign, anyway. The kid was into music. Maybe his own music knowledge and interest would come in handy after all.

"Deanna, my flower."

She pivoted away from the copy machine and threw a glare at Todd. "Don't call me that. I'm not yours and I'm no one's *flower*. Didn't like it before and I don't have to put up with it now."

He snickered and moved to her side. "You might want to reconsider being mine, at least part of the time."

"Not in a million years. Now go away so I can work."

"No? Even if I can help you get farther up than this? You know there's an opening for an art director."

"Yeah, so?"

He stepped closer. "I can put in a good word."

"Bet you could. Problem is, I don't work on your side of things, so why would they listen to you?"

"Know why there's an opening?"

"Doesn't matter in the slightest. I'll put my name in the professional way, with my credentials to speak for me."

Todd laughed. "And you're still naive enough to think that'll work?"

"Get lost, Todd."

"Fine, but you might want to know something before you brush me off. There's an opening because they moved me up. I'm now head creative director for the whole department, one step under the big boss man, and you're working under me."

Deanna froze a moment and turned enough to see him huff away, swaggering. Head creative director. She felt her shoulders slump. She now had no chance of rising in the company without his say so, and he would never okay it without her *cooperation*. She might as well move companies and start at the bottom again.

Forcing herself to continue what she was doing, the thought rattled her brain. Maybe it was worse than no promotion. Maybe the jerk would cause trouble for her otherwise, try to push her out or force her hand.

He could try. She did her job well. Everyone knew she did. He couldn't fire her with no good reason. Although if he did, she'd have a reason to move. Maybe even across the state.

========

Not that he didn't have better things to do on a Saturday, but Daws didn't see what else could be done. And it very well wouldn't work.

The four hour drive made him wish he'd headed farther south, driven the extra hour and a half, and landed at his own apartment. He still could, after he took care of business. He wouldn't rule out the idea.

Finding the National Guard Armory, easy enough as it sat along Main Street, Daws studied the old building and its fenced area with a few Humvees and some storage buildings behind it as he pulled in and around to the front. There weren't many vehicles in the parking lot; must not have hit a training weekend.

He made his way up the few steps and through the glass doors to a reception desk.

A PFC behind the desk stood in greeting. "Can I help you?"

Daws removed his dark sunglasses. "Is your commander in, by any chance?"

"Can I ask why? If you're looking for recruiting, it's down the street..."

"I'm not looking for recruiting." He pulled his ID card from his wallet and held it where the private could see. "Staff Sergeant Fred Dawson."

"Regular Army." The PFC, who looked to be around nineteen, relaxed. "What can we do for you, Staff Sergeant?"

"This isn't an official call. I did hope to talk to someone in charge."

"Our lieutenant colonel's here. I'll get him for you." The young man half disappeared at a door opening and spoke to someone in the next office.

They came out together. Daws gave the tall, thin man with gray hair and friendly face a nod and introduced himself.

"Where are you out of, Sergeant?"

"Fort Drum, New York."

"And to what do we owe the pleasure of a regular Army sergeant from New York visiting our Vermont Guard post?"

"I'd like to request a favor, Sir, if I could have a moment of your time."

With a curious expression, he asked Daws back to his office and closed the door most of the way. "I like to keep an ear out up front. If that's all right?"

"Of course. It's nothing official, mainly personal, so I may be overstepping my bounds but thought it wouldn't hurt to ask."

The commander leaned back in his chair. "Go ahead."

Explaining briefly about the major and the accident, Daws continued. "I wondered if you had any community programs in conjunction with civilian youth, or kids of military families."

The man frowned and scratched the back of his head. "Not as of now, other than appearing at local festivals for the sake of recruitment and such. What did you have in mind?"

"A mentor of sorts for the major's fifteen year old. He's having trouble dealing with his father's death and his older brother is helping as he can, but I hear he was just pulled out of a local jail for underage drinking, at a bar where he was playing with some older guys in a band."

"A loose cannon, huh?"

"Afraid it's heading that way. The major said he was much like him as a youngster and he turned out a fine officer, highly respected. Got all of his men into Kuwait and out again with only a couple of minor injuries. Flew into incursion areas and pulled quite a few of our ground troops to safety himself."

The commander sat up straight. "You were there with him?"

"Yes, Sir."

"See a lot of action?"

"Enough." Daws shoved the fleeting image from his mind and returned to the business at hand. "I'd be glad to return the favor as I can for anyone willing to look after the kid."

"Why are you doing this, Sergeant?"

Daws dropped his eyes only for a moment. "The major was like a father to me. Brought me through a lot of hard times. His last breath was concern for his son. I intend to do what I can to keep the boy on the right path. Being stationed four hours away makes it a challenge."

The man studied him for too long, silent. Daws wondered if he was trying to decide if he was telling the truth or had an ulterior motive. What that would be, he couldn't imagine. "My CO is Captain Hodgkins of the 3/64th. If you need time to check into things before you decide whether one of your men can help..."

"How long are you staying in the area?"

"Planned to go back tonight, but I can stay as late as tomorrow afternoon if needed. Have to be at PT at o-six-hundred Monday."

"Well, Sergeant, I may have a solution for you. A man who may be willing. His regular job is as high school coaching assistant, so he'd be used to the age. I need time to reach him and see what he thinks."

"Of course. I'd like to talk to him, also, if you don't mind."

"If he agrees. What's the kid's name? He may know him."

"Ryan Reynauld, but I don't want him to know what I'm doing."

"Reynauld." The lieutenant colonel leaned forward. "Major Edward Reynauld's kid?"

"You knew the major, Sir?"

"I knew him as a young man. Used to live around here. It was front page news every time he was decorated. His death was a real tragedy to the community. You said his family is nearby?"

"North Bennington. Moved back after the funeral."

"Hadn't heard that." He shook his head. "My guess is local law enforcement will be fairly lenient with the boy, for his parents' sake. Still, if we can help prevent the need.... Have you had lunch yet?"

"Hadn't thought about it."

The man grinned. "I recommend the little family restaurant just down to your right. Good food. Friendly service. Tell 'em I sent you. I'll see what I can do over the next hour. Come back and see me then."

=======

Deanna dropped the letter on the table. What right did the neighbor lady have to scold her for not visiting her mother? And how did she get her address? The woman knew nothing about her life. Or did she? How much had her mother said?

And while she'd fussed to the neighbor that Deanna didn't visit, did she also bother to say just how much Deanna had already given of herself? Did she tell the busy-body how her thirteen-year-old daughter had to take over the house, and the kids? How she'd made dinner and packed lunches for her siblings and got them all to the school bus on time and done their laundry and sat with them at night when they couldn't sleep? All because their mother "needed a break"? Had she told her that? Did she mention how ungrateful the little brats were for all of it just because their father blamed it all on "her" father for "up and leaving"?

Just how long was she supposed to have stayed? The next oldest was nearly seventeen when Deanna left. And their mother was back home. It wasn't like she left them while still incapable of managing.

Scolded by a neighbor for not visiting. Because her mother was "weary" and overworked. Why was she? Most of them were adults now. It was their turn to help.

Visit why? So her mother could constantly tell her she was "just fine," as she always had? She was so "fine" with help from her nerve pills that she ended up "visiting relatives" for a very long time. In every letter her mother sent, she was still "just fine," no matter how often Deanna asked her to be honest, to tell somebody if she wasn't.

No, she was strong, she said. She kept it to herself.

The same pills Freddy had in his cabinet. And she couldn't make herself ask him. He was okay, though. He wasn't taking them. Deanna had to wonder if he didn't because he was sure he was "just fine," too. He did seem like he was.

How was she supposed to visit? Between Todd breathing down her neck and saving vacation days to visit Fred, Deanna couldn't possibly. Her weekends were used for working at designs, studying ads for the newest techniques, and watching the papers for a different job.

=======

Pulling into his parking space, Daws turned off the engine and looked west at the bright orange-red sky. Cumulus clouds low to the earth reflected the colors, their edges glowing as though on fire. A gorgeous sight. He wondered if Deanna could see it from where she was. He wished he'd been able to see her over the weekend.

Corporal Kelly was set to keep an eye on Ryan, in guise of recruiting him for the high school track team. His Guard status wouldn't be mentioned, and neither would Daws. He'd had to stay overnight in the little Vermont town since the corporal was away all of Saturday and in church the next morning. The lieutenant colonel got word to him well enough during the hour Daws enjoyed a large meal at the recommended restaurant for the man to agree to meet and discuss what Daws wanted exactly.

He didn't know, exactly, only that the kid needed a strong hand and a shove in the right direction. After meeting the corporal, Daws figured he'd found the right man to do it. He hoped he had.

As the red began to fade, he got out of the car and headed up to his apartment. The last time he'd talked to Deanna, she sounded annoyed. She wouldn't say why. He hoped she'd be more willing to talk this time.

Part of Deanna was annoyed that he'd driven all the way to Vermont for the sake of that kid instead of coming to the city to see her.

Only a small part. She respected what he was doing, or trying to do.

The phone pulled her from the balcony where, wrapped in her thick sweater, she watched the last bits of red fade behind the city skyline. She wondered if he had seen it. Or if it looked the same at the other side of the state. Or if he was irritated at her still since she hadn't been very friendly last time they talked.

The caller ID showed his number and she gave him a cautious greeting.

"Did you see the sky tonight?"

She smiled at his voice, the friendliness in it, and at the repetition of her thoughts. "Hey, you're home."

"Just got in."

"And I was just out on the balcony, wondering if you saw it."

"Wish I'd been out there with you."

"Yeah." She lowered onto a chair. "Me too. How'd things go?" Deanna unwound and listened to Freddy relay his meeting with the corporal. She had a thought of telling him the kid's family could look after him and he shouldn't have to worry so much, but it would be wasted breath. He'd promised his friend; he would never back out, however much work it made for him, however much of a struggle it would become. Deanna could do nothing but support his quest, and hope the kid wouldn't push too far.

At least he didn't sound like he held her earlier mood against her. His voice was a salve and she finally moved to the couch and pulled the afghan over her legs as he told her about his visit to the Armory. If she closed her eyes, she could nearly make herself believe he was right there.

"What have you been up to today?" Fred clinked pans together in the background. "You've hardly said anything all weekend."

"Oh. Well. I've been kind of frustrated and you didn't need that on your mind during your trip." She grabbed a cup of cool coffee.

"About what? Is the jerk hitting on you again?"

"Worse."

"Worse? What did he do?" His voice grew sharp, angry.

"Not what you're thinking. Lower your weapon, Sergeant." She grinned, hoping he'd hear she was. "Worse means he was promoted. He's my boss now. Directly."

"You have to be shittin' me."

"I wish. Maybe it's good though, right? Maybe he'll have to mind his Ps and Qs better?"

"Wouldn't count on that."

"No." She sighed. "Any advice?"

Silence filtered over the line and Deanna gave him time to consider what she'd asked as she got up to go reheat her coffee.

"I have advice. Sure you want to hear it?"

"Of course. Doesn't mean I'll do it, but I want to hear it."

"Quit. Start your own business. Be competition for them."

Deanna stopped, stunned. That, she never expected.

"Still there?"

"Yes." She closed the microwave door and pushed one minute.

"You could do it."

"Oh, I don't know. That's ... I don't have the connections for that. I'm only an assistant. Who would hire me? What would I use for funds, for office space, advertising, not to mention computers and supplies and..."

"You've thought about it already."

"For years. I even checked into a loan once, but I have no collateral and had no one willing to cosign. How do you start when you have nothing to start with? I've been trying to save, but that's going so slow on my pay. Yes, I've thought about it."

Silence. The microwave beeped. She pulled it out and stirred creamer into the already light coffee.

"I could help you."

Deanna nearly lost all strength in her legs and was afraid she'd wind up on the floor. "No."

"Deanna..."

"Freddy, no. I'd risk my own funds for the chance but not yours. Thank you. You're incredible. But no. I'll just have to hang in and try to move up until I get to the right place to venture out. But thank you."

"All right, but the offer's open. Don't feel stuck. Don't put up with anything from him."

"Oh, don't worry. I'd go back to waiting tables first." She moved back out to the couch and pulled her knees up, clasping them with one arm as she held her coffee and focused on its warmth.

"If you're going to do that, you could do it here."

Deanna pressed her eyes together. "Would you want me there? Full time?"

"Gladly, but not at the expense of your career."

With a deep breath, she swallowed hard. He'd want her there full time. For a moment, she could see herself in his little one bedroom apartment, waitressing during the day and cooking for him at night, sitting together on the little couch, lying beside him in bed...

"Deanna?"

"I'm here."

"I'm trying to get a few days off over Thanksgiving. Don't get your hopes up. It's doubtful, but I'm trying."

"Oh. Too late. My hopes are already up."

"Shouldn't have mentioned it, then."

"Of course you should have. I'm glad to know you're trying." Another month. Maybe she could see him in another month.

"What else is bothering you?"

Setting the cup down again, Deanna went out on the balcony, to the fall chill in the dark sky, to the sound of cars below, to the twinkling lights...

"Talk to me, Anna."

She bit her lip to prevent tears.

"Hey, don't make me drive down there tonight to check on you."

A chuckle escaped. "Don't tease. You would not. You just got back."

"Don't be so sure. What's wrong?"

"Be careful, I'll not tell you just so you'll come."

"Deanna."

"Okay, so I won't. I, um ... well, a couple of things. I feel like an idiot, though. How hard is it to unplug a drain? I thought about calling a plumber. Well, I did, but they'll only come during the week and I want to save my days off for when I can visit you and..."

"Wait. What drain?"

"The bathtub. It started to fill and the drain's open. I found drain cleaner and I've been plunging so much my arms are sore and I tried putting an auger down there to pull it out but it won't go down enough to reach the blockage and I don't know what to do with it..."

"Okay. Slow down. The drain cleaner isn't working?"

"No, and it's been two days. Shouldn't it by now?"

"Yes. It may not be a clog."

"The water won't go down. I pulled it all out using an old glass and dumping it into the sink. Took forever. And I tried more cleaner and scalding water – don't ask how I know it was scalding – and it won't drain."

"Try to ounscrew the lever piece from the wall to see if it's still lifting the plug. There's a tool set under the kitchen sink."

Letting his voice calm her, Deanna followed his instructions and found the lever disconnected from the stopper thingy. She grabbed it inside the hole and pulled it out. The water drained. She rolled her eyes. "Are you kidding? After all that plunging? Now what do I do with it?"

"Leave it out. Pick up a rubber drain plug so you can use the tub, and I'll fix it when I get back."

"You're amazing. You don't have to even be here to know how to fix what I couldn't figure out."

"Sorry you had to deal with that. Did you burn yourself?"

"Yeah, but it's not bad. Just annoying. I always called the superintendent when I was renting. You don't have one, though, and ... I feel like an idiot."

"You shouldn't."

"Really? How many brain cells does it take to figure out to unscrew the lever?"

"You'd have to understand how it works. Most don't. You're not an idiot. You're one of the smartest people I know."

"Am I? That's sad." She shoved moisture from her eyes.

"Deanna, relax. Next time tell me instead of worrying about it. I'll help walk you through it or I'll call someone..."

"You have enough on your mind." She didn't get an answer. "I'll learn how to do these things. There has to be a book or something, right?"

"You're fine, but you don't have to hide things from me. I'm not going to break because you ask for help."

"No?" She sat at the edge of the now-drained tub.

"You think I will?"

She grabbed a deep breath. Bit her lip. Took another breath. "I ... I did something I shouldn't have." She stood again and returned to the main room, out to the balcony. She wanted the dark, the stars. "When I was there. I snooped. Not on purpose. Well, it didn't start on purpose, but..."

"I know."

Deanna backed up against the window. "You know what?"

"Why did you need the eye drops?"

He knew. She lowered, crouching, her head tilted up to see the sky above the balcony's metal railing. Shivered.

"I know you saw the pills, but why did you need the eye drops?"

She told him. Unable to lie and unable to refuse, she told him how it upset her, not the blood but the thought of him being hurt, that it could have been worse and she could have lost him. "I didn't want you to know. I'm stronger than that. I am. I have never in my life ever cried over a man. Never. Not even that first one. But I did. For you. And I didn't want you to know. I don't want you to think I can't handle it. I can."

"I know you can." His voice was soft. It reached too deeply into her soul. "They gave me those pills after the crash, after the major's funeral. I wasn't sleeping. I did nearly go off on some moron who deserved it: my lieutenant. He asked for it, as he often does, but I didn't have the control I normally do. They sent me to the clinic, after they pulled me away from him. Said I didn't want the pills. That's why they're still there."

"Not all of them."

"No. Started to take them so I could sleep. Only needed one good night's sleep. Things made me more irritable, so they tried to give me something else. I refused. A direct order from an officer, the doctor who saw me. Could've written me up. Instead, they sent me home to unwind."

"And that worked?"

"That's when I met you. Haven't needed anything since. Sleeping well enough now."

Deanna shoved a hand through her hair and stood again, went to grab the balcony railing.

"Anna, it doesn't make me weak to have used a few of them anymore than it made you weak to be upset after what you did for me. I'm not. I won't break. And neither will you. It's okay to cry on my shoulder or ask for help."

"I don't ask for help. I've learned not to. It always backfires."

Silence. Then his voice was even quieter. "Not with me, it won't."

The tears started again. She tried to shove them away.

"In all honesty, I'm flattered to be the only one you've cried over."

Deanna gave up trying to control them. An impossible task. "I miss you. I finally find my prince and he's five hours away and I don't drive. Just seems really unfair, you know? After I waited so long for you. After all the horny toads. I'm sorry. It's just been a rough week and I'm moody and..." She grabbed a quick deep breath. "I'll be fine tomorrow. Promise."

"If you're not, you can say so. I'll try to help. And I'll try to get there for Thanksgiving. Going to hold on that long?"

"Yes. Or longer if needed. I'm not going anywhere, Freddy. I'm not. I'd miss the closet, you know."

He teased in return until she relaxed and lowered onto the couch. She wasn't going anywhere. How could she? She was in love with him.

Deanna stretched her shoulders and sat forward in her seat, peering out the window toward the depot and wishing for the bus to just get there already so she could go find him. He couldn't get more than one day off for Thanksgiving, so she invited herself to his place. He hadn't seemed to mind. She hoped he actually didn't.

Finally, the bus jerked to a stop and she grabbed her bag and pushed toward the door. She did excuse herself when she accidentally bumped a man on the way, but he let her through. This time, she found Freddy as soon as the door opened. In uniform. Walking toward her.

The way he held her made her quite sure he didn't mind. One arm circled her waist and the other pressed against her shoulder with his palm cradling her head.

"Now I can see why you were in a hurry."

Deanna looked over at the amused voice – the man she'd bumped. She apologized again but he stopped her and said there was no need. He set a hand on Fred's arm, thanked him for his service, and told them both Happy Thanksgiving.

She explained as he walked away again, and watched Freddy's face, the expression that was always so calm, so controlled. "You are sure it's okay I invited myself?"

"Glad you did. I didn't think I should ask you to miss more work."

"But you wanted to ask?"

"Yes." His thumb brushed her cheek. "I wanted to ask. I thought about it more times than I can say."

"Did you?" She gave him a light kiss. "Just as well, since I am here and I'm staying until Monday."

"Guess I'm stuck with you, then."

"Stuck with me." Deanna chuckled and wrapped her hands up around the back of his shoulders. "So take me home, soldier, and I'll show you how *stuck* with me you're gonna be."

===

Daws fought against the flashing images. It wasn't real. Something inside told him it wasn't real. But it sure as hell felt real. The heat, flames, smoke ... real. But where? Not a desert. Too green. Too wet. Misty. The chopper. On the ground. He ran, his heart pounding. He ducked at gun fire. No. Not gun fire. Explosion. Flying debris. He had to get out. Away. He couldn't. His men were in danger...

Someone took his arm, called his name.

He couldn't leave. He had to get him out. Andrews. No. Not the desert. Not the building. The chopper. The major...

"*Freddy*. Wake up."

Freddy. No one called him...

"Wake up now. It's only a nightmare."

Nightmare. He opened his eyes and jerked to sitting, checked his surroundings. Dark. Quiet. Too quiet.

"Are you okay?" A soft voice, and soft hands. Deanna. She touched his face.

He forced his breaths to slow, released the tension in his body as her fingers ran along his cheek, around his ear. "I'm sorry. I woke you."

"No." She pressed closer. "Don't be. Are you okay?"

"Yes." Except he was wet, sweaty. He took her hands and pulled back. "I'm going to run through the shower. Go back to sleep."

"What was it? Where were you?"

He touched her eyes as well as he could in the dark. "Don't worry. Doesn't happen often. You're all right? I didn't..."

"You were terrified. I could hear it in your voice."

"It's all right, Anna. As long as I didn't swing and hit you or..."

"No." She pressed her lips against his. "I'm so sorry, Freddy."

"For what?"

"For ... you were back in the war, weren't you?"

He couldn't answer. He wasn't even sure where he'd been and wouldn't let himself go back to the nightmare enough to try to figure it out. It didn't matter. Just a nightmare. And now Deanna was right there with him. Everything was good again. He raised the hand he still held and kissed her fingers. "Go back to sleep."

Deanna let him go and watched him make his way from the bed to the bathroom. He didn't bother to cover himself and didn't close the door before turning the shower on to warm. It *didn't happen* often. She wondered how often "not often" meant. Would it help if she got him to talk to her about it, or would it make it worse? Did she even want to know?

She couldn't help the honest realization that she didn't want to know, not much, anyway. She didn't want to see the images he had in his head; she was very visual and they would stick too well. It wouldn't help get rid of his nightmares to have her own.

With a sigh and the sound of him getting into the shower and pulling the curtain, she lay back against her pillow and focused on the water, on the open door. An open door. Was it an invitation? Todd never left the bathroom door open, even if only shaving. He wouldn't have even stepped out of bed without pulling his robe on. Always too secretive, hidden from her. She should have known.

Fred was ... well, even a thought of a comparison was laughable; there wasn't any comparison.

He hadn't ever mentioned nightmares, though. What else hadn't he mentioned? There was too much she didn't know, too many things she couldn't learn at the distance they had, physically. She felt no distance mentally. At least not other than what she still didn't know.

There was time. He was open enough with her whenever she asked him anything, Deanna had no doubt he would open even more the more they were together. Maybe she could help get rid of his nightmares. He'd calmed immediately upon her touch, her voice. It could take time. She had no doubt it would. For the moment, though, she could at least help him relax afterward.

She made her way through the semi-dark and the open door, glad he didn't startle when she opened the shower curtain. Instead, he pushed water out of his face and offered a hand as she stepped in, then wrapped around her and met her lips.

===

Shivering as she got out of the car beside him, Deanna held her long coat together with one hand so she could accept his arm with the other. She was surprised he hadn't worn his uniform since they were having Thanksgiving dinner at the mess hall. He looked nice in his Dockers and collar shirt, but part of her wanted to request he wear his military gear. She hadn't. Although she had to wonder if he would have given in to the request.

The constant greetings on the way into the long brick building both relaxed her and made her nervous. They often used rank and name, even out of uniform. Otherwise they'd nod or throw a generic how are you or such. But she was again amazed at how often they spoke to each other.

He held the door for her and greeted someone else by last name. Deanna had no idea of his rank until they were introduced. He was a sergeant, like Fred, except she'd learned that could be either sergeant or staff sergeant since they often didn't bother putting the "staff" in front of it. The younger ones did. At least she thought she noticed that those who called her boyfriend staff sergeant instead of only sergeant were generally the younger ones. Privates, maybe. Although several privates she'd met weren't so young. Some joined much later than others. Freddy told her they either became bored with their nine-to-fives, wanted an escape from somewhere, or had trouble finding the kind of job they wanted in civilian life. She understood that and had to wonder what kind of possibilities there would be for an art director in the military. Not much, she supposed. And she didn't want to be sent away from New York.

Deanna tried to keep up with the introductions as they made their way into the mess hall, but her attention was on the building and on the mixture of people, men and women, some uniformed, others not, and children. Lots of children of all ages. Somehow, she hadn't expected children.

They moved into a large open space full of long rectangular tables covered by white paper cloths. Orange and brown paper streamers twisted together ran down the middle of each, and small bags of candy pumpkins and candy corn wrapped in tulle sat at each place. A separated row of tables placed end to end sported real tablecloths in squares of brown, orange, and white layered atop each other. It was packed full of cakes, pies, cookies, and other types of desserts, interspersed with fold-out paper turkeys and pumpkins.

Music came softly from somewhere she didn't see yet. Pop. And she'd half-expected it would be either elevator music or patriotic songs. Not Michael Jackson. A few younger kids were dancing to it along the sides of the room. Other kids were eyeing and being held back from the dessert table. The older ones were sitting at tables quietly waiting to eat or standing around in groups talking.

"Told you it was nothing fancy."

She squeezed his arm. "Oh. It's ... probably most like the first Thanksgiving I've ever seen."

He raised his eyebrows. "Calling us Indians or pilgrims?"

"Pilgrims, of course, since none of you have your chests and legs uncovered. Unfortunately. That could be nice." Deanna grinned at his expression and glanced over to where three kids chased each other around a table nearly running into people. "Although maybe some of the kids are more along the wild Indian line."

"You get used to overlooking that."

"Oh? Not sure I could. But then, I'm not sure I could be a mom and try to deal with it myself, either."

"You don't want children?"

She found his gaze. "I don't think so. Did I just blow it? Looking for a housewife type? Cause that's not me."

He grinned. "Didn't think you were. And no, that suits me okay. I've seen how hard it is on these kids to have one or both parents gone so often. I know how hard that is. I don't plan to do it myself."

Deanna rubbed a finger along the inside of his wrist. Suggestive. But secretive. "Be careful, Fred Dawson. You're appealing to me more all the time."

"Is that so?" He gave her an unmistakeably flirtatious look.

"*Deanna.* I'm so glad you could make it."

Deanna started at Mandy Hodgkins' voice and accepted a hug. She greeted Captain Hodgkins with a simple smile, since she wasn't sure how to address him. "This is nice."

"Yes, it is good when you're away from family to be able to have a big party with your second family."

"I just hope I can remember some of the names he's throwing at me." She teased Fred with a glance. "I did remember two or three of his men, at least their last names."

Mandy rolled her eyes. "Well then you're doing better than I did when I was first pulled into all this. I felt like a bright red Ferrari in the middle of a bunch of green jeeps. And they all looked the same to me. Not to mention how all the wives in the company were best of friends at every gathering though we might not have seen each other outside company gatherings or at Commissary runs. They'd throw out their names and expect I would know it next time I ran into them. I learned fast to learn their names fast."

"Well, I could learn them, I think, except he never uses first names. It's always either last name, rank, or Mrs. someone."

Mandy laughed. "We get used to introducing ourselves to each other. I swear none of them even know any first names."

Her husband objected. "Not true. I know the sergeant's first name. But I also know he prefers his last. And he knows my first name. How would he not after seeing it twenty times a day on paperwork?"

"I'm impressed, then." Mandy wrapped her arm around her husband's. "I didn't give either of you quite enough credit." She threw Fred a wink.

"Story of my life." Captain Hodgkins nudged against his sergeant. "In charge of a whole company of soldiers and she still treats me like a ten-year-old boy."

With a playful pat to her husband's chest, Mandy excused them both and said they needed to make the rounds.

"Do you ever double date with them? Or go hang out somewhere?"

Fred shook his head briefly. "Can't do that, except at military functions."

"Why not?"

"He's an officer. It's against regs."

Deanna wasn't sure she didn't hear a bit of regret in his voice. "So you can only hang out with enlisted soldiers?"

"Some of them. Depends."

"On what?"

"Where we are. Which rank. If I have direct control of them at work, or vice versa. Anything that would look comprising to my career or theirs, I can't do."

"Like bosses dating secretaries."

"Similar, except our regs are firmly upheld. It's not worth losing rank or promotion ability." He nodded across the room. "Let's claim a spot at the table before we're stuck beside the little Indians."

Deanna wasn't surprised when he took them over beside a few men in his unit. A corporal and another sergeant, if she remembered, and one she barely recognized. He asked if she remembered them by last name. They gave her their first names. Then a gray-haired man in uniform called attention from the crowd and it was suddenly quiet. He thanked everyone for coming, told them to enjoy the day and eat hardy, thanked the decorating committee which turned out to be the enlisted wives' club, and introduced a chaplain.

He called for prayer and his first prayer request went out to those serving overseas, especially in dangerous missions. She felt the tension in the air become thick for a moment, emotional, or maybe it was only her. She'd never before stopped to think about American troops who spent the holidays away from their families. Her cheeks warmed. She wouldn't forget again. Even if things didn't work out with Freddy, Deanna would remember to remember.

When the call to dig in came, several groups of people jumped right up and headed to the buffet line. Others went more slowly. Many sat and waited the line out, continuing conversations instead. Freddy waited. Most of the jumpers were young men and women, single soldiers, he said, who were used to regular mess hall food or fast food and had relished this feast for days beforehand. Most of those who waited were families or older.

The smell made Deanna half wish she dared jump up as the singles had. She was single, after all, and generally did no more than soup and sandwich or microwave meals. There wasn't much point in going to the trouble for herself. She wasn't really single, though. She was Staff Sergeant Dawson's date. Even so, she hoped there would be more than scraps left at the bottom of the pans.

Finally, he held her chair and set a hand on her back while they walked up to take a place in line. He gave her a heavy white plate with a blue stripe around the edge. Not very decorative, but functional, she supposed. And she wouldn't have needed to worry about lack of food. They walked in front of a line of large metal trays set down into the counter and several men and a couple of women stood with large spoons, forks, and gravy ladles to dish out whatever they chose.

Deanna glanced at Freddy when she noticed one of them was Captain Hodgkins. He teased about making sure the sergeant ate enough to fill up and added an extra scoop of mashed potatoes against Freddy's wishes. On the way back to their table when no one was close enough to hear, she had to ask. "Is your captain a cook?"

Freddy threw her an amused glance. "No. The cooks prepared the meal. It's traditional for higher ranked officers to serve the men on holidays, in thanks for following orders and making the mission go, a way of saying we're all in this together."

Her thoughts went to their company parties as they took their seats. If she ever saw the boss or upper management team serving food, she'd very well fall down in a faint. She'd like to see it, though. Apparently, so did some of the younger soldiers, since they joked with their commanders who wore long white aprons.

It was truly much like the first Thanksgiving as she'd always imagined it: the two seemingly opposed sides that, in reality, had the same goal sitting together, working together, sharing their own harvests with each other. Even when she'd been back home as a girl when they had a bunch of relatives visit and talk loudly and eat loads, she didn't remember feeling the spirit of the holiday so strongly.

She'd also never felt so warmly welcomed.

Try as she might, Deanna couldn't possibly remember the names of all of the women who came up to chat, dragging her away from Fred and the other men. Uncomfortable at first with their questions about her relationship with him and about what she did in New York, she soon relaxed and had fun being one of the girls. One of *them*, their own family of sorts. They were from all different states and had been to several others, and some had lived out of the country, mainly in Germany. Two of their husbands had gone to Kuwait from there, one just before the war, another several months before. The young woman relayed how he lived in a large stifling concrete building and was constantly bitten by incessant sand gnats.

Deanna saw such a mixture of expressions in her face as she cuddled her child on her lap. Remembered fear, pride, and resolute determination. It reminded her of herself when she was younger. She turned her focus to the little girl. "How old is she?"

The woman, all of about twenty-three or four, grinned and stroked the child's curly blonde hair. "She's two. She turned two while he was over there, the day the cease fire was called. Our celebration baby. Her first birthday was the day he found out he'd be promoted to specialist. He was away for that one, too, out in the field. Maybe he'll be home for one of them some year. So far she's not old enough to know, anyway."

The woman beside her chuckled. "I think Jim's been home for only one birthday and I have three kids. Oldest is six. But at least he's always made Christmas, so far. He was supposed to have CQ duty for it last year, but...." She paused and looked at Deanna. "I think it was Sergeant Dawson who took it for him so he could be home."

The blonde woman nodded. "Probably. Corey's mentioned he should take holiday duty for his men because Sergeant Dawson was making him look bad. Is it horrible I wouldn't let him do that today? But she's such a handful, I wouldn't have been able to make myself come on my own."

"Oh, it's different. You need him around, and..." She looked back at Deanna. "You don't have children, right?"

"No." Deanna tried not to look shocked. "We're not married, and I've only known him for about six months."

"Well, sometimes they do get involved with women who have children already. Kind of pathetic to say those kids are glad to grab onto the stability of their mom's boyfriends, especially since this isn't very awfully stable, but these guys do appreciate the value of children, especially when they have to be away from them so much. The kids can feel they do, you know."

Deanna let the thought sink in as they chatted about kids and stability, or lack of, and how they wished they could drop their kids off with grandma and grandpa for some free time on occasion, for a date night with husbands they don't always get to see very often. How they often wished their babies could grow up around their grandparents and cousins and aunts and uncles, and if they were wrong for keeping them always away.

She couldn't help wonder whether Fred was more against having kids so as not to put them through it, or because it would be too hard to leave them, to not be there. Or maybe, judging by how he apologized for Deanna having to deal with little things like the plugged drain by herself, he was afraid to leave all of the child-rearing to her. She'd be afraid of that, too. Listening to some of the horror stories of illnesses and accidents and tantrums they dealt with, often alone and after a full day's work, and about friends they knew who had their babies while their husbands were deployed, Deanna was just as glad she didn't feel any urge for her own.

"Ready to go?"

She looked up as Fred set a hand on her back.

"Corey, tell your sergeant he needs to go ahead and marry her already so she can have all this fun, too."

Deanna looked from the woman to the man beside Fred. He threw his hands in front of him. "Don't get me in trouble."

"Oh come on. We all know he's a gentle ben inside. You guys just want us to think you have it rough at work." She laughed.

"Yeah. Right. How about you don't get me extra duty?"

Deanna stood and put an arm around her boyfriend. "Guess I better let you take me home."

He gave her an amused grin and a quick farewell to the group.

As soon as they were outside, she had to ask. "You wouldn't actually give extra duty for something one of their wives said?"

"Wouldn't be the first time. A soldier is responsible for his family's actions. Their wives need to remember that."

"You're serious." She breathed in the fresh, crisp air at a gust of wind against her face.

"They're warned before they get married."

"Warned for what, exactly?"

He nodded at a couple as they walked by and waited until they were out of hearing range. "I've seen men busted back a rank because their wives kept bouncing checks, although they were away at the time and had nothing to do with it. I've seen them get kicked off post because of something one of their kids did. And I gave one of my men extra duty when his wife came onto post and yelled at me about how he shouldn't be doing PT until his cold was better."

"She did that?" Deanna felt her jaw nearly drop. "What would make a woman do that? How embarrassing for him would that be?"

"More when I pulled him up in front of everyone and asked if he needed to go home to his mommy. Made her mad and she yelled again, even through him telling her to stop, to go home. She didn't do it again, though, after I kept him on post every weekend for the next month on cleaning detail. Also didn't put him in for promotion when it came time. He can't even handle his wife well enough, he doesn't need to be in charge of troops. Shows a lack of interpersonal skills and judgment."

"Should have put *her* on cleaning detail. What a moron."

"Wish I could. But they have to understand this isn't a game and it's not just a paycheck. If he has a cold out on the battlefield, he can't pull up a mat and blanket and sleep till he's better. If he can't handle it in training, he needs to get out. If she can't handle it...."

Deanna watched his face. He didn't quite want to say what he was thinking, that a woman who couldn't handle it needed to get out. It was why he'd asked her that night if she could. Maybe he still wanted to know. She never realized how much these men, and women, had at stake from choosing a partner. Of course, everyone did and too many jumped without considering the stakes. But their jobs at least couldn't bust them if their spouses bounced a check. They weren't likely to be busted in civilian jobs even if they bounced a bunch on their own.

Fred was right to be careful. Part of her had to wonder if marriage had never come up for that reason, because he wasn't sure enough of her yet. She couldn't quite blame him, given her history of bad choices.

Daws knew time in Vermont would mean less time he could take in New York over New Year's, if any. Still, Corporal Kelly's report made it necessary. The major's kid had scheduled himself to play an hour from home in what the corporal said was a scroungy bar in a rough part of the town. His mom and brother didn't know. Ryan only started talking to the Guardsman he thought was only a track coach assistant after he was assured Kelly would keep things to himself and not go to his family. Kelly couldn't go to this show. He had duty all weekend. So he called Daws.

Grabbing the phone after everything he'd need for a couple of days was packed, he stood and paced until she answered. He got her machine. "Deanna, are you there?" He waited to see if she was screening calls as she had been recently. She didn't say why. "Sorry I missed you. I have to be out of town for a couple of days or so but I'll call as I can."

He frowned at himself when he hung up. He should have said more, or said it differently. Should he call back and try again? No, she'd think he … he wasn't sure what she'd think. He'd have to let it go at that and call from the hotel.

Deanna heard the phone and grabbed at her keys. Fingering through until she got the right one, she twisted it into the lock. "Hold on, I'm coming!" It had stopped. "No, wait." She heard his voice as she dropped her things on the floor and kicked out of her wet galoshes. *…call as I can.* "No Freddy, five seconds. *Get off.*" Stupid galoshes. She hated the things. She also hated having to wear stupid heels to work in the winter instead of something sensible, like mountain boots. It was the northeast, after all, not Florida. They should all be wearing boots and heavy sweaters. Who was anyone trying to fool, anyway?

She got to the phone a few seconds after he hung up and started to grab it to call back. It rang when she touched it and she pulled it to her ear. "Hey, I was hoping you'd try again. I just got in…"

"You were hoping who would call again?"

She cringed at Todd's voice. "Why are you calling me? This better be a work emergency."

"Of course it is. Who did you hope would call again?"

"Not your business and I can't talk now."

"You kind of made it my business by saying so over the phone."

"I wasn't talking to you. And I can't talk now. Bye Todd."

"*Deanna*, wait. It is for work."

"Fine, but I'll call you back."

"Must've been a gorgeous hunk. Who else would you worry about missing?"

She wished she could tell him in person to see his face. "Actually, yes. And I have to catch him, so..."

He laughed.

Deanna hung up and picked up the receiver again so he couldn't interrupt. She dialed Freddy's number and waited through the rings. "Come on. You didn't leave that fast, did you?" She paced and stared out at the darkening sky. She had no choice but wait for him to call again.

As soon as she hung it up, it rang. This time, she checked the number first. Todd. He could be ignored.

"Come on, Deanna. Pick up. Don't be childish."

She glared at the machine and went to the kitchen to see what she had as far as leftovers.

"I need you."

"I bet you do, slime ball." She talked at the phone while finding a bowl of potato sausage soup. That would work.

"I mean at work, Deanna. Come on, this would be easier if you'd answer."

Good darn luck. She was at home. Off duty, as Freddy would say. She didn't have to talk to the jerk.

"Okay, I'm sorry I laughed. I figured it was Patrick Duffy again. A joke. You know, like before? Pick up..." The machine cut him off.

She poured the soup into a microwavable dish, added a touch of garlic salt, and turned it on for four minutes. That might be enough. It would be ready by the time she changed.

The phone rang again. Todd's voice, again.

"Look, you still have a shot at that promotion."

She rolled her eyes and kept walking.

"I'm serious. On your credentials only. Nothing more. And you have this on recorder now so you could very well use it against me if I'm lying. I have a project that has to be done this weekend. I need you on it. It's a step up, Deanna. I've been a jerk and I'm sorry so this is my way of making it up to you. Come on, pick up the phone."

Deanna stopped at the bedroom door and eyed the machine as it again cut him off. She didn't trust him. She wasn't an idiot. As she changed, she was glad it didn't ring again. Maybe she was. Was he serious? She knew they had a big new client. She knew the first presentation hadn't gone well. Maybe he was desperate enough to be nice to her. But why her? He had plenty of artists to choose from. Why her when he so obviously didn't respect her work?

Returning in her heavy sweats and slippers, she pulled the bowl out of the microwave and set it on a hot pad on the little kitchen table. Four minutes was plenty long enough. It was too hot. As it cooled, she grabbed crackers from the pantry.

He had said he did. When he first introduced himself to her, Todd said he'd seen some of her work and was quite impressed. She'd come to think it was a line. It was possible it wasn't. He'd commented on the unique flavor of it, the way it pinned the product sharply and hit the target exactly. In fact, he'd borrowed the idea for a campaign of his own not long after. He wouldn't do that if he didn't think ... so that was it. So often when he talked about his campaigns with her while they were dating, he'd asked her opinion.

Maybe he did think she had talent he needed.

A few bites into the soup, she got up and dialed his number.

"Yes?"

Still arrogant. Not hello, but yes, as though whoever it might be was bothering him. She'd always hated that. Still, a possible promotion made her hold her tongue and play nice, somewhat. "So talk. What is it about?"

"That was fast. Thought it might take you till tomorrow to give in."

"Tell you what. How about you go jump off a bridge tonight and I'll wait till tomorrow to see if I can spot you in the river."

"Okay. Okay. Wow, you're on a roll tonight. Did your hunk stand you up?"

"Work, Todd. Nothing else. Talk."

He snickered. "Okay. So you know the Hough account, right? You've heard about it."

"Hard not to when Mr. Look At Me is working on it." Deanna rolled her eyes at the thought of the guy, the other one up for the promotion she should have.

"Yes, well, he was. He's off of it. Couldn't see eye to eye with the client."

"So what's unusual about that?"

"This time, the client's not budging. She wants something more 'female friendly' as she says, something women would buy into. That's her biggest market..."

"So you want me to give you advice and then you take the credit. As you have before."

"Hey, you gave me permission to use any advice you gave."

"Yeah, because you were competing with that moron and I cared about you just a teensy bit. I don't anymore."

"If you say so. Then why did you call back?"

"I deserve a promotion. Tell me you're not jerking me around with this."

"Help me on this one and I'll see what I can do..."

"Liar." She hung up. And she went back to the table and took a couple of careful swallows of soup before it rang again. Just before the machine picked up, she did.

"What was that about?"

She rolled her eyes. "You know what it's about. I heard that before. Help you with it and we'll see? Not this time. So try again."

"What are you asking?"

"Don't play stupid with me, Todd. I know you too well. I heard too much. You want my help, you make me a partner on the project; put my name on it."

"Deanna, you know assistants don't..."

"Want my help or not? Make me a partner on it and I'll be glad to do whatever I can to make the client happy."

"I'm not that desperate."

"Fine. Don't call back." She hung up again and set the receiver off the hook so he couldn't. She leisurely ate as the phone buzzed and then a computer voice told her to replace it. She had no need to do so. It could buzz all night.

Except Freddy might call. She supposed Todd had heard enough busy signals if he'd bothered to try to call over the past fifteen minutes to get the point. If not, he could talk to the machine.

With a sigh, Daws replaced the pay phone receiver on the hook and went back to the car. He'd wasted fifteen minutes trying to get through. Who was she talking to for so long? He'd have to wait until he got there. Stopping again would put him in later than he wanted and he was tired already. A hell week on top of the news about Ryan. Little sleep. Little time to talk with her. When he did, he couldn't stay on long and still stayed on longer than he should have.

Pulling back out onto the interstate, he considered a detour to talk to her in person instead of running after some kid who he imagined wouldn't even appreciate help if it was offered. If it was needed. Daws hoped it wouldn't be, hoped he could sit in the back of the scroungy little bar and just watch to see it wasn't needed. He didn't want the kid to know he was watching. And he sure didn't want to get into another brawl and need more stitches. Deanna would have a fit. Not to mention since he wouldn't be bailing out one of his soldiers, it would likely go on his record as a mark instead of a commendation.

He wasn't quite sure why he worried so much about his record. Considering how marked it already was by no fault of his own, enough to hold him back from anything that a scrape at a bar would bother, he didn't have need to worry so much.

It could go against future promotions, he supposed. But a promise was a promise. The major had asked. He would do what he could.

Besides, he was growing less sure he wanted to stay in. If he did, he would be moved to a different post before long. There were murmurs about a tour in Korea. A year-long tour. With only one short break in between.

She would never stick around and wait for him for a whole year. That was asking too much. How could he?

"Deanna, all right. I am that desperate. Pick up the phone."

Jerk. She'd finally settled in with a blanket and hot tea and a mind-numbing movie. She didn't want to be bothered. She didn't even care about the stupid promotion anymore.

Yes, she did. She'd worked too hard to turn the chance away.

Throwing the blanket aside and setting the cup on a coaster, she stomped over to grab the phone. "Ready to be reasonable now?" She couldn't help but rub it in. If he was ready to give in, he was obviously desperate.

"Come over to the apartment. We need to get this going immediately. Time's short..."

"No way in the world am I going back to that place. You're out of your mind."

"Okay, so I'll come to your place. Then you won't have to put your galoshes back on..."

"No. And you mean tonight? It's after seven and I'm tucked in."

"Bed? Already?"

"Couch. With a movie."

"Oh? Where's your hunk?"

She didn't answer. No way would she admit where he was. And she wasn't real sure at the moment.

"Sorry. That was unnecessary. Tell me where you live, since the office apparently doesn't have an updated address for you, which, by the way..."

"You tried to look up my address?"

Silence. "I was curious. Hoped you weren't stuck in a bad part of the city. Are you? Because if you need a place that's safe, I have the extra room..."

"I don't need a place. I have one, a nice one, and if I did, I sure wouldn't call your place *safe*."

He took a breath deep enough she could hear it over the line. "Okay, I was only worried. I'm glad I don't have to be. So let me come over and we'll start working on this."

Part of her wanted to let him come, let him see just where she was staying, how incredible it was. But she didn't want him there. She didn't add her new address to the work records so he wouldn't know where she was. Turned out to be a good idea. "No. You're not coming here."

"Deanna, it's work. It's not like we haven't been alone together..."

"And look where it got me."

"All right. Point taken. You win. But now you know I'm married and I know you're not interested. So let's focus on this project."

"I want something signed that says I'm a partner on this thing before I put any work into it."

A pause. "Fine. But I can't do that until Monday when the office is open."

"Then we'll start Monday."

"Can't wait that long. Deadline is Monday afternoon to have a decent proposal."

This time Deanna sighed.

"Come on, you know I realize you deserve the promotion. Let me help you get it. It's the least I can do. And you know, if we work on it over the weekend, by Monday I can know better what to put on that admission paper you want as to what part of it was yours. Sound fair?"

"Yes. If I can trust you."

"Well. I guess that has to be your call."

"Let me think about it tonight and I may be willing to meet you somewhere tomorrow. Not here. Not at your place. Somewhere neutral and public."

Dishes rattled as though they'd been dropped in the sink. She hated when he did that, too. "Too much work to do to wait that long. If you can't do it tonight, I'll call Chelle and ask her instead."

Deanna froze as though she'd been shot. "Chelle is a secretary, not a marketing assistant."

"For now. But she has some good ideas..."

"You mean you're sleeping with her now."

He cleared his throat. "I thought we were talking work only. And I'm not threatening. I'd rather have you, for the project, but I'll make do if needed. Your call. I'll give you ten minutes to call back if you're interested. If not, I call Chelle." He hung up.

"*Jerk!*" She yelled at the phone and slammed it down. Call Chelle. He'd just grab a secretary he was screwing and weasel free work out of her for the female perspective. The girl didn't have a creative bone in her body. It showed in her clothes, bland and monotone. She'd never come up with anything half decent for a particular client. He was bluffing.

But maybe he wasn't.

Daws set his bag on the luggage stand and stretched his shoulders. He needed a shower. And food. And then sleep.

First, he needed to call Deanna. The four hour drive made him sure the message he left wasn't good enough. Dialing through the hotel operator, he was glad to get a ring instead of a busy signal. Four. Five, and the machine picked up. At nine o'clock. Was she in bed already?

Damn, he should've thought up a better message just in case. But he expected her to be there. "Hey Anna, I'll be out for a while, so I'll try again later."

"I have to go." Deanna pushed away from the table of the coffee shop close to Todd's apartment, where they'd once used to meet, before she moved in with him.

"It's early yet. Tomorrow's not a work day..."

"It's not early. It's after ten. I'll think more about it as I unwind, but I'm tired."

He stood beside her and tried to hold her coat until she pulled back. "Okay, look, we're only a block from the apartment. Come on over and use the spare room. That way we can work longer tonight and get up and at it again..."

"Not a chance, Todd. Good night." She walked away, to the counter to ask if they'd call a cab.

He followed. "How far are you? Should I walk with you instead of paying for a ride home?"

"So you can see where I live? I don't think so. I'll manage as I always do."

"What's the big secret? Is it even worse than your other place? If it is..."

"No. Because I don't want you to know. You have no need to know."

"It should be in your work records."

"And this is why it's not. One more word about it and my work on this is done."

"Okay." He threw his hands in front of him. "Till tomorrow, then. Say ... nine a.m.? I'll buy breakfast."

"Say eleven-thirty. It's Saturday and I'm catching up on my beauty sleep."

He started to make a comment and apparently thought better of it. "Ten thirty? Good enough?"

"You start at ten-thirty and tell me where we should meet at eleven-thirty. If I like what you choose well enough, I might try for eleven."

"You've become quite the negotiator."

"Have I? I guess I did get something from our little arrangement. Where?"

"You choose."

She thought about it for long enough to make him think it was hard to decide where. "Cheap Shots on First Avenue. They won't be open by eleven but I know someone who'll let us in. And it'll be quiet until evening. We'll have plenty of space to work."

"That bar you go to?"

"One of them. Don't dress up."

He started to balk, but again, held his thoughts. "Fine. But we'll have to move once it gets noisy."

"I don't plan to be there that long."

"Deanna..."

"Good night, Todd." She buttoned her coat, wrapped the scarf around her neck, and stepped out into the cold air. At least it was still, no wind to add to the cold. She pulled her gloves on, crossed her arms in front of her and gave him a warning glare when he took her side.

"Hey, I'm only being a gentleman and standing with you until you're safely in the taxi."

"Why? You never did before."

He shrugged, his arms full of paperwork. "Maybe I've become better at some things, also. I am sorry, you know, for hurting you..."

"Stop there. Just go on home. I'm fine."

"Where are you staying, Deanna? Would you tell me only so I don't have to worry?"

"You don't have to worry."

"But you don't have anyone else in the city, other than those bar friends and..."

"Be careful."

"All right, but..."

"And what makes you think I don't?"

"Deanna, level with me. This talk of a hunk ... be truthful. Patrick Duffy or someone else this time?"

She stepped away from him, watching the street for the yellow that would signal her escape.

He moved up. "There is no one. I know there isn't. We could..."

"There is. I'm in a relationship, Todd. A real one. With an actual gentleman, not one who is trying to act like he is only to earn my favors. There will be no more favors from me. Ever. I made a promise to him, and unlike some of us, I keep my promises. I am faithful."

"Is that so? And yet you were free to come out here on a Friday night and stay until after ten."

She wanted to punch him in the jaw. The jerk would probably sue her for assault, though. Deanna didn't figure Freddy with his immaculate record would appreciate bailing his girlfriend out of jail. If he could hold his control, so could she.

"Come on up to my place."

She walked farther away, closer to the sidewalk, her focus on the smell of snow coming. She expected it would cover the ground by the time she got up.

"Deanna." He touched her back.

She swiveled away. "Don't touch me again. I'm not available. Believe what you want, I don't care, but don't touch me again." She saw the flash of yellow, hoped to heck it was hers.

"All right, I'm sorry."

The taxi slowed and she waved at it. "Any mention of anything between us tomorrow while we're working and I walk out. And there won't be another chance. Got it?"

"He's not much to worry about if he let you out here with me tonight so late. You can do better."

Deanna felt her cheeks warm and her hand fist. She wouldn't do it, no matter how much she wanted to do it. "You have no idea what you're talking about." Congratulating herself for staying calm and in control, she escaped into the taxi.

Ten thirty. Daws shoved the pillow up against the headboard and stared at the phone. Still no answer. At least this time he'd thought to leave a number so she could return the call. If she would.

He nearly jumped off the bed when it rang. "Hello?"

"Freddy."

His breath caught. "Are you all right?"

"Yes. I'm sorry. Where are you?"

"Vermont. Where have you been?" He caught himself and restated. "It's late and I've been worried."

"I was working."

"This late? You just got home?"

"No. I was home. I went back out. A ... well, to help meet a project deadline."

He waited for her to explain better. She was silent. "Okay. I'm glad you're in and you're sure everything's fine?"

"Yes. I am sorry. I nearly caught it earlier when you called and I tried to call back but you didn't answer."

"It's all right." At his apartment, when he'd considered calling again. He should have.

"What are you doing in Vermont? Is everything okay with that kid?"

"That's what I'm trying to find out, but I'm going to have to let you go. I'm nearly asleep now and I don't want to fall asleep on the hotel phone and let them run it up."

"Oh. Of course. Can you call me in the morning?"

"I will. Good night, Deanna."

"Glad I caught you. Good night."

He hung up and lowered into sleep position. Out, after work, on a Friday night, for a project deadline. And she'd volunteered no further information. He could have asked, he supposed, but he didn't want her to think he was prying, or not believing. He had to believe her. It would never work if he didn't. At least he could sleep knowing she was safely inside the apartment.

She heard the phone click and lowered onto the closest chair. He was annoyed. It filled his voice.

And he had every right. Well, maybe he did. After all, she had done nothing wrong. She was working. She had the right to further her career.

Then what? What if she got the promotion after all this work and he was sent elsewhere? Would he want her to move with him? It was too soon for all that. Maybe. Except he'd said he'd be glad to have her there, to stay. Could she leave what she'd worked so hard to gain?

Getting up again, she shuffled through turning off lights and went to run a bath. She needed to soak and get clean after spending the evening with the idiot. Come home with him. He had to be crazy.

She did wish Freddy was there, though, so she could find a way to introduce her hunk to the idiot who didn't believe her.

=======

Daws sat in the back of the smoky dark bar watching the kid on stage. His guitar technique needed work, as Harding reported, but he had a damn good voice. Especially for a fifteen year old. It was smooth but with just a touch of an edge that made it sound older than he was, and more experienced. He had a possible future in music. If he couldn't get the electric guitar sounding better, though, he'd have to leave that to someone else.

No one else seemed to mind. They paid him little notice, except for several girls up front who tried to get his attention. It worked. He took too much pleasure in them getting his attention. And they were too old for him. That could be trouble. Daws figured they thought Ryan was older than he was. Not that he looked it, but he sounded it, and he was playing in a bar where he probably said he was eighteen. Most owners weren't particular, as long as they got a good crowd.

A couple of girls had asked to sit with Daws, also, or asked him to dance. He refused, even though it wouldn't be cheating. He had no interest.

Even if his conversation with Deanna had been strained this morning. He hadn't called early since he knew she slept in on weekends. He got up and showered and went to find breakfast and returned to the room to find the phone light blinking. He'd missed her call.

She was on the way out the door when he called back. She said it was fine, that she'd be late to her appointment so she could talk to him. Work again. Most of the day. He felt her rush and said he had to go, anyway. He didn't, but it was too hard to keep the annoyance from his voice.

Daws had spent the day first at the Guard center talking with the commander and then at the local library to do research on music careers for non-musicians. He read about roadies of all kinds, what he could find, which wasn't much. But one job did stand out. A bodyguard. A personal bodyguard who would take care of many details for someone who needed protection. Driving. Keeping an eye out on surroundings. Arranging extra guards as needed. Standing between the musician and anyone trying to get to him who shouldn't. He could do that. It would keep him mentally aware and would be at least a touch prestigious, if not publicly. Publicly prestigious, he didn't want. As long as he was comfortable in the fact that he was doing something worth doing, and it was challenging enough, it would work.

Ryan talked to his audience in between songs. He was good at that, too. Playful. Friendly. Quick with comebacks, sarcastic as they were. Confident on stage. Already. A few nerves showed, barely, but Daws had no doubt he could get over that.

The kid pulled the electric off and reached for an acoustic. It was the one Daws left for him.

Something about that touched him. Ryan had accepted the anonymous gift and had taken care of it. The way he held it said he relished it.

And he was worlds better on the acoustic. The sound was gentle, smooth as his voice, precise. Yes, the major's kid had definite potential in the music world.

As the song ended, Ryan announced that he'd written it.

Yes, a hell of a lot of potential.

Daws stayed through the end of the show and kept distance as he watched drunks swirl around the boy, but no one bothered him beyond talking. And the boy didn't seem to mind. Ryan especially didn't mind the two girls hanging on him.

Calling a waitress over, he showed her a ten dollar bill. "Need a favor."

"Hey, I only serve drinks. I'm not..."

"I just want you to go tell those two girls something for me. Quietly."

She eyed the money. He added another ten to it.

"Tell them what? It depends."

"Only those two girls. No one else, including your boss."

"Why?"

"Don't want anyone in trouble. Trying to prevent that."

"You a cop? 'Cause we ain't had trouble here in a long time. Cleaned it up good."

"I'm not a cop. And I'm glad to hear it. Can I trust you?"

"Depends."

He nodded. "That singer?" He motioned toward Ryan. "He's under eighteen. Could get them in trouble if they try to push things too far, and there's someone here who will press the issue if they do. Just let them know, quietly, to prevent trouble. He's a good singer. I'd hate him to be unable to come back again."

"Yeah, he is good. The boss knows he's a minor."

"That so? Well, then you're not causing any trouble for anyone. Just let those girls know, and if he comes back again, maybe keep an eye out?"

"All that for twenty bucks?" She eyed the money again.

He added a twenty to it. "How about now? I'm not going farther than this. I'll ask someone else..."

"No. I'll do it." She grabbed it from his hand. "I got a kid brother I watch, too. Some of these tramps are just stupid. I'll keep an eye on 'em for ya."

"Thank you."

"No problem. And hey, I know a woman who's had an eye on you all night. Want me to introduce her?"

"Thank you, no. I'm attached."

"'Course you are. Figured." She shrugged and moved away, slipping around customers and pulling one of the girls away to talk in her ear. The girl's expression said she was surprised, but she backed off and took the other girl with her.

Ryan raised his hands in protest and called to them as they left. Yes, he'd have a rough road ahead of him. The major hadn't understated that one. He had a good face, though. He was doing his best to cover it, with hair stringing down into his eyes, but it didn't quite disguise friendly eyes and a well-taught respectful demeanor. Daws could see it. It was in his whole attitude, underneath the cockiness he worked hard to put out there as his real nature. There was also an unsureness about him. Maybe that's what Daws noticed that he'd placed as nerves.

The boy pulled away and strutted to the bar, brushing someone off along the way. Daws edged just close enough to hear, on the other side of a young couple.

"Great job, kid." The bartender pushed a glass of what looked like soda toward him.

"Ryan. Don't call me kid. The name is Ryan Reynauld and someday it's gonna be everywhere so everyone knows it." He took a long swallow.

The bartender laughed. "Yeah? Well, for now, if I was you, I'd keep that under my hat so mommy doesn't find out. She doesn't know you're here, right?"

The boy straightened his shoulders and looked the graying man in the eyes. "And she won't. Part of the deal for me to pull more kids in for you, right? After tonight, there'll be more. The ones I got here will spread it around, and so will others."

"Pretty damn sure of yourself."

"Hey, if I'm not sure of myself, no one else is gonna be sure of me, either. Right?" He took another swallow. "How about slipping some gin into this?"

The bartender leaned forward on the counter and said something too low for Daws to hear.

Ryan pulled back. Daws turned as though talking to the waitress going by, but kept on eye on him as he moved away from the bar to the table with his band mates. No need to warn the bartender. He apparently had enough sense not to give in to the kid.

Turning toward the bar, with enough angle to keep an eye on Ryan, Daws asked for a Coke.

"Want something in that?"

"No, have to drive. You know that kid? The singer?"

"I know his family. Good people. Not close or anything but they're real friendly to everyone and well-liked. Why?"

Daws shrugged. "Curious. Is he playing here again? I know some people who might be interested in coming out to see him."

"Yeah? You don't look the type to be into his kinda music."

Accepting the cold glass, he took a sip. He didn't really want it. He'd be up all night. "I like a lot of different kinds of music, but I meant..." He threw a glance back at Ryan, as effect. "Just between us, because I don't want him to know, but I have contacts. People who might be interested in him. Thought I'd send them this way if I knew when he'd be here next."

"Yeah? He's young."

Daws nodded. "And that electric guitar work needs help, or he needs to ditch that and stay with the acoustic. But that can be dealt with."

The bartender leaned forward. "You know music. You're for real?"

Daws took another swallow, and another glance over at Ryan where a different girl was leaning in over him. "That's going to get him in trouble. He'll be finished before he starts."

"Nah, I'm keepin' an eye out. He thinks his mom doesn't know he's here tonight, but she does. Not sure how she does, but someone tipped her off. She gave me a call and asked me to keep an eye on him."

With a nod, Daws leaned back and tried to look like he was considering the man's words. He knew how Mrs. Reynauld found out. He'd assured her he'd be there and would be sure he got back out safely again.

"Got a card or something?"

He turned back to the bartender. "Why?"

"Not sure I should give out the kid's schedule without knowing you're who you say."

"I didn't say. Don't worry about it. I'm sure he'll get picked up elsewhere as soon as word gets around. I'll find a place to send them." He started to get up.

"Wait." The guy walked over to grab a paper from beneath the bar and came back. "January twenty-fifth. That's when he's scheduled next."

With a nod, Daws returned to the little table in the corner. It had been wiped down already by the waitresses getting ready for the bar to close, but he'd leave a good tip to make up for it. While the band packed their equipment and began carrying it out the front door, Ryan remained at their table and flirted with the girl, until the waitress Daws had paid went over and said something and the girl left. The boy shoved back from the table to go help carry equipment.

Yes, he was going to be a handful. On the other hand, Daws saw plenty of his father in him. The line about being sure of himself came from the major. Probably all of the troops who'd served under him had heard it. If Ryan was clinging that much to his dad's words, Daws had no doubt he'd do well.

Deanna turned toward the ringing phone and reached over to click on the bedside lamp before answering. "Yes?" She covered a yawn and cringed at the fact that she'd imitated the jerk by saying yes instead of hello.

"I woke you."

"Freddy. No. Well, yes, but it's okay. How was your night?"

"Went well. No trouble. The kid actually has a great voice and a lot of potential."

"Oh? That's good. What does he play?"

"Hard to say. Some kind of Eighties pop and metal mix with a touch of punk thrown in. Odd. He'll have to change sounds if he wants to go anywhere."

"Think he will?" She turned onto her back and tried to stay awake.

"He has every intention of it."

"Yeah. Well, I had every intention of working up to creative director, too, but that's not working out so well."

"What happened?"

"Nothing worth talking about. Same old thing. So is he doing okay, then? You'll be back home tomorrow?"

"No. I'm using the few days of leave to stay here. There are things I want to look into."

"Oh."

Silence filtered across the line. "We'll talk more later. I'll let you get back to sleep."

"No, it's okay."

"Glad it is, but go to sleep, Deanna. We'll talk in the morning. Eleven?"

"Oh. Um, better make it around nine."

"Why?"

"Working."

"On a Sunday? That early?"

"You don't work early weekends?"

"Yes, but it's not the same."

"Why isn't it?" She sat up. She had to sit up before she fell asleep.

Silence again. "Okay. Nine, then."

"Wait. Why isn't it?"

"Deanna..."

"I want to know."

Silence. "An office job is generally Monday through Friday, isn't it?"

"Depends. For secretaries and such it is. When you get higher up, it isn't always. We have mission deadlines, also."

"Okay. I'm just concerned. You sound beat."

"It's late."

"All right. Go back to sleep. I'll talk to you in the morning. Night, Deanna."

"Night. Sleep well."

"You too."

She reached back over to return the receiver to the base. She'd sounded too testy. It was unintentional. But Todd had irritated her all day long and she didn't want to tell Freddy he did. And she didn't like that he was spending a few days barely north of her instead of with her. Petty. Telling herself she was being too petty, she grabbed a deep breath and cuddled back down into the pillow.

Waiting to hear who was on duty, Daws identified himself and asked how things were in the company.

"Quiet. Almost wish for some excitement to help me stay awake."

"Try coffee."

"Hell, I've had so much coffee I've had to piss five times in the past hour."

Daws switched the phone to his other ear. "Guess that gives you something else to do. Hey, I have a weekend pass there. Find it?" He waited for the acknowledgment. "Put a note on it that I'll be in New York City tomorrow instead of Vermont. You can call the number on my home of records if needed."

"Says you only have a four day pass. Lot of driving for that little time."

"Necessary. I'll be back Tuesday night."

"Got it. Drive safe, and wave at the Statue of Liberty for me. Still have to get out there one of these times."

=======

Frustrated nearly beyond what she could stand without screaming at the top of her lungs, Deanna shuffled through to find her keys. "*Ugghh!*" They were in there somewhere. Her handbag wasn't that big. Time to clean it out again, but right now, she just wanted her darn keys...

She jumped as the door opened.

"Are you all right?"

Catching her breath, she stared at him. "What are you doing here?"

Fred raised his eyebrows and backed up so she had room to pass. "Thought we might need to talk."

Deanna dropped her handbag and shrugged out of her coat as he closed the door behind her. "You drove all the way down here to talk? What happened to the phone?"

"How about some wine? Or a lemonade?"

"I don't have any. Ran out and...."

"I noticed. Went out for more."

"Why? Am I going to need it?"

"You tell me." Fred moved in front of her.

"Well. I figure if you drove down when you had other things you planned to do, there has to be a big reason, right?"

"Yes."

She stared into his brown eyes. "Well, go ahead. I'm PO'd anyway. Might as well get it all over with at once."

"Come sit down." He touched her arm; the warmth of his hand seeped into her cold skin.

"No." She pulled from his grasp. "I think I can do this better standing up. So go ahead."

"Do what?"

"What you came here for. After barely talking to me the past two days because I had to work or because ... whatever the reason is."

"You were either on your way out or nearly asleep."

Frustrated with how calm he was, how he just stood there studying her, Deanna walked away, to her room. She needed to be out of her work clothes and in something large and warm and comfy. Did he expect her to break down and beg him not to leave? That wouldn't happen. It never had before, and it wouldn't. Even if he did mean more to her than anyone else ever had.

She found the warmest, bulkiest, ugliest thing she could find and wrapped herself within it, then scrubbed her face with warm water and brushed her hair out. She could handle this, even on top of the intolerable day. It wasn't like she saw him much. She was still in the city on her own. Still dealing with Todd and his garbage on her own. Except for phone calls, and she didn't say much about the jerk. Freddy would overreact, or he'd worry, and he had enough going on without her adding to it when he was too far away to make any difference.

You get used to crying those tears in private.

The memory of the words offered by the long-term Army wife nearly brought the tears to the surface. But she couldn't. He was there waiting for her to return to him. He liked her strength. He needed that. Maybe if she held herself together well through this, too, he might reconsider. If she wanted him to reconsider. Maybe she just wanted something normal for once in her life. Maybe she needed a man who was home every night, who didn't need her to be so strong. At least not always.

But she would be.

With a deep ragged breath, she went back out to him. He was standing at the table looking over sketches she had done. For the project. The one she hadn't told him about.

His gaze was gentle when it touched her. "These are good. They're yours?"

"Yes. I did tell you I was working." She walked past and went to the kitchen.

"Deanna." He followed and stopped in the doorway. "What have I done to make you mad?"

"I'm not." She stared into the pantry. There had to still be something quick and easy to snack on. She'd barely eaten during the day.

"Aren't you?"

Gritting her teeth a moment, she closed the door and turned to him. "Tell me why you're here."

"I just did."

"You didn't tell me anything."

"I want to know what's wrong. Can't get you to talk over the phone."

She shrugged. "As you said, I was always on the way out or nearly asleep."

He was silent a moment and then nodded.

Deanna watched him turn and go back out, to the living room, she supposed. What was it with men? Why couldn't they just be straightforward? She wasn't going to dissolve at their rejection. She wasn't going to throw a fit or beg them to stay. So she'd have to get her own place. She'd done it before.

Returning to scan the pantry, although there wasn't much point since she knew what was there and she knew what she really wanted wasn't there, she grabbed a snack bar, opened it, and set it on the counter.

She didn't care about the place. She cared about him. And why would he have driven all the way down to break up with her when he had the perfect excuse to do it over the phone? She'd dealt with phone break ups before. The pathetic, spineless cowards. Freddy had driven all the way to see her ... to ask what was wrong?

She wanted answers. It would be better to know than ... well, maybe it would be. It had always been a relief before. Maybe it wouldn't be this time. She couldn't imagine feeling any little bit of relief if he was done with her. Not this time.

Treading back to the living room, Deanna stopped when she didn't see him. He wouldn't have left. Not without saying so. She crept toward the hall that led to the bedrooms. "Fred?"

"Back here."

Deanna went to the guest room and watched him from the door. He was hanging a shirt in the closet, the tiny little closet she should have been using. Did he plan to stay in the guest room instead of with her?

"It's late." He didn't look at her. "I'll be here tomorrow if you want to talk."

"I have to work." Stupid thing to say. She gritted her teeth.

"I know. Before. Or after. I have things I need to do during the day but I'll be here sometime tomorrow night."

"Only one more night?"

"Have to be on base by Tuesday morning." He walked toward her and stopped. "I'm going to shower."

From his expression, she figured he didn't want her to interfere, or to scrub his back. So she moved out of his way and went to the couch, flipping on the television as a distraction. She should go ... what? Talk to him? Tell him why she'd been so grouchy? He'd be annoyed about her working with Todd all weekend. Would he believe that's what she was doing? If he didn't, there was nothing to worry about saving.

She heard him go from the bathroom to the guest room.

As she considered going to find him, he came back out, in sweat pants and a gray Army PT shirt. He claimed the big chair and at least acted like he was watching the show.

"Is the business you need to take care of tomorrow why you're here?"

He tilted his head toward her. "Deanna, I told you why I'm here. I want to know what's wrong."

"You didn't drive all the way down here just to find out what's bugging me." She tried to find something in his expression to tell her otherwise. "Your ... things to take care of tomorrow..."

"I'd planned to do them from Vermont. Changed my plans."

"You really came all this way because...?"

Fred leaned forward and rested his forearms on his legs. "Have you decided you can't deal with it?"

"What?"

"Say so if you have. I won't kick you out. If that's what you're worried about. It wasn't part of anything."

She felt her head shake. Had she decided she couldn't deal with it? "No."

His head lowered just enough he had to open his eyes wider to keep her gaze.

"No. Freddy..." Pushing herself off the couch, she went to him and lowered onto his lap. "No. I can. I told you I can."

"Deanna, I don't want you to stick to this commitment if it's only because you said you could. You don't have to prove anything to me..."

She pressed her mouth against his, felt his surprise, then his arms wrap around her. He didn't feel like he wanted to break it off. He held her in, his grip firm, secure. A lengthy kiss, beautiful and passionate, and everything she'd thought a kiss should be. Every kiss with him felt that way. Deanna caught her breath upon the release. "Does it feel like I'm only trying to prove something?" She brushed fingers through his short hair. "I was afraid...."

"Afraid of what?"

"That ... my edginess was making you change your mind. And I know I have been, and I can be. I'm not always easy to deal with. I rant and rave a lot and I don't have a lot of patience and I'm stubborn and outspoken and not really much of a lady. I know. It's hard for men to deal with. I know it is. But you, well, you're stronger than anyone else I've known and I thought maybe..."

"Do you still want this?" He peered into her eyes.

"Oh." She traced fingers down his face. "Yes. I still want this. I've never stopped wanting this. I was afraid you had."

He helped her to her feet and stroked a finger down her face. Then he switched off the television, went to turn off the lights, and came back to grasp her hand. Without a word, without asking, he led her back to the bedroom.

Deanna kissed his neck and felt the stubble against her face. She slid her hands up under his shirt...

"You haven't brought your things yet."

It took her a second to realize he meant her things out of storage. "No. Not other than my music. Most of it." She moved her lips to the base of his shoulder.

"Why?"

He smelled of soap, fresh, clean. She breathed him in and slid her hands up farther, caressing the firm muscles of his back. "As I said, I wasn't sure you'd keep wanting this."

Freddy rubbed a thumb along her cheek and under her chin, raising it until he found her gaze. "And as I said, if you decide you don't, you can still stay. I won't kick you out."

"But you might want rent I can't afford."

"No. Deanna, this..." he slid his fingers down her arm. "This has nothing to do with the apartment. It's separate. I'm not here much, and normally much less than I have been. When I'm in town, if this doesn't work out between us, I'll either stay in the guest room or at a hotel. I want you to stay, either way."

"Fred?"

"Yes?"

"I'm too tired to talk tonight. How about we save the energy for more important things?"

Satisfied with how much he got done, Daws went back to the apartment, cleaned up and changed, and headed to pick Deanna up at the office. He wouldn't go in. He'd park as close as possible and wait outside. She'd said she would be off exactly at five and wouldn't let them keep her one minute more.

It was cold, and the wind chill dropped the temperature to beyond cold: twenty-three. Polar Bear weather, not human weather, as she said. He didn't mind much as long as he had his coat and wasn't out long. He didn't want her walking to and from the bus in this, though.

She needed to learn to drive. If he ever found enough time, he'd teach her.

He parked fairly close, pulling in as someone pulled out, returning a hand gesture to someone behind him aggravated that he dared wait a few seconds for a parking spot although it was the only way to get one. Moron, as Deanna would say.

Still five minutes to five, he sat in the warmth of the car and watched the front of her building, his radio keeping him company.

At three minutes after five, she came through the glass doors. He got out to meet her and paused when a man caught up and took her arm. Daws couldn't see her face to know whether or not she was annoyed. He wandered closer, watching.

She pushed the guy's arm away and stalked from him, ignoring whatever he said as she left. Her head was down and huddled into her scarf. The guy moved in the opposite direction.

"*Deanna.*"

The expression on her face when she turned and saw him showed half surprise and half ... alarm? "Hey. What are you doing here?"

"Brought the car. Too cold to wait for the bus." Daws moved up to her since she'd stopped walking.

"That was sweet. I'm not used to this kind of service." She gave him a light kiss on the cheek.

He noted the man she'd pushed glance over and pull his gaze away as he noticed that Daws saw him. Deanna didn't see it. He decided not to say anything. Walking her to the car, he held her door and looked back in the man's direction as he moved around to the driver side. Talking to some other woman. She didn't look concerned.

Starting the engine, he turned the heater up. "Would you like to stop somewhere for dinner?"

Deanna unwrapped her scarf. "Sure, if you want. If it's warm and not too noisy. I've had about all the noise I can deal with today."

"Who was that?"

She jerked toward his gaze. "Who?"

"The man you got away from so fast."

"Oh. That was nothing. The ex. The lying cheater ex. Still as big a jerk as ever. Or worse."

"Is he why you've been so annoyed?"

Biting her lip for a moment, she looked away and rubbed her hands together. "Yes."

"Why?"

Her chest rose and fell heavily enough he saw it even under her coat. "We'll talk tonight when we're home, okay? I promise. I just ... it's been a long day and I'm afraid I'll bite your head off if I don't relax first."

Daws brushed the side of her face. It was cold. Soft. He gave her a light nod and pulled out to find a nice luxurious warm quiet restaurant to help her unwind.

He was going to explode. After he was so sweet to pick her up and take her to that too-expensive beautiful restaurant and push for a table close to the fire, Fred was going to explode. He stayed quiet when she told him about the project Todd needed her help with, although disapproval was all over his face. He paced when she mentioned the long nights and the way the jerk kept asking her to work at his place or let him come to hers. But now, he was doing all he could to hold it in. She could see he was.

"Turn him in, Deanna." His voice was low, rough.

"I can't."

"Of course you can..."

"They won't believe me. They'll believe him. It's his word against mine."

"Maybe they will. They've seen his work. Yours will be different enough they'll know he didn't do it."

"Well, the problem with that is that I've helped him on too many of his projects so some of my work has been in a lot of what he's already done. No, they won't know the difference. And since that paper I made him sign is still in his possession, there's nothing I can do to make anyone believe me. I'm an idiot. I should have known better."

"You're not an idiot."

She eyed him as he stood half way across the room. His rebuttal didn't sound very convincing. And why would it? She was. She'd done all that work and simply believed he'd let them know she was working on the project, as he said he had. She didn't push for the written proof because a couple of others saw her working on it. That was evidence enough.

Except they turned on her. She was only "helping him organize" as far as they knew, since that was her job.

Deanna could get him to admit the truth. He'd told her how she could. But she'd go scrub toilets before she ever moved back in with him.

"*Move in* with him? He asked you that, as *condition for promotion? Turn* the asshole *in.*"

"Don't yell at me about it. It's not like I agreed."

"I'm not yelling at you. I'm yelling about him. Didn't you tell him you were involved?"

"Yes, I told you I did. It doesn't mean anything to him. His *marriage* doesn't mean anything to him. Why would my ... *involvement* be different?"

He stopped pacing and stared. Deanna supposed she shouldn't have hesitated in trying to decide what to call their relationship. Still, they weren't exactly living together. The one night of sex when she visited during his promotion and four nights while she was there over Thanksgiving and again when he'd surprised her in the city didn't exactly add up to living together. She hardly saw him.

His chest rose fast and fell hard and he walked over to the windows overlooking the balcony.

Deanna sat still and watched him, his back straight, head up, thumbs hooked in the pockets of his Dockers. He looked out over the city at night, at the bright white-yellow lights of building windows drawing a geometrical design across the landscape. The towers of the World Trade Center stood head and shoulders above the rest. They often reminded Deanna of two lovers standing strong against the rest of the world: separate yet joined, stalwart and unshakeable through whatever storms came their way.

With a sigh, Deanna got up and walked over to him. She set a hand on his back, enjoyed the warmth, the sturdiness, the life within.

"Would you still be living with him if he hadn't cheated on you? If he wasn't married?"

Fred's question, soft and gentle, felt like a punch in the stomach.

He turned, waiting for an answer. She wasn't sure she could. She saw too much vulnerability at the moment, so rare to see from him. And yet, it made her angry that he'd even ask.

"Deanna?"

She walked away. She'd told him he could trust her, that she was faithful and wanted to be. She'd done nothing wrong. Maybe stupid. Working all weekend with him hadn't been a good judgment call, but she hadn't even allowed the jerk to put a hand on her arm without pushing him away.

"I'm taking a shower." His voice sounded resigned. "The bathtub drain is fixed. It shouldn't give you more trouble."

"Fred." She turned to stop him as he headed toward the hall. "That's impossible to answer. I don't know. But I'm glad I'm not. It was a stupid thing to do in the first place. How am I supposed to know if I would still be putting up with him since I did for too long, even at all, when I shouldn't have. But I'm glad I'm not. That's the best I can say."

He stared a moment, nodded and continued toward their room.

Deanna fumed as she went to refill her coffee. Two nights. She had only two nights with him until whenever they could arrange another visit, and they had to spend one of them arguing about the jerk. It's why she didn't tell him; she didn't want to argue. She missed him too much when he was away, which was nearly always. She should have skipped work. But she was backed too far into a corner at the moment. One misstep could cost her too much.

She missed him and she was edgy and he had to leave again at o-four-hundred to be at work on time. After only two nights. And he'd only gone to the extra trouble to drive down to the city because she was edgy.

Setting her coffee on a coaster, Deanna shoved a hand through her hair, sighed, and went to find him.

He stepped out of the shower as she stepped through the open door. He glanced over at her but continued to dry himself as though she wasn't standing there staring at him. Admiring him. Gawking, really. And she loved that he didn't care.

"I would never take him back, you know. If that matters. Even if he wasn't married. Even if I was single. I don't want him. I'm not sure I really ever did. Like I said, it was stupid."

Fred wrapped the towel around his waist and came closer. Waiting for more.

"And now, when bonuses come out, he'll get a huge one for keeping that account they nearly lost, because of my ideas, my sketches, and I'll still get nothing but the fifty bucks I always get. If I get that. And since he's in charge this year and I'm being so *unfriendly*, I may not even get that. But you know, it's not about the fifty bucks, not that I couldn't use it. I'm just really sick of fighting so hard to get what I've earned and still not getting it. I've worked hard. I've done my time and everything I was supposed to do. I earned a certificate and a degree while I was working almost full time and it's gotten me *nowhere*. Why should I even keep bothering? And the whole time the jerk is holding me down because he can, he thinks it's *funny*. I can see he does. No, I don't want him back. I want to knock his freaking head off."

Deanna didn't realize she was shaking until Fred took her in his arms and held her in. "I'm sorry. You didn't come all the way down here to listen to me complain. I'll stop now."

"I did, actually." He pulled back to meet her eyes. "Since you wouldn't tell me over the phone. And I have to admit, when I saw his hand on you earlier, *I* wanted to knock his head off."

"Did you? You're telling me you were jealous?"

"Hm. I'd rather say protective. Doesn't sound as bad."

"Were you?"

His light brown eyes peered deeply into hers. "Every day. At least every work day when he gets to see you and I don't. Didn't help to find out he was with you all weekend and you didn't tell me."

Deanna brushed a hand up alongside his face. "I'm sorry I didn't tell you. And if it makes you feel better, all day when I'm at work and every night when I'm here alone, and the whole time I was putting up with him over the weekend, I was thinking of you. Wishing I was with you. Wanting to cuddle in next to you and get lost in your arms. It's part of why I've been so frustrated. I've wanted to come home and hold onto you. I've never in my life wanted to be with someone so badly. You remember that." She gave him a light kiss.

"Anna, I'm sorry I yelled. It wasn't at you."

"I know." She gave him another kiss and hugged him tight. "Sure you have to leave in the morning?"

"I'm pushing it staying tonight. I shouldn't."

"Okay." She found his eyes again. "But promise me something. If the jerk gets out of hand, let me take care of him. I don't have rank to lose. Actually, I don't have much of anything to lose. Good thing about that is it gives me more freedom."

He frowned. "Well. I'll at least make sure I'm not in uniform. And defending the innocent against aggressors is still allowed. If I do it carefully."

"You know, my guess is all you'd have to do is walk toward him like you intend to do more. He is an actual pansy. I can imagine his reaction at seeing a six foot, two hundred and fifteen pound Mack truck coming at him. Probably give him a heart attack."

Fred raised his eyebrows. "Six foot, two fifteen?"

She shrugged. "That's what your ID said. Yes, I was snoopy enough to look that close. Is it right?"

"It is at tape and weight time."

"At what?"

"Periodic checks to be sure we're keeping in shape enough. I pause the weight lifting and eat less for a couple of weeks before to keep the weight down. Harder to pass the bigger you're built."

Deanna ran her eyes down his body, his perfectly toned, svelte and solid body. "Really? They can't tell by looking at you?" She teased his bare skin with a finger.

"It's all about the numbers. Not a good system. Plenty of overweight and out of shape lazy asses still pass because of their lanky builds. I pass PT well enough they don't bother me much."

"Why do you do this?" She could see he wasn't sure what she meant. "You have the apartment, paid, and the ability to do nearly anything. Why do you put yourself through this with all the restrictions and..."

"Someone has to do it, Anna. We will be the number one target if we ever let our defenses get weak. As you said earlier, the more you have, the more you have to lose, and the more careful you have to be to protect it. What else could I do that would make this much difference?"

Number one target. The thought made her cringe. And it made her feel guilty. She hadn't even found the backbone to return the letter to the nosy neighbor. Or to her mother. She supposed she would.

To get away from the too-serious conversation, Deanna teased his skin. Admiring. Gawking. "How about we go to bed early and unwind together?"

"Careful, Ms. Meyers, I'm starting to think you only want me for my gears."

"Maybe I do." Deanna pressed into his mouth and pulled in as close as she could possibly get. "Or maybe for a couple of other things, too." She lowered her lips to his neck. "After all, I don't get to shift your gears very often, but I still look forward to hearing your voice every day. It helps me make it through all the garbage."

He ran his hand down her shoulder to her hand, and clasped her fingers. "Good to know I'm helpful to some extent long distance."

Deanna pulled back and found his eyes. "Oh Freddy, you have no idea. I feel like a whole new person now that I'm with you. Wow, did that sound as corny as I think it did?"

"It did. But I'll let it go this once."

"Hm, that's nice of you."

One hand still clasping hers, the other brushed hair back from her face. His body pressed closer. "Not much choice on my part. The thing about big trucks you should know: the engine may be slow to start, but once you get it going, it's made to keep going for the long haul. Steering it away from where it's heading can be tricky. You have to be sure of what you're doing when you do it."

"Yeah? Well, I think maybe it's time to shift into higher gear, since I only have you for a few more hours, and I'm pretty sure I know what I'm doing."

=======

Part of the reason she was so frustrated.

Daws pulled through the gate and headed to the Dunkin' Donuts on base. It was a small one but he only wanted coffee. He'd left too late. He barely had time to run into his apartment and change into his BDUs. Even if he'd made coffee before he changed, he would have had to take it. This time, he'd settle for a cup on the go.

It was well worth it. Deanna showed no hesitation in letting him know how much she'd missed him, wanted him. She barely allowed him out the door. He barely made himself go.

Part of her recent frustration was being away from him so often.

It was flattering.

It also worried him. She said again she could handle it. She'd also said it was good they weren't married, so if she didn't keep her temper in check and actually went off on Todd, it couldn't reflect on him.

He supposed she was right. A girlfriend's actions didn't count the way a wife's did, particularly a girlfriend in another city. Still, Daws wouldn't be with Deanna if he didn't trust her. And it bothered him that she thought their relationship meant less because they were only "involved" and not married. And yet she said it was good they weren't. He had to figure it was a hint to not even ask. That worked okay for him, as long as she knew it did not make it mean less.

=======

She supposed it was a bad sign that she left work considering how she wouldn't get Freddy in trouble if she went off on the jerk. Something needed to change. Soon. Nothing Deanna said to him made him stop expecting she'd give in. He apparently didn't know her well. Just because she gave in too fast once didn't mean she ever would again. She was far too stubborn for that. Trusting maybe, but well able to hold a grudge when she had reason. And he gave her more reason every day.

Letting herself into the apartment, she felt a huge breath take over. Home. Time to go change clothes, grab something quick for supper, and talk with Freddy. Then a hot bath to rid herself of the last remnants of winter's chill and television or a movie. And bed. Alone. Still, one of these days, it wouldn't be alone. One of these days, he would be with her every night. At least she told herself he would.

At the phone's ring, Deanna frowned. Too early for Fred. Maybe a telemarketer. Kicking off her shoes, she made her way over and checked the number, then grabbed it. "Well hey there, Sergeant." She took the phone over to the couch and sank into the cushions. "You're earlier than I expected. Haven't even changed from work yet."

"We do shorter days when we can at December's end. Gives them time to finish shopping."

"Oh? That's sweet of you."

"Not my idea, a general tradition."

"Even if it were your idea, you wouldn't take credit."

"How was your day, Anna?"

She smiled at the way he changed the subject. "Same as normal."

"That good?"

"Well, maybe a little better than that. I heard rumors that my name did make it onto that project at least to some extent. Not holding my breath, but something might still come of it. I have a meeting tomorrow. I guess we'll see."

"A meeting with who?"

"With ... well, a few people. Yes, he'll be there, but a few of us will be. It's fine. And you know I can handle the jerk myself, right? Don't worry so much."

A sigh came over the line. "Wish I could be there, close by, in case. At least pick you up afterward."

He sounded tired. Deanna wished she could wrap her arms around him and soothe him to sleep. "You have more important things to take care of. They're counting on you."

"Maybe I want you to be able to count on me."

"Oh, Freddy. I do. I count on talking to you every night, or at least every night you're not in the field. You are here for me. And I do count on you. I know I can."

"Anna, tell me you're sure it's all right. Working so closely with him."

"He's married. If he gets carried away, I'll tell him to back off or I'll let her know. Not that I shouldn't, anyway. I think about doing it every day, just because she should know. It's unfair and I'm a part of it, and..."

"No you aren't. And I wouldn't threaten that. Leave her out of it. You don't know what kind of a situation they have."

"I know he's cheating on her."

"But you don't know what she's doing, or if she knows."

Deanna pulled the blanket over her legs. "Maybe so." She fidgeted, trying to get comfortable. "So how are things with Ryan? Any word?"

"Hm. He needs watching as much as the jerk does. My connection, the Guardsman who's been playing coach to him, did get him on the track team and apparently he's good at it."

"Track? It's freezing. How are they doing track now?"

"In the gym. Running. Hurdles. Pre-spring training."

"Oh."

"You're not much into sports?"

"No. Well, I played basketball one year. Hated it. Loved when we did weight training and that kind of thing but not otherwise."

He chuckled. "Anyway, with Christmas coming up, the kid is getting snappier with him and in general."

"A kid who doesn't like Christmas?"

"The first without his dad."

"Oh." Deanna threw the blanket off again and went to the kitchen. "Yeah, I kind of know that one. The year I moved out here. Couldn't afford to go back home and didn't know anyone. I ate too much of a canned ham and most of a cheesecake while I sat and watched TV all day. I think I was sick for two days afterward."

"Wish I'd known you then."

"Yeah? Would you have come to keep me company?"

"That or I would have invited you here. Not here, but to Fort Carson where I was stationed at the time." Silence invaded while she shouldered the receiver and twisted off the lemonade cap. "Would you have gone that far?"

She took a swallow. "Like I said, I couldn't even afford to go home and that's closer."

"I would have bought the ticket."

Leaning against the counter, she set the bottle down again. It was cold. She was already cold enough. "Well Fred Dawson, gotta tell you, at this point I'd have to say I'd jump on a plane and visit you anywhere in the world if I had means to get there. I shouldn't tell you that, but I would if it was at all possible."

Silence intervened again. Deanna grabbed a small kitchen towel from a drawer and wrapped it around the bottle. She took another swallow. "So. I don't suppose you can come down for my office party and let me show you off?"

"Anna, I can't. I've already taken off too much recently. We have several out on leave and someone has to stay and mind the store."

"But you said you do that every year."

"Yes. To save those with families the chance to get away. I've had no reason to get away."

Wandering back into the living room, she returned to her spot and pulled the blanket back over her. She wanted him there. In flesh.

"Their leaves have been in for a month or more. Already said I would be here."

"I know. It's okay."

"You don't sound like it's okay."

"No. It isn't. But it is. It's hardly the first holiday I've spent alone."

"Come up to Drum."

"Why? You're working, even Christmas Day. Don't you have duty or something?"

"Staff duty. You can come in for dinner. There's a lounge. Nothing fancy, just a couple of Army couches and some chairs and a television. I'll order food in." A pause came over the line. "Not the best way to spend our first Christmas together."

"Well, it's better than poor Ryan and his family, right? At least you're still here. Even if we spend it on the phone, it's better..." She didn't bother to finish.

"Will you think about coming up?"

"I'll think about it. If I can get a ticket this late."

"I'll get it. If you say yes."

She grinned. So sure of himself. When anyone else sounded so sure, she scowled at their arrogance, but somehow, he wasn't arrogant. His self-assurance was entirely different. Eventually, she'd figure out why it was. "Let me see how hard it might be to get a couple of days off so it's worth the trip there and back. Not that a day or two with you isn't worth it, but..."

"Understood."

=======

"Thank you, Sergeant."

Daws held the door he opened for Mrs. Brymer, spouse of one of his newer soldiers he barely knew. Being platoon sergeant made it harder to keep up with each of his troops – he couldn't say men anymore, now that he had females in his charge, also – than he could when there were only eight or nine. He now had twenty-seven and had no idea what the family situations were for most.

Dealing with their personal issues was the hardest part of his job, even harder than ducking as mortar fire flew overhead. Maybe not quite that. But much of him wanted to put out an order that until they made at least E4, they should refrain from marrying and having children.

Of course he couldn't. And it was ludicrous that with as many hours as his men – his troops – worked, even at the lowest pay grade, they had so much trouble paying their basic living necessities. The young singles, he didn't feel for. If they ran out, it was due to too much club hopping or too much beer when they were out hopping. They lived in the barracks. Their pay was fine for one person to live on with no rent, utilities, or mandatory groceries.

It was the married soldiers who could hardly make it. Even supporting only a wife on their pay was tight; adding a kid or more made it near impossible. In the civilian world, they'd get government assistance, and more assistance for more kids. It wasn't allowed for the military, even at the same pay levels. Other than WIC, which provided some limited food item assistance. Most refused to take it. They represented the United States Military; it was a matter of honor. He couldn't help think they should worry less about that particular point since those providing their funding didn't worry much about it.

Daws sighed and tried not to think of Private Brymer's wife's tears of embarrassment as she asked for someone who could help. A two year old on her lap squirmed. He tried not to notice the child's coat was too small and too thin. An old blanket was wrapped around the coat until the child pushed it away. Mrs. Brymer explained how she'd worked as long as she could, but the child was often sick and the day care wouldn't allow him to stay, so her new job let her go for missing work too often. Just before Christmas. When they were still trying to pay off the bills from moving onto post after a month's worth of hotel and eating out bills while they waited for housing. The Army paid ten days of temporary living; the rest was on them, although it hadn't been their choice to move and they hadn't wanted to move. Even the cheap hotel that smelled of something she couldn't even explain racked up their credit card debt that was only used for necessary things: clothing for the kids and the groceries his paycheck didn't always cover. She talked of going back home to stay with her mother until they could get their finances straightened and letting the private move back into the barracks. But then they'd have even more moving expense and she couldn't imagine how they'd pay it.

Personally, Daws thought it might be a good idea. Except it seemed hard enough on Deanna to have him away so much and it was only him, they didn't have kids. He tried to consider it from Mrs. Brymer's view. Forced separations due to training and such played enough toll on young mothers who didn't even have family around to help. Finance problems shouldn't add to their time apart. No, he would go with her to Family Support the next morning and see what they could do, and then he'd send the change can around to the higher enlisted ranks. Quietly. Without names attached. Only Daws would know who it was for.

And he would grant Brymer permission to take on a part time, although he staunchly objected to his troops doing more than they already did. Down time was essential. Daws would have to watch him more closely to be sure he could still function well enough.

Deanna managed to maintain her fake smile throughout the phone conversation with the exasperated client and was terribly relieved to be able to hang up. Why did the reception desk always funnel those calls to her? That wasn't her job. They weren't her clients. She wasn't the one who ticked them off by not staying in touch well enough, by not having their projects ready on time. If they were her clients and her projects, she'd be glad to keep them informed. And she'd have the projects done.

Most of the creatives at McCallister's, she enjoyed. They kept the name up to standards and kept it going. The two or three who didn't shouldn't be there. Deanna could easily replace one of them.

At least she was always able to calm the clients when they were angry. McCallister's almost never lost a client. It was why she applied there. When she did work up, she wanted that reputation still intact.

But she was sick of those calls. If she was the swearing type, she'd do that about now. Since she wasn't, she contented herself with finding a couple of old papers, crumbling them into tight balls and throwing them at the wall above the garbage can. One went in, the other bounced off. Good. She could grab it and try a slam dunk on her way to refill her coffee.

"You missed." Todd bent to pick it up and dropped it in.

"I would've done that."

"Now you don't have to." He leaned back against the wall, in her way.

"Excuse me."

He curled his lips into a sneered grin. "You're welcome."

"I didn't say thank you. I could've done it myself. Would you move? I have work to do."

"Your desk is behind you."

"Get out of the way, Todd. A girl is still allowed thirty seconds to refill her coffee, isn't she? The nose rubbing twins over there find plenty of time to do it, and then some."

He shrugged and leaned toward her. "Attitude will get you everywhere, Deanna. You should know that by now."

"Attitude? Is that what you're calling it these days? Move."

"Now that's no way to talk to your boss."

"You shouldn't be my boss and you know that as well as I do. By the way, I just handled Mr. Tomas for you. He wants the draft for the campaign yesterday since you promised it last week. I let him know you'd have it by tomorrow. Guess you have to work tonight."

Todd edged in. "Interested in helping with it tonight?"

"When does my name go out for the promotion as you promised?"

He stepped back, a confused expression covering his face, instantly, and well planned. "Promised? I don' t recall any such promise."

"The heck you don't. That was part of the bargain for help on the last project, which my name is supposed to be on."

"Is it?" He shrugged. "My error, I guess."

She stared at him as he started to walk away, into his office. With the opening clear, she shuffled in and grabbed the big cardboard tube of sugar and a matching one of creamer then poured stale-smelling coffee in the mix. His error?

With a light shake of the head, she went to set her cup on her desk and then followed him, into his office. One of his playmates, or buxom secretaries, was there.

Todd raised his eyes to hers. "Yes?"

"I need to speak with you."

"I'm in the middle of something. Would you wait outside?"

"No. I won't wait outside." She crossed her arms in front of her.

In a feeble attempt at a staring contest to get her to back down, he finally shifted and glanced toward the girl awaiting his instructions. "Leave for a minute."

She didn't bother to act insulted by the order. Deanna guessed she was too used to taking his orders.

"Okay. You have one minute." He leaned back into his thick leather chair.

"You promised to put my name in for the promotion if I helped with that project. And you know you only kept that client because of me, because of my ideas. Fulfill your part of the bargain."

He pulled one leg over the other. "I made no such bargain."

Deanna felt her mouth nearly drop. "*Liar.* You filthy *liar.*"

With a jerk, Todd jumped up from his chair, moved closer and shut the door. "Don't call me that again if you want to keep this job. And if you don't, I can arrange for other companies to know why you didn't."

"Fine. You tell them why. But try the truth for a change, because you are a liar, and you know you are."

"Deanna." He stepped closer. "Be careful. Our past relations have helped me be more lenient with your attitude but I do have my line and you're awfully close to crossing it."

"I don't care about your line. You crossed the line long ago. You're lucky I haven't told your wife that I was living with you. So don't get too full of yourself with me, and don't threaten me."

He snickered. "You think she doesn't know? She knows. It keeps me out of her hair so she can run around with her *friend* who she's known longer than she's known me. Tell her. Just a warning, if you do, she'll do everything she can to embarrass the hell out of you. She's done it before. It doesn't matter who I'm with as long as I keep them away from her." He moved closer yet. "So again, be careful."

"Back up."

He ran his eyes down her body and moved the hand hidden from view of the windows up her thigh, under her skirt.

She shoved him. "Keep your hands *off* me. You will never touch me again. *Never.* I'll file sexual harassment."

"No you won't. Because if you do, you'll never get a decent job in this city again. Who wants a trouble maker in their employment? Who do you think they'll believe? I have plenty of *friends* in the office who'll say you're lying."

He was right. Deanna knew he was right. Especially if he brought up her past relationships, of which he knew too much. She would never let the jerk intimidate her, though, not so he could tell. "You know what, Todd? Maybe I don't care about working in this city again. Maybe I'll sue for a bundle of money so I can take my time finding another job in another city, away from scum like you who won't know who I am. Maybe I won't win, but it will mark your name and scare clients away, and right now, that would be good enough for me. So don't be sure I won't. Try it again and find out." Deanna held him with a glare.

His expression said he was taking her seriously, at least for a moment, until he laughed. "Okay, good attempt at a threat, but I know you. I know how much you want to be a big name in New York. So your bluff won't work."

"Hm. Maybe that used to be true and maybe that's why I've put up with as much of your garbage as I have, but it's not anymore. There's somewhere else I think I might rather be, even if it means changing jobs. So in all honesty, it won't take much more to push me that direction. As I said, try it and find out."

"You're lying."

Her back stiffened, her chin raised. "I don't lie. You should know that much about me. And forget the lawsuit, *Mr.* Bodin. One more move like that, and I'll let my boyfriend know he has free rein to handle you as he wishes. He's been wanting to meet you."

"Boyfriend?" Todd's lips curled.

"The reason I'm thinking I might want to be elsewhere. A real man, not a pathetic excuse for one like you are."

He grabbed her arm and moved in. "Be careful."

Deanna broke out of it and returned the stare. "*Don't* touch me again. That's a warning, not a threat." She didn't give him time to answer and wouldn't give him the satisfaction. Instead, Deanna swiveled and strutted out the door as if he hadn't bothered her in the slightest.

In reality, she wanted to go home and take a two-hour bath just to wash him off.

She also wanted to call Freddy.

Rubbing her hip, she gritted her teeth and waited impatiently for the elevator to take her up to the right floor. Stupid ice. Why hadn't the sidewalk been better salted at the bus stop? She almost managed not to fall as she stepped out but the idiot behind her brushed her side and she couldn't recover from it. There would be a bruise, she figured. Wonderful. Not that it would show to anyone but her.

She pulled her keys out and checked her watch. Past time he usually called. Her anger kept her from getting done what she had to do on time, so she made herself stay an extra half hour, then she fell on the stupid unsalted ice. It made the walk to her building slower than normal.

The phone was ringing. She heard it as she got to the door.

This time, she didn't even bother to drop her things. She hurried to the phone and greeted him, hoping it was him and she hadn't hurried for a telemarketer. It wasn't. She asked him to hold on while she got out of her coat and shoes and took the phone to the couch, wrapping the blanket over her legs.

"Okay. Sorry. I can talk now."

"What's wrong?"

"Why do you ask?"

"I hear it in your voice."

"Very perceptive, Sergeant. I bet your people don't get away with anything. Am I right?"

"They don't tend to try. Not more than once."

With a chuckle, she imagined curling up into his arms.

"What happened, Anna?"

"Hm. Not sure if I want to say, but I guess I better, since I kind of involved you. I shouldn't have, and he didn't believe me anyway, I don't think…"

"He. Todd?"

"Yes."

"What did he do?"

Deanna bit her lip and held her breath a moment to calm herself. Through the rest of the day, her anger kept her together. She managed to see past the stares directed at her ever since she left Todd's office. She even convinced herself he hadn't gotten to her. Almost.

"Talk to me. Don't keep it in."

With another deep, shaky breath, she tried to decide where to start. Slowly. Letting herself work into it, starting with the project and ending with him not only rubbing his hand along her thigh but grabbing her arm.

He was silent.

"Freddy?"

"I'm here."

"I know I shouldn't have mentioned you. I can fight my own battles, and I will. I was just so angry, and…"

"Did he hurt you?"

"No. Other than the acid pouring in my stomach all day." She bit her lip again. "I may have a bruise but nothing to do with him."

"From what?" He sounded like he was about to jump through the phone.

"Ice. The bus stop was covered in it."

"Bruise where? Did you break anything? What did you hit?"

"My hip, but not hard. I mostly caught myself. Nothing broken, other than a bit of my pride, but I've had to fix that before." She forced a grin, hoping he could hear it.

"Keep an eye on that. If it gets worse, get it checked."

"Are you a doctor now, Fred Dawson?"

"We all get basic field training, enough to know an injury can be worse than it seems at first."

"Oh? Is falling on the ice a big problem out there in the field?"

"Doesn't matter much what caused the fall."

"And what else did you learn in your field training?"

"Cold weather injuries and symptoms. Heat exhaustion. How to splint a bone. CPR. Signs of shock. Basics."

"Oh. I was joking, but you all learn that?"

"Part of training. Medics aren't always close and there are only so many."

She wanted to touch his face, to run her hand back into his short light brown hair. "I think I've said this before, but you'd be handy to have around on a regular basis."

"Are you going to turn him in?"

Fidgeting, she hesitated. "I don't know. I'm not sure what to do anymore. I think ... I may just quit. Give up. I'm not ... I'm not the type to give up, you know, but I won't ever get anywhere there and if I try a different company, he'll be sure to mess that up for me, too. I just don't know that it's worth it and ... I've been thinking..." No. She couldn't say it. He wanted her in New York to watch his place.

"Thinking what?"

Pushing the blanket off her legs, she got up and paced.

"Anna? Thinking what?"

"That maybe I could find a job in Watertown or somewhere close. I can learn to drive, right? You'd teach me. It doesn't have to be marketing. I don't think I care anymore..."

"You're thinking of moving here?"

She stopped pacing. "Maybe. Depends what you say."

The line was quiet. Too quiet. For too long. Not a good sign. Deanna brushed at the tears she couldn't stop. He didn't want her there. She was pushing...

"I have orders." His voice was low. "Came today."

"Orders?"

"PCS. Permanent change of station. I'm being reassigned."

She couldn't reply. Was there a base any closer to the city? Not likely. And if there was, fat chance that's what he meant.

"It's a one year tour. I can ask to come back here if this is where you want to be, but I can also try for something else. Anywhere you'd like to go?"

"Oh. Can I?"

"After the year is over. You can't accompany me on this one. But when I return, if there's somewhere you'd thought about living, I can try to get close to there. Kentucky maybe, to be close to your family?"

"You'd want me to move with you?"

"If you're willing. After the year's up."

She made her way to the couch and propped herself on the edge of it, ignoring the pain in her hip. "The whole year? Where?"

"Korea. Up by the DMZ. Not a sponsored tour. No families."

"Korea? For a year? What's the DMZ?"

"Demilitarized zone. The neutral boundary. We're stationed there to help keep the peace between north and south."

"Why?"

"The war."

"What?"

"You know it never ended. The Korean War. It's on a long-term cease fire, but if we leave, it starts again. The north will move back into the south."

"Oh." Suddenly, she realized just how little she knew about world events or history or military action. Where had she been that she didn't know that? "So. A full year straight?"

"I'll have about three weeks' break halfway between. Still think you can wait it out?"

"Yes. I won't say I'll like it, but yes. I'll be here." She stood and paced again. "Guess there's not much point in moving, then. When? When do you leave?"

"Spring. I'll tell you more when I see you."

Spring. At least it wasn't immediate.

"Have you thought more about coming for Christmas?"

"Yes." Actually, she'd hardly stopped thinking about it, but her head kept telling her she couldn't. It was too much time off, or too far to go with little time off. But he was leaving in the spring. For a year. "Yes. I'll be there. Will you object to two weeks so we can start the New Year together, also?"

"Anna, I would love you to be here for two weeks. If you can afford the time."

She sighed. "Well, like I said, I don't think I care much. If they fire me, I'll find something else. Might as well at this point. I'll make reservations tomorrow."

"Let me. I'll take care of it."

"Freddy, you're doing too much already..."

"Not nearly enough. You're still fending off the idiot on your own because I can't be there."

"That's my job. It's my career. You're doing yours and I can't help with that, either."

"Of course you do."

She frowned and headed toward the kitchen. "How is that?"

"Support. And your willingness to wait. The fact I know I can trust you. I can't tell you how much that means to me every day."

Biting her lip, she stopped and leaned back against a wall for support. "Always. I mean that." She tried to keep her voice steady.

"I know you do. And so much of me wants to tell you to quit tomorrow and move up here until spring. I can't ask it, but I'd like to. When I get restationed in the States again, I'd like you to move in with me, if it won't mess up your own plans. If it does, we'll keep making this work. Agreed?"

She wiped at the moisture under her eyes. "Yes. Wherever you go. Yes." The following silence was hard to take. Deanna had to pull herself together. "Are you going to be home all night?"

"Yes. Working on a counseling statement. Bad part of the job."

"Who got in trouble?"

"No one I've mentioned. New guy."

"Did he mess up bad?"

"It's minor, but it has to be nipped in the bud. He refused to salute an officer because he doesn't like him. I hardly blame him this time, since I don't like the guy, either, and I know he doesn't deserve the respect of a salute, but his rank does. Have to put that on paper, carefully."

"Oh. Good luck."

"Yeah. Want me to let you go?"

"No. But I want to go bathe and get comfortable and my stomach's growling."

"Better eat first, then. I'll be here if you want to call later."

"Count on that, Sergeant."

"Deanna?"

"Yes."

"You're more than welcome to tell him I'm anxious to meet him. It won't be a lie. And I don't mind being dragged in. I'd drag myself into it if I could."

She gave him a quick farewell, since she couldn't think about Todd at the moment. Freddy wanted her to move in with him. Not only to take care of his apartment, but elsewhere. She just had to hold out at her job for another year and a couple of months. Then she'd move with Freddy and tell Todd just what he could do with himself.

Of course, she could go ahead and quit after Freddy left for Korea. She could go home. The Christmas letter she got from her mom was short, rushed. Deanna couldn't help think something was wrong. She could say she was moving back to help out, to visit, temporarily. Get a little job. Find a roommate and rent a nearby trailer. Return to the city for the three weeks he would be home...

Except he needed her to take care of his apartment.

And she wasn't sure she could handle being among her family so steadily for so long. There was a reason she'd escaped so early. Funny how she'd nearly forgotten. Had she been away that long?

Fred offered to try to get stationed close to them.

No. A sudden, sharp cringe in her stomach vetoed that idea. Deanna wasn't even sure she'd ever take him there. Some things were best left alone.

Daws opened a can of soup, dumped it in a stoneware bowl, and shoved it in the microwave. Cracking a couple of eggs into the hot pan, he watched them and thought about the asshole's hand on Deanna's thigh. It made him hotter than the eggs crackling. He was sure as hell anxious to meet him. The asshole didn't believe her? He would.

By the time she called back, he'd made new arrangements and had his plan formed.

"Did I interrupt your work?"

"Not at all." Daws took the phone over to the coffee table and set the base down. He supposed he should have bought a cordless like he had for the New York apartment, but the regular landline was required. If the power went out, he had to be able to use the phone, to receive calls. And he didn't need both.

They talked about everything except the asshole and Korea, until he heard her yawn. "I should let you get to sleep."

"What time is it? I don't see the clock from here and I'm too lazy to get up and look."

"Ten-seventeen."

"Is it already? And you still have work to do. You should have cut me off."

"I was enjoying the talk." He stood and stretched his shoulders. "But you're tired. Before I let you go, you do plan to go to your office party?"

"I don't know. I don't think I will after today."

"You should go." He heard silence. "Don't let him win, Deanna."

"He already has."

He sighed at the despair in her voice. "No, he hasn't. And we won't let him. Go to the party. You'll have an escort."

"What?"

"Someone from the city who'll pick you up. Someone you can trust."

"Oh. Freddy, don't do that. Don't bring someone else into this..."

"Already arranged. It's fine. Just tell me you'll go."

"You don't plan for me to say he's my boyfriend, right? Because I can't..."

"I would never ask you to lie. You know that. Just be ready." Silence. "Anna, trust me. You can't let that guy win, or think he scared you."

"Maybe he did."

Daws grabbed a deep breath. It would take everything he had not to throttle the asshole when they met. "He won't again. Avoid him at work and don't stay late. But go to the party. Trust me."

She didn't answer right away, but he waited. "I do. Okay."

"Okay. Stop thinking about it tonight. Get some sleep. Wear flat shoes tomorrow so you don't aggravate your hip. Tell him it's health reasons and you'll turn in a complaint if he objects." Waiting for a light agreement, he wished her a good night and hung up.

Yes, he looked forward to meeting Mr. Todd Bodin.

=======

Smoothing her skirt, Deanna moved in front of the door-length mirror to check her attire. She'd splurged too much on the dress, but the deep green silky material pulled her right in and wouldn't let her go. It was complimentary to her auburn hair and brought out the best of her coloring, and her curves. At the office, she kept her curves at least partly concealed for a professional look. Not that anyone else thought of her as a professional, but she tried. This, however, was a party. Most of the girls and some of the wives would be much more splayed than she was. It would make her look both understated and just glamorous enough.

At least that was her hope. She also hoped she could pull off the matching attitude.

Satisfied, she thumbed through her jewelry to find something that would work with it. A plain gold chain and small diamond earrings would have to do, even if she wore them last year. No one would remember. With another check, she went out to the living room.

She hoped whatever escort Fred set up would happen to also be at least somewhat attractive. No, honestly, she hoped he would be drop-dead gorgeous. Just to be able to show up with a head-turning escort. Or would Fred be more wary than that and choose someone a little less appealing? No, she figured he knew he didn't have to worry. He likely didn't think about the guy's looks at all, only how much he trusted him.

With a light chuckle, she sat and hooked her strappy black heels to her feet. They would be cold on the ride over and back but she'd deal with it. She couldn't wear sensible shoes after taking such pains with her looks, even if her hip was still slightly sore. Her galoshes were staying home.

Maybe she should stay home. She could invite him in. If Fred said it was safe, it was. They could watch something silly on television, or a Christmas special, and eat popcorn and stay warm and avoid Todd. *Don't let him win.* Fred's voice filtered through her thoughts. He wanted her to go.

But since when did she let a man dictate what she would or wouldn't do?

With a sigh, she realized she only agreed because he was right; she didn't want the idiot to win, either. Yes, she would go. And she would at least act as though she was enjoying herself.

The doorbell made her jump. He was there.

As she started toward it, Deanna realized asking him to come in for a movie was a ludicrous thought, anyway. He probably wouldn't even step foot inside the door.

She hoped he wouldn't be too horribly stiff at the party.

With her hand on the knob, she paused for a deep breath. And she opened it with a resolved smile.

A bouquet of white Canna lilies tinged with green and blue streaks was the first thing she saw. Then her eyes traveled up to the man holding them. He was in a dark blue uniform coat with lighter blue pants, striped down each side, a dark blue hat in his hand ... and several rows of small ribbons pinned over one breast, with two medals hanging beneath.

"I did say you'd have an escort you could trust." Fred offered the flowers.

Her eyes tried to water. She couldn't answer. She stood. And stared. Oh, how he filled it out nicely, how sharp he looked, how...

He stepped forward. "You look amazing."

She felt her head shake, then she moved up into him and pressed her mouth to his. The arm still gripping his hat went around her back. She felt it against her, the rim, his strong arm, as though they were all connected.

"Fred." She managed to find her voice. "You said you couldn't be here."

"After your little meeting with Todd, I changed my mind. Made it work. I can only stay two days. Two nights, that is. A day and a half. Best I could do."

"You are the most wonderful man I have ever met." She kissed him again and gripped the front of his jacket, pulling him inside.

"We'll be late if you keep that up." He gave her a teasing grin.

"Is that a promise, Sergeant? This is nice." She ran her fingers along his chest, over the stiff fabric.

"Dress blues. For special occasions. Thought we might reiterate to your boss just how well trained I am in protection."

Her eyes pulled to his medals, hanging below four bars of ribbons, in particular a purple ribbon with a heart and man's bust. "Is this what it looks like?"

"Purple heart." His voice was low, his eyes pulled away.

"Why? I mean ... you didn't say you were injured over there."

His chest rose and fell. "It wasn't much. Got hit in the leg. Not bad enough to keep me down. Tried not to accept it."

"Why wouldn't you?"

"Some things are better forgotten."

Deanna grabbed a breath as she tried not to picture how he must have been hit, and focused on the medal beside it: a gold-colored star hanging from a red and white ribbon with a thin blue stripe. "And what is this for?"

"Bravery during battle, or *heroic or meritorious achievement or service*, to be technical."

She met his eyes. "What did you do that was so brave, more than just being there, that is?"

"Pulled one of my men from a building that was falling in around him. More instinct than bravery."

"And I bet there's more to it than you're saying."

He didn't answer and she raised fingers to his face. "Will you forgive me if I repeat that tonight? Or at least what it's for?"

He met her lips. Softly. Only for a second or two. "This is your night. I am here for you. Other than any personal information I may have said about my troops, or my personal background, there is no off limits. I am here for you."

Shivers ran from her shoulders to her toes.

"And this." He leaned to set the flowers on a table, then stepped back to eye her attire. "This is you. Fiery and elegant. Sexy and mature. Very nice. You were going to the party like this without me?"

"Well, you said I'd have an escort I could trust. I took your word for that."

"Maybe you shouldn't have." He moved in again and slid both hands behind her back, pulling her in, pressing his mouth firmly against hers.

She no longer wanted to go to the party. She didn't care about Todd or what he thought or believed. He didn't matter. She wanted to keep Freddy home, for the two nights they had and the day in between. When his lips moved to her neck, she pressed closer. "We could skip it."

He moved back. "No. I want to meet this guy. And I want you to show up, your head high, with every bit of knowledge of who you are written all over your face. I want him to know just who he's messing with."

"It won't matter."

"I'm guessing it will."

She saw that look on his face again, the one that made her think anyone would hope he was on their side, not against it, the confidence, the knowledge of who he was and of what he was capable. Deanna expected she only had a rough idea about just how much he was actually capable of. "Let me put these in water."

Fragrance drifted around her as she went to find a vase and filled it. She knew she was spending too much time arranging the cannas, soothing herself with their scent, touching their soft petals. Blue and green. She'd told him she bought a new green dress for the party...

"Ready?" He moved in behind her, stroked her nape, so rarely uncovered as it was tonight.

She closed her eyes and concentrated on his fingers, the warmth of his body next to her. Who cared what Todd or anyone else thought? This man was so much more worthy of ... of everything. His opinion squashed theirs to nothing. And she was the one he chose.

"Before we leave, there's something you should know about your flowers."

Deanna leaned back farther against him, and grasped his arms to wrap around her stomach when his hands touched her waist.

"They're not lilies, technically, although they're called Canna lilies. Cannas are a special breed and more rare than lilies, yet they've been unfairly pegged as something far more common. They remind me of you." He kissed her neck. "Rare. Beautiful. Unique. So much more than anyone sees."

Deanna had to force herself to continue breathing, and turned to face him. "There's something you should know, too. I don't know how I was lucky enough to find you, but you better plan to stay around long term, because I can't imagine anymore not having you." She moved her hands up alongside his head, separating her fingers in front and behind his ears. "I love you, Fred Dawson. And I have never in my life said that to anyone but my mom." She kissed him, purposely not giving him time to answer, or not answer. No pressure. He didn't have to return the words. He only had to keep holding her the way he did, looking at her the way he did, and kissing her the way she'd never been kissed.

She did have to regain her footing, and quick, if they were going to make it out of the apartment. "So." She dropped her head nearly to his shoulder and fingered his uniform. "Should I ask how a hard-core Army sergeant knows so much about flowers?"

He chuckled. "I don't, not other than these. It's the only kind I remember seeing in my grandma's yard, on the rare occasions I was there. Didn't think much about them, since I was a kid and they were flowers." He shrugged. "Until I saw them at my first duty station. Still a kid, first time out on my own and wondering what I'd gotten myself into. An officer's wife had a big patch of them in all colors and I literally stopped during a run when I realized they were the same. Guess I had a touch of homesickness. Also rare. She saw me stop and gave me a grin. So I screwed up the nerve to ask what they were called. Didn't hear the end of that until I moved again."

Deanna laughed. "No, I bet you didn't. Macho guys aren't supposed to care about flowers, right? Unless they're giving them to some girl to get themselves out of trouble."

"Something like that. Also got fifty for it."

"Got fifty what?"

"Pushups. Had to drop right there and do fifty before I continued the run."

"For talking to her?"

"For getting distracted from my duty."

"Bet you wish you hadn't, right?"

"No, I'm glad I did. Never would've figured it out on my own. Easier to ask."

"Fifty pushups in the middle of a run is easy?"

"I was ten years younger then. Could still do it, but wouldn't ask for it as I used to." He stroked a thumb across her cheek. "Nothing else I've seen would fit you as well. Worth the pushups and the ribbing."

For the second time in the past ten minutes or so, Deanna had to force herself not to cry. Instead, she kissed him. He caressed her neck, softly, avoiding her hair she'd put up in a semi-elegant knot, sliding his fingers up to her ear and playing with her earrings.

He studied her ears a moment when he pulled back from the kiss. "I have something for you before we go." Fred reached inside his jacket and pulled out a long jewelry box. Deanna had felt it as she leaned against him, but through the thick material, she couldn't tell what it was. It had crossed her mind it might be a weapon in a chest sling, as she'd seen in movies. She was quite glad it wasn't.

"Part of your Christmas gift. Thought you should have it now."

"Oh. You shouldn't have ... you've done so much already, coming all the way down here..." She felt her mouth gape as he opened the box. "Those aren't real."

"I would never give you anything fake, Anna." He pulled the string of pearls and the matching earrings from the box and set it aside. "Will you wear them tonight? Or is what you have on..."

"Yes. Of course. But Freddy, it's too much."

He moved around behind her. Warm fingers exchanged the gold chain and tiny diamonds with the pearls. Setting her older jewelry beside the box, he kissed her neck, ran his hands down her arms. "When you walk in there tonight, I want you to put aside anything they've said about you and replace those thoughts with how highly I think of you, how I've considered turning down Korea just to stay closer to you, although it would mean a mark on my record and little chance of another promotion..."

"Don't do that." She turned to find his eyes and set her hands on his stomach. "No. I won't be the cause of any mark on your record or any interference. Don't. As much as I hate to think of how hard it will be, I ... I want you to go. I want you to keep excelling. And I'll be here when you get back. I'll also be thinking about those three glorious weeks you'll have in between that I sure hope you'll spend right here with me."

"Count on it." He kissed the side of her head.

Daws rubbed the back of her neck after dropping her coat at the check window. She was tense. As they approached the hotel ballroom, she gripped his arm and leaned closer. "Come on, soldier. Help me make an impression and then take me home."

With a light nod, he opened the door and held it for her as music and voices belted through. A large party. Larger than he expected. And they were all dressed to the hilt, sparkly and dripping with real money, fake money, and charade. She kept hold of his arm, her dainty fingers pressed firmly just above the crook of his elbow. And she at least looked relaxed and confident as people turned to stare at him. He'd expected it and pretended not to notice. Part of him wished it was an outdoor party so he could have kept his hat on instead of checking it with her coat. As low as it came over his eyes, it helped hide the direction of his gaze.

A middle-aged woman with a painfully shrill voice came up to Deanna and asked if he was real and where she picked him up. With a roll of the eyes, and while Daws considered saying he had a wind-up spring in his back, Deanna introduced him to her, and then to another woman who was thankfully much quieter and less obnoxious.

The shrill woman glanced between them and then to others nearby paying attention. Her expression was amused when she turned it back, her voice still too loud. "This is for show, right? Trying to make Todd jealous?" She looked directly at Daws. "The boss man. You know they *used to* date, right? Rumor has it he still has a soft spot for her."

"I do know." He slid his hand up Deanna's back, rested it at the base of her shoulder, and caressed her neck with his thumb. But he kept his eyes on the shrew. "His problem. She's not available."

"Honestly?" She looked back at her coworker. "I just can't see it. He doesn't look your type."

Deanna's body relaxed under his touch. "And how would you know my type, Jess? We barely ever speak."

"Well." The woman raised her chin. "We've seen who you were with before."

"Which was a huge mistake, since *boss man* is not my type. And I couldn't care less if he's jealous or if he's not. Is his *wife* here? She might care, but I don't."

"Yes, first time she's ever come to one of these, and she's been attached to his side since they arrived. On the lookout, they're saying. So be careful."

"I have no reason to be careful." Deanna claimed his hand and moved away from the women.

Daws checked their expressions as he passed them and met the eyes of anyone who seemed to be disputing her, only long enough.

Other than stares and a few quick greetings to Deanna, they were left alone as they checked out the buffet and picked at shrimp and a few finger foods. She eyed the chocolate cake but bypassed it, taking him over to an out-of-the way table. He excused himself and went back for it, nudging against her back and shoulder as he set it beside her plate.

"Oh, I shouldn't. I've been horrible recently."

He followed her hand with his eyes, down to where she set it over her abdomen, and let them slowly move back to her face. "We'll work it off this weekend, not that I can tell you have anything that needs to be worked off." As he took his chair, he let his eyes drop again, to the beginning of cleavage above her low V-neck bodice and down to the fitted waist of the dress.

"Careful, soldier. You're in uniform." She leaned closer, daring him. "What you're thinking might get you in trouble."

"I'm in uniform at the moment. Won't be later." He skimmed the side of her neck with the back of a finger.

Someone behind them gasped. Deanna glanced at the woman and

leaned closer to his ear. "Think it's too soon to get out of here?"

"Yes. It's too soon. Haven't met *boss man* yet."

"Oh. Probably unnecessary. I'm sure he'll hear..."

"Not unnecessary. It's a big reason I'm here tonight."

"Fred..."

"Don't worry." He pierced the cake with his fork and offered the piece.

She kept his eyes as her lips caressed it off the prongs. "Hm, the one from the restaurant on our first date was far better. And I'd rather skip the office politics tonight and be home with you. Alone. Without the uniform."

"Soon." Daws pulled back and picked up a shrimp, glad she continued with her chocolate. He didn't want her to worry about every little pound. She'd stay in shape enough; he knew her that well. He'd never been attracted to stick figures. He liked her curves, and he wouldn't complain if there was ever a touch more of them. He wanted her to be able to indulge herself at times. Her spirit craved it. It was one of her best assets, the craving. The lust for full, vivid life. It showed in everything she did. He never wanted that to change.

With a need to distract himself from those thoughts, he scanned their surroundings, noting the looks and the avoidance, figuring he could tell which were employees and which were managers or more. Listening to bits of conversation he could make out around them. Funny how she talked about showing him off and then chose a table as far out of the main activity as possible.

"Mr. Bodin wants you."

Daws followed Deanna's gaze to the girl. Young. Casually dressed in skinny black pants and a baggy black shirt, with more earrings than ear and more attitude than experience.

"Does he?" Deanna's tone was friendly. She didn't dislike the girl, but she didn't introduce her. "He can come find me if he wishes. Thanks for relaying the message."

The girl glanced from Daws back to Deanna. "I think he wants you to come to his table."

"I wouldn't be surprised if he does, but I'm not at work. If he wants to speak with me, he can come to me."

"Really?" She shrugged. "I'll be glad to tell him that. The creep's a full-out jerk-off. Glad someone's got the balls to stand up to him."

Daws pushed his chair back and got up to hold Deanna's. "Let's oblige the man." Her eyes touched his and he knew she was about to argue. He leaned closer. "If you make someone think you're about to give in, the blow you deliver is far more effective than when they brace for it."

She still argued with her expression, but she gave in to him.

"Ah, Deanna." A skinny pasty-white man who appeared to be in his mid thirties stood and walked around the table. "We were just speaking of you." He threw a glance at Daws and dismissed him, taking Deanna's hand. "Come. Maybe your friend would like to go find more punch as we talk."

She pulled her hand away. "We're not staying long. Jacie said you wanted to see me."

Before Bodin could reply, a woman with taut skin and hair pulled high into a tight bun held in by some kind of black wrap-around thing took his side. She peered at Deanna. "So this is the girl I've heard so much about."

Deanna returned the stare. "I'm sorry. Have we met?"

The woman offered a few fingers disguised as a handshake. "We haven't. I'm Audrey Bodin, Todd's *wife*. I've been hearing about you from some of your colleagues."

They were being watched. Carefully. By everyone around.

"Then I'm at a disadvantage, since I only recently learned Mr. Bodin was married."

Bodin half choked and tried to make it sound like he was clearing his throat.

"Well." The woman glanced at her husband. "Yes, I know he doesn't like his personal life to mix with his work life. The two should be separate, don't you think?"

"I agree more than I can say." Deanna turned her gaze on her boss. "Was there something you needed since you called me over?"

With a quick silent warning, he forced a smile. "We were discussing the Hough project."

"Oh?"

"I mentioned to Mr. McCallister that a couple of the rough ideas were yours. He wasn't sure he'd met you."

An older gentleman with a friendly round face came up to Bodin's other side and extended a hand.

Deanna took it with a light dip of her head. "Mr. McCallister, it's a pleasure."

"Likewise. I'm afraid I don't keep up with my employees well enough. A shame not to have met such a charming one like yourself."

Daws shifted and the man turned to him. "And you are Deanna's...?"

"This is Fred Dawson." Deanna slid a hand up his back to behind his shoulder, showing possession.

McCallister offered a firm handshake. "An honor to meet one of our finest. Staff Sergeant, I'm guessing from your insignia. Am I right?"

"You are." Daws said nothing more for the moment as he wondered how the businessman knew his rank's symbol.

"You have been in for how long?"

"Ten years. Nearly eleven."

The man gave him a light nod. "And highly decorated. Impressive. Purple Heart. Glad to see it must have been a minor injury. Is that a bronze star?"

"It is."

"Admirable. Truly admirable. My father was military, an Air Force colonel when he retired. He hoped I'd follow in his footsteps. Bad knees prevented that. Fell off a horse I was warned not to ride. Lots of rehabilitation, and had to let him down on the lost Air Force career, but otherwise, it was worth every minute I stayed on that stallion."

Daws grinned, a light half-grin. "I imagine."

"Ever ride horses?"

"No. Grew up in the city. Went from there to the Army."

"I have." Deanna's soft voice joined them.

McCallister turned back to her. "You ride?"

"Used to as a child. Had my own, one dropped off at our place because he was too old to be *of use*. I claimed him. He still had plenty of strength for me."

McCallister smiled. "Always nice to meet a fellow horse lover. No surprise, then, that Todd has spoken highly of you."

"I have to say I'm surprised he has."

Daws stifled a grin as Bodin's back stiffened.

"Are you? He recognizes talent well, as I've found. He said a few ideas for the Hough campaign started with you, before he tweaked them, and there's a possibility for your growth within our company."

"Before he tweaked them?" She looked at her boss for a moment, at his eyes warning her to stay quiet. "Yes, well, no disrespect meant, but I'm not seeing much growth potential here. This is only a step for me. He was generous to say so, though." She threw Bodin another look.

"Oh?" McCallister watched the exchange. "Is marketing not your intended career? I was led to believe it was."

"Yes. I just think I'm going to take it in another direction. Or to another area. I like to have my possibilities open. Something that won't hold me down to one place, perhaps." She linked her hand back over Daws's arm. "In fact, Mr. Bodin, I intended to find you tonight, as well. I'm going to need the next two weeks off."

"Absolutely not. You've taken a fair bit of time off already. It would be unreasonable to allow since no one else has so much lenience."

"No one else works all weekend long for no pay, either."

Bodin cleared his throat as both his wife and McCallister questioned him silently. His expression was again a warning, but he recovered quickly. "Well, that. I am sorry it has taken so long to get your overtime for that weekend. It will be coming. It doesn't, however, allow for two weeks..."

"I'm not asking. I'm telling you I won't be here. Fred has time off for the holidays and I intend to spend it with him while I can. Fire me if you wish, but I won't be here."

Daws figured he was about to do just that when McCallister interrupted. "Todd, I think in this case we can make an exception. We allow our Guardsmen the time they need for their duty. We will do the same for Ms. Meyers."

"But, she's not..."

"You have your two weeks." McCallister cut him off. "If it goes beyond the time you've saved, I'm afraid it won't be paid vacation, but your job will be safe. And I do hope you'll reconsider staying with us. I have a feeling your chances of growth may not be as slow as Todd has suggested." With a nod at Bodin's wife, he wished them happy holidays and left.

Her boss moved in. "That was unnecessary. You should have come to me directly, and alone."

"You would have refused."

"That's my right."

"You and I both know it shouldn't be. Now if you'll excuse us, I've been here long enough and I need to pack."

"Deanna. This should be a private discussion, as it is work related."

Bodin's wife turned farther away to talk with another woman, although Daws knew she was close enough to hear every word, and would listen.

Deanna didn't budge. "I tell Fred everything, anyway. No need for more privacy than we have now."

Bodin eyed Daws, a touch of nervousness reflected in the thought, and glanced over at his wife. "Well then, let me just say I have put a good word or two in for you and you'll find that reflected in your bonus. Be sure to get it before you leave." The man's eyes dropped to her cleavage, only for a second.

"If you expect my gratitude, you're crazy, unless it includes the promotion you promised."

Bodin's wife cast her eyes over, only for a second.

"And I believe you must have misunderstood." He threw Daws a sly grin and raised his voice. "Why is it that we men have such a hard time communicating with the fairer sex?"

"You are so full of it..."

Daws squeezed her hand lightly with his arm. Too many were listening. "I have no trouble communicating with her. She has incredible comprehension skills. Any error in understanding would be on your part, not hers, my guess." He eyed Bodin long enough to be sure he knew which error Daws meant. Then he turned to Deanna. "Mind if I take you home now?"

She hesitated. Only for a second. "I would love for you to take me home now. But you should know that Todd understands very well what I say to him, and vice versa. It's a matter of concern, not of comprehension. Don't let him fool you. As if he could." She started away, mentioning she would go pick up her check and be right back, but she paused by Bodin's wife. "If you have questions about me, you should ask me, not the others in the office. And if we happen to meet again, which I doubt, don't call me *girl*. I'm not twelve and you're not my superior." Tossing her head, Deanna sauntered off, leaving the woman to gape after her.

When Bodin tried to slip away, Daws grabbed his arm and moved in close.

"Release me."

He squeezed harder. "Wouldn't struggle unless you want what I have to say to become very public."

"I have nothing to say to you. Except you're an idiot to play along with her little show and tell game. She's using you to get to me. Is that from a rental shop?"

Daws stepped closer. "I know you realize what you lost when you lost her. I also know you put your hands where they don't belong the other day. I strongly suggest you don't do it again, and if you want my credentials, call the 3/64th on Fort Drum and ask for Colonel Hitchcock. I'll let him know he's free to tell you about my training and capabilities. And I suggest you keep it in mind, because there is no one on earth I care about more than that woman. She is off limits to you. And I am never far away."

"Are you threatening me? Maybe I should turn you in to your *colonel*."

Daws released his arm. "My word against yours." With a warning glance, he walked away.

Deanna studied him when he took her side. "Everything all right?"

"It is. And it should be. Would you like to dance before we leave?"

She graced him with a smile and took him front and center on the small dance floor. Not only did she wrap her arms around his shoulder and play with his hair, but she sang some of the lyrics of *Unforgettable* along with Natalie Cole, and kissed him when it ended.

=======

Claiming the eighteen month old from Clara Jenkins, Deanna stroked his fine reddish blond hair. "Are you always this much of a handful? Or are you just excited about what Santa brought?" The baby studied her with a frown.

His mom assured her he was on his normal behavior, with a roll of the eyes. Deanna suggest Clara go relax with her husband and let her entertain the child. It had been some time since she'd held a little one. Still, it came right back to her, the way she'd spent so much time holding onto her youngest sibling who never wanted to be put down. The girl was … Deanna had to think about it … fifteen? Was that right?

"He looks comfortable with you."

She grinned at Fred as he came around from the hallway, back from whatever check he had to make. "Giving his mom a break. They're in there playing pool."

He took the chair behind the staff duty desk and made a notation on a chart. "You don't need to stay. As I said, I'll be in and out."

"Better than not seeing you all day. I did tell them whenever they want to go, I'm ready. I hope it's really okay as they say it is."

"I imagine. With no family around, there's not much else to do on a holiday. Especially since they're getting free help with the kid." He tousled the baby's hair. The child turned to look at him and made a lunge, arms out and reaching.

"Hey." Deanna threw her hands up as Fred caught him. "What's wrong with sitting with me?" She tried to take him back. He refused. "See? A good thing I don't want kids. They'd rather be with anyone else."

"It's the uniform. Looks like his dad. I've seen little ones run up and hug the wrong soldier's legs just because of the uniform." He caught the baby's frown. "Not me you want, is it?"

"Look at this."

Deanna turned toward the door and grinned. "Well hello, Private Anderson. Charlie, right?"

He returned the grin, his hand on a girl's back. "Yes, ma'am. Except I'm a specialist now. And you have the sergeant holding a baby. Now that's something to see. Getting him in practice for your own some day?"

"No." Deanna retrieved the baby as he fussed. "This is as far as I want to go with kids. And congratulations on the promotion."

"Thanks, but are you sure? 'Cause he could use one of those to help mellow him out."

"Ha." Clara Jenkins returned. "You only think it mellows you because you don't have any yet. Actually, it makes you tired and cranky. Come here, buster, and relax, you're fine." She cuddled the boy into her shoulder with a kiss to his head as Charlie introduced his date. "But look at the ring she got for Christmas. I'd say they're on track to this." She raised Deanna's hand to show off the delicate silver pearl and diamond ring.

Deanna couldn't help a grin. It was stunning, as was the way he gave it to her, on Christmas Eve, in front of the little tree she insisted they had to have, after he helped her decorate it. She'd been sitting on the floor adding the last of the tinsel to the bottom branches and he sat behind her, wrapped her in his arms, and told her he loved her. That he had from the night they met. And he slipped the ring onto her finger. Onto her left ring finger.

Charlie teased his sergeant about not getting a wedding invitation and told Deanna they were there to steal her away. "This is no way for you to spend Christmas. His own fault he has to if he didn't get out of it. Plenty owe him. No reason you should suffer."

"Oh. Well, I'm not exactly suffering, but he'll probably be just as glad I'm out of his way so he can work." She slid over and accepted Charlie's arm. "Where are we going?"

Charlie shrugged. "Here and there. If it's all right." He checked Fred's reaction.

"We're going with." Corporal Jenkins interrupted. "And Zakowsky and his wife and a couple of friends of theirs."

"Going where?" Fred frowned at the ringing phone and turned to answer. As he talked, Charlie told her quietly they'd all return together with Christmas dinner so she could spend it with him.

When he was off the phone, she went to give Fred a quick half hug.

He spoke into her ear. "If you'd rather not, say so and I'll take the blame."

"But you don't mind?"

"Not if you don't. As he said, no reason to be stuck here."

"Hm. I enjoy being stuck with you, Fred Dawson."

"And I'd argue for you to stay, but I have to run out again and long-term visitors are frowned upon while on duty. It's more relaxed on a holiday, but not exactly within regs."

"We'll make up for it tomorrow." She gave him a kiss in front of his ear and left him to work.

========

Daws stroked a strand of hair from her face and thought about how comfortable she was in his world. She'd readily agreed to the New Year's party Captain Hodgkins threw at his on-post quarters for any of his company who wanted to drop in. Even for officer's quarters, it was hardly big enough for as many as showed. The pale mustard yellow WW2-era box house with a tiny screened porch looked like every other house in the officer's section, with white walls and over-shellacked wood floors and the captain's rank and last name boasting its temporary ownership beside the front door. His wife had it decorated as personally as possible, though, and it was as homey as any post housing was.

Deanna wasn't bothered by the crowd. She laughed when his men gave her their regrets for having to start the New Year with him and hoped the rest of it would be better for her. As she laughed, she held him tighter and said she'd manage all right.

They complained when Daws said they were leaving. Early. But he wanted to be alone with her at midnight. He barely had her inside their apartment before she showed him he'd made the right decision.

He hoped the nightmares were done for the rest of her visit. He'd had them twice in the week and a half she'd been there. It worried her. He could see it did, although he insisted he rarely had them anymore. It annoyed him to no end that they had to be more frequent when she was there than when she wasn't. Still, it was damn nice to have her there calming him afterward. Waking up alone from them made it much harder to recover and return to sleep. Often, he didn't.

She breathed deeply, her body pressed against his, and he kissed her head. "Anna. It's one minute until midnight."

"Mm, is it?" She kissed his chest, her warm breath whispering onto his bare skin.

Daws rolled her onto her back, gently, and propped himself up to where he could see her face.

She turned her head toward the window. "It's raining." The building's security lights cast a glow through the drops as they filtered toward the ground. She turned back with a grin. "The earth's playing our song."

He raised his eyebrows in question and waited.

"It was raining when we met. A new beginning for us both. I think it's appropriate we begin our first new year together with rain. Should we go out in it?"

"No."

She chuckled. "You're sure? I'll warm you up again."

"It's more sleet than rain. I say we watch it from here."

With another glance to the side, she returned her gaze, slid her hand up around his head and pulled him closer. "It's midnight."

He leaned down into her. Her grip tightened around him.

The train started to board as snowflakes settled onto Deanna's hair like powdered sugar on an unfrosted half-burnt spice cake.

"I'll come back as soon as I can." She rested a hand just below his shoulder and shivered.

"You should board, Anna. Get warm."

"Not until I have to. Any idea how much I'll miss you?"

He nodded. Yes, he had an idea.

"I could still quit, you know, just stay here."

He forced a deep breath. "Don't tempt me."

"Freddy..."

"Keep working on the direction you want to go. If you're ready to quit, do that, and start that business of your own. Don't worry if it takes a while to get going. It doesn't matter. I'll be back in the city before long. Need to make an appointment with the accountant. I want you to have access to my accounts while I'm oversees..."

"Oh. No. I don't need you to support me. I've always supported myself..."

"Anna, I want you to redesign the loft. I've never liked the furniture in it. I don't want it to be theirs anymore. I want it to be ours. Redecorate it. New furniture, new curtains, new paint ... whatever you want, other than knocking down walls. Will you do that for me?"

"But, what if you don't like what I choose? You want me to send samples or pictures?"

"No. I want you to wait until I go to Korea and just do it. We'll set up a budget and anything you want to do with that, go ahead. Hire who you need to help. Painters, designers ... whatever you need."

"Fred..."

"I trust you, Anna."

She hesitated. "I think that's the first time anyone's ever said that to me."

He stroked the hair back away from her face, melting the flakes of snow in his path. "Will you do it?"

"Well ... how about if we talk about what you like and what you don't first. I can't do it without your feedback, without at least knowing..."

"Okay. We have until spring to talk about it. Ask what you want until then. But I trust your judgment. We also have until spring to teach you to drive. I'm leaving the car with you." He held her in close and kept her as warm as possible until the last call to board.

PART 2

"In the final choice, a soldier's pack
is not so heavy as a prisoner's chains."
General Dwight D. Eisenhower

She waited through four rings and then could barely hear his greeting through loud background music she only somewhat recognized. "What are you listening to?"

"Deanna. Hold on."

She hoped she hadn't called at the wrong time. They'd already talked once. She wasn't due to call him again until their "dinner date" as they'd set it up. Saturday nights at six, they would meet on the phone as they ate, and pretend they were at the same table. It was Freddy's idea, when she told him much of what she missed when they were apart was talking with him over dinner.

At home, before she moved to New York, dinner meant "grab what you can before the men get it all and eat silently and quickly." It was a running joke in their family. She never thought it was funny. She liked to linger over a nice meal, not shove it down her throat fast enough she wouldn't be hungry all night.

The music quieted and Deanna pushed the thought from her head.

"Hey, sorry."

She wanted to touch him. "Don't be. I'm calling unexpectedly. Is it okay? What did I interrupt?"

"Always okay. Working out. Nearly didn't hear the phone."

"Hm, wish I was there to work out with you, or just watch you work out. That'd be nice, too. Want me to call back? Or you can when you're done."

"I'm done enough. What's up?"

"Nothing." She sank into his big chair. "Wanted to hear your voice. Now that I did, I'll let you go."

A pause. "Wish you wouldn't."

Her body stiffened. "Wouldn't what? Call just to hear your voice?"

"Anna, you can call anytime. Stop apologizing when you do. I meant I wish you wouldn't let me go. I was working out to try to keep from thinking how much I want you here. This is more helpful."

A deep breath took over and she stared at her ring. She had to stop thinking any day would be the day he changed his mind. "Good. Although I'd still love to sit and watch. Admire. Gawk. Whatever you want to call it. And nothing's wrong, before you ask."

A light chuckle came across the line. "What have you been doing today?"

"Going through decorating magazines. Still think I should do this for you while you're not here to supervise?"

"No doubt in my mind."

"Brave man."

"It's just furnishings."

"Yeah. Guess after everything else you've dealt with...." She let that thought slip away. Almost. "How are you sleeping?"

A pause. "Not as well as when you were here, but well enough."

She grinned and shifted in the chair. "No nightmares?"

"No."

"Good." Deanna searched for something to talk about. Decorating, maybe. But she planned to do that over dinner, after she pulled a few more ideas together. "So, I'm trying to figure out what you were listening to. Sounds familiar, but not quite. Hard to tell over the phone."

"Queen. *Innuendo.* Their last album. Came out just before I left for Saudi. Listened to it a lot for a few days. A year ago. Hard to believe it was only a year ago."

"Long year, huh? I haven't heard that one. Maybe I should."

"Has some darkness to it. He was sick and nearing the end."

"Maybe something lighter would help those nightmares better."

"Don't know. I like the purging quality, and the sound is incredible, vocally and musically. Good listen."

She nodded. She hadn't wanted to go there, to talk about anything heavy. But maybe he did. He had, to some extent, over the holidays, as they cuddled together at night. He gave her hints of what he saw in his nightmares, but only hints.

"I'll bring it to you in April."

"Oh." Deanna shifted again. "You don't want to take it to Korea?"

"No. I'll be taking most of my music to the apartment before I leave. You might plan plenty of CD and album storage while designing. And space for some cassettes I still have hanging around."

"Okay." She couldn't help but grin. That, Deanna had already thought of. She'd spent time scanning his collection while she was there, getting a feel for what he liked. A bit of a lot of things, all at the quality end of the scale rather than the more popular. Some she'd never heard of. A few he'd played for her. There wasn't any she didn't enjoy, but then there was hardly any music she didn't enjoy to some extent.

When she started to get the idea he wanted off the phone, to either finish his workout or shower, Deanna said she looked forward to their dinner date, unless she'd bothered him enough already.

He insisted she keep their date as promised.

She shouldn't have called. Now Deanna had the image of him at his weight bench, his muscles flexing, straining. And the times she'd sat and watched him, how she'd joined in his workouts, how many weights he'd removed before she could lift the bar, and how she'd tried to distract him once by lying on top of him while he was doing pushups. How it didn't stop him. How amazed she was that he could continue with her weight added.

How she wanted him home with her.

=======

A good thing he liked to drive.

Daws pulled into the hotel parking area and checked the time. Traffic was good; he still had an hour until he met with the A & R Rep he'd coaxed to Vermont. Grabbing his duffle, he forced civility, mostly, through a slow check in, accepted his room key, and headed the pointed direction. On his way up, he considered that he may have been ruder than necessary. But he was exhausted in between not sleeping well and trying to get over the remnants of a flu. He nearly canceled Vermont until another weekend. There wasn't much time left before he would be out of country, though. He couldn't risk waiting.

He was glad he'd had time to give Deanna a quick call after he showered and dressed. Although not personally crazy about Mister A & R, Daws admitted he seemed to know his stuff, and he was willing to share information. The guy insisted on picking up the dinner tab, which he would forward to the record company, gave Daws a few contact names for a possible job in the near future, and talked about some of the acts he'd pulled into the company. Impressive list, if he could be believed. There wasn't much point in not believing him, since Daws would know if he'd been worth contacting by whether or not he had interest in Ryan, regardless of who he'd found before.

He took his own car to the show. Daws wasn't about to be tied to the guy's whims of when he wanted to leave, and he couldn't risk being in the car with him if he drank while he worked. Lack of judgment was not a valued attribute for NCOs. He didn't suppose it would be for his new intended direction, either.

The guy spent more time flirting with the waitress than listening to Ryan. He complained about the bassist. Daws agreed but said the bassist didn't matter; it was only Ryan he had been called to check out. Still, he commented on what he liked and didn't about the other band members, admitted the boy had a decent enough voice for a bar act, but shrugged off anything else.

"He has a couple of big name managers biting to represent him."

Daws was stretching the truth horribly, since the 'big names' were only big locally, so Ryan's mentor informed him, and neither had experience in New York or L.A., but this guy wasn't paying enough attention.

"Yeah? Names?"

"Can't say that without their permission. Nothing in stone yet."

"Uh huh." He tossed back the rest of his drink. And he shrugged again, folding his arms on the table. "Well. I might be interested in another couple of years or so, when he's had a chance to grow up. Depends. Some of them get worse as they get older, not better. Kind of have a feeling that'll be the case with this one. Not worth putting my reputation on the line for. Not yet, anyway. If he improves, in another year or so, call me. I'll see if I have time to get back this way." He shoved his chair back, stood, and offered a hand. "Nice yakking with you. Good luck, but don't get your hopes up. He's a dime a dozen. I can find one like him in every town." With another shrug, he walked away.

A dime a dozen. No. Maybe the guy was a professional, maybe he was well trained in what labels wanted, but this time, he was wrong. His loss. There were plenty more where he came from.

Deanna sniffed and shuffled into the bathroom to grab a new tissue box. Stupid people who had to go to work sick. She was sure more than once her head would just go ahead and explode if she pressed a finger anywhere on her face. And that might be preferable to having to swallow one more time. Gargling with salt water three times during the day hadn't helped an iota, that she could tell.

Stupid cold season. Why couldn't they make a medicine that actually worked without knocking her out?

At least they could tell when she called in sick that she was.

She also cancelled her weekend plans. Even if she felt better, she wouldn't risk passing it along.

This time when Deanna met a few women at Cheap Shots, she'd mentioned her Army boyfriend, on purpose, to get their reactions. They'd asked to meet him, and whether he was "super buff," and how "well armed" he was. She was supposed to meet up with them again over the weekend. That would have to wait.

Plopping the tissue box on the night stand, she crawled under the covers.

A ringing in her ears woke her. It wasn't in her ears. The phone. In the living room. Deanna considered ignoring it but checked the time. After six. Freddy.

She fought the muscle aches to force herself to go answer. It had stopped. She'd heard his voice, a message. She hit his number and took the phone back to the bedroom. "Hey, sorry. I'm here." She cringed at the pain in her throat.

"You're not feeling any better."

"No. But I'll live. How was your day?"

"Anna, go to the doctor. It's been three days. You should be better."

"Can't. No energy to walk to the bus stop."

"Call a taxi."

"For that either."

"You don't have anyone there who'll take you?"

"No. It's okay. A virus. They can't fix that. Waste of time to go."

"Deanna..."

"It's okay. I always take care of myself. Somehow, I live anyway." She slid beneath the covers. It was too cold.

"Should I come?"

Tears filled her eyes. Yes, she wanted him there, but it would use leave days and take away from how long he could stay in April before his year of being overseas. "No. I'll be okay tomorrow. Sorry. Can't talk. It hurts."

"Okay, go back to sleep, but be sure you're keeping fluids in. You can't get better without them."

Maybe that was her problem. She'd hardly had anything for three days. Too tired to bother. "Okay."

"Hang up now, Anna. Don't answer me again. Get water or chicken broth or something, then go back to sleep. I'll check on you later. Just hang up now so I can hear that you did."

She didn't argue. Hanging up, she tried to make herself go get water, but closed her eyes instead.

Daws paced. She had no one. He knew she'd just met a couple of women she hoped could become friends, but he also knew they weren't friends enough she'd ask them for help.

And he couldn't go. He was getting his E5-P ready to take over his job when he left. Points would drop soon. There was a growing shortage of E6s. The man had to be ready by April so Daws could go on leave without hassle. Before he had to leave Deanna for a year.

An hour later, he called her back, heard the gruff hello. "Hey Anna, don't talk. In a few minutes, someone will be at the door. I had chicken soup delivered. There should be enough for tonight and tomorrow. It's already paid and they'll leave it at the door. Just stay on the phone with me until I know you have it. Don't talk. But eat tonight, even if you only want the broth. At least do that."

"Freddy?"

He frowned at the pain he heard. "Yes?"

"Thank you."

"Don't thank me. Just get better. That's an order."

Scooping up all of her sketches, her ideas, her logos she thought had real potential, Deanna dumped them in the garbage.

One year. During that year he'd be away, she wasn't doing one thing more than she had to in order to keep her job, her paycheck. Her creative urges would go entirely into redecorating the apartment.

He would be home in three weeks. Before he left her for a year.

A whole year, minus three weeks in between. Deanna was sure they would go much faster than the next three would, while she waited for him to get there. And much faster than the rest of the year-long assignment.

What made the Army think taking them away for a year at a time was okay? What was the saying she'd heard from another wife on base? If the Army wanted you to have a family, they'd issue you one.

She grabbed a deep breath. Other women did it all the time. So could she. And at least she didn't have kids to worry about. Although, if she did, at least she'd have company every evening. And those Army wives had each other. Deanna knew they looked out for each other. What did she have? She wasn't one of them. She wasn't an Army wife, only a girlfriend. In the city by herself.

Going out "man hunting" with Jenn and the others the night before had been a huge mistake – one more huge mistake. Deanna enjoyed her new friends. They were fun to hang around even if she didn't quite connect and they didn't always understand her thoughts. One of them mentioned how "artsy" people were just different, with a friendly smile. Deanna figured it was meant as a compliment, but it wasn't quite. She wasn't looking to be different. She was looking for others who understood.

Even so, she agreed when they asked her to go bar hopping. *Man hunting.* Deanna refused until Jenn said she could be their antenna. Since she wasn't looking for a man herself, she could help them decipher which might be safely dateable. The thought nearly made her laugh out loud, considering her brilliant judgment calls in the past. Still, she did finally hit a BINGO so they figured that was qualification enough.

And she was tired of being home alone all weekend. Not to mention, she didn't want them to give up on her completely.

She shouldn't have gone.

On top of the *artsy types* conversation that threw her too far back into the idea of being *different* that she'd worked too hard to avoid, it took little time for the other girls to find guys to hang out with for the evening. Deanna was too often left alone sipping her hard lemonade, too often hit on. Her friends said it wouldn't hurt to at least dance with a guy now and then, to have some fun. They didn't get it. If she did, she'd either have to tell Freddy or not tell him. Neither was a good option. If she told him, he'd worry about her out dancing with other guys the year he would be away. If she didn't tell him, it would be constantly on her mind, nagging her for hiding it. It wasn't worth it.

She called it a night early.

It didn't matter. Freddy would be home soon. He would take her out.

The three weeks were going far too fast. Two of them were already gone.

Deanna had coaxed Fred out to the dance floor when he'd grinned about her singing to Lynyrd Skynyrd. He liked the music. He preferred slow dances. But he gave in to her.

Making it easy on him, she pretended *Sweet Home Alabama* was slow dance music and held her arms over his shoulder. Todd had made fun of her the one time he caught her listening to the southern rock band. He said it showed her hillbilly roots. She'd turned it up louder and ignored him. He'd gone out by himself to find somewhere "more cultured."

Idiot. All he knew about music was what he was "supposed to" listen to, for appearances. He didn't feel it.

She shoved him back out of her thoughts. He hadn't been worth her time in the first place; he sure wasn't now.

Fred's fingers alongside her face and around the back of her neck pushed the moron farther out. Her eyes closed in response. It always did that to her: the way he caressed her nape, so softly, lovingly. He knew it did. She loved that he would do it even knowing she wouldn't be able to be with him when they went home. Stupid female complications. They could have waited until he left.

Still, he caressed her just as much, kissed her just as often, held her against his body at night. He'd even waited on her when she didn't want to move, and brought pain reliever. Since he'd never had a live-in, Deanna wasn't sure how he'd react. He never once even complained about it interrupting their time.

The song ended and merged into an actual slow dance.

"Are you okay or do you want to sit down?"

She smiled up at him. "I'm fine. But thank you for thinking to ask. How did you learn to be so understanding of women? Since you weren't close to your mom?"

He nuzzled his face against hers. "My sister spent plenty of time lecturing me as I was growing up about how a girl should be treated, whatever the situation. She was very open."

"Did she? Good for her. A shame you aren't still close."

"We were never close. She had a string of boyfriends. When they upset her, I heard about it, as though it was my fault for being male."

Deanna couldn't help but chuckle. "Well, I'm only half sorry you did, because it sure is nice for me. How selfish is that?"

He grinned and kissed her.

Deanna held him close, trying to grasp every moment they had together. How could she let him leave for a year? Not a year; six months. Twice in a row. She'd make herself think about six months and the three following weeks. The other half, she'd think about when the time came.

She was glad to be home again, and went directly to the bedroom to find her sweats. When she returned, he had two mugs of instant cappuccino waiting, and he held her against his side.

Jenn and company had finally shown up. They didn't often go to the little club that was a step up in atmosphere from Cheap Shots and a few steps down from Verlaine's, but Freddy liked it. So did she. Deanna said they would be there if the girls were actually interested in meeting him. Then she nearly wished she hadn't.

If she was the blushing type, she would have been beet red when Jenn told him Deanna had mentioned he was "very well armed" and Jenn was impressed that his build didn't hide other shortcomings. Fred raised his eyebrows as he met Deanna's gaze, but he didn't look embarrassed. He told her, in front of them, he was glad she was satisfied with his full armature.

Sergeant Dawson was also not the blushing type. If she hadn't been sure before, the night at the club settled it.

As they settled in, he told her he was glad she'd found what seemed a nice group of friends, some she could probably trust. She knew what he meant. He was glad she wouldn't be fully alone while he was away. For a year. Six months. Only six months. Then she'd deal with the rest of it.

=======

"I have to go, Anna." Daws held her face in his palms and touched his lips to hers.

She nodded but showed no sign she was about to release him.

"I'll call when I get to Vermont."

"I think I should resent the kid for taking a half day away from me just so you can check on him."

"It's not his fault. He doesn't even know."

"I know." She sighed. "But if he'd grow up and stop acting like a jerk, you wouldn't be so worried..."

"He will." Daws hoped the bits of maturity he'd started to see would continue to grow, anyway. He thought they would, if the boy was handled right. "He's sixteen next month. Still a kid. Still angry. But I see a lot of potential. And I owe it to the major..."

"Somehow I think you've gone way past that by now." Deanna ran a hand up his chest.

"How's that?"

"I think you're starting to care about the kid, just for who he is, not because of the request."

Daws couldn't quite deny it, but he wouldn't admit it, either. It was business. A favor. No more. Well, possibly more in time. The kid would need help on his way up. Daws was working on positioning himself to be part of it. He'd spent too many of his off-duty hours trying to figure out just how to do it. He was making some good headway with his next career. The farther he delved in, the more he wanted to jump into his next phase.

He didn't particularly want to go to Korea. During the past eleven years, he'd lived in Germany for eighteen months and toured several of the surrounding countries. He'd lived in Colorado, Texas, and Alaska. He'd done training in Virginia and South Carolina. He enjoyed the travel, the new places and faces and experiences. He was interested in seeing another country, in learning about it from within. He wasn't, however, interested in leaving her alone for a year or in leaving all of the work of looking after Ryan to whoever he could trust to help.

That bothered him maybe more than anything else. Deanna was strong and capable and she'd be fine. The major's boy ... was still horribly rebellious. Daws decided he had to go speak to the brother. Watching in obscurity and recruiting others to do the same had become too much like stalking for his taste. Still, he didn't want the boy to know he was being watched. At least Daws didn't want him to know *he* was watching. It could hamper his future plans.

"Hey." Deanna's voice pulled him back. "It's all right, you know. I've already accepted that this kid will be part of your life, at least for several years to come. I was joking about resenting him. I don't."

He kissed her. "I know. And yes, I expect he will be. Unless he tells me to take a hike. Always possible."

"He doesn't know..."

"He will. When I get back. One of the first things I plan to do."

"Well." She ran her hands up around his neck. "You better come find me first or I will resent him for sure."

"Guaranteed. And keep October free."

"Oh don't worry, soldier. I'll be here waiting with open arms."

Something inside him wanted to argue, to not allow himself to believe she would be. "Hope you won't change your mind."

Her head shook and she kissed him. Full force. No holds barred.

He had to catch his breath when she released him.

"I won't change my mind. I am your other half, Fred Dawson. You might as well accept that." With a deep breath, she backed up and took his hands. "And you better go while I'm still willing to let you. I know you don't want an AWOL on your record."

For a brief second, he wasn't sure he didn't. "Take care of yourself. Keep that number handy. Andrews is right here in the city and he'd be glad to help if you need. Don't hesitate."

"Fred, I told you I'm not..."

"I know what you said, but I want to make sure you know you can. I kept the man from cutting his own foot off, at least. He won't mind helping you for me. Hold on to that number."

"Okay."

With a light nod, he forced himself to open the door. And he hesitated.

"It's all right." She ran a hand over the side of his head. "Just take care of yourself and call me when you can." Deanna gave him a soft kiss, slow and gentle, and then ran her thumb over his lips. "I love you. And I'll be here."

Damn, he didn't want to leave her. He felt himself nod again, an attempt to act like it was all right. "It'll make everything easier knowing you are." He brushed her lips briefly and set his forehead against hers. "I love you, too, Anna."

He pulled into Bennington thinking about the look on her face as he walked away from her, out the door. Strong, resolved ... strained. Holding everything in. But what else could she do? When he told her at the beginning he didn't want to make things harder for her, this was what he meant. She'd said she didn't care. But how could she have known? They never knew what they were getting into when they made vows to soldiers. Warnings and stories could only do so much. Living it was entirely different. He'd seen it; he'd seen spouses come in full of knowledge they were strong and could live on their own when necessary, the excitement, the pride, the love for their soldiers so obvious. Daws had seen the same proud starry-eyed girls change in as little as two years, though usually longer, sometimes up to ten years for the more stalwart. Until it hit them how much time they were alone and how much time alone or not they spent worrying, about money, about moving, about living in places they hated in tin cans substituting for homes, about the reality of the dangers their husbands faced they tried hard not to see, not to allow in their thoughts. How they'd given so many of their "best" years to men who were hardly around, always tired, who worked late and went home grouchy, who usually helped with the kids as they could but wanted that to be playtime, not parent/discipline time. They had enough of that during the day.

Single women could go to clubs and flirt and date when they felt alone. When they needed companionship. Soldiers' wives had to be more careful. Their actions could easily undo their husbands, not only career-wise, but personally. It could so easily devastate them to hear rumors of what their wives may be doing, even if they weren't actually doing anything. It only took being in the wrong place with a man and one person to see it and assume. Not to mention they often had family pulling at them to come home. And they had kids much of their family had never even seen because of distance and money restraints. And they always had to be guarded around anyone non-military, to be careful about what they said, to always consider security in every conversation. Many opted to avoid communication with civilians for that reason; it was easier. They stuck with military friends. The ones who understood.

Daws had seen it build to explosion point too often. He'd seen them age three times as fast as other girls who didn't have to become so fully responsible so fast with so little help available.

At least some of those things, Deanna didn't have to deal with. She didn't have kids. She never talked about her family so he had to figure they weren't pulling at her. She had a nice apartment, a career of her own – something that was hard to find for those moving every three years or thereabout. Her friends were likely to stay right there, also, once she found them.

Her biggest concern because of his job would be the lack of male companionship. It did matter to her. He knew how much it did. It was the only thing that really worried him. Of course she could still go out and dance, even flirt. Being away from base meant no one to spread rumors on base. And she wasn't twenty. She was twenty-eight, already fully adult. Already out on her own.

Still. Six months was a hell of a long time.

He would do what he could to still be there for her. The first bouquet of flowers would be delivered to her later that night. Yellow cannas. Light. Fun. With a card saying he was thinking of her. In five days when he was on the plane heading overseas, the white cannas would arrive. He'd left money and instructions with Andrews, now a scaffold-climbing civilian again, to add to the deliveries at certain times.

Daws wasn't at all sure she'd actually call Andrews if she needed help. She was too thoroughly independent-minded. Not a bad thing, except it bothered him. Maybe he would give his former soldier instructions to drop in now and then. Would she mind?

Deciding to consider it later, he followed the little side roads that led to the major's house. It was a school day. Ryan wouldn't be home. Will was expecting him. He wasn't sure what kind of reception he'd get, since he hadn't told Will or Mrs. Reynauld yet that he'd had Ryan watched, but he figured if it was her husband's idea, she might understand.

Memories of the funeral flashed through his head upon seeing the house. It was a small white and black square, neat and well landscaped, but without much adornment. The major had often said his wife wasn't terribly feminine. A former lieutenant herself, she valued neatness and precision more than decoration. Still, Daws would have expected more ... something.

A dog barked when he pulled in the drive. Daws didn't see it, but he remained aware as he got out of the rental. His old Chevy was parked in his building's garage, for Deanna. She'd learned fast and was a natural. Still, she was doubtful she'd use it other than driving around the garage to keep it from sitting idle, after she had a friend take her in to turn the permit into a license. He hoped she would soon.

A glimpse of the barking animal showed him on a chain at the side of the house.

"*Hunter*, knock it off." Will Reynauld stepped out onto the concrete slab that served as a tiny porch. "Don't mind him. He's been running wild and isn't happy about being chained. We're trying to find him a home where he can run around a yard. This one, too." He picked up an orange and white cat that circled his feet. "And where have you been? We've been looking for you." He returned his gaze to his visitor. "Hope you're not bothered by animals."

"Not if they aren't bothered by me. I'm Fred Dawson..."

"I recognized you. Will Reynauld." He offered his hand. "Come on in."

Daws gave the house a quick scan as he followed through a small entry into a small living area. It was more than the outside ... more homey, more comfortable. Quaint. It still didn't fit his image of the major's wife.

"So you're headed to Korea? Dad did a year there. Have a seat. Mom'll be down in a minute."

"Thank you. Yes, he said he did. Recommended it to any of his soldiers who were single." Daws accepted an arm chair that looked like it wouldn't sink too far down.

"You were close to him, from what Mom said." The young man perched at the edge of the couch and stroked the cat he set in his lap.

Daws didn't answer, since he couldn't figure an appropriate way to answer.

"And you were there?" Will's face tightened. "At the crash site. We were told he wasn't alone, that you were with him."

"Yes." Daws wondered just how much they were told, if they knew he was the one in charge of bringing the choppers in and maybe if he'd done it sooner, or later...

"Staff Sergeant Dawson."

He stood at the woman's voice and held his place as she came toward him. "Mrs. Reynauld. Good to see you again."

She accepted his hand and held it with both of hers. "We were surprised at your request to visit, but we're very glad to have you."

"I hope it's not an intrusion..."

"Not at all. Any friend of Ed's is always welcome."

"Thank you, ma'am."

"How about coffee? William, did you offer the man anything to drink?"

"No. I'm sorry." He coerced the cat to the floor and stood. "Look who I found, by the way. On the porch."

Mrs. Reynauld gave it a frown. "Out creating more homeless kittens, in all likelihood. You need to call today for an appointment to get him fixed since you haven't found him a home yet." She turned back to Daws. "Sorry about the zoo around here. This one's heart is far too soft and he keeps bringing in strays. I do wish he'd wait until we find a bigger place. Go put him in the back room and tell that dog to hush." She motioned toward the chair Daws had been using. "Please. Is coffee all right? We have tea..."

"Coffee would be good, if it's made. Don't bother otherwise. I won't be in your way long." He did sit again as requested.

"Oh, it's usually made. One of my bad habits I don't feel the need to change." She lowered onto the couch beside where Will had been.

"May I ask how you and your sons have been?"

She grinned, a sly quick grin. "It's my understanding you know how we've been."

"Ma'am?"

"It's all right, Sergeant. I know Edward asked you to watch over us. Captain Hodgkins said we should call if we needed anything and you'd likely be the one to take care of it."

He nodded. Maybe she knew about Ryan then, as well.

"And thank you. It is comforting to know we weren't simply pushed aside now that..." She dropped her eyes, only a moment. When she raised them, she was in full control again. "As I believe I said at the funeral, Ed did speak of you often, and a couple of others. The other two, we haven't heard from at all, not that I expected it. However, from the way he always spoke of you, I was comforted in knowing you were at his side during the war. And when his helicopter went down." She accepted a cup from Will and waited while he handed the other to Daws.

"I did wash my hands. There's no cat hair."

Daws threw him a grin. "I'm not that particular. Thank you."

Mrs. Reynauld set a hand on her son's shoulder as he sat next to her. "William has been a real life saver, not only since the funeral but consistently whenever his father was away. My right hand man."

"Yes, I heard." He took a swallow of the coffee. Nice and strong, stronger than he expected. "And are you still attached to the young woman who was at your side?"

"Tracy. We're engaged. But we're trying to take it slow so Mom doesn't go into total shock."

She gave him a friendly scowl. "You're too young."

"I'm nearly twenty-two. How old was Dad?"

"Never mind." She returned her gaze to Daws. "She's a lovely girl. It's hard to think of, though, when it's your baby making such a leap instead of yourself." With another loving glance at her son, she took a sip of coffee. "Are you married, Sergeant?"

"No, ma'am. Not married."

"And no children?"

"No."

Mrs. Reynauld considered that for a moment. "I've never been sure whether that's harder or easier. For the single soldiers, that is. To not have to worry about leaving someone behind when duty calls or to not have someone waiting for you. Ed and I met and married so young, we hardly had a chance to know anything else."

Daws grabbed a breath before he tried to answer. "I do have a girlfriend I'm leaving for the next year. This is our first long separation so I suppose I'll find out."

"And she'll wait for you?" Mrs. Reynauld seemed hesitant to ask.

"Yes. I have no doubt she will." At least he kept telling himself, since he drove away from her earlier, that he had no doubt.

A smile preceded another swallow, which she used to switch gears. "So tell us, is there a particular reason for your visit or did you simply tire of checking in on us through others?" A twinkle in her eye belied an attempted scold.

"I do hope you understand, it's only because the major insisted. I promised him..."

"She's teasing." Will threw a sideways glance at his mom. "We're not bothered that you do."

"Well. I think it may be more than you realize." At her raised eyebrows, Daws decided he better clarify. He explained about the major's last words and how he had the local Guardsman helping to watch Ryan through track practices and such. How he'd gone to that show not expecting much, but finding a mark of true music talent.

Marianne Reynauld nodded. "Yes. I hear him improving all the time."

"He also has good stage presence. A good voice."

"Does he? He's never let us hear him sing."

Daws took a long swallow of his coffee. "I think he could get somewhere in music. I plan to try to help him. But I did want to speak with you first. To let you know..."

"You plan to help him how?"

"Soon after my tour I'll be due to reenlist. I've been looking at other options. Mainly within the music industry. I'm from New York City and plan to settle there. I've been making contacts, researching..."

"All of this because Ed made you promise? I'm quite sure he didn't intend you to go to so much trouble, or to pull you out of the Army."

"I don't consider it trouble, and it's not the only reason. As I mentioned, I have a girlfriend. She's settled in the city with her career. Between the two.... I don't have permanent plans yet, only considering. With your permission, I'd like to help guide Ryan as he moves toward his music path, watch out for him..."

"He's not easy to deal with." Will eyed him, trying to figure out what he really wanted, Daws supposed.

"I can see that. He's hardly the first young man I've had to handle with both kid gloves and a lot of patience."

"Why are you doing this, Sergeant? What is your interest beyond your promise to my husband?"

In order to explain, he would have to delve deeper into his own history than he wanted. But she wasn't a woman to talk around. "To be honest, I see a lot of the major in him. I also see a lot of myself in him. I see him walking the line between two paths, the same as I was when the major saw it and pulled me to one side. I could have easily stepped the other direction. I don't mean any offense, but I think Ryan could be ... wavering at the moment..."

She nodded, more emotion seeping through. "Yes. We see it. It scares me every day of my life."

"I'd like to step in and try to pull him to the path that will let him follow his passion. Something he can throw himself into heart and soul. I think he's leaning that direction, anyway, but I want to help make sure he is. As the major did for me."

Marianne Reynauld remained silent, her fingers twisting the wedding ring on her finger. Then she nodded. "If Ed trusted you with him, so do I. But there are things you should know. How long can you stay?"

"Until there's a chance he'll be home. I don't want him to know yet." He saw an objection coming. "I'm headed out of country for the next year. There's no point in trying to build any kind of trust with him until I can be around for him. It won't work. With some it might. I have a feeling, though..."

"No, you're right. He's..." She hesitated.

Will didn't. "He's a leech. Very needy. Demanding. And don't get me wrong, I adore the kid and I love him to death, but yeah, you tell him now you'll be here and then you're not, it won't work. He's still plenty mad at Dad for not being here when they'd planned so many things, even if he knows it was an accident. He's still angry. Not only that, but he resents having to leave the friends he made on Drum. He doesn't make real friends easily. The attitude hides what's underneath. He used to get picked on a lot, because of his build, because he was always the new kid and he has such a sweet natural personality that girls like a lot, but other boys didn't. He learned to hide that with his smartass attitude. Still doesn't get along well with most guys because of it, but they ignore him instead of picking on him. He had finally made several very close friends just off post and resents that we had to leave. Won't even try here. Says he's not staying long enough to bother."

Will sighed. "Another reason we're taking the wedding plans slow. I'm afraid it'll be hard on him for me to move out." He looked over at his mom.

It was a story Daws had heard often: kids shutting others out or clinging to whoever they could find in between their moves. Sometimes they got lucky and made good, helpful, supportive friends. Many times their new "friends" led them straight into trouble. Losing his dad at that moment in his life...

"It'll be between us until you get back." Mrs. Reynauld gave him a gridlock stare. "And then what?"

"Then I arrange to run into him at one of his shows. He won't know we talked. He won't know his father asked me to watch him. I'm sure it sounds underhanded and I don't typically work that way, but it's the only way I can do this. Not so as it looks like a favor. It needs to look all business, at least until I think he's ready for the full truth."

"And you plan to take him deeper into the music business?" She looked wary.

"I plan to be there when he decides to go deeper. He will. Whether I help or not. He'll get there."

She frowned. "You think he has that much talent?"

"Yes. And the charisma to go with it. I think he'll do well."

"Funny." She shook her head. "We'd talked about whether he might follow our footsteps. He's incredibly smart, which is something you probably haven't seen. His dad thought West Point might be a good idea. Will thought he might head toward teaching since he's always been good at helping his classmates who were struggling. And he volunteers during the summer at the rec center working with boys. Or he used to. Music, we never saw coming. Until someone dropped off that old guitar."

Daws tried not to react, since he wasn't sure Mrs. Reynauld was happy about Ryan's direction. "I was opposite. My parents constantly pushed artsy things at me, told me the only way to make a real difference was to add something of beauty to the world. I didn't disagree, but I have no talent for it."

"And then how did you end up military?"

He felt his body tense. "Enlisted the day I turned eighteen to get out of the house. To do something worthwhile, as opposed to ... whatever they were doing. And to have someone pay attention to what I was doing for a change. Once I had it I wondered why I thought I wanted that. But I think he does, also. The strong constant hand."

"Oh, I don't know. He's not taking mine very well, and trust me, I have one. Although he never gave his father an ounce of trouble. Infuriated me, to be honest. Now I'm too constantly worried to be infuriated. I've calmed down some with my rules, but he still balks."

Daws had no trouble imagining Mrs. Reynauld, former Lieutenant, with a firm hand. "Which is why I want our relationship to look purely business, so he doesn't think I'm trying to control him, or ... to act like his father. I don't want him to think that."

"Mom, he'll be home in about twenty minutes."

She checked the clock at Will's warning. "Yes. Well, let me ask this, then. Why did you come to us now instead of waiting until you return?"

"There's a chance someone will find him at a show and want to sign him before he's eighteen. Now, from what I've read, it's unlikely since the contract won't hold up once he's legal age, but they might."

Mrs. Reynauld straightened her back. "Not without my permission."

"No. Not without your permission. And that's why I'm here. I'm hoping you'll wait..."

"Oh, they're not grabbing my son out of school and throwing him in that mess before he's legal. That's not going to happen. He stays right here as long as I can still make him."

Daws gave her a nod and pulled a slip of paper from his pocket. "This is my address and phone. My girlfriend, Deanna, will be there and I'll call her often to check in. She knows you may call. Please do if you need. I've been making contacts who can help ... with music questions and so on."

Will looked at it and then threw him a questioning gaze. "I have to ask, and I kind of understand about wanting to help, because of Dad and all, but it seems like a lot of hassle, and trust me, you take him on and it will be a lot of hassle...."

"William."

He paused only long enough to shrug. "Well, he oughtta know the truth. Ryan's a firecracker. It will be a hassle. So what are you going to get from all of this to be worth it? You'll have a job and such even when you get out, right? Because Ry is really full time and he can be exhausting..."

"I plan to work for him." He caught their exchanged glances. "As I said, I think he'll do well. He'll have to have a team he can trust. That'll be my job, to surround him with the right people and keep an eye out..."

"You want to be his manager."

"No. I'm a security specialist, with logistical training. That's what I plan to do."

"Security. You think he'll need it?"

"My guess is he will."

Mrs. Reynauld stood and paced several steps. "And maybe I should encourage him to go into something where he won't need security."

"Ma'am." Daws stood, also, holding his place. "You can always try, and I mean no offense, but his mind is set. I see it. You can hold him off until he's legal, but afterward, he's heading that direction."

"But if you don't help him, maybe he'll stay small time and do it as a hobby…"

"Mom." Will took her side. "You can't do that. You can't set him up to fail."

"I mean no such thing. He's smart, William. He can do anything he decides."

"This is the only thing he's ever been passionate about. If he can do it and support himself doing it, he should. And I'll tell him that."

"Then it doesn't matter much what I think since he's always listened to you better. As much as he looks up to you, you could help guide him another direction."

Will shrugged again. "Maybe. But you know what Dad would say about now."

Daws stood back and watched the silent exchange. He had to wonder if she would tell him to get out and not come back, to stay away from her son. And he knew damn well what the major would say. As he always did. *Don't be here if you're not passionate about the job. Be where you are passionate. Love it or get out.* One of his tag lines.

She moved her gaze to him. "Just how good are you at security? No offense, Sergeant, but this is my baby we're talking about."

"Yes, ma'am. I understand your concerns. But there's far less hazard in music than there'd be if he'd gone to West Point. The Gulf War might have ended, but I don't see it as done. Neither did the major. He insisted it wasn't and he worried about Will following in his tracks because he figures it'll be a lot messier than the first one, a whole different mission. I agree." He cringed at her expression. "I'm sorry. I only meant that with the right people around, even if he gets up to top name status, he'll be safe. If needed, I'd step in front of any harm to come his way. You have my word."

"Why would you do that for him?"

"I made a promise. And I would have done the same for his father if I could have."

He nearly blew it all by staying too long. Pulling out, he spotted the same car that had been at Ryan's show zoom down the road toward him and he swerved behind one parked along the street. In his rearview mirror, Daws watched the kid zip into the driveway, jump out of the old deep red Camaro and shove the door closed. Throwing a wave at another kid next door, he swaggered toward the house and let himself in.

A firecracker.

Daws sighed. Yes, he imagined that was true. It could be easier to stay in the Army than to jump out into the fire that would be Ryan Reynauld.

=======

"Already?" Deanna frowned at the vacuum cleaner. Or vacuum non-cleaner in this case. Stupid thing wouldn't even suck up a bit of shredded paper. The deployment curse, as she'd heard one of the wives call it: the moment the soldier left, everything started to happen, every little thing that could go wrong, would. Murphy's Law for the military.

She sighed. His plane left today. He was in the air on the way to Korea. And the stupid vacuum chose now to revolt.

Coincidence. And a little thing. She was smart. It was only a simple machine. She'd fix it.

A half hour later, Deanna had removed about two thousand screws – well, maybe about twelve in reality – and hoped she'd be able to figure out where to put them back. It was the third time she'd taken it apart, each time a step farther, and pulled out hair and carpet fuzzies and whatever else was in there. Still, no sucking.

With a frown, she decided to go farther. If she broke the thing, she'd go get a new one. The phone rang as she started again and she was glad for the interruption. "McCallister and Sons, this is ... oh, no, sorry..." She stopped at a click. "I did *not* just answer his phone like I was at work. Ugh! Way too many calls today. And I'm talking to myself. Great." She tried to check the number. Private. Well, they'd have to try again.

Deanna barely returned to the mess and torn-apart machine when it rang again. *Not McCallister's*: she reminded herself on the way to grab it and managed to say hello instead.

"Are you all right?"

She rolled her eyes. Definitely a curse. "Todd, why are you calling me?"

"You seemed bothered today. I wondered if you were all right."

"I'm not at work. It's none of your business. Don't call back." She hung up. Did he think he'd dialed the wrong number earlier? The thought made her chuckle.

Elbows deep in dusty itchy garbage that had actually been sucked up before the rebellious machine stopped working, Deanna found the problem. It was all up inside the hose. Now to find a way to pull it out. She searched under the sink in the tool box. Nothing long enough. A wire hanger. Did she have any?

Searching through her closet – the big closet Freddy still teased her about – she found a blouse recently back from the cleaners, on a paper-covered wire hanger. She tore the paper off and started to unwind the crimped wire. "*Ouch.*" Deanna surveyed her finger, grimaced at the torn fingernail, and went to find the clippers to cut the nail the rest of the way off. If she was the cursing type, she could just imagine what would be flowing out of her mouth. Good thing she wasn't. Anyway, she supposed it was good. Soap in her mouth one time was enough to discourage another attempt.

With a deep breath, she lowered onto the bed. Why had she thought of that now? She'd been eleven. Forever ago. And it was hardly a curse word. Her brothers all said much worse. They didn't get soap. Their father taught them every bad word they knew. Deanna wasn't sure whether it was more the soap or the way she felt disgusted when he talked that way that discouraged her more. The last thing on earth she wanted was to sound like him.

Gritting her teeth, she shoved him from her thoughts and stood. The vacuum wouldn't clean itself out. She chuckled at the thought. Maybe she'd invent one that would. Then she wouldn't need to ever go back to McCallister's. She could do what she pleased. Maybe fly ... to Korea once a month just to see him, hold him.

"*Stop it*, Deanna. You can't do this already." With another deep breath, she stomped out to the living area and shoved the hanger up into the hose, repeatedly, in and out, squeezing the tube, trying to loosen the congestion and get it to spill its contents onto the ... she laughed at the thought, the image. She laughed until tears ran down her face and her sides hurt. Would she tell him that when he called? No. She'd start laughing again and he'd think she lost her mind.

Maybe she had. After all, it ran in the family.

The thought sobered her and she wiped at her eyes. It wasn't funny. And she had to quit talking to herself.

Finishing the task, she managed to reassemble the thing, using all of the screws that were hopefully in the right places, and not loose as her own were, and plugged it back in. "Please just work." The noise sounded right, and it picked up the scattered mess she just made.

Jubilant in self-congratulations, Deanna gathered the tightly wound stuff she'd pulled out of the tube to drop into the trash and went back to vacuum the rest of the carpet, the ugly beige carpet Freddy wanted replaced with whatever she chose. The doorbell grabbed her attention, barely, and she frowned at the interruption. It rang again. "Okay, I'm *coming.*" Checking with the chain still hooked, Deanna had to fight herself not to cry.

"Deanna Meyers?" A young man in a labeled shirt held a bouquet of flowers.

"Yes. Hold on." She unchained and opened the door and told him to wait while she found a tip.

"It's already covered. Thank you. Have a nice night."

She couldn't answer. She held the pure white cannas to her face and breathed them in. "Oh Freddy." Her knees weak, Deanna went to the big chair he always used and laid them on her lap to open the card:

You are with me everywhere I am.
I Love You, Fred.

The tears wouldn't be held back. She cuddled the flowers against her chest, pulled her legs up on the chair, and immersed herself in a good cry. Oh, how she missed him already.

Sealing the envelope, Daws wrote Tracy's address on it and added the twenty-nine-cent stamp. He'd wanted to keep in touch with the Reynaulds and didn't want to use overseas phone time to do it. Will suggested he could send mail to Tracy and she'd get it to them without Ryan knowing. He should have written sooner, so they'd have his address.

Two months had passed already. In ways, it seemed longer, but at least his days were busy enough they made time move along. Except on weekends he didn't work and decided not to go out. Today was dragging so slow he'd written the letter just to make a few more minutes pass.

The Reynaulds had Deanna's number. They could have called her if needed. Daws talked to her most every day, only for a few minutes.

He got up to set the letter beside his hat so he wouldn't forget to take it to the mail in the morning, and switched his stereo on. It was one of the few things he'd taken with him other than personal items. He'd sold the inexpensive furniture from his apartment to a young newly married soldier. Cheap. He figured it made more sense than to store it for a year since, if they got stationed elsewhere upon his return, Deanna might want to choose her own. And what he had was only meant to be temporary. He'd moved it twice already. Cheap furniture didn't stand up well to multiple moves. At least it didn't matter much when it got banged corners and lost pieces, as always happened.

Rifling through the few CDs he'd shipped over, he changed his mind and turned it to the radio: Armed Forces Radio, the English language station that played only music he'd hear stateside. He enjoyed local music when he was out in the economy, but at night in his barracks, he wanted the feel of home, as much as possible.

Tom Petty's *Learning To Fly* streamed into the small too-white, too-bare room.

Daws grabbed the book he'd been reading since he arrived and opened it to where he'd left off. *The Business of Music.* With the book's help, along with the research he'd already done, he figured he'd have a good start on another direction when he decided to take it.

Deanna hesitated, and dropped the letter in the mail slot. It was addressed to her oldest sister, asking how her mom really was, since she couldn't get a straight answer from the old horse herself. Most of Deanna's hesitation was how she knew there was every chance there would be no reply. And she would much rather have an angry reply than none at all, as was normal. Still, she had to try.

The five flights of stairs up to her apartment, Freddy's apartment, were torturously long this time. She shouldn't have sent it. She should have sounded friendlier, filled her sister in on more of her own life. Deanna couldn't make herself do it, not until she at least had an answer. She'd nearly waited to re-read it the next day first. But she wouldn't have sent it. It would have been dumped in the trash like her last work designs if she'd given herself time to think about it.

Maybe she could go get it – wait for the mailman to come and ask for it back. He wouldn't give it to her. Once dropped into the box, it could go nowhere but to the addressed recipient.

Maybe her sister had moved long enough ago it would be returned to sender. Deanna could only hope.

Back in the apartment, she turned the radio on as a distraction. Wilson Phillips was singing about someone being in love with someone else. At least she didn't have that problem. Freddy belonged to her, only, even if she hardly ever saw him.

Deciding she didn't want the radio, Deanna switched it to CD and put in one of her favorites, Bread, fast-forwarding to *Baby I'm A Want You*. She closed her eyes and allowed Freddy's image in her head until it ended and she restarted the CD at the beginning.

She didn't want that, either. She needed upbeat. Rifling through some old cassettes she hadn't heard for a while, she grinned when her finger landed on Raucous's *Intoxication*. Deanna had been thirteen when it came out and she had to be careful not to let her mom hear it. The deeply suggestive songs amused Deanna, made her wish for a love like Susie's, and for someone to write songs to her that way. And she still wished she could meet even one of the Raucous guys, one in particular, but any would be a childhood fantasy come true.

The heavy beat and incredible vocals calmed her as they always had. With a deep soothing breath, she returned to the table and her latest decorating magazine. She needed to get going on the project Freddy asked her to do. He would be home in ... four months, there were four months still ... and she hadn't done much of anything other than consider styles and colors. It was time to jump in.

Daws checked the clocks displaying Korean time and Eastern U.S. time. Nineteen-hundred in New York. O-nine-hundred for him. Had it only been an hour and a half since he called her? At least their time difference worked well, since he was in between PT and his work day as she got home. It didn't give him long to talk, though, since phone time was limited and valuable and had to be shared among them. His only other option was after he got off, but at that point, she was getting ready for work and time was still limited. Except on weekends, but too many waited to use the phone on weekends and it was hard to get on then.

She was unhappy earlier. He could hear it although she insisted otherwise. Deanna said all was fine and they were being more pleasant at work, partly due to Mr. McCallister taking such an interest in her boyfriend, she assumed. If that had helped her in any way, Daws was eternally glad he'd gone to her party in uniform.

She said she'd thought of him during fireworks as she watched with her friends from the balcony of his apartment. The perfect place to see them, Deanna said. He agreed, for the most part. His parents refused to do anything for the Fourth of July but he didn't care since he could sit out on the balcony and watch the light show over the Harbor. Of course, several buildings blocked part of the view and he'd determined some day he would get up close where there was no obstruction. He still planned to do it, and take Deanna.

Her words about the significance of the explosions bursting overhead hitting her harder than it ever had before rang through his thoughts. She wanted him to talk more about his experiences during Desert Storm. He couldn't do it, not over the phone, and maybe not in person. He wasn't sure he ever would, other than a few basic things that everyone knew already, or distorted, from what the papers and news reported. He might tell her more about what was distorted.

Daws wondered about calling her back. As soon as he found a few minutes no one would miss him, he would do that. She was unhappy, no matter what she said.

His captain, the moron who made him truly miss Captain Hodgkins on a regular basis, gave him an excuse not an hour later. A paperwork run. And no, a private couldn't do it; it was too important. Daws didn't bother to remind him he was an E6 and not to be used as a runner, which would be easy enough to fight. This time, he didn't. He used it to give himself time to make a quick call. It wouldn't keep happening, though.

It rang several times until the machine picked up. She was out at seven-thirty at night. He should have left a message; his number wouldn't show on the caller ID. Three more months before his halfway point. It was going to be a long three months.

Her jog had felt incredible. Running through a quick shower, Deanna dried well and slipped into a long thin nightshirt. Then she sat down at the table with her newest decorating magazine and the large sub sandwich she'd grabbed on the way back to her building. Loaded with different kinds of lunch meat, including one of her favorites she knew she shouldn't eat, salami, she let herself ignore the calories in the thing and indulge carelessly. She deserved it. She was back on track and would be in shape again well before Fred got home.

Flipping through pages, she stopped at one that showed a tall bookcase that had not only regular books but photo frames and photo books highlighted. The colors all brought out those in the rest of the room and gave it a homey, personal touch.

She loved it. She wondered if he would.

Deanna knew he wouldn't want his parents highlighted, even if she could find photos of them somewhere, but maybe he had military pictures ... and she could do them as a gift. Did he have any, though? If he didn't, maybe she could find someone who did.

Considering whether or not she should do what she was thinking, Deanna kicked back and finished her sandwich, washed it down with hard lemonade, and let the idea fester. She hoped it wasn't the effect of the lemonade and rush of food after being too hungry that made the decision, but she got up and found the phone number Fred left for her.

Andrews. One of his men.

Deanna held the phone in her hand for some time, considering again, and then took the plunge.

Her line was busy when he snuck in another call. At least she was home. He supposed he would rest easily enough with that.

But he couldn't. He doubled back and tried once more, and grabbed a deep breath at her voice.

She beckoned to the caller again, a question in her voice.

"Anna, sorry, I'm here."

"Freddy? Hey, what's wrong?"

"Nothing."

"No? You called earlier. You never call twice."

"Wanted to hear your voice. Is everything all right?"

"Yes. I told you earlier it was, but it's nice to hear your voice again."

She sounded happier, more relaxed. Maybe she only needed time to unwind after work. And go ... where? The store maybe. It didn't matter. She was home and happier.

"Fred? What's worrying you?"

"Nothing now, and I have to go. Wanted to be sure. You sounded ... not yourself earlier."

"Oh. Well, sometimes I'm not, but don't worry about it."

"Hard not to."

She didn't answer. Maybe he was pushing too much again.

"You're still worried I might not be here when you come home."

This time, he couldn't answer.

"Well, don't." Her voice grew soft. "I will be. Fred, I will be here when you come home, and I can't wait to see you, to hold you in my arms again. Don't ever worry about that. You just keep your head low and take care of yourself and come back to me. Don't worry about anything else in the world."

His eyes closed and he faced the wall in case anyone walked past. "You deserve someone who's there."

"Fred Dawson, don't you start that. I deserve you. That's not humble of me to say, I know, but I don't care if it is, because I do. Because I've kissed my fair share of frogs and I didn't give up and I waited until I found you and I do deserve you. And you better not forget that, because I have this ring you gave me and I'm not letting you back out."

Damn, he wanted to wrap her in his arms. "Have no intentions of backing out. I love you, Deanna. Hang in there with me."

Her breath came over the line, a quick gasp. "I love you, too, and I'll be here. Waiting."

A couple of his men came looking for him and he gave them a nod to let them know he'd be right there. "I have to go. Sleep well. Not sure if I'll be able to call the next couple of days, so don't worry if I don't."

Deanna shook her head as she hung up. Silly man. If he had any idea how much time she'd just spent on the phone not only with Andrews, but also with Mandy Hodgkins, just to gather photos and stories for the scrapbook she had planned, he would realize how silly he was to think she might not wait. She was going nowhere. Not without him.

=== August ===

Deanna wondered how hard it would be to learn to make Kimshi and Bulgogi.

Her specialties were steak – she had it down to perfect timing for any way someone asked for it – and chicken dishes with an emphasis on casseroles, plus she was good with seafood. If she tried, she could do a simple stir fry without anything getting too overcooked. But Korean? She wasn't sure she'd even tried it.

Fred said they'd have to find a place so she could.

He was enjoying the country. He even went on a sight-seeing tour with other soldiers, American and South Korean. Other than the first couple of weeks of his system adjusting to the different food, he'd grown to love walking around off-post sampling new dishes. He hadn't yet found the nerve to try the octopus, at least not the ones that were still moving when the server set the bowl in front of them. That was one step farther than he thought was necessary.

Four months. Only two-thirds of the way to his mid-year break. It was harder every day to get up for work knowing he'd be on her mind all day long. She was even late a couple of times. It was unlike her.

It was so unlike her, Todd stopped her to ask if she was all right. It was sweet, she supposed, but Deanna brushed him off. The other girls stopped harassing her. One of them even offered to refill her coffee once. If she'd known they would become so placating, she would have started going in late and dragging her heels sooner.

The phone still in her hand asked if she wanted to place a call, and she sighed and set it down. Her stomach growled but she didn't want to bother to make anything. Instead, she shuffled back to the master bath and started the hot water.

After she relaxed in the tub, she'd return to her magazines to find ideas for smaller furniture pieces that would finish out the loft. The big pieces were already replaced; the previous furniture had been trucked off to McGuire Air Force base on Fort Dix to donate to MWR for auction. It was the one thing Fred insisted she do. He said officers would pay a fair amount for it and the money raised would help provide funds for enlisted with emergency needs. It was closer and less expensive to ship it there than to Drum. Deanna figured it would also keep his donation more anonymous, which was more his intent.

And he didn't want any of it. He wanted it gone.

It made her nervous redoing his place with the very little input he was willing to offer. He trusted her. Part of her wished he wouldn't quite so much.

Soaking in the wet heat with the whirlpool jets massaging her skin, Deanna fingered the pearl and diamond ring that matched her necklace and bracelet and earrings. He'd asked tonight if the Reynaulds had called in, if they got his letter. They hadn't called. Maybe she would call them. His mind, more and more often, was in Vermont, on the major's son.

They would have to get the kid to move to New York when he was old enough. It would be easier for Fred to keep an eye on him without pulling away from Deanna too much. She scorned herself for the selfish thought, but still, she wasn't too horribly selfish. After all, she told him to go do his tour overseas as he was supposed to instead of staying with her. There were many days she fussed at herself for it.

This morning had been one of those times. She missed him. While fixing her hair for work, she'd caught a glimpse of the ring in the mirror and broke down in tears. No wonder Todd asked if she was all right. She looked horrible when she finally got to work.

He would never know. She would never tell Fred. She'd told him she could do it, and she would.

Squeezing her eyes together, Deanna leaned her head back to rest against the plastic cushion. Four months down. It would get easier from there. At least she told herself it would.

She never expected it would bother her so much. After all, she'd spent most of her adult life alone, and only had a few minor boyfriends before then. It wasn't like she had to have a man in her life. She did well by herself. Movies kept her company and there were few she hadn't watched. She loved following the stories, studying the actors and their methods, watching several times for anything she might have missed or just to hear the lines she loved again. Plenty of her music collection was soundtracks to her favorites.

Maybe she'd bypass the magazines tonight and put in a comedy. Decorating made her think too much about him, about what he'd want, about him finally seeing it and his reaction, his expression, his eyes, mouth...

"Stop, Deanna. *Just stop it.* You're fine. You're an *adult.* Just stop it."

The water was growing cool so she let it drain and dried, slathering herself with scented lotion meant to soothe and refresh. Citrus and vanilla mixed, one of her favorites. As she gave the lotion time to absorb, she found her tweezers and plucked errant hairs from beneath her brow. The memory of his fingers stroking over top of each, that night after he'd found them red from plucking, and the way he nuzzled into her neck against her moist lotioned skin, mentioning how he loved how she smelled, drifted in and became too strong. "*Ugh*. This *isn't* all right."

She dropped the tweezers back into her drawer and stared at herself in the mirror. She needed to get back to her workouts. How often during the past four months had she started again just to give up and go back to moping, to indulging in chocolate and pasta with rich sauces she told herself made her feel better? It didn't, though, not for more than a few minutes. And she knew better. It had to stop. She had to pull back into herself, had to keep moving forward.

Pulling her thin robe over her shoulders and tying it loosely, she went to check the time. Nearly seven. He'd called a few minutes after she got home and could never talk long anymore. She missed their long rambling conversations.

A good workout was what she needed. So she had bathed already. She could again, just quick to wash off the sweat.

She'd let her gym membership lapse, but she supposed they still had space. If not, she'd go walk/jog around the park instead.

Actually, that thought was much more appealing. It was too hot earlier, with the normal New York in August humidity making the heat worse, but she figured it would be decent enough by now.

=== September ===

Nothing but garbage.

Deanna sighed and closed the mail box. She shouldn't have sent the letter. Two and a half months and no answer from her sister. Nothing new from her mom. As far as she knew, her mom could have taken "a vacation" again. Who would tell her?

On top of a lousy week at work, while Todd continually "let" her screen his angry client calls and then pretended to worry about her, Deanna didn't need attitude from some mouthy kid on the bus blaring nasty music through headphones. She'd asked him nicely to turn it down so she wouldn't have to hear the lyrics – the music she could handle – and he rolled his eyes and closed them. She was less nice the next time, after she pushed at his shoulder to get his attention. The kid cursed her with a word even her step-father didn't use. If he'd been at least eighteen, she would have knocked him down, but she knew better than to assault a minor, no matter how much he deserved it.

The bus driver brushed off her complaint, afraid to tangle with the little moron. So she got off the bus early. And walked an extra three blocks home. In her heels.

Her feet were killing her by the time she started for the stairs, so she gave in and opted for the elevator. Deanna normally only settled for the thing when Fred was with her. He didn't like stairs. She thought it was funny. The Army Staff Sergeant who could do ten mile runs with a heavy backpack didn't like stairs. Like flying, he said: he could if he needed but he preferred cars, and elevators.

He couldn't call tonight, still on a mission he wouldn't talk about, or couldn't. She was never entirely sure which, but she'd learned not to ask questions.

Deanna scanned the bookshelves. They were still too bare, especially her side, but they were coming along. Deciding he might not want private information visible when they had company, she put the two tall shelving units in the master bedroom instead of in the main area. They were just what the room needed to make it cozier. After getting them in place, she decided there should be a chair and small table in front, to fill empty space and invite sitting and browsing through the books right there in the bedroom. Two of the chairs from her apartment fit perfectly in front of the bookcases and were now reupholstered in matching colors and contrasting prints to go with the room. The low square spinning cassette holder with most of its slots filled sat in between, covered with plain fabric squares that matched both chairs and made the line flow between. It made a nice little table to rest her coffee or tea on as she sank into a chair.

It was so cozy, she'd found herself cuddling in the bedroom at night while she looked through magazines or skimmed one of the books she'd found on the closet shelf of the guest room. Mysteries. A bunch of them in different age ranges, beginning with the Hardy Boys and Ellery Queen and working up to Mickey Spillane and Tony Hillerman and John MacDonald. They now filled about half of his bookshelf. A few photos in frames helped to make them look less bare. His bottom shelf was full of LPs. It was too full to fit them all and so the rest overflowed onto her bottom shelf along with the few albums she had.

The rest of her space included mainly movies she'd pulled out of storage with everything else she had in there. Any of her furniture pieces that fit in the apartment without throwing the design scheme, she kept. The rest she gave to Goodwill. She'd had second thoughts of doing so, with full knowledge that keeping them in storage would possibly be less expensive than rebuying if he ever kicked her out, but she didn't expect anymore that he would. She didn't plan to let him very easily.

He would be home any day. He couldn't give her an exact date, for security reasons, but he'd let her know as soon as he could. And she had the place as ready as she would for this time. Partly on purpose, she'd left it not quite complete; she wanted his input on what she'd done so far.

Deanna had mentioned once how she loved being surprised but how hard it was to surprise her.

Daws hoped his plan wouldn't cross the line between surprise and fear. He didn't want to scare her. She knew he would be back any day and by all rights, he could have warned her once he reached the airport, or he could have had someone let her know. He didn't want to warn her. By the time he got to JFK, it was late, past midnight. It was also a work day. Wednesday night. He knew he'd have a hard time letting her go in to the office the morning after six months of being apart. He should have warned her, allowed time for her to get a couple of days off.

Grabbing his luggage from the belt, he went directly to where taxis always waited.

The first in line jumped out of his car as he approached, asked where he was going, and put his bag in the trunk. He also asked where he'd just come from and chattered to Daws as he drove, asking about his service. The idea made him wary. He said little, only enough to be polite.

He was required to leave his duty station in uniform. In a perverse way, he was glad. Watching reactions had become somewhat of a game, as he guessed from a distance what kind he would get and tried to read possible danger zones. More often than not, he was right. Several people gave him a warm nod. Many pretended not to see him. Either was fine. He wanted nothing more than to get home, to Deanna, and unwind after a long half year and the back-breaking, nerve-wrenching, cramped, long flight back to the States. Possibly, he wouldn't mind flying as much if the seats were made for his build. He was stiff and exhausted and needed a shower.

A couple dressed in shaggy coats with peace signs emblazoned on their T-shirts had headed toward him as he approached baggage claim. Daws cursed under his breath, threw them a glance as they moved closer, and kept walking. They tried to block his path as they called him a murderer and spewed hate loudly enough to catch attention from everyone nearby. He threw a 'stop annoying me' look and swerved around, thinking how easy it would be to just knock them out of his way and wondering if they knew how easily he could. As he'd told Deanna, knowing he could was enough for him. In general.

When they moved around in front of him again, purposely shoving into his side as they did, a few young people stepped between and became a wall, yelling back at the raving lunatics.

Daws would rather have handled it himself, but he wasn't allowed to lay a hand on them, other than in self defense if absolutely necessary. He also couldn't say anything rude, regardless of what they said. There was no need. Airport security moved in to assist and he thanked the young people and walked away from it. If the two American chickens considered that "peace," he wanted no part of it and they weren't worth his energy, more than he already gave so they could spread their vulgar hate freely. Objecting to war was one thing; yelling at soldiers was another.

In the taxi, he shoved them out of his thoughts and looked out at the city that was never actually dark, regardless of how small the moon was on any given night. Tonight it was full, and he gave it his attention until the taxi turned and blocked his view. In an attempt to keep his eyes open in the relative dark, Daws took in the bits of moving life on the sidewalk offsetting the cold, immovable structures in their background.

There were similarities between New York and Seoul: the hustle and crowds and side-to-side buildings and mix of speeding cars and scurrying pedestrians. Seoul was modern and also well lit and didn't lack for activity of any kind. The largest difference he'd found was the language and the food, and most spoke English well enough to communicate as much as needed. He'd picked up several Korean words and phrases and at least tried to be polite enough to use their language. It was simply easier for them to use English, which they knew much better.

It was fairly quiet in New York since it was after midnight, but still there was plenty of life to be found. Home. The longer he was away from it, the more he wanted to be there.

Finally, they pulled up in front of his building and he tried to pay his fare.

"No, I do not want your money." The driver, dark skinned and solemn-eyed, shook his head.

"Why?"

"I have relatives in Kuwait. They are safer now because of you and those like you. I will not take your money. Thank you and bless you for helping my people."

Daws tried to argue, but the man wouldn't give in, so he thanked him and wished him and his relatives well.

As he claimed his bags and headed to the door, he thought about how the recent surge in praise for the troops wouldn't last. It wouldn't take long for people to forget and go on about their lives as though nothing had happened. He supposed it was good. They felt secure and that was part of his job. But he knew it wouldn't last. It never did. There would be calls for cuts again before long. It never failed. Never mind the old barracks with peeling paint or that they were already far below civilian level pay.

Shoving that from his head, also, he took the stairs instead of the elevator, as Deanna usually did. It felt good after the long flight home and easier than standing in a moving box waiting for the thing to get up to his floor. He was sure it didn't actually take longer to climb the stairs, but it felt less time when he was actively moving.

He turned the key in the door quietly and still wondered if he should have warned her. It was dark. Except for a soft glow from the hallway. Daws set his bags down, unlaced his boots enough to pull them off, and scanned the room while he began to unbutton his shirt that had lost much of its stiffness over the fifteen hour flight. He hardly recognized the place, as much as he could see of it. Thoughts of turning the light on dissipated as quickly as they came. He'd wait and let her show him. More important thoughts filtered in.

He stopped in the bedroom doorway. She was propped against pillows and the headboard, the little bedside light on, a book open on her lap, her fingers still holding the page although her head lolled back in a deep sleep. A glance to his right made him sidetrack. He went over to the space that used to be empty. Two chairs and two bookcases tucked cozily in the large corner. The edges of the shelves met as though holding each other in place and a vined plant sat on top and stretched itself across both. One side held all of his old books, at least the ones he'd managed to hide well enough they didn't get tossed by his parents. He'd had a ton more. Garbage, they said. He was supposed to read Steinbeck and Tolstoy and Lee and Sange and ... so many other names they'd shoved at him. And he had, to an extent. While he saw their value, they didn't fascinate him the way private eye novels did.

Daws picked up a picture frame that grabbed his attention. Him and the major at a company picnic. Where had she found that? Daws had never even seen it. Next, he scanned through a photo album. Army photos. A few his, most he hadn't seen. How did she get them? Her shelves held mainly movies. A few fancy boxes, closed. And one photo. He gazed at it through the shadowed light. Deanna. Much younger: a teen, maybe. And a woman he guessed was in her late twenties, her hair pulled back tightly, a simple black dress, modest, concealing, and a sadness in her eyes. In Deanna's eyes ... hardship. He could see it. Worry. Even through her smile.

Returning his gaze to his sleeping angel, he put the photo back and went to her. Soft messy curls trailed along her face. Her shoulders were bare, the thin straps of her nightgown and the V edge of black lace contrasted against pale skin.

"Deanna." He ran fingers through the curls.

She jumped.

"Hey. It's just me." He lowered onto the bed and stroked her hair as she woke enough to recognize him.

"Freddy."

"Sorry I scared you."

She threw her arms around him. Her face nuzzled into his neck, fingers slid up into his hair. "You're cold."

"Think it's only about forty degrees out there."

She pulled back to see his face and moved her hands to each side of it. "You're home."

"I'm home, Anna, and all yours for the next few weeks." Daws held her in, breathing her warm feminine scent, nourishing himself with her softness, her tenderness, as her fingers pressed against his back, her face nuzzled into his neck.

"I've missed you." She met his lips in a long, deep kiss.

Daws still wasn't sure how he'd answer if he was asked whether it was harder to be away when he hadn't left anyone behind or when he had. As hard as it had been to come home to no one after Desert Storm, he was at least able to convince himself it was better that way.

Now, though, with Deanna pressing as close as she could get, showing him how much she'd missed him, he knew he could never convince himself he wished she hadn't waited. Yet it would be hard as hell to make himself leave her again.

Her lips moved to his neck. She continued to unbutton the shirt where he left off.

Daws teased the strap of her nightgown. "You are so beautiful."

"I'm a mess." She ran a hand through her hair. "You should have warned me."

"A beautiful mess." He fingered one of her curls. "I'll warn you next time. This time, I wanted to catch you as you were."

"Next time." Deanna pulled her eyes away and set a hand on his chest, running the tips of her fingers just above the hem of his T-shirt. "What if I don't let you leave me again?"

"Hm." He kissed the side of her head. "What if we don't talk about it tonight? I want to be enjoy being here with you while I can be."

With a light nod, she returned to his lips and slid her hands to his shoulders, tugging his shirt out of the way.

"I need to shower." He helped pull the thing the rest of the way off.

"It doesn't matter. Just come to bed." She moved her hand around the back of his head and pulled him forward, holding him in as she lay back against the pillows.

"Mm, Anna." Daws found her gaze, the beautiful hazel eyes, more brown tonight than green. "I've been in this thing for close to twenty-four hours. Give me five minutes."

"No. I'll give you two. Make it quick, soldier."

Forcing himself away from her and to the bathroom, he gargled mouthwash as the shower warmed – he'd dig out his toothbrush in the morning – and ran through the steaming water to wash off the travel grime and the cold. If it was longer than two minutes, it wasn't much longer, and he wrapped the towel around his waist, only partly concealing just how glad he was to be home with her.

As soon as he was next to the bed, she pulled him close and wrapped bare arms around his bare waist, her head against his stomach. "I know you have to be wiped out. Just come to bed and hold me."

He was wiped out, exhausted, but he'd been away far too long to let that interfere.

===

When the alarm blared, Deanna grimaced and rolled over to stop it. Except she rolled right into Freddy and nearly hit him in the face. "Oh. I'm sorry."

"Morning." He reached over to push the button and gave her a grin. "Not used to someone in your way anymore?"

"No." She snuggled in against him and kissed his chest, enjoyed its warmth, its mix of hard and soft, the few little patches of curly hair. "But I could get used to it." She trailed kisses along his shoulder and neck and breathed in his so-masculine scent. "In fact, I'd love to get used to it."

He caressed the bare skin along her spine, pushing the blankets down to her waist as he lowered his hand. "Careful, or you'll be late for work."

Work. Not likely. Not today. "Want to hand me the phone?"

"No." He stroked his fingers along her bare hip. "You'll have to reach for it if you want it."

"Fine, then." Deanna crawled half over him and propped herself on top as she grabbed the phone. The man did not want her to go to work. Or he at least had every intention of making her late. From her current position, that fact was too fully obvious for him to even try to deny. He caressed her thigh as she dialed the office and waited for the machine to list its office hours, which hadn't started yet. She left a message that she'd be out the next two days.

"Anna, don't get yourself fired." His voice was husky as he brushed a thick clump of curls from her face.

"Doesn't matter. I'll find something else if I do." She leaned down farther against him. "I want all the time with you I can get while you're home. I need that. And from the feel of things, so do you."

He chuckled and gave her a quick kiss. "If it helps, I managed to get four weeks instead of three. Adds another week at the end, but figured we needed some real time together. A week or two now and then isn't doing it."

Four weeks. Four whole weeks. The idea nearly made her cry. Four whole weeks of seeing him every night and every weekend and whatever time she could manage otherwise. "I love you, Fred Dawson. And I'm still going to be greedy with your time. And other things. Going to keep up with me?"

He gave her a light grin. "I'll do my best to meet your expectations."

They didn't leave the apartment through the weekend. They talked and she showed off the details of what she'd done with the decorating. They went through the Army scrapbook together and she insisted he tell her about each photo. He wasn't sure whether to be flattered or feel invaded when she said she called not only Mandy Hodgkins but also Andrews, begging for photos, as well as going through a couple of boxes he'd hidden in the back corner of the guest room closet. She said she hoped he didn't mind and she ignored anything but the photos, including a few letters.

Part of him minded. Some of the photos were with old girlfriends, those who mattered enough to keep their photos. She teased him about it and it led into discussion of some of her old boyfriends. She didn't have photos. Of any of them. No memorabilia, either. Once she was done with them, she was done. Associated stuff went out. He wasn't sure whether to be jealous of that ability or to feel sorry for her that she couldn't even hold the good memories. Or maybe she did and couldn't admit it. For as open as she said she was, Deanna had at least as much baggage hidden as he did. Possibly more. At this point, he was quite sure it was more. There wasn't much left of his life she didn't know after the picture hunting escapade.

The letters were from his parents. She had to know they were. She didn't ask.

He told himself he was flattered she was so interested, but thoughts of moving the letters elsewhere flashed through his brain now and then. He wouldn't. She could read them if it mattered to her enough to do it behind his back. She would keep it to herself; he at least was sure of that.

Monday morning, he talked her into going back to work. Regardless of what she said, Daws knew Deanna wanted her job, and wanted to hold it long enough to either advance or find something better. As part of his coercion tactic, he drove her to work, walked her to the door, and promised to meet her for lunch. "Eleven-thirty?"

She slid her arms over his shoulders. "Yes. What are you going to do until then?"

"Check into a few things."

"Can I know what?"

"Tell you at lunch. Better get going or you'll be late."

"Hm." She played with the hair at this nape. "I'll work easier knowing you're right here in the city and I get to see you in a few hours."

He grinned and backed away, waiting until she was inside to return to the car. Daws was actually more concerned about being late to his own appointment. On his way to mid Manhattan, he pondered what he was about to do. He'd called Will Reynauld on Friday to check in and thank him for sending the cassettes to the apartment. After a friendly greeting and a couple of minutes of conversation, Will told him Ryan's band had hired a manager, but Will didn't trust the guy. He'd been going to most of his brother's shows and the manager did have them fitting better into one genre than into their strange mix, but it still wasn't quite right for Ryan's voice. And the manager planned to have them hit quick and make what they could as fast as they could. He didn't think it sounded good for the career Ryan wanted.

Daws agreed. Still, he could be overstepping his bounds since he hadn't even talked to the kid. But he would be clear about the situation, feel her out, get an impression, and leave it at that.

It took longer than he appreciated to find a space in the nearby parking garage, and he strode quickly to the elevator that would take him up to Virginia Gray's office. After sounding out several of his contacts, he decided she was the place to start.

A secretary announced him through the phone as he peered out the window over the city. A nice view. Not as nice as his.

"Mr. Dawson?"

He turned to find a sturdy, rather tall woman of around forty with dusty brown hair cropped short. Going to meet her, he offered his hand and thanked her for seeing him. She led him into her office, closed the door, and beckoned him to a chair. Her office was sparse, neat, efficient. All business. So far, so good.

"So you're here about possible representation of a new artist? Is it you? The message was unclear."

"No, ma'am. Not me."

"Don't call me ma'am. You can call me Virginia until we get to know each other better and then it's Ginny. I don't answer to ma'am." She grabbed a pen and pad of paper. "Male or female? Single or group? What relationship to you?"

"Male, in a group currently but I'm only here for the lead who should be solo."

"Does he do anything but sing?"

"Plays acoustic guitar well, electric not so well last I heard. Could have improved by now. Writes some of his own."

At that, she looked up, eyebrows raised. "Songwriter? Decent?"

"From what I've heard."

"What relation is he to you?"

"None."

Her eyebrows rose. "Then why are you here?"

"He needs a good manager."

"And you think that's me?"

"From everything I've heard, yes. They say you have a firm hand and a fair amount of patience."

"Wonderful." She leaned back in her chair. "Another trouble maker?"

"No. Good kid. Just has a lot of energy and can get kind of smart. Don't think he'll be too hard to back down, though."

"Okay, so no relation, good kid, good songwriter ... what's in it for you?"

"I plan to be in charge of his security."

She laughed and leaned forward. "Getting way ahead of yourself, aren't you? You know very few singers end up needing private security. Most don't get half far enough to even need more than a small road crew who can double as security."

"He will."

Her amusement turned serious. "How much do you know about music? I don't recognize your name."

"You wouldn't. And not much, but I learn fast, and security I already know. I know what it entails. I know most don't need it. But he will. And as far as he knows, I'll only be security."

"As far as he knows?"

"We haven't formally met. I've been watching him, with his family's okay."

"Wait." She stood and walked around the desk to lean back against it. "You have a kid you think you can turn into a celebrity so he'll need your services and you can get paid well for your efforts? Why not start with someone who's already up there? I can give you recommendations. Tell you how to get started if that's all you want..."

"No. This isn't about me. It's about him. A favor. Nothing more."

She studied him silently a moment. "You have military training."

He waited.

"The haircut. The bearing. *Ma'am*. It adds up. Am I right?"

"U.S. Army. Eleven years. Still active."

"Then we're talking sometime in the future with this kid? How old is he?"

"Sixteen. By the time he's legal age for a contract, I can be out and ready to take him on."

"Why'd you come so soon?"

"Wanted time to check things out as I can. I'm not here much currently."

"Hm." Virginia Gray gave him a thoughtful frown and wandered to her window, then she turned. "How many managers are you checking out?"

"Three. For now."

She nodded. "Well, you should know I'm not lacking in clients. I nearly didn't let you in, as I'm constantly busy with a couple of local start up bands along with my big name. I don't like to be too narrowed since they tend to come and go. So maybe you should come back when he's legal and you're set up in the industry and we can talk again. My guess is you'll get the same answer from everyone worth talking to."

Daws stood. "That's fine, but he already has a manager trying to steer him the wrong way. I don't have a lot of time to search for others, but I also can't risk not having someone else lined up to at least consider him when it's time to pull him away into something more serious, so I will keep looking." He reached into his pocket and pulled out a cassette. "Listen to him. My contact information is there. If you wait more than a couple of weeks, you'll have to talk to my girlfriend instead. She'll handle things for me until I can." With a nod, he turned to leave.

"Mr. Dawson." Virginia Gray caught up. "Just so we're understood, if I have any interest at all, just how much a part do you intend to play, other than security?"

"I have veto power. Any major decisions go through me. And he doesn't know until he figures it out on his own."

"Why?"

"Has to be that way. I'm not saying more."

"Don't tell me he's some kind of dignitary or something I can't know about, because I have enough on my hands..."

"Nothing like that at all. Just a kid whose father did me a favor. And he can't know that, either."

As he left the office, he knew Virginia Gray would call. Still, he had two more appointments before he met Deanna for lunch. He supposed he should have asked her before pulling her into handle things for him as necessary, but he had no doubt she'd agree. And she'd be good at it. Marketing was her job, and she was damn good at it. Eventually, the right person would see that.

"Of course." Deanna reached across the table and took his hand. "Anything I can do to help, just ask me, okay?"

"You're busy already..."

"I need to be busy. Helps me deal with you being gone. And don't look at me like that. It's okay. Really. Well, okay enough. I want to help. Just tell me what I need to know."

He gave her a light nod. "I'll show you what I've found tonight. I'm not sure you'll need to do much, but in case, go with your judgment if you run into something we haven't talked about."

"You're trusting me an awful lot, Fred Dawson. The apartment, redecorating, your account ... and now with this kid who seems to matter to you more than I really understand. That's a lot of trust for someone you've known barely over a year."

He eyed her a moment, then got up and moved around the table to sit beside her. Raising her hand, he rubbed a thumb over the pearl ring and met her gaze. "I think you don't understand how I meant this."

Deanna remained silent, since she had no idea how to respond.

"I'm not sure I believe in marriage; at least I'm not sure I believe in it for myself, but I believe in the theory, in the promise of it. Those other things ... are minor, compared to this." He glanced down at the ring again. "I trust you to believe in this relationship the same way I do. Fully. Honestly. Openly. Anna, you are my partner. I don't want that to change. I would never take a partner I couldn't trust fully, with anything." His fingers stroked hers, but his gaze remained firm. "I need to be able to depend on you. I need you to be able to depend on me. Through anything. Am I taking your agreement as more than you meant it?"

Marriage. He didn't want their partnership to change.

Deanna pressed her lips together as she leaned in to touch her face to his. "No. I meant it, too. Fully. I want to be by your side forever, Fred Dawson. Yes, you can depend on me, for anything I can possibly do."

He pulled back enough to catch her eyes and he kissed her. In the little cafe where many of her coworkers tended to eat since it was close. She knew a couple of them were there and had glanced over more than once. She supposed they'd darn sure believe her now.

When it was time to go back to work, he walked her all the way up to the office and set a light kiss above her ear when they reached her desk. "Have a good afternoon. I'll be back at five."

"Oh. You don't have to. It's a lot of extra running..."

"I don't like you taking the bus. You won't as long as I can help it."

"You plan to drop me off and pick me up every day while you're home?"

"Yes."

She couldn't help a grin, and set a hand on his chest. "Well, I'm not going to object. I kind of like being treated like a lady for a change."

"As you should be." With a light touch to her face, he strode back to the elevator, returning a greeting to those who bothered to say hello.

Deanna barely had her handbag back in her drawer when the office gossips accosted her.

"So he is still around. And we half thought you were making it up just to annoy Mr. Bodin."

"Half?" Deanna 'half' ignored they were there. "You fully thought I was making it up. And I couldn't care less. Excuse me, I have work to do because I'm out of here precisely at five tonight."

"You can't." One of them looked at her wide-eyed. "There's a meeting right after work. Mandatory for everyone."

"I hadn't heard of it."

"Well, the memo just came through while you were at lunch."

"Did it? From who? Mr. McCallister?"

"No, from Mr. Bodin."

"Is that so?" Deanna pulled out a file. "Meeting for what?"

"It didn't say."

"Well, I won't be there. If it doesn't say, he probably doesn't even know and it's not horribly important." She heard a gasp and knew one was pulling the other away from her desk as they whispered to each other. She didn't care if they did. A last minute meeting with unannounced subject meant one thing: Todd was trying to annoy her by keeping her from her boyfriend as much as he could. It wouldn't work. She was bound from nine to five and to pre-planned meetings, but no more than that, not without the promotion that would allow them to assign her more hours.

She was just getting her head into the current must-do-now file when she felt a body approach from behind.

"Ms. Meyers."

Not Todd. The other jerk. "Yes?" She didn't bother to look up.

"You got the memo about tonight's meeting?"

"No."

He cleared his throat. "I am aware that you know about it."

"I heard second-hand. I never give that much credence."

"Yes, well, now you're hearing it first hand. It's at five, mandatory."

"About what?"

The sharp air intake told her he was trying to control his frustration. "Does it matter?"

"Yes." She finally raised her chin. "I have plans."

"You'll have to change them."

"No."

"Excuse me?"

"No. My work day ends at five and I'm leaving at five. If it had been last week, I might have been willing. This week I'm not. I won't be there."

"*Miss* Myers. Refusing mandatory meetings is grounds for dismissal."

"Is it?" She turned back to her file. He wouldn't do it. McCallister was in her corner. She did too much of his work for him. He wouldn't do it.

"Be there tonight or you have two weeks." He pivoted away.

She held still, staring at the file. He meant it. Maybe she didn't care. Then she'd have two full weeks with Freddy instead of only weekends and after work before he left. She didn't want to be fired, though. She could quit first. But if she quit, she wouldn't get unemployment. How fast could she find another job? And if she quit over a stupid meeting, who would hire her? They would put it on her record. It would look like she wasn't willing to go whatever distance it took to get the job done, and that wasn't true. At least it didn't used to be true. Before she'd been so burned by them, she was. Now, she wasn't. She was biding her time.

Until what?

With a sigh, she went back to the file and put her head in her work. At break, she would call Fred and tell him about the meeting, see what he said. Would she tell him about the warning? Yes. He wanted openness.

Full honesty. She had to tell him.

Daws frowned at Deanna's message and checked the time it was left. Three. And it was nearly five. He'd been out all afternoon, had just stopped in to drop off a few groceries for the dinner he planned to make her. A meeting.

He grabbed the phone and returned the call. The operator answered first and directed him to Deanna Meyers. She sounded relieved to hear his voice. And she explained quickly.

"Anna, go to your meeting. What time is it over?"

"Are you sure? I don't know. Hopefully not more than an hour. He won't say. You know he's doing this on purpose. The creep actually said he'd take me home afterward. I told him he was out of his mind."

"Call as soon as you're done, or if you know you're close to done. I'll pick you up. Use this number." He read off it from the slip of paper.

"What number is that?"

"Mobile. Picked it up today."

She apologized for the hassle and for being later than expected, but he assured her it was fine and let her return to work. It wasn't fine. Daws wanted more than ever to knock the moron to the ground. But he didn't want her to lose her job, at least until she found something better. He would suggest she start looking, and use that better one as an excuse to leave. Appearing to want more, to move up, would look better on her record than quitting outright or getting fired.

He put the groceries away. The dinner would have to wait. By the time she got off work and they got back, it would be done too late. He'd take her out instead.

Second call he'd missed that day. As Deanna was changing from work, meeting, and then dinner, Daws checked the machine. Virginia Gray's voice asked him to call back as soon as possible, even if it was late; she was always up late, and up early. She left a different number. He let the thing run to see what else was there, deleted the garbage, left the one from Deanna's friend, then went back to replay the first one and wrote the new number on the message pad.

Deanna came over to meet him as it ended. "One of your appointments today?"

"Yes, the one I most wanted to hear from."

"So call her."

He turned and set his hands on her hips. "It'll wait until tomorrow when you're at work."

"It's okay. You had to wait an extra two hours for me. Still can't believe he found a way to make it last that long while saying nothing. But go ahead."

"She'll wait. You have a message from Jenn." He didn't want to appear too anxious with Ms. Gray. "Coffee or wine?"

"She'll wait, too. Coffee. I don't want to get sleepy too fast."

"But you do need to sleep so you can get up for work tomorrow."

"I'll catch up when you go back to work." She met his lips. "And we're going to talk more about Ryan, aren't we? If I have to improvise, I need some basis to go on."

"Coffee it is."

"How about I make it? Don't you want to get more comfortable?"

"Hadn't thought about it. Guess I will." Daws watched her amble away toward the kitchen. Incredible woman. Strong, independent, fiery, smart ... and still willing to allow him to treat her like a lady without balking. A true lady, knowing she could do anything herself but confident enough in that knowledge to let him hold doors and be protective. She had to know he couldn't be anything else.

Daws pulled into sweats and a tee and came out to the smell of strong coffee brewing. She was on the couch, her legs curled beside her. He grabbed the packet of information he'd collected during the day, along with some he already had, and took it over. Before he sat, the phone rang and he went to grab it.

"Mr. Dawson?"

"Yes."

"Virginia Gray. I wasn't sure you'd actually call back after hours since so many have problems with that, so I thought I'd call instead and see if you were in."

"Barely. Just got your message."

"You weren't going to call tonight."

"No. Would have in the morning."

"I can see you're going to be interesting to deal with. Straight-forward. I like that, but I don't see it much. So, I listened to the tape since I had a few minutes in between appointments. I only meant to listen for a minute or two but I ended up late to my next appointment. The kid has a good voice. Tell me those songs are his own."

"They are."

Silence. "How did your other meetings go?" She sounded wary.

"One was pointless. One might not be."

"Ah. You haven't signed anything yet?"

"Can't sign anything yet. The kid doesn't even know."

"Right. Well, what'll it take to give me first shot when he does know?"

"What kind of offer are you making?" Listening to the terms, he jotted notes and said he couldn't promise anything, that it was up to the kid, but when the time came, he'd encourage Ryan to set up an appointment to talk with her. And he agreed to let Virginia speak with Deanna to get acquainted.

Accepting the phone, Deanna put on her full business attitude. Daws stepped back and listened a moment, then went to pour coffee. She was still chatting when he returned, talking of her market experience.

"I'll look forward to hearing from her. Thank you. I'll put Fred back on."

Daws wanted to hang up and ask Deanna just who she would hear from. Her eyes sparkled with excitement. Instead, he let Virginia Gray know he was back on the line.

"You didn't tell me your girlfriend was in marketing."

"Should I have?"

"I half expected some little airhead good at following orders. No offense. I'm glad she's not. Is there any way we can all meet for lunch sometime this week?" Running it back and forth between the two women, they agreed on Thursday, close to Deanna's job since she had the shortest time allowance.

Finally off the phone, he sat with her again.

She grasped his hand. "I hope Ryan is smart enough to let you lead him toward her. I think she's a wonderful possibility. How'd you find her?"

"Network. Andrews is a roadie, does electrical work for shows. He led me in the right direction. So, this is what I have." He opened his first folder. "I'll be digging more while you're at work. Trying to set myself up to where I need to be."

"Okay, but, how are you going to do this around your job? I'll do what I can, gladly, but he'll be out of school in a couple of years and you still have ... eight to reach retirement?"

"Anna, my current enlistment is up in a year. I don't plan to reenlist. I'm getting out."

"What?" She stared, surprise and possibly a touch of hopefulness covering her face. "But I thought this was who you were, what you wanted the way I want to be in marketing, at least through twenty."

"I always figured I'd hit at least twenty. Things have changed."

"Not because of me?"

"Who do you look forward to hearing from?"

"What?"

"The phone just now."

"Oh. She might have a lead on another job, smaller but friendlier. Better possibilities. But it's just a lead."

"You should follow up on it. Check it out."

"But ... if we're going to move..."

"We're not." He pulled her hand into both of his. "I have six months left overseas and then only six more until I get out. They won't bother to move me from Drum for that. If I stay in, they'll move me. Could be anywhere..."

"I'll go with you. I told you I would."

Daws kissed her fingers. "I've done my time and I'm ready to move forward. This may not work out. If it doesn't, I'll find something else based here. Don't worry, Anna. And don't hold yourself back for me. I want you to go whatever direction you need to go. We'll make it work."

"I don't want you to leave me again."

Grabbing a deep breath, Daws moved the paperwork to the table and urged her closer. "Not much longer." He kissed her head. "Hang in there with me."

"Always." She brushed his lips. "No matter what we end up doing. It'll be together, right? After this."

"Yes. And it is now."

=== November ===

Tying his boots as tight as he could get them, Daws stood and took her in as she wrapped around him. She still smelled of sleep and their bed and she felt so vulnerable in her pajama pants and thin tank top, her shoulders and arms bare, her head resting against his shoulder. Against his pressed stiff uniform.

"Come on, Anna." Forcing partial release, he took her hand and led her back to the bedroom.

"Changing your mind and staying longer, soldier?" Her voice teased although her eyes were serious.

"Wish I could." He drew back the blankets. "You're getting cold."

"No, I'm fine. I'm staying at your side as long as I can. Guess I should at least get my robe before I go to the elevator." She brushed a hand through his hair, what there was of it. He'd had it cut again the day before, back to regulation.

"I don't want you to come to the elevator. I want to leave you tucked in and warm, not standing alone in the hallway. Can't do it."

"Freddy..."

"I'll sit with you a couple of minutes." Daws waited for her to slide underneath the blankets and he pulled them most of the way up. He wanted to see her bare shoulders.

She fingered his uniform, the pocket flap, the buttoned hem, the rank pinned to his collar. "You do know how proud I am of you?"

In answer, he leaned down and claimed her mouth. He didn't want to leave her.

"Freddy." She whispered next to his ear, her arms wrapped up around his shoulders. "You take care of yourself and come back home to me. I'll be here waiting. I love you."

"I love you too, Anna. Don't let anyone treat you the way they shouldn't. Do whatever you need. I'll stand by you." He found her lips again. "I have to go."

"Be safe, Sergeant Dawson."

"You too. Call Andrews if you need." He saw her nod and made himself get up. With a quick brush of his fingers through her hair, he moved away and left the room. He couldn't let himself look back at her again. It was too hard already.

He would get through the next six months telling himself it was for her; what he was doing was for her, for her family, for the major's family, for every American family able to go about their own lives and keep the country running from within. He'd seen first-hand how important it was to protect their ability to remain strong. He wondered how many of them realized how important it was to maintain their own businesses, their own jobs, their own strength. To stay in control of their own futures. He'd seen what happened when it was all left in other hands. He would gladly live the way he was for the next year or so on top of his nearly twelve served so he wouldn't have to live the way he'd seen. Powerless. Defenseless. No. He would sacrifice everything before he would live that way.

Deanna held herself together until she heard the door close. And then she gripped his pillow to catch her tears and thought about running after him, just to hold him once more to help her last another six months. Such a long time.

She considered not going to work, calling in sick. She was sick. Sick of dealing with so many days alone without him. Sick of looking like everything was fine when nothing much was fine. She hated her stupid job by now but her leads that he pushed her to try to find led nowhere. Too many in her field knew Todd, or they knew her boss, or Mr. McCallister. They wouldn't hire away from the owner, or they'd been warned away by one of the jerks. How so many doors in such a big city could be closed to her, she didn't understand. There had to be something she was missing, something she could do better. Maybe she would follow Virginia Gray's lead as he said she should. Maybe not. She was sick to death by this time of having doors slammed in her face. Right now, she couldn't begin to think of dealing with it once more.

And she didn't want him gone another six months. The four weeks together every day spoiled her too much; she wanted more of it, not in six months. Now.

Burying her face deeper in his pillow, the sobbing tears turned to quick breaths. She had to pull herself together. She wasn't about to call in. They knew he was leaving today. She'd taken the past two days off. She would never give them the satisfaction of thinking she couldn't handle it. She could.

She would, whether or not she could. For him. For their future.

=======

She nearly ignored the phone. It wasn't the right time for Fred to call.

The ringing annoyed her, though, so she got up to grab it just to make it stop.

"Deanna?"

"Who's asking?"

"Ellis Andrews."

"Oh. Of course. How are you?" Deanna pulled up a chair. She was too tired to stand. And she felt like an idiot not recognizing him after talking with him about the photos and then meeting him and his wife for lunch when Freddy was still home.

"Good, thank you. I wondered if you had plans for Thanksgiving."

The question caught her off-guard.

"My wife and I are having a couple of friends over and we thought, with the sergeant away, maybe you'd like to come, as well. She wanted to be sure you wouldn't spend it alone as she did our first year of marriage."

"Oh."

"Unless you have plans."

"No. I don't. But I don't want to impose..."

"We'd love to have you. She loves to cook and always makes far too much for the few of us. It's just another Army couple and a couple of her friends from work. Nothing fancy. I'd be glad to come pick you up."

"Um. I'm sorry, this is unexpected."

"No need to answer now. Just let me know if you'd like to join us. It's not at all an imposition. As I said, there'll be plenty of food."

"Thank you. I'll think about it."

"No problem. Tell him I said hello when he calls and wish he could come, also. Maybe next year."

"Yes. Maybe. And I'll let you know either way. I do appreciate it. Thank you." She hung up wondering why she didn't accept. But she didn't know them well. They both seemed nice enough. Freddy trusted him. But she wanted to ask him first. Andrews was his friend. She had to ask what he thought.

Maybe he understood she had to ask first. That could have been what he meant by telling her to say hello for him. She'd ask. It had to be better than sitting home alone. The little turkey breast she'd picked up could wait.

Daws dug into his mix of turkey and stuffing plus Kimshi of various sorts and tried to take part in the conversation surrounding him. His thoughts were on Deanna and the way they spent it together the year before, how she took everything in and amused him with her questions and flattered him with her unending interest in understanding as much about his world as she could. He was glad she was with Andrews and his friends today. He would have hated knowing she was home alone.

He was also amused that she'd asked him first. He knew that

wouldn't last long. As soon as her feet were better under her and he was there all the time, Daws was well aware things would change. She was assertive. An in-charge type. He loved that about her. He couldn't wait to see more of it.

"Sergeant?"

He raised his eyes across the table to his lieutenant.

"You're in another world today. Mind sharing it with us?"

"I do mind. Did I miss something?"

"Home with the little lady, am I right?"

He didn't answer. There was no point.

"So do you plan to make it permanent with this one?"

Daws looked over at him again. "It is."

"I thought you weren't married."

"We're not. Technically. Doesn't mean it's not permanent." He scooped spicy cold radish onto his fork. That, he'd have to learn to make.

"Never would have thought you to be commitment-phobic."

"I'm not. Already have the commitment."

"Still, she could leave easier without the contract. How do you know she's not hanging out with someone who's around? What's to stop her?"

With another forkful and a swig of hot tea, he gave a light shrug. "Same thing that stops you, or doesn't, if you're married. If she wants to break it off, she should. A piece of paper won't make a difference. Wouldn't try to hold her against her will. Couldn't live that way."

It was enough to shut him up and turn the conversation elsewhere.

As soon as he could escape, he called her. It was early the next morning her time, but he wanted plenty of chance to talk before work. Except she didn't have to work. He'd forgotten about Black Friday when everyone but retailers and restaurants were closed. She had plenty of time to talk. Her voice was sleepy, but he held her as long as he dared, and listened to her talk about how nice it had been to spend Thanksgiving with his friend if she couldn't be with him, how she'd enjoyed the Army stories.

Daws cringed. He should have called Andrews and requested he not tell stories. Wouldn't have mattered, though. Andrews was a talker.

And his wife sent a bunch of leftovers with Deanna, wanting them out of the house, she said. She also invited Deanna to go to lunch with her sometime on a weekend when she didn't have plans.

Maybe they'd have her for Christmas, also, since he couldn't be there for that, either.

Deanna hadn't planned to spend so much of her Saturday on the phone, but at least she finally got to talk to Mrs. Reynauld. She figured the young male who answered was Ryan but he didn't give his name and she didn't give hers. She asked for his mom and he called to her without bothering to cover the phone.

Brazen kid. It was all through his voice. But there was something sweet about it, as well.

In between trying to juggle the music stuff she hardly understood, including a quick chat with Andrews, she got a call from Todd. He wanted her to work all weekend. This time with pay. She turned him down.

Deciding she needed a break from the phone and the apartment, Deanna wrapped up in layers to fight off the cold and went for a walk around the park. Her near daily walks, even when only up and down stairs in her building or at the mall were improving her figure and her good-energy level. They were also therapy, releasing some of the pent-up energy from nerves, from job anger, from missing him.

It was snowing, only flurries, but at least there was no wind. She pulled her scarf around her nose and mouth to deter the cold and quickened her pace. There were few people out and she enjoyed the near silence of walking alone among the snowflakes that stuck to the trees and carpeted the grass. She wasn't quite alone. A few winter-hardy birds braved the cloudy chill. Deanna slowed to enjoy a small group of black and white chickadees, her favorites, as they fluttered down from a bare tree like heavy-falling leaves. They were quick to grab at the small crumbs of a near frozen hot dog bun. Before long, bigger birds would come along to fight for it. They had to grab what they could while they could. Deanna often felt the same. It was nature. You were either one of the big birds or you learned to use your resources to work around them.

If she let herself, she could hear cars along the outside of Central Park, but they were easy to tune out. It was only part of the city and hardly more notice than a gnat behind her head. Of course she didn't have to worry about gnats or other bugs with the thirty-five degree temperature. That was the good thing about the cold.

One month down. Today was the one month mark from the day Freddy went back to work. She was doing well. It didn't go as slow as it had the first time. They were over the halfway mark and she told herself the rest would be easier. This time when he came home, he would stay. Well, he would stay at Drum until he got out, but at least he would be in the States and she could go visit if he couldn't.

Or she could move with him.

If she let her job go, and it was more tempting every day, even without another lined up or the promise of one, she could go with him. They'd have to pay someone to watch the apartment, but with as much as she'd saved by doing the redecorating work herself, and since she'd put her own funds into it as well, she figured it would be okay short term. He'd loved her decorating scheme. He didn't complain about anything she'd done, including her mismatched coffee mugs added to his and moved to the shelf with the glass door. He even used hers instead of his when he poured coffee. Freddy urged her to continue decorating as she wished.

Maybe she'd go shopping the next day. She didn't have Christmas gifts to buy, since she gave him his already – a few CDs of bands she thought he'd enjoy to take back with him – and she'd mailed a pretty sweater to her mom. No one else needed anything from her, so she could search for things for the apartment instead. At least she would feel part of the December shopping rush that way.

Work was having an exchange again. And again, she refused. She didn't like the idea of mandatory gifts for people she didn't particularly care about. Too hypocritical. They could think what they wanted and continue their little farce as they wished, without her.

A raucous bird pulled her attention to a tree in the near distance and she caught glimpse of a large man in a bulky long coat. His collar was up around his neck hiding part of his face. He was headed her direction, crossing the grass instead of on a trail. Deanna realized with a cringe that she'd left her pepper spray behind. In all of the times she'd been out walking alone, she'd never had need to even think about it. So she hadn't. With another glance, she was sure he was watching, his path on an intersect with hers. She turned and headed back. Her walk would be long enough.

Deanna sped her steps, carefully, watching for slick points on the path from unmelted snow and touches of ice, and glanced back over. He'd changed direction, again on an intercept. He'd chosen his spot well: she wasn't at an open part of the path; a large cement wall blocked the way to the road. She had to keep going. He sped up. So did her heart. Would he run if she did? Or would he give up? She wanted to look in control, whether or not she was.

Up ahead she could get out to the road. Her quick walk became a jog as Deanna hoped not to hit ice. Fred. She wanted him there. She wanted to call his name, or his number ... the phone. She did have his phone with her, in her pocket. He'd asked her to carry it in case he could call.

She slowed enough to pull it out, making sure the man could see she had a phone, and hit a number. It started to ring. She had no idea who she'd just called but a voice at the other end would be comforting.

"Virginia Gray."

Oh. No. That wasn't a number she wanted to call.

"Hello?"

Deanna looked back at the man; he was closing in. "Yes, I'm in Central Park near the tennis courts and there's a man following..." She spoke loudly, looking at him directly now, studying what he wore, his height, complexion.

He turned away.

"Hello? Who is this?" Virginia's voice called out.

"I'm sorry. I didn't mean to call you." The guy continued to retreat. She kept an eye on him as she slowed her pace.

"Deanna?"

She stopped walking long enough to catch her breath. Her lungs hurt with the too-fast intake of cold air.

"Hello? Are you all right?"

"Yes." She bent over and held herself with a hand against her knee.

"Is this Deanna? I think I recognize your voice. What about the man? Wait, I'll call the police from the other line. Don't go..."

"No, it's okay. He left. I'm sorry. I just hit a number. I didn't mean to bother you."

"It's all right. Are you sure he's gone?"

"Yes, he saw me on the phone. Figured I'd been smart enough to dial 911, I suppose. Guess I should have. I panicked. That's not like me. I don't panic."

"Okay honey. Catch your breath. You're alone?"

"Yes, but it's okay now. Thank you."

"Wait, Deanna, don't go. Keep talking to me. Head to the nearest restaurant or shop and let me know where you are."

"No, it's fine. I'm going home. Sorry I bothered you."

"Listen to me. He could still cut around. Do as I say. Go now. Don't take your time. You're still by the tennis courts?"

"Just south of that, close to the reservoir."

"Okay. Get to the street as soon as you can and let me know where you are. I'm staying on the phone."

Deanna heard her muffle her voice and talk to someone else. She should have thought to dial 911 instead. It would be far less embarrassing. She gave in to Virginia, though, since she'd bothered her.

And it was comforting, more than Deanna wanted to admit.

They chatted while she kept an eye out for the man and quickened her pace again. Ginny asked about her walking alone. Deanna told her about stair walking and how her returned health kick made her feel better. She knew it was no more than rambling, maintaining the connection. Finally, she got to the sidewalk and found a sign. "I'm at 93rd. Thank you. I'll let you alone now. And I'm sorry..."

"Don't be." Virginia repeated the street number and mentioned a restaurant. She asked Deanna to meet her there and to give them her name. She tried to argue; she'd taken too much of the woman's time already.

"I want to talk with you anyway. This is as good a time as any. I'll meet you there." She hung up.

Stopping at the light, she felt like a huge idiot. She could have just acted like she'd called the police. He wouldn't have known. Now this woman she'd barely met, a contact of Freddy's, was coming ... why? She'd told her she was fine. She *was* fine. Only shaken. But there were plenty of people out on the street. Too many witnesses. She was fine.

Still, Virginia Gray was headed to meet her. She couldn't very well not be there.

Her lungs still hurt from cold and sudden exertion when she reached the place. Heat pressed against her as she opened the door. She was suddenly too hot, still breathing too heavy, with so many layers.

"Do you have a reservation?" A skinny balding man in a black and white suit eyed her.

"No..."

"I'm afraid this is reservation only, and we maintain a dress code."

The way he glanced at her jeans made Deanna think he equated them with a bum. They weren't her best jeans, since she was only out walking, but they weren't holey, either. "I'm meeting someone here and then I'll gladly get out of your way."

"I'm afraid you'll have to wait outside. This isn't McDonald's."

She wanted to haul off and deck him. "Tell you what. Take your snooty attitude and your fake accent and leave me alone. As I said, I'm meeting someone here. A regular, I think."

"I'm sure you are, Miss..."

"*Ma'am* or *Ms.* Don't call me Miss. I'm not twelve and assuming my marital status is not your place."

He cleared his throat and shifted his shoulders. "Yes well, unless you can give me a name as to whom you're meeting, I'm afraid you'll have to wait outside. This is a business and a private establishment. We have a certain class of clientele..."

"Oh I'm sure you do, but you can kiss off because Ms. Gray asked me to meet her. Otherwise I'd be just as happy not to stand here and be leered at by an over-glamorized waiter."

He stiffened. "Ms. Gray?"

"Virginia Gray. She said to give you her name." Deanna had to stifle a grin. The guy recognized the name.

"Hem, well." He skimmed through his book. "I don't see her reservation so my guess is you're throwing out her name erroneously..."

The door opened again and brought a swift rush of cold with it. Wrapped in a thick suede coat, Virginia swept in nearly as quick as the wind and came up to take her hands. "Deanna, are you all right?"

"Yes. And thank you again, but I didn't mean to interrupt your day..."

"No, not at all. Some days beg interruption and this was one of them. I was glad for the excuse." She peeled leather gloves from her fingers and turned to the smug man who was suddenly less smug. "I do realize I didn't call in but this is rather last minute. Would you have a small cozy table somewhere private and warm?"

He gave her a light bow. "Of course. Right this way."

Daws undressed and got under the blankets, still thinking about his conversation with Deanna. She'd called Virginia accidentally? Deanna was too together to not pay more attention than that. There was something she didn't say. No amount of coercion made her spill it all. Something happened she didn't want him to know.

He raised his arms and hooked his hands under his head. He'd try again. Maybe she needed time first to sort it through her own head.

Their meeting went well, though. Deanna liked the woman, although she mentioned Virginia was rather abrupt and it could be hard for a young kid to deal with, particularly one who was somewhat rebellious. That's what would make it work, though. Ryan would have to have a strong hand, like his mother. Mrs. Reynauld didn't pull punches, either. She was firm and determined. He would be used to that. Anyone unwilling to push him would never get anywhere with him. The boy would walk all over them once he felt secure in his role as even a slight celebrity. Daws figured he would try, anyway. He'd likely be one to get arrogant fast if it wasn't reined in, to his own detriment more than to anyone else's.

Hard to deal with. His own brother's words. Daws needed someone like Virginia Gray to help rein him in. Ryan wasn't a soldier. He couldn't give him orders. The kid would take more finesse.

=======

"*Moron.*" Deanna slammed her file down on her desk. The creep had only recommended a twenty cent raise, citing her days off and her few late days, never mind all the extra work she'd been doing and time she'd stayed late to make up for it. And no bonus. Still, Todd asked her again about working all weekend. Again, she said no. It was a ploy to get her alone, to use her skill and give her nothing in return. She wasn't stupid enough to do it more than once.

"Deanna, can I speak with you?"

With a sigh, she turned to Phillips. "What?"

"In my office."

She trudged in behind him and refused the chair he beckoned her toward.

"I want to know your interest in continuing with our company, since some of us are starting to wonder if you want to be here."

She tried hard not to laugh. "I do my work well. I don't gossip as some do. I don't whine and complain. I work. So I'm not sure why you're asking."

"Be that as it may, your attitude is causing problems."

"My attitude?" She shook her head and forced herself to stay calm. "I'm friendly to clients. I've had no complaints filed. So just what's wrong with my attitude?"

He leaned forward, arms crossed on his desk. "Your hostility toward Mr. Bodin is causing undue stress around the office. That needs to stop."

"My hostility. Oh, you haven't seen just how hostile I feel toward Mr. Bodin because I am at work and I am professional and I have done or said nothing worse than he's said or done to me, and not nearly as bad. If he wants me to be less hostile, he can start treating me as fairly as he treats his other employees."

"Except we know there is history between the two of you that makes that rather impossible."

"Of course it doesn't. That history was a long time ago, long before he had any administrative power over me. It means nothing. I am a paid employee here. I do my job better than most. And yet he treats me like dirt. My attitude is a reflection of that and until he decides to grow up and get over himself, my *attitude* won't change."

He stiffened and stood again. "Mr. Bodin is in charge of this section. I suggest you remember that. And I suggest you might accept his offer to work this weekend and start making up for the tension you're causing."

Deanna stared, unable to believe what the man was suggesting. She didn't at all believe he meant she should actually work, and yet, she could prove nothing.

"Are we clear?"

She remained silent a moment and then returned to her desk, pulled up a new document, and started typing. As she left, she handed the jerk her resignation, stating another job possibility she needed time to explore, and her unwillingness to work any longer in a *hostile* environment. He'd have to put it in her file. She'd sent a copy of it to the admin office when the mail came around an hour earlier.

Two weeks. She'd given them that much because it was in her contract. She could handle them for two more weeks. By the New Year, she would be free of it all. And unemployed. And alone for the holidays.

She grabbed a paper on her way home to start skimming the want ads. The bus ride was noisy and animated, as was more normal close to Christmas when people decided to be nice to each other temporarily. She was more than ready to get off at her stop and walk away from it. Her heels annoyed her as they clicked down the sidewalk and up the five flights of stairs, slowing as she went. With a sigh at her closed door, she kicked out of her shoes and pulled off her coat, switching the paper and the mail she'd grabbed from the box to the other hand, and flopped on the couch to rifle through the garbage.

One wasn't garbage. A Christmas card from her mom.

Deanna held it in her hands a while before she lay it on the table and got up again to dump the junk mail. The answering machine light was flashing but she ignored that, also. She wanted to be left alone. The thought nearly made her laugh. She was alone. How much more alone did she want to be?

Going in to change, she decided not to walk tonight. She hadn't since that day. It was time to join a gym again instead, except she couldn't do that, either, not without an income. Pulling on her oldest, most comfortable pajamas and thick robe, she went to find something for a quick dinner. Leftover casserole would do. Again. She stuck it in a microwave bowl, added a touch of water, and started it for two minutes.

Fred would call soon. She'd feel better after she talked to him.

As she waited for the microwave, she pressed the review button on the machine.

Todd. What an arrogant jerk. Asking her not to quit. News had traveled fast. She hit delete before he stopped jabbering and moved on to the next message.

Virginia. Inviting Deanna to lunch on Saturday. With a frown, she saved the message and went back to get her food, adding extra garlic to enhance the leftover blandness and grabbing a lemonade. It was her first since Freddy had restocked them for her.

She so desperately wanted to hold onto him. Just hold him and feel his arms around her.

Shoving that thought aside, she retrieved the new decorating magazine that had come and set it on the table to flip through as she ate. She was still sitting there, finished eating, nursing her drink and considering possibilities from the pictures when the phone rang and she jumped up to grab it.

"Deanna, wasn't sure you'd answer."

Her stomach clenched. "Todd, why are you calling me?"

"I don't want you to quit. I made them hold onto your resignation until I spoke to you. We can work it out."

"No, we can't. It's done. Well, in two weeks it will be, and I have to get off the phone. Don't call back." She hung up as he was asking her not to. At the next ring, she checked the number first and relaxed immediately at Fred's greeting. "I'm so glad to hear your voice." She lowered onto a chair, her elbow propped on the counter to support her head.

"What's wrong, Anna?"

"I quit my job today." She explained maybe more than she should have, even telling him the jerk had just called.

"I'm glad you quit. Don't worry about it and don't job hunt until after the New Year. Give yourself time to relax."

"Oh, but I don't want to go through my savings. I've been so careful to save and it may take a while to find another one and it may not be high enough pay to keep saving as I have been..."

"You have access to the account. Use it."

The account. His. She felt her head shake. "No, Freddy, that's ... for the apartment, for decorating..."

"And for anything else you need. That's why I put your name on it."

"No. I mean ... I'll find another job. I've always taken care of myself..."

"We're partners, Anna. With as much as you're taking care of for me, you shouldn't have a second thought about letting me help you in return. Use it as you need."

"Oh." She didn't want to continue that line of conversation and so grabbed the opening. "Speaking of, Virginia left a message. She wants to have lunch on Saturday. I can't imagine why. I don't know anymore than I've already told her."

"So go find out. If you want. Say no if you don't. She can wait and deal with me. There's nothing urgent since the kid isn't ready for her yet."

"No, that was my thought."

"Call back and ask. Say no if you don't want to go. She could be a valuable contact for you, though; has a lot of connections."

"Oh, I don't want to use that..."

"Why not?"

"This is about Ryan, about you. I'm not imposing."

"Deanna, that's how business works. It's not imposing. It's networking. If she offers contacts, use them. I assure you none of them would think twice about doing the same."

"Maybe."

"And if that jerk calls you again, tell him to stop or you'll file a restraining order. He has no business calling you at home."

"I don't have grounds for that..."

"Did you tell him not to call back?"

"Yes."

"Than you have grounds if he does. He'll know that." Silence came over the line as she pondered whether she could actually threaten Todd with legal action. "I wish I was there for you to tell him myself, and to go with you to meet Virginia."

She chuckled. "If you were here, he wouldn't dare call." Deanna bit her lip, wishing he was there. She wouldn't allow it to show in her voice.

"Be careful with him."

"I am. Don't worry, okay? I can handle it." She pressed her hand against her eyes to prevent tears. She absolutely would not do that over the phone. She would not worry him. He had enough to think about, to keep his mind on. She would not add to it.

"Hang in there, Anna. I can hear in your voice you're more upset than you're admitting, but hang in there. I'll be home soon. For good."

A tear escaped and she swallowed hard, then grabbed a deep quiet breath and wiped it away. "I'm all right. Just one of those days. I'll take a long bath with plenty of bath salts and think of you in there with me and I'll be fine."

"You're going to think of me in the bath with you?"

"Yes."

"Hm. Hold onto that thought until I can make it real for you."

She chuckled. "Oh, trust me. There are a lot of thoughts I'm holding onto that directly involve you. But I better change the subject, I think. Everything okay there?"

A pause. "Yes, nothing interesting going on, and that's always good."

"It is good. Save the interesting for when you get home."

"I'll do my best, but I thought you were changing the subject."

"Well, I'm trying. I'd rather not. But you're kind of in public at the moment, right?"

"Yes. And I have to go in a couple of minutes; there's a line." His voice lowered. "But you should realize I'll be thinking about you in the tub thinking of me with you. Going to make the day interesting to get through."

"Yeah? Should I encourage that thought and make it even more interesting?"

Another pause. "I think we better leave it there. You're sure you're all right?"

"Yes. And I can't wait to have you in my arms again."

"Same here. I love you, Anna. Have a good night and don't worry about the job. Just look forward to the end of it. It'll all work out."

Deanna returned the sentiment and let him go, although she wanted to keep him talking, to keep him a few minutes longer, or an hour. As she grabbed her lemonade and went to tuck herself onto the couch, she thought of the way *I love you* had become so second nature for him to say. She could tell at first it was hard, that he had to push himself. By now, though, he was at ease with it, and he told her every time they talked. It was so sweet. She wondered if he knew how much difference it made to her just to hear it.

Wiping a few more tears, she picked up the Christmas card from her mom. She was apparently home still. Or again. There had been no word since summer; her sister never answered. Deanna supposed it was possible her mother had "taken a break" and returned again. Did she even want to know?

How long had it been now since she'd been home? Thinking back to what year she moved, she nearly gasped at the realization it had been eight years. She'd been nineteen. For the first year she'd called home often, checking in, keeping the connection. As time went by, she called less often. She didn't even remember the last time she'd called. Home felt like a world away by now. She felt a whole different person than she had been.

She set the card down again and headed back to take a long bath.

The doorbell interrupted. With a frown, Deanna wondered who would be at the door at nearly seven, or at all, for that matter. Checking the peephole, she clenched her teeth. Todd. How did he find her? She'd never added her address to work records. She was completely unlisted; her name wasn't even on the phone or the apartment.

Deanna considered ignoring it, but she wanted to know how he found her. Or she could pretend he didn't. If she didn't answer, he wouldn't be sure he did.

He rang again, then knocked.

She didn't want him there, in the hallway, where neighbors could see him. With her foot against the inside of the door so he couldn't push it open, she cracked it just enough. "How did you find me here?"

Todd gave her a grinning sneer. "Easy enough, once I decided to try."

"Really? I'm unlisted. Who did you talk to?"

He shrugged. "No one. You may not be listed, but Fred Dawson is. I expected that's where you were. Not hard to figure out."

"Go away. You have no right to be here."

"Deanna, let me in so we can talk about you quitting."

"There's nothing to talk about."

"You're not seriously leaving. Deanna, open the door." He tried to push it.

She held firm. "Try that again and I'll call the cops. You're not coming in."

He slid a foot against the door frame. "And when you go to the phone, I'll come in behind you. Stop being ridiculous. It's not like we haven't been alone before."

"I don't have to go to the phone. It's right here." Raising the cordless where he could see it but not reach it, she savored calling his hand. "Leave, Todd."

"Come on, little flower. You're blowing this whole thing way out of proportion. I only came to talk, to see what we can work out so you'll stay. I never thought you'd leave. I thought you were more of a fighter than that. So come on, fight for what you want. I have no doubt you'll figure out a way to win. That's what I've been waiting for."

"Get out." She pushed the door but he stopped it.

He chuckled. "What do you want? You want me to leave the wife? Is this whole thing with the soldier who's never here a ploy to make me jealous?"

"I don't care enough about you to bother making you jealous. And I don't care what you do or don't do with your wife. I don't even care if you're taking every other girl in the office back to your apartment. I don't care. I made the mistake of you once. I'm not stupid enough to do it again, especially when I have exactly what I want. He's incredible. He's committed to only me, and that goes both ways. He knows what honor and respect and decency mean and he is all of those things..."

"Then why would he want you?" A smirk covered his face.

Deanna reached out to shove him, hard, knocking his foot out away from the door. And she slammed it. He knocked again, called her name. She called building security. They asked if she was all right.

All right? No. She wanted Freddy. Of course she told them she was fine.

She had three sick days left. She would use one tomorrow. She couldn't face Todd tomorrow.

The next morning, she opened the card.

With strong coffee in hand, and having called in to work after talking to Freddy and telling him she'd be home, Deanna curled up in her robe that she planned to leave on all day and unfolded the sheets of notebook paper. Six pages. Most would be about neighbors and the town and such, as usual.

She was right. And she skimmed through to go back and read later. It was sometimes interesting, but she most wanted family news and that was always toward the end. Deanna frowned that it took until the last page. It said almost nothing about her mom or siblings. Most was about how her dad, her step dad, was failing in health and maybe it would be a relief to have one less thing to take care of, before her mom backtracked and said she didn't really mean it, only on certain moments.

She signed off: *Love, Mom.*

Deanna stared at it a while. Love? She never signed off that way. She'd rarely said it and only in person on "certain moments" meaning rare and to be remembered. Why had she not mentioned Deanna's siblings? Her last letter suggested she could call her brothers and sisters more often. She had called a few times in the beginning, but they never called back. She'd written but they never wrote back. Why should she make the effort they wouldn't?

"Fine." She threw the letter on the table and stared out the large windows overlooking the balcony. Wouldn't they be shame-faced for their words when she left home if they knew how she was living now? They swore she'd come home broke and needing help. She swore she wouldn't. Maybe that's what they expected, that she'd failed and was barely surviving and didn't want to admit it. Well, they could just think that. What did she care?

She did, though. She at least didn't want her mom to think so. She'd always worked so hard to make her mom proud. And what would she write back? That she was unemployed and living with a man who would probably end up supporting her when her own funds ran out?

No. She wouldn't bother to write before she said that.

Her half siblings could think what they wanted. She had to write her mom. It would be unfair to make her worry. Maybe she'd just write about Freddy and say she was doing well and leave it at that.

Getting up, she went to the window and sipped her coffee as she looked out over what she could see of the city from there. Maybe she'd go shopping. No. She didn't want to go out. She wanted to stay in her robe and ... and what?

She needed to return Virginia's call.

Gathering the nerve to do it, she refilled her coffee first and dialed the number. Her secretary answered; she was with a client. Deanna left a message and thanked her.

She went back to stare out the window. The day off would give her extra time to plan the rest of the apartment decorations. A tree. They didn't have a Christmas tree. If she had to spend the holiday alone, she would at least have a tree. Artificial. She didn't want pine needles all over the floor to step on in her bare feet. She didn't want to have to water it. She particularly didn't want to think that the poor little tree had been cut down instead of being allowed to grow and flourish. No, plastic and metal wouldn't make her feel guilty.

Not today, though. She wasn't going out today.

The phone rang and she took another swallow of rich coffee as she ambled over to answer. In a quick conversation, Virginia convinced her it was necessary to meet over the weekend, but Deanna insisted on somewhere less pretentious than before. They compromised on a coffee house.

With nothing else she wanted to do, she went and gathered three of her favorite movies and brought them back out. Why not really play sick and watch movies all day? Tomorrow, she'd look at the want ads.

Daws hung up with Andrews. Deanna turned them down for

Christmas dinner. He wondered why. She said something about plans as an excuse but she hadn't mentioned plans to him. She'd had a nice time with them on Thanksgiving, or so she said.

There was no one waiting for the phone, and she said she'd be home all day, so he dialed her number.

Noise in the distance made it hard to hear. The television.

"Hey, hold on." In a few seconds, the noise stopped and she returned. "Sorry, I wasn't expecting you. What's up?"

"Sneaking an extra call since you're home. Am I interrupting?"

"Yes. Hugh Grant. But he'll be a good boy and wait for me."

"Good to know. Enjoying your day off?"

"Very much. I'm being a bum, still in my robe and slippers watching movies. Haven't even brushed my hair. Turned on yet?"

He grinned and wished he could see her, cuddle up beside her. "Did you call Virginia back?"

"Yes. We're meeting Saturday. I still don't know why. Any clue?"

"No. I haven't had contact with her. I save my calls for you. Except I'll admit I just called Andrews." Silence. "Deanna?"

"Yes?"

"You have plans for Christmas?"

"No. That was ... well, sort of. I plan to stay right here and talk to you and watch every Christmas movie I can find."

"Why won't you spend it with them?"

"Freddy, they're great people and it's not that I don't want to, it's..."

"What?"

"They'll have family over and they're all couples together and it was hard enough on Thanksgiving. I can't do that again, not until you're here to go with me so I don't look so pathetic. I'm not sure why it's harder to be single on a holiday when you aren't actually single than when you are, but it is."

He dropped his head and rubbed his neck. "Have you thought about going home this year?"

"Home?" She laughed. "No."

"Why?"

"Because I ... I don't know, I just don't."

"Maybe you should. I don't want you to be alone."

"I won't be alone. You'll call me."

"It's not the same."

"No, but it's better than any other Christmas I've had since moving up here, except last year. Last year was amazing and I'm hoping for a repeat next year."

"I'll be with you next year. And not working."

"Then it'll be amazing, too."

"Anna, you should consider going home."

"You won't be home."

"I would be if I could."

"I mean, when did you last see your sister for Christmas or any other time?"

He paused, taken aback. He couldn't even remember the last time he'd thought about his *sister.* "Not the same. She's half my sister and didn't want to be that much."

"Mine are half, too. All of them. I'm the odd ball. She married their father because she had me, not because she wanted him. She wanted my father and he didn't want to be married. They all know it's my father she wanted and she tended to treat me as ... well, it was too obvious. Makes it awkward, although it's not my fault and I never tried to get special attention."

"You never told me that."

"No. I don't ... it doesn't matter. They haven't bothered to contact me since I moved, so it doesn't matter."

"Your mom does." He waited through her silence. "Or invite her up there with you."

"She won't leave them to come here."

"Well." He waited as someone walked past. "You might at least think about it. I'll let you get back to your movie..."

"No. Freddy, talk to me. Do you have to go?"

He should. He knew he shouldn't tie up the line. But he agreed to a few minutes longer.

It turned into nearly twenty and a couple of people were waiting so he wished her a good rest of the day and made himself let her go.

=======

"McCallister wants you."

Deanna looked up at the new girl. "*Mr.* McCallister, you mean?"

"What do you care? You're supposed to go up to his office." She sauntered away with a toss of the head.

The owner's office. Deanna sighed and covered the files she was working on with plain paper. For privacy. As she got up, she paused in the jerk's door to tell him she'd be back soon and clarified when he said it wasn't time for break. The elevator lurched up to the highest floor and left Deanna's nerve down below.

His secretary sent her in.

"Ms. Meyers." He stood and came around the desk, offering a chair and then closing the door before he reclaimed his. "I have to say I was chagrined to see that you're leaving. It's hard to lose a valuable employee."

She kept herself from saying *valuable employees* should be treated better.

"I'm also concerned about the 'hostile environment' mentioned in your resignation. I haven't seen any complaints come through. Have you filed any I missed?"

"No. I haven't filed a complaint."

"But you've had problems in the office?"

"It doesn't matter anymore. I'm not trying to cause trouble."

"What trouble have you had?"

"Mr. McCallister, I'm not comfortable with this. I've taken the matter into my own hands and I'm leaving the job to someone who will be better suited for it. It's that simple."

"I'm afraid it's not. I have to investigate the hostility claim. It's my business name at stake."

"Oh, but I'm not doing anything with it. I had to give a reason for leaving. I'm not pressing the issue. And I have nothing against the company as a whole or against you."

He moved from his chair behind the desk to the one opposite where she sat and shifted it to face her. "Would you be more comfortable talking about it with Miss Adams here, as well?"

His assistant? "No."

"Please. Deanna, let me know what trouble you were having. Even if I can't convince you to stay, I do need to prevent it in the future. I won't have my company ruined by anything inappropriate."

His eyes were kind, friendly, concerned. She couldn't quite refuse. "What if I give you the general situation without names? It is partly my own fault and I'm willing to take the blame for that."

He gave her a light grin. "You're welcome to do so, but my guess is I'll know who you mean. You and Mr. Bodin were close for a time."

"You know?"

"I make it a habit to know as much as I can of what might affect my business. I did warn him when he was promoted that it could have no bearing on employee relations, and he assured me your relations with him had been severed."

"Yes. As soon as I knew he was married. Because I didn't."

"I expected as much. I knew nothing about the affair until it had ended. He did say it would not affect your work relationship."

She looked away.

"I take it his assurance wasn't quite accurate."

"No." Briefly, she described the weekend she worked with him, the way he left her name off the project, the way he continued to badger her about working weekends, and that he came to her apartment the other day.

At that, he stood and paced. "I wish you'd told me."

"I have to work in this city. He's already spreading my name around. I can't afford more of that."

He started to answer and then stopped. "Where do you plan to go next?"

"I don't know. I'll find something."

"If you need a recommendation..."

"I won't agree to let them call here for a reference. He'll slam me if he gets hold of it."

"I was going to say, have them call my secretary directly. I'll give you a good reference. Personally." He came back around again. "Or if you'd like to move to another department not under his control, I'll do that. Of course, you could always press charges against him, internally, and it would give me reason to replace him. Then I could move up what's-his-name who took over his job and give you his."

Deanna stared. Give her Todd's old job? An actual marketing executive, a creative, not an assistant.

"You look interested. I've checked your files. You have the qualifications. In fact, I was surprised you weren't moved into Bodin's job."

"I would have been, if I'd been friendly enough. There's not a job in the world worth that."

His chest rose. "I am sorry. If there's a way I can help correct the error now, I'm glad to do it, along with getting rid of Bodin."

She shook her head. "I can't stand to be here anymore. It's too hard. Too many stares. The staff would never give me enough respect, especially if you fire him. He has a lot of *friends* here. I appreciate the offer and I'm tempted, but I can't. I'll finish my two weeks since I have to, but..."

"Well." He paced again. "If I can't convince you to stay, the least I can do is give you the two weeks paid vacation. Starting today. Plus whatever sick time you have left."

"Oh. I'm not asking..."

"I realize you aren't. And I respect that. I'm also grateful you're not making this an issue that could reflect badly on my name. I will talk with Bodin and I'll wait until a better time to get rid of him so it doesn't look connected. But if you're sure about leaving, don't force yourself through more hostility. You have your two weeks vacation, starting tomorrow. If you would, come up before you leave and sign paperwork. Miss Adams will have it ready for you."

"My contract says two weeks. I don't have that much vacation left. I won't have my record marked worse than what Todd's already done."

"It won't. I'll put it down as settlement for our issue and nothing will be said." He approached again and offered his hand to help her up. "I am sorry to lose you. Keep our number in case you need it. And have a nice holiday. Go spend your time shopping or with friends and family." He set a hand on her shoulder. "Tell Sergeant Dawson Merry Christmas from us, as well."

Surprised he remembered her boyfriend's name, Deanna couldn't do more than nod and let him walk her out. She nearly chuckled as she headed down the stairs to her desk. Two weeks paid leave, plus her two unused sick days. That would help. She could job hunt instead of shop.

"Should have pushed him for more."

Daws took her silence as a rebuke. Still, two weeks' pay was nothing considering how long it might take her to find something else and that what she found could be at lower pay, plus the hassle of job hunting. It wasn't enough. McCallister had to know she could have sued and received enough she wouldn't have to work for a year or more. Any concern she heard from him was in fear of his pocketbook and his reputation, not for her. Since she signed the paperwork, though, settling her claim for two weeks' pay, she no longer could. Smart on his part to get it done before Deanna had time to talk with anyone else, with him. He figured there was no point in mentioning it. And it was her job, her call. She was still silent. "Anna, I'm glad he gave you that, and I'm glad you're out of there. I can quit worrying about it now."

"You didn't need to worry. I know how to handle myself." Her voice was sharp. A warning.

"Yes. I know you can. Doesn't keep me from worrying." Again, she didn't answer. "Deanna, what is it? You're quiet tonight."

"I'm ... tired. And I've been thinking."

His breath caught. He forced its release. "About?"

"Um. I just don't know anymore if I'm cut out for this. My family said I wasn't and I was determined they were wrong. But everything I've done, all the stupid choices I've made – and from what you just said, I guess I did it again..."

"I didn't say that."

"Should have pushed for more? Maybe I should have. Maybe you were right and I should have listened to you and I should have filed suit against the jerk but I didn't, and I've kind of put myself against a wall now and ... leaving that job should feel like a relief, shouldn't it? It doesn't. It feels like I failed. Due to my own fault. If I'd had the judgment not to sleep with that lying user, then maybe I would have moved into his job and ... I'm just tired, you know? Tired of making such stupid decisions. I'm not stupid. And I don't know why I can't, just once, make the right choice instead of the wrong one."

He heard warning sirens and had to convince himself they were only in his head this time. "We all make bad choices at times. Not all of them are."

"No? What have I done that wasn't?"

Daws had to wonder if that was supposed to be rhetorical.

"You can't think of anything either, right?"

He rubbed his neck. "I could. But it doesn't matter if I can if you can't. Tell me something you've done that wasn't a bad choice. You tell me."

Silence overwhelmed him. Was it that hard to come up with one thing? The silence lasted too long and he couldn't figure how to break it.

" 'Bout done?"

He looked behind him at the guy standing against a wall. Without answering, he turned back. "Anna, I only have a minute, but I'll call back if I can. Getting harder to find time, too many rotating through right now, on the way in or out. I'll try."

"Okay." She sounded much too resigned.

"Hey. Before I go, tell me one thing. Give me one thing that comes to your mind that was the right choice." Silence again, but he wasn't letting go until she did. Something. Anything. "Anna?"

"Taking the cell phone with me when I went for a walk. That was a good idea. Except it was your idea, not mine, so I don't think that counts."

"What?"

"Never mind. You don't have to understand. At least I could name one."

Daws thought back to their recent conversations. When had she mentioned the cell?

"Anyway, I'll be in a better mood next time you call. Promise. I'll let you go."

"Deanna..."

"Love you. Bye, Freddy." She hung up before he could reply.

"*Damn.*" He slammed the receiver back on the hook.

"Problems with your girl?"

With a quick glance at the guy, long enough to see two more lined up behind him, he headed back to his room. At least she'd said she loved him, but it was quick, more like a habit than intention. He should have refused to leave her for a year. They hadn't had enough time together first. Their relationship was still too new. So it would have marked his record. What did it matter? With the direction he was headed, it didn't. He should have refused.

Deanna set the phone down and went to find tissue. She was not going to let him know she was crying. She didn't do this. She didn't. It was stupid, one more stupid thing.

Wiping her face, she froze. "Oh." She lowered her hands and looked over at the phone. "No. That's what he meant. What an idiot I am. *He's* my *not stupid* choice, my one really smart decision. I'm *such* an idiot." Making her way back to the stool beside the phone, she lowered onto it. Maybe he'd call right back. Once he let whoever was waiting use it, he'd call back. If he could. She hoped he would.

She was tired of this, tired of the long distance conversations when she held so much back just to try to keep him from worrying. He could do nothing; why should he worry? And he had to hear that she was holding back. Which was worse? Telling him or not telling him? Once she told him, she couldn't say forget it, because he wouldn't. If she told him about the man in the park, he would only be aggravated that he wasn't there for her and she didn't want that. She wanted him to keep his head in his job, to come home safely.

She was an idiot for telling him to go, not to let her stand in the way. She wanted him home. She wanted to take him home with her, to meet her mom, to let him more into her life. She wanted him to really know, to understand better than she could explain with words. "Freddy, call me back."

Deanna dropped her head on her hands, elbows on the counter, and let the tears flow. Privately. She'd get used to the tears in private. No, she didn't want to get used to them.

The phone rang and she nearly jumped on it.

"Deanna? Everything all right?"

"Who is this?"

"Virginia Gray. I'm sorry if I'm bothering you."

"No. Sorry. I didn't recognize you." She wiped the tissue over her nose.

"I called to ask if we could move lunch to ... say an hour later on Saturday? Or I can do ten-thirty Sunday. We can have brunch."

"Any time is fine. Let me know which is better. If a weekday is better for you, that's fine, also."

"I'm not sure I can do that well around your schedule and I don't want to be too pressed for time."

"I don't have one. I left my job, so anytime works." She struggled to make her voice sound normal.

"You're not all right."

"Yes. I'm fine."

A pause. "What are you doing now?"

She couldn't stop a snicker. "Now? Sitting by the phone hoping Freddy will call back because I was horrible to him a few minutes ago and I can't call him..." She bit her lip and pressed at her eyes.

"Give me your address. I'll come to you."

"What? No. I'm not..."

"Don't argue. And don't say you're not ready for company. I couldn't care in the slightest. Give me your address, or I'll look it up."

Just like Todd did. Feeling helpless to refuse, Deanna gave it to her. "Now what have I done?" Rolling her eyes, she went to the bathroom and shook her head at the sight. No one ever saw her this way. Ever. She'd have to cover it up as well as possible.

"Come on, Deanna. Pick up." He should have been at work by now, but everyone else was and so the phone was free. He supposed she could be in the tub ... the ringing stopped.

"This better be Freddy."

Pulling back and looking at the phone as though it could explain, he returned it to his ear. "Are you all right?" Her voice was odd.

"Yes, and I'm so sorry and I'm so glad you called back. I kept telling you to call back and you didn't and I'm so sorry but you're my right thing, the one most right thing ever, that I've ever done and I should've said so but it's so much true I didn't think I should need to say you are but you are and..."

"Anna. How much lemonade have you had?"

She giggled. "No, it's peach schnapps and raspberry schnapps and ... with something mixed. Wow, they're good. It's been forever since I've had them. Not that much, really. I was just tired and ... and Freddy, you are my right thing. My biggest right thing."

He wasn't sure whether to laugh or worry. Damn, she was cute drunk. But he didn't like that she was so far out of it without him there.

"Freddy?"

"I'm here. Are you alone?"

"No." She giggled again.

"No? Who's there with you? Your girlfriends?"

"No. They all had shopping dates, guy dates, who shop. Isn't that hysterical? They asked me but I don't want to shop with no guy date and no job and..."

"Okay, so who's there?"

"But it's okay now because I don't have to live off of you. I have other opportunities."

His stomach tightened. "Anna, tell me who's there with you."

A giggle, half stifled, came across the line. "He wants to know who's here."

"Anna? Come on, baby. Talk to me." He heard noise and muffled voices. "*Anna.*" A couple of guys looked over at him but he didn't care. Who in the hell besides her girlfriends would be there with her, drinking?

"Fred?" A different voice. Female.

"Who is this?"

"Virginia Gray. Don't worry. She's fine, only unwinding. It didn't take much. She's less used to it than I expected."

"Why are you there? Who else is there?"

"Just me, hon. I called to change her appointment time and she was in tears so I dropped by."

"In tears?" He lowered his voice and turned away from the privates. "Why?"

"Oh, hon, things kind of added up and overwhelmed her for a moment, but she'll be fine now. Had to let it out girl style, with someone who understands. But I promise, she's not as far out of it as she sounds…"

"No? Because the balcony … don't let her out there."

"It's far too cold to be out there. We're fine. I'll stay until she settles in. Coffee's brewing as we speak … here, she wants the phone back. Don't worry, I'll take care of her. I have a contact who I think will be thrilled to have her skill…"

"Freddy. I think I have a job already. She's great, isn't she? Ryan has to agree to her. She's great. And I miss you so and I'm so sorry about … about before. And…"

"Okay, it's fine. But switch to coffee now, all right?"

"Yes, it smells wonderful. I'll get it."

He heard mumbling in the background.

"No, Ginny's getting it for me so I can talk to you. Are you okay? You're not mad at me?"

"I'm not mad at you. I'm glad you're feeling better."

"Yes, all's okay and you're my wonderful, wonderful right thing. Don't forget that even if I don't say it and I can't wait to hold onto you again and cuddle against your strong chest and your shoulder and your arms and … and all of you. I love you so much, Freddy. You come home to me safe."

He gritted his teeth for a moment. Damn, he wanted to be home with her. "I love you too, Anna. Have your coffee and settle in. Drink some water before bed so you're not dehydrated tomorrow. I'll call in the morning."

"Yes. In the morning. Good night. Have a good day. I love you."

A clunk told him the phone had hit something.

"I think she'll be asleep before much longer." Virginia Gray sounded amused.

"Make sure she's all right before you leave. She doesn't drink much."

"No, I figured that out around three shots ago. I may stay over if that's all right with you."

"You don't have family who'll be concerned?"

"They're well used to it by now as much as I travel with my artists. They don't pay much attention to where I am."

"Fine, then. Use the guest room. And thank you."

"Oh it's been fun. She's a riot, very sweet. And it's hardly the first time I've had to babysit someone who's had too much. First time it was my fault, though."

Hanging up, Daws still didn't know whether or not to be relieved. He barely knew the woman. She did have incredible references and a good name in the industry, not only well-known but generally well-respected. He hoped to hell they were right.

PART 3

"Don't be afraid to see what you see."
Ronald Reagan

Deanna stared out the train window as it edged into New York. Back to reality.

Her visit home for the holidays hadn't felt real. Instead of returning the card with a long letter, she decided to go home. Fred encouraged her. Said she'd be glad she did. She supposed she was.

Although, it was hard to see how the few years had aged her mom. The woman was too tired, too worn down. And she cried when she opened the door and found Deanna standing there. It made Deanna cry, also. She'd held onto her mom for the longest time, until voices in the living room asked who it was and came to find out.

Her sisters were all there helping to make a ton of cookies as they did every year. The two oldest were married, both within the past year. Neither had sent her an invitation. Deanna expected maybe that's why her mom hadn't mentioned anything about the family. She didn't want to admit the weddings she hadn't been invited to or even told about. At least her mom hadn't been "away," only busy.

They were all cool to her, except the youngest. Fourteen year old Rosie was too much like her, as the others grimaced. She was exuberant and dressed in just the right fashions and outspoken. And she had a boyfriend already. When the others made comments about Deanna being away, Rosie jumped in and said it was 'cause she was the smart one to get out of the little nowhere town and go make something of herself and she planned to do the same just as soon as she was old enough. The girl was half Deanna's age but they spent a fair amount of time together talking, just the two of them. Deanna hardly knew her little sister; she'd been only six last time she saw her. She was glad for the time with Rosie.

And with her mom. Deanna was horribly glad she'd gone to see her mom. She helped her with everything: cooking, dishes, laundry, and whatever else she could find that needed done. They spent every evening at the kitchen table talking alone after her father had fallen asleep in his recliner. Deanna told her everything she could about Fred. Her mother adored the ring he gave her and asked several times if he was really the one and to be sure before settling. She also asked several times if she was protecting herself well enough. As long as Deanna had been away, she found it funny, but sweet.

She assured her mom she would bring Fred back to meet her. And if there was ever a wedding, she'd see to it her mom got there.

Now, with the railroad wheels clicking beneath her along the track, taking her back to New York, Deanna wish she'd stayed longer, tried harder to make peace with her siblings. They finally gave in enough to talk to her in a civil tone and she looked at albums of the two weddings and praised them on the dresses and colors although the eldest's bridesmaids' dresses were truly horrendous. Things were peaceful enough when she left.

Deanna was awfully glad she had at least the possibility of a new job, through Ginny's connections. She made it sound as a done deal, so her mother wouldn't worry. At least she told herself that's why she did. Ginny did make it sound fairly certain, if not with her first contact, then with another. Deanna wasn't sure the manager wasn't using the offered help to try to coerce Fred to bring Ryan to her as a bit of an exchange, but if so, Ginny didn't understand Fred well enough. He wasn't one to be coerced into anything. He would only take Ryan to her if he thought it would be best for the kid.

When she got home, she needed to call Mrs. Reynauld and check on him.

Daws knew he offered to go home with Deanna at some point, but after what she said, the thought made him cringe. He supposed there was no point worrying about it until it happened. He still had three months left in Korea and he knew she wouldn't want to spend his time off with her family.

Three months. They'd come to the three quarters point that he'd been told was in some ways the easiest and other ways the hardest. Didn't matter much. He didn't let himself think about hard or easy. He was there. He was doing his job as well as he could. There was talk of him going to the E7 board already, so he figured he was doing it well enough. Whether or not he'd go if offered, he wasn't sure yet.

Either way, he was glad she was back at their apartment. They had too much trouble talking when she was at her mother's with the relatives swirling around and only one phone in the house. He'd heard a comment when she told him she loved him. Laughing at her.

Maybe he did want to go home with her.

Pulling his heavy wool sweater over his T-shirt, he added the camo shirt. He hated how stiff it made him, but it was well below freezing and he'd be outside much of the day. As he left his room, he grabbed the lined winter cap with added ear protection. January in Korea was worse than

January in New York, although he never would have guessed it. It was the altitude, they said. The air was much colder up in the mountainous regions.

Deanna bundled herself into a nice thick sweater over her shirt and thick pants, wrapped a soft knit shawl over her head, and topped it with her warmest long coat and gloves. Ginny assured her casual dressy was fine, and boots, not heels. The woman they were meeting didn't believe in a bunch of showy clothes she felt were too impractical for actual work. She wanted work, not show. Deanna had her fingers crossed tightly for this job to pan out. She wanted to work, not to be showy. And she was so glad to be able to wear mostly flat boots. And the boss was female. In her eyes, that was a huge plus.

Making sure she had her keys, she locked and closed the door, and strode down the hallway. As she ventured out, she forced positive thoughts. She could do this job. She could convince the woman she could do it. And it would work well, be a nice atmosphere, unstifling. With any luck, it would also be free of creeps, although that was possibly too much to wish for. At least this time, she wouldn't get involved with any of them. She had, after considering it for some time, given Mr. McCallister's name as a reference. Deanna hoped it was the right move, but then, refusing to give any reference at a job she'd been with for six years wouldn't look good.

The meeting was at a coffee shop, not an office, which seemed strange to her, but less nerve-wracking. Maybe. Ginny would be there for introductions. Deanna would owe the woman a huge favor if this worked well. She would *not* transfer the favor over to Fred, though. His business with Ryan was separate.

Ryan. The kid had often been on Deanna's mind since she'd called his mom the day before. He was fighting with his band members, largely because of the manager they'd found who kept playing him up and pushing them in the background. Deanna knew how he felt. It wasn't fair for any of them. Mrs. Reynauld was having serious doubts about supporting her son's chosen path. Fred would have a time trying to convince her otherwise, Deanna was afraid. But maybe she was right. Too many kids who went into music or acting or anything else very public ended up having such a hard time, with the press, with alcohol, with drugs. She would hate to see Ryan end up the same. She woondered if Fred had considered all that.

Of course he would. And he'd be watchful of it. Still, there was only so much he could do.

The coffee shop bustled as shoppers and employees on breaks headed in to warm up, but Deanna found Ginny easily enough. The other woman was with her. Deanna headed toward them as she made herself appear calm and collected, and she studied the woman who could possibly be her new boss. The first thing Deanna noticed was gorgeous blonde curly long hair drifting over her shoulders. For someone Ginny said was casual and no-fuss, she looked as though she spent a long time on it, and paid plenty for that perm, if it was. But as she got closer, Deanna noticed a lack of makeup, not a total lack, but not overdone. And her face was kind.

She got up and took Deanna's hand. "It's wonderful to meet you. Can I call you Deanna?"

"Of course. It's nice to meet you, as well."

"Have a seat. What's your favorite?" She motioned a young man over to take Deanna's order for low fat mocha no whip as they took their seats. "I'm Libby McCartney, no relation to Paul, I'm afraid. Wouldn't that be nice? Are you a music fan?"

Deanna couldn't help but grin. "Yes, actually, and it would be nice. I'm a big Beatles fan."

"Ah, early era or later?"

"Both; I prefer the early stuff, though. I liked the more innocent sound of it, although I have respect for their innovative techniques that came later." Music. She could talk music all day.

"Yes, unfortunately the price of fame and innovation tends to come at a high cost. That is sad. Do you play an instrument at all?"

"Oh. No. I sit around listening to those who can and wonder why I never tried. I suppose it seems more mystical to me that way. Or I'm simply too lazy to try."

The woman laughed. "Understood. Both."

"I have a hard time seeing you as lazy." Ginny raised her eyebrows. "Don't let her fool you. This girl knows how to work."

"Relax, Virginia." Libby caught Ginny's eyes but returned to Deanna. "She's such a serious thing, isn't she? I'm constantly telling her to relax."

Deanna avoided the question. "You've known each other for some time?"

"Forever. We were in school together, although we hardly spoke. In fact, I'm not sure we did. She was always serious back then, also, while I was focused on socializing. As it turns out, neither way worked better as far as our futures. We came out fairly equal there." She took a hefty swallow of her coffee. "So, I called your Mr. McCallister. Charming man."

"Yes. He is that."

"We had a nice conversation. He asked me to send you back to work for him."

"Did he? That was nice." Deanna felt a stare and glanced over. No one she knew. He was trying to get her attention, although maybe he hoped she'd introduce him to the beautiful blonde at her table.

"Will you consider his request?" Libby didn't appear to notice anyone else in the room. She was highly focused.

"No." She thanked the young man who brought her coffee over and stirred it to help it cool. "He is a nice man, I agree, but I went as far as I could go there. It's time to move on."

Libby McCartney nodded as she studied Deanna. "What are your career goals?"

"Simple. I want to be a recognized name. I want to be respected for what I do and what I can do. And I want to work up to where I have some leeway in my campaigns and in my work hours." Deanna cringed inwardly. She didn't intend to mention that last bit of information.

"Leeway in your hours? Can I ask how?"

Deanna took a sip of her coffee and allowed herself time to consider her answer. She shouldn't have mentioned it. Still, she was taking a plunge already and figured she might as well stand up for what she wanted. "I'm going to be horribly straight forward, and I'll understand if I don't fit your needs." She returned Ginny's questioning gaze, but dove right in. "I'm in wait and see mode to some extent. Because of my boyfriend, actually, and never before would I have let a man interfere with my work. However, this is different, and at least for some time, I may have to do so."

Libby didn't show any sign of annoyance. "Yes, I know the situation, about his short trips to the city when he can get here. I also know Virginia hopes to work with him. If that turns out, he'll still travel. Do you mean you intend to travel with him every time he goes out on the road?"

"Oh. No, I don't think so. I enjoy travel but I'm more a homebody than that and I don't enjoy hotel rooms an awful lot. If he goes that direction, we'll work it out, but I intend to stay in the city most of the time."

"Then you're only asking for time off when he's around?"

"Not so much time off as a varied schedule. Much of what I did at McCallister's, I could have done from home. I do get the job done, Ms. McCartney. I only ask for some leeway as to where I am when I get it done."

"Libby. Please." She took another sip of coffee, eyeing Deanna over the top of the cup. "I have to say it's unusual for someone looking for a job to make such a demand up front."

"It's not a demand; it's a request. Although I will need time in April when he comes home from overseas. By then it will have been six months since I've seen him and that's not negotiable. As I said, I understand if I'm asking too much. But I've been pushed around about all I'm going to be and I want more than that by now. I'd rather go sell tickets at the theater and provide them my available hours than be chained to an office most every day of my life. There may come a time I'm willing to do it again; right now I'm not. I want to work. I'm happiest working on something I enjoy and feeling productive. I don't, however, want to give all of my freedom to some job again. No offense."

Libby McCartney broke into a beautiful smile. "I think you'll fit right in with us. Welcome to the team, if you're interested."

"Possibly. I'm still rather unsure just what the job is, though."

"Ad designer, brand manager, client liaison – kind of an all-in-one position. A team member. We all help each other as needed. We only compete with other businesses, not with each other. And as long as the job gets done, where and how you do it is not my concern. I need self motivators who won't let the client push them around, who'll stand up to the standards of my company. I will say some of our clients are quite pushy, some ruder than they should be. I don't expect you to take it. I expect you to back them down until they can be respectful, preferably without losing the job. Think you can do that?"

"Yes. I can do it."

Libby offered a folder. "Some basic information. Read through it. If you're still interested, come by the office on Monday and we'll get you started. My card's inside. I have to run." She stood and began pulling her coat over her shoulders. "By the way, I look forward to meeting your boyfriend if you do decide to join us."

Deanna couldn't help a grin. "And I'm sure he'll be anxious to meet you, as well."

"To size me up, yes?" A sparkle highlighted her eyes. "As assumption from what Virginia says."

"A fair assumption. No offense."

"None taken. I'll see you Monday, Deanna. Have a wonderful weekend."

"She works with a lot of artsy clients."

Daws accepted a chair the private brought close to the phone and lowered into it before answering. He didn't want the grimace to go through the line. "Does she? Should make it interesting. And you got along well?"

"Yes. Freddy, I think this could be what I've been looking for all this time. I should have left that place earlier."

"Earlier might not have been the right time for her. Don't worry about should haves, Deanna." He flinched when he moved his leg.

"What's wrong?"

"You start Monday?" He pressed a palm against the throb, or just above the throb, in an attempt to numb the nerves enough to be able to talk.

"Yes. But something's wrong. What is it? Does something not sound right about it to you? Am I jumping too fast?"

"No." He forced his voice to normalize. "It sounds perfect. I look forward to hearing more about it when you start. It's nice to hear you so excited. You deserve this. Congratulations." Silence came over the line. For too long. "Still there?"

"Yes. But tell me. What are you hiding? I can hear it in your voice."

Damn. He should have waited longer to call, until the pain medicine had better chance to work. "Don't worry, it's minor." Minor was a stretch, but it would heal. He supposed that was minor enough. Considering.

"What's minor? What happened?"

"Banged up my leg this morning. Taken care of, just needs time."

"How? And how bad?"

"Anna, it's all right…"

"Freddy, *tell* me. I'll think worse than it is if you don't."

He doubted it. But he'd downplay it as much as possible. "Might be another scar you'll have to overlook."

A pause. "What happened?"

"Hit a covered pothole. A set up. Probably been there for years and hadn't been found. We found it. Turned the Humvee half over. Lucky we all got out of it with cuts and scratches and such. Could've been a lot worse." He pressed harder. The pain made it hard to talk.

"*Oh*. Are you still walking?"

"Yes, still walking on it. Not more than I have to, but it is still attached." He meant it as a joke, but the private raised his eyebrows since Daws was supposed to stay off his feet and use crutches for the next couple of days. He wouldn't. It made the pain worse to swing his leg forward than to walk on it. Deanna's silence said she didn't think it was funnier than the private did. "Some pain and nothing you want to look at, but it'll heal."

She sent a deep sigh through the line. "I wish I could be there to take care of you. You should come home. You can't work that way."

He chuckled, making the private raise his eyebrows again. "Might get a day off. Maybe two. Then back to work."

"No, but you need time…"

"Anna, it's all right. They'll put me at a desk until it heals enough. Tell me more about your new job." The medication didn't seem to help the pain much, but it was making him tired. He didn't want to talk. He wanted to hear her voice.

He only half remembered hanging up and then he was back in bed. He hoped he'd told her he loved her. He didn't remember whether he said it or only thought it.

Deanna wrapped her coat around her, the new smart and sexy but very warm coat she'd treated herself to upon starting her new job, carried her boots to the balcony door, slid them on, and stepped outside. She shivered as the frigid wind brushed along her face and down her front, and pulled the coat tighter. In this blizzard, she was terribly glad she often worked from home now. Still, the constant snow and polar bear temperatures had kept her in far too often. She liked to be out and about. Before it got so nasty, a short fast walk up and down the sidewalks sufficed. She was cold hardy, for the most part, but this....

She sighed and immediately regretted it. The cold burned her throat. It had to be barely above zero. Yet she wanted to be outside. Even through her gloves, her fingers started to burn. So she closed her eyes and took one more slow breath of fresh air – at least cold air was cleaner than hot New York air – allowed the tiny sleet-like snowflakes to cover her cheeks and hair, and gave up, returning to the apartment's warm shelter.

Never, several months ago, would she have thought she'd get tired of being in his home. Maybe she wouldn't be if he was there to help distract her, to give her restlessness a place to land.

As she slipped out of her boots, leaving them on the ceramic landing just inside the balcony, and pulled her coat back off her arms, Deanna had the sudden realization she was annoyed at him. He should have warned her better. Fred should have told her ... but he did, or he tried. He warned her about the separations and she said she could handle it. Of course, she expected the two months apart with a week or two in between. She agreed to that. She hadn't agreed to a whole long mostly rotten at-times-unbearable lonely and too-long year without him. He didn't warn her about that. Never even mentioned the possibility until it happened. He should have.

Storming to the kitchen to refill her coffee and shove it in the microwave since it had cooled, Deanna had thoughts of grabbing hold of him and shaking. Or beating on him until he apologized for not warning her about a whole year separation.

Not like it would have mattered if he did. With another sigh, she realized she would have bravely said it was okay, she could handle it, like it didn't matter what came up, she'd just handle it.

Of course she would. What choice was there?

Her body loosened from its grip of anger and she pulled the coffee from the microwave and stirred in skim milk. He was getting out. In less than a year. She could handle it that long.

What choice was there? She was in love with him. She'd wait. It was a good thing, she supposed, that she didn't know what she was getting into when she allowed herself to get close enough to fall for him. Would she have done this voluntarily if she had? All of the lonely nights, all of the times she needed him there and had to settle for a quick phone call, on his part, she couldn't even call him, which ticked her off to no end many times. When she had news or needed to talk, she had to wait for him to decide to call. There was nothing at all fair about the arrangement. All of the power was in his hands. Well, in the Army's hands, really, but there wasn't much difference that she could see. And she never intended to let anyone run her life as much as he was running it, as the Army was running it. He wanted to be there with her. Or so he said. He loved what he was doing. Would he really get out or would he decide he couldn't do it? It was his choice; the power was all in his hands. Or would he give in to her if she insisted? Then what? He'd resent it? If his new path didn't work well and he had to struggle with a job he didn't want, as she had for so long, would he take it out on her for pushing him out of the Army?

A deep breath led her back to the window. To the hard icy snow spattering the panes, adding to the drifts on the cement balcony. That was what still needed to be done: the balcony. She hadn't even considered doing anything with it while obsessed with the inside. He had a couple of metal chairs out there. Or his parents put them out there and he hadn't bothered to move or replace them. They needed to be replaced. They were showing what the weather had done to them over time. The design was nice but the black had faded and ... some textured spray paint would work. Plus cement paint to turn the ugly common gray into something to match the apartment. Dark green? She'd done the place in dark green and cream with coral accents. She could paint the cement floor and the part of the wall below the black metal railing in dark green. Maybe paint the metal in cream. Could she? She supposed she better ask before she painted the balcony. That was a whole different thing than painting walls.

Maybe she wouldn't ask. He told her to decorate as she wished, other than taking walls down. She didn't have to leave all the power in his hands. It was her place, too. More or less. Not technically, but he said it was. But it was just paint. She could make that decision alone. If he got mad, he'd get over it. In her current state of mind, she half considered taking a wall down just to irritate him, also.

Of course she wouldn't go that far. And she needed to calm herself down before he called. She didn't even want him to call tonight. It was too frustrating and she was already too frustrated. Maybe she wouldn't answer. Maybe she'd answer and just tell him she wasn't in the mood to talk.

Pacing around the room, Deanna knew what her real annoyance was about. The last day of February. She always resented the end of February because it shorted her two to three days and threw her schedule. She'd mentioned it to one of her boyfriends once, how three of every four years she was so annoyed at February's end. He looked at her like she was nuts. Only a couple of days, he said. So what? He didn't get it.

That wasn't her only annoyance. It was her most fertile time, the time she most hated her nights alone. No, she better not even answer the phone when he called. Too dangerous. Maybe she'd go out and get paint ... but for what purpose? The blizzard was raging. She couldn't paint the stupid balcony until spring, until she was assured of two or three warm dry days in a row, which could be an issue in New York in spring. She wanted it done before he came home. He might stop her otherwise.

Daws let the phone ring until the machine picked up. "Damn." He slammed the receiver down. He was cold, his leg was throbbing because of the cold and he had started back on PT, his captain was doing his best to drive him insane, and she wasn't even home. Why wasn't she? It was a week day. She made her own hours now. She could damn well be home during the two times a day he was able to call. The last time he'd snuck a call in during work hours, his moronic captain said he was setting a bad example for his men. The hell he was. His work was always done, and it was done well, and his team had the best record for having theirs done, also, for their safety record, for the quality work. A *bad example*. He supposed he would be if he allowed himself to go off on the captain who still didn't seem to understand the line between officers and senior NCOs. Although the officers were technically in charge because of their commission, they rarely knew the job as well and hadn't been in nearly as long, and most of them were smart enough to realize both and to take advice and work as partners. This guy ... was a moron.

With a frown, he realized his thoughts were echoing so many of Deanna's while she was still at her last job. She'd done it for six years. Daws couldn't imagine dealing with one idiot for that long. One good thing about his job; they moved people around a lot. There was always someone he preferred to avoid, but it was not often the same one for too long at a time and there was something to that.

He hurt too much to hang around and try to call back. If she'd wanted to talk, she would have been home.

She should have answered.

Trying to focus on her work, her new campaign that had lots of potential to make a nice mark on her career, Deanna looked at the phone and admonished herself. Childish. It was horribly childish not to answer, and now she'd have to tell him why she hadn't answered. She couldn't say she didn't want to; he might not bother to call back again and she wouldn't blame him. So she'd have to make up an excuse. Lie. She didn't want to lie to him. How could she?

And how could she tell him the truth? Maybe she could avoid saying why and simply apologize. But if he wanted to talk to her badly enough, he would have called the cell.

Oh. With a sick feeling in her stomach, she remembered it was off. Charging. She was home; it didn't need to be on. Had he tried that, too?

Maybe it was better. She was in the wrong mood to talk to him. Safer not to, whatever she had to say to excuse it. It was for his own good.

Showered and changed into his fatigues, Daws had relaxed enough to think about calling the cell. She didn't have to be home at the right time to talk; he'd forgotten, in his anger, that she was still available. Bad example or not, he stopped at the phones and gave it a try. Number not available. It wasn't on. Maybe she was back home. Did he dare give it another try? It would only frustrate him if she didn't answer again.

But he wanted to hear her voice, if only for a minute.

"Hello?"

The sound of it eased his tension and he grabbed a deep breath. "Hey, Anna. Just get home?"

"What? No."

"I called twenty minutes ago."

"Oh. I'm sorry. Aren't you at work by now?"

He frowned. An apology. Avoidance. "Heading there. Everything okay?"

"Yes."

Yes. Nothing more. "All right. Have to go. Just wanted to check in."

"Have a good day."

"Yeah." He nearly hung up. He couldn't quite do it. "What did I do?"

"What?"

"You're mad. Why?"

"I'm not."

Daws clenched his jaw for a second or two. He shouldn't have called back. "Then what is it?"

"Thought you had to get to work."

"I do, but what's wrong?"

"Nothing. It's fine. Don't get yourself in trouble for me."

He rolled his eyes, clenched his jaw again. "Okay, I don't have time for this so can you just tell me?"

"Tell you what? Go on to work. I'm not stopping you."

"Deanna, I don't need this today. You don't answer but you weren't out and the cell's off and now you act like I'm bothering you by calling and nothing's wrong? My leg hurts like hell and they're shoving me back behind that desk today never mind I'm up to doing PT by their standards, and I'm not in the mood for games. So if you're mad, say so and get it over with."

Silence came from the other end.

"Did you hang up?"

"No." Her voice was half angry, half ... insulted?

"I'm sorry. I didn't mean to yell. Could you just, for this week, not make me guess or beg for answers?"

"Everything's fine. And you don't have to call if you don't want to talk."

"I wouldn't call if I didn't want to talk."

"You don't sound like you do."

"I was thinking the same."

A pause. "I'm always glad to hear your voice. Why is your leg so sore?"

Her friendlier tone and concern eased his tension. "PT."

"Are you supposed to be doing that yet?"

"Yes. Which is why I am. Started today. Leg doesn't seem to agree it's time. Didn't mean to be an ass to you."

Another pause. "I didn't answer earlier because I'm just in one of those moods and I didn't want to make you mad. Bad decision, I guess. Sorry."

"What's wrong, Anna?"

"Nothing. Just ... nothing. Did you take something for the pain? Can you tell them it's too soon?"

"It'll be fine. Anything I can do to make your day better?"

"Yes, but you won't, so no point in asking. If you haven't taken something, do that."

"I won't what? What do you want me to do?"

Silence.

"Anna, I really have to go, but tell me first. What can I do?"

"Get on the next plane home and come take me to bed."

His body stiffened. At the thought, so did the rest of him. Damn. Adding another ache wasn't about to help his leg. Particularly with the two so close. He turned to face the wall in case anyone walked by.

"Told you you wouldn't."

"Anna. Hell. That was about the last damn thing I needed to hear right now." He pressed a palm beside the leg wound, hoping it would cut off nerves to both. And he realized she hadn't answered. She was taking it wrong. He knew without a doubt she was. "Okay, so I can't do that. Luckily, I still can when I do get home. Another inch or so to the left and it would've taken that out of play so you could go find someone still able who's actually around for you. Should have aimed better."

"That's not funny."

"No, but accurate."

Silence. And the thought of her finding someone else served its purpose. At least the part of him that most needed to relax did.

"Is that what you think?" Her voice was upset, soft. "You think I'd leave you if…. Do you?"

"Anna, I was joking. Distracting myself since you made me…."

"You think I would leave you. You … all those times you teased about it, you were serious. You think that's what matters most to me?"

"No, I was teasing. Come on, I have to get to work and I don't want you upset…"

"Fine. Go to work. I need to get back to mine, too. Have a good day. Take something for your leg."

"Anna, don't hang up."

"You have to go to work."

"They'll wait. Listen to me."

"No. I can't. Not now. You're going to have to give me time to calm down before this gets worse. Go to work. Don't call back tonight. Bye, Fred."

He heard the click and cursed. Damned woman. He *was* teasing. Did she think he'd be with her if he believed that? She didn't even let him finish telling her that she'd made him hard as hell and he was too much in public view not to fix that fast and…. *Damn.* Did she think he minded how much she wanted him, wanted to sleep with him? How in the hell could she think he minded? The major had assured him the right woman would appreciate his sense of humor. Damn sure didn't seem like she did.

Don't call back tonight. Fine. He wouldn't call back tonight. And maybe not in the morning, either. If she wanted time to calm down, she could have it.

As he headed in to the damn desk he would be stuck behind, her words suddenly returned. She didn't answer because she was in a mood and didn't want to make him mad. So she was home. She just didn't answer. He laughed. Something about the straight-forward truth of it was too funny, too charming.

One of his men turned to give him a strange look. "Can I ask what's so funny, Sergeant?"

"Just had the most stupid fight in the world with my girlfriend."

"And … that's funny?"

"Suppose it shouldn't be." Still, he chuckled. He damned well *would* call her back.

Deanna opened her eyes to a ringing. It was dark. In her slumber, it took her a while to figure out it was the phone. At ... one in the morning? Her mom. Something happened. Grabbing it, she gave a cautious hello and braced herself.

"Don't hang up on me again. I'm giving up lunch to talk to you and I know you were asleep but I plan to keep you on for long enough I'll have to settle for a bag of chips to take back so you might as well wake up and listen to me."

Freddy. "Hey."

"Just listen a minute."

She didn't dare argue after she'd been so awful earlier. She sat up to try to keep herself awake, since it had taken forever to get to sleep, and pulled the comforter as far around her shoulders as she could. "Okay."

"I do know better, Anna. I damn sure wouldn't ask you to do all of this with me if I didn't. You could find that anywhere; don't think I don't realize you could. Hell, I see the stares when we're out. I know you could have anyone. And I don't always know why you're going through all of this when you could do better, but I'm glad you are, and I am teasing."

"Freddy..."

"I'm not done. I realized what time this is for you after you hung up and I can't tell you how much I'd love to be there to take advantage of it, and I would, and I will, so be warned. If it helps at all, I can tell you *how* I'd take advantage of it over the phone, since no one's around and it's the best I can do. Or would that be worse?"

"Oh." Deanna closed her eyes and shook her head. "Probably would be."

"Up to you."

"You would?"

"Want to find out?"

Her body tensed. Yes. And no. "Hm."

"Is that a yes or no?" He was teasing, taunting. Daring her.

"Um."

He chuckled. She wanted to pound on his chest. And then kiss it better. She wanted to check his leg, rub it down with lotion to keep it moist and help it heal. "No."

"No? Sure?" He sounded almost disappointed.

"No, and I'm not sure, but ... won't that make things kind of ... hard for you? Or did you find a private phone?"

"A private phone would cost a hell of a lot, but I can if you prefer. Might have to be quick."

"No. Oh, Freddy, I'm so sorry. I didn't mean to be such a witch. I'm sorry…"

"I love you, Anna. I would do anything I could for you."

"I know." She brushed at the moisture under her eyes. "And I hate knowing you're in pain and I can't do anything about it. It's been bothering me since you did it. I want to be there…"

He chuckled again. "That's nothing compared to what you did to me earlier."

"What I did? By being such a jerk?"

"By asking me to take you to bed in that horribly sexy voice of yours. It absolutely made things … hard for me. But don't let what I said throw you. I loved every damn second of it."

"I think that makes you as crazy as I am." She grinned to herself, thinking about how easy it had been to get to him.

"Hm. Good thing no one's around at the moment."

She chuckled. "Is it? Want me to return the offer?"

"No."

"That sounded definite."

"I don't have time to go take a cold shower before I have to be back at work. Getting tortured twice in the same day is liable to make me go commando on some jerk who deserves it."

"Can I volunteer? I deserve it. I've been very bad today. Even made myself a pan of brownies and ate nearly half of them, after sucking the batter off the spoon and running my finger inside the bowl to lick it off." She scrunched the comforter closer and lay down again.

"Anna. Damn."

She grinned at the distress in his voice. "Sorry. Couldn't resist."

"Payback is hell."

"Go ahead."

"Hm. Think I'll save that challenge and stand up to it in person."

"You do that." She stretched out on his bed and grabbed his pillow. "I miss you."

A pause. "I miss you, too. And next time you're in a mood where you don't want to talk, just tell me that when you answer."

"And you'll let me go, just like that?"

"No."

"Then why should I tell you?"

"So I'll be careful about not teasing."

"I love you so. But go eat now. I don't want you hungry half the day. And I think maybe I'll be able to sleep since you're not still mad at me." Deanna listened to his quiet reply and his wish for her to sleep well and managed to hang up before her eyes closed and she pulled his pillow in against her chest as though she was holding him.

=== April ===

Daws left his bags in the PFC's trunk and headed in to in-processing. He'd slept some on the flight but was still exhausted. He hadn't had a decent night's sleep since he messed up his leg. It was pretty well healed but still pulled at him at times, and it was now stiff from the long flight and the long ride from the airport. Still, the only thing he wanted was to get settled and get a ticket to New York. Bus to Syracuse, then train. He'd rather take the trouble to transfer from one to the other than to ride the bus all the way. Deanna assured him she'd meet him at the station whenever he could get there, although he said he'd grab a taxi. She was driving the Chevy now and then, he knew, but she didn't seem horribly comfortable with it.

He had his assignment – a desk job. For the moment, he wouldn't argue. First thing was to check in and find a place to stay. He could have gone straight to the city, but he'd be able to relax more while there if he at least had a place to lodge when he returned to Drum.

"Incoming or outgoing?"

Daws handed his paperwork to a clerk in fatigues. "Incoming. From Korea."

"Welcome back, Staff Sergeant. How was your tour?"

"Interesting, thank you, Corporal. How fast can I get in and out of here?"

She grinned. "Don't want to spend time with me?"

"No offense, but no. Want to take care of business and go home a while."

"I hear that. And I'll make it as quick and painless as possible. Have a seat."

It was fairly quick, he supposed, but he was impatient. Restless. He signed the paperwork reassigning him at Drum, glad that with only six months left and his intention not to reenlist, they wouldn't send him elsewhere. Although Deanna said she would follow him, there was no way he could let her leave the job she loved, now that she had just what she wanted.

The E3 who picked him up from the airport stayed until he was done, although Daws told him he'd find a way to the billets. He'd let his apartment lease go, put a few things in storage, so first on the agenda was to find a place to stay. He wanted that settled before he went on leave.

When he stood, the E3 got up from the waiting area and joined him. "Anywhere you need to stop before I drop you off at the guest house?"

"Guest house? Thought I had space in the billets for a few days."

"Change of plans. No space. You have a room set up already. Need anything from the Shoppette on the way?"

"No. Just a bed and a phone will do fine tonight."

The corporal grinned and stepped back to let him lead the way.

He was hungry. Nearly starving, actually. But he'd get settled first and then walk up to the NCO club. He didn't need the private to shuttle him around. Daws guessed the man would be off duty as soon as Daws didn't need him.

They pulled up in front of the building and Daws told him to go on home, with his thanks again. The man gave him a card with a phone number and said he lived on base and could help with transportation until he was settled.

Checking into his room, Daws set his bag down, sat on the bed, and grabbed the phone. Five fifteen. She wasn't home yet. He yanked the comforter down and reclined atop the rough over-bleached blanket, hands folded under his head, and considered getting up and changing, going to find food. Except he wanted to catch her first. He didn't want to leave a message that he was in New York. He wanted to hear her voice.

He was nearly asleep when the phone rang and he reached to grab it.

"This is the front desk. Can I ask you to return for a moment? I'm afraid there's something we forgot to have you sign."

"Can it wait? I'll be headed out soon."

"I'm ... sorry, Sergeant. It does need to be taken care of."

"I'll be right down." Sitting up, he stretched his shoulders. And he tried Deanna again but hung up before the answering machine kicked on.

The base hotel had only two floors and no elevator and his leg pulled at him as it always did on stairs, but more so since it was stiff tonight. The same girl who checked him in greeted him.

"You have paperwork for me?"

"Actually..." She gave him a sheepish grin. "No. I was sworn to secrecy." She nodded behind him.

He turned and Deanna threw her arms around his neck. "Oh, it's good to see you."

"How did you get here?" She felt incredible and she smelled soft and sweet and clean, so much better than anything he'd smelled in the past six months.

She smiled. "I drove, of course. Thought you might need your wheels and I couldn't bear the thought of you being so close after so long and still having to wait. So I imposed on Mandy. And I'm staying until you can come home with me."

Daws threw an acknowledgment to the captain's wife but he met Deanna's lips, unable to resist. He did make it soft, gentle, and so much shorter than he wanted. And he held her close again.

"We're taking you to dinner. Are you ready to go?" Mandy Hodgkins intruded with an amusement-filled voice.

Go? Hell no, he wasn't ready to go. He stroked Deanna's hair as his eyes took her in. He wanted to take her upstairs and take her in with more than his eyes ... but he needed to eat first. And Captain Hodgkins' wife was right there. "Left my hat upstairs. I'll have to get it."

"I'll give Shel a call to tell him we'll pick him up in a few minutes while Deanna walks you up. That is, *if* you'll be down again in a few minutes?"

Daws gave her a nod in return for the teasing and led Deanna up to his room. She kissed him in the hallway as soon as they were out of anyone's sight. In the stairwell, she stood one step up and wrapped her arms over his shoulders, just looking at him, until he gripped her around the waist and pulled her head down to his. She kissed him again beside his door before he could get it unlocked. When they were finally inside, she pressed him up against the door and made it deeper, her hands roaming freely, slipping up under his shirt to caress him through the thin tee.

"Mm, Anna, we'll never get to dinner if you don't stop."

"Don't tempt me." She ran a hand through his hair, kissed him again, then studied his face. "You look exhausted. Should I go tell her we're staying in?"

"Just let me look at you for a minute." Daws slid his fingertips over her face, brushed them back along her hairline, behind her ear, down her neck to her shoulder, over the fitted soft sweater that highlighted her curves. "You are so beautiful, and I can't thank you enough for being here waiting, not only here on Drum, but here. Figured the next few days till I got things lined up and got out to the city would be torture."

"Yeah, I figured they would be, too. Couldn't stand to wait that much longer. Hoped you wouldn't mind."

Mind? He felt his head start to shake and couldn't refuse his impulse to pick her up and take her over to the bed.

"I should let Mandy know if..."

Daws kissed her, sitting at her side, leaned down against her. Then he went back to studying her face. "No, I am tired, but I'm also starving. Might need the energy later." He kissed her neck, her jaw. "Want a few minutes alone first. She'll understand."

Deanna slid her arms up around him and held him in tighter. "Am I allowed to stay here with you?"

"Why wouldn't you be?" He kissed the soft spot in front of her ear.

"Wasn't sure how strict regulations are, since we're not...."

He caught her eyes. "No regs against having a girlfriend if you're not married."

"Then I can stay here tonight? Mandy offered space if I need it."

"No way in hell. You're staying here. I'll let the front desk know, as if they don't already. Any complaints and I'll say you're my fiancée."

She grinned. "Come on, then. Let's go eat so we can come back and act married. They're moving, by the way." Deanna claimed his hand as she stood.

"Who?"

"Mandy and her husband. They're in the middle of it now. You barely caught them."

He didn't answer. Just as well. They were changing his unit. And his job. Daws would be more in administrative work than he had been. Not by his choice. And he wouldn't stay there long.

========

Deanna ran her hand along the inside of his thigh, over the long, wide scar he said he didn't care about. She wasn't sure that was true and she'd been putting vitamin E cream on it every day to help it heal. He said it was unnecessary and after three months would do no good, but he didn't stop her.

She finally had him home, in their apartment. The most recent rubdown followed a long whirlpool bath that he said relaxed the tension in his leg. She would insist he do it often, although she thought the neck massages she gave him while he bathed might have as much tension relief effect as the jets of water.

Deanna called her boss earlier in the day to let her know she was back in the city. Libby told her to take the next week off and then check in to see if she was needed the week after. He was staying in New York for two weeks. It wasn't enough, but they'd make do. She'd adjust her schedule and go up to visit him often. He promised to find her a fax machine nearby so she could relay paperwork quickly, and he was leaving her the cell phone so Libby could get in touch wherever she was.

Of course, visiting him would be awkward for a while. He had arranged to share space with an E5 in a little two bedroom trailer. Fred apologized for not having better accommodation for her, but with his ETS date coming up in less than a year, he didn't want to rent anything on his own.

Deanna assured him it was all right. At least she could see him more often. She could easily take her work with her and spend the bus ride each way going through ideas and messing with sketches. During rest stops, she could use the cell phone to make calls. It would work. Until he came home for good. And until then, she planned to make full use of any time they did have.

"I have something for you."

She raised her eyes from where they followed her hand on his thigh. Her fingers returned the favor and traced her gaze up along the top of his hip to his bare chest. She kissed the softness alongside his pecs and teased with a grin. "Already? You recover fast."

He stroked her hair. "Hm. Not what I meant."

"No? I think I might be disappointed." Her fingers teased, as well.

"Are you? You haven't seemed to be."

"Oh, Fred Dawson, you know that's not what I meant. And you know I'm not."

"Glad to hear." He rolled her onto her back and leaned over top. "And I mean I brought something for you since you asked about it."

"Okay." Deanna searched her mind for what she might have asked about that could have been brought.

"Sure you want it?"

"Maybe I should ask what it is?"

With a quick grin, he got out of bed and unzipped a pocket in his suitcase. Returning, he handed her two dark green sealed plastic pouches. Printed on the outside: Meal, Ready To Eat. Meatloaf with gravy.

"Oh. MRE." Deanna turned one of them over in her hands. "This is a whole meal?"

"At times."

"How does it open?"

He turned to pull a pocket knife out of the bed stand, slit the top, and handed the package back.

Deanna pulled out a menagerie of little wrapped items: a box of meatloaf, a package of crackers sealed so tightly the little hole indentations showed, a tiny chocolate bar Fred said was meant to be dessert, waterproof matches, salt and pepper, tiny wrapped napkin, and plastic spoon. "This is meatloaf?"

"More or less. Probably don't want to try it."

"You have."

"When there's no other choice."

"You've actually lived on this as a meal?"

He brushed fingers through her hair. "Lot of nutrition, so they say. A load of calories for energy. It'll keep you alive. Not appetizing, and plenty of water with it is a must."

"To wash down the taste?"

"To rehydrate your insides after all the dehydrated calories."

"Oh. Can I try it?"

"At your own risk."

She wrapped in her thin robe as he pulled into his boxer shorts and went with him to the kitchen table. She didn't get far with the "meal, ready to eat." Especially when he mentioned each one had over a thousand calories. Deanna could imagine how fast she'd gain weight living on a thousand calories per meal, per dry, nearly tasteless and nearly inedible meal.

"Still ready to join up?"

She caught his teasing grin. "Well, if you were staying in and I could be by your side every day, I might still consider it. You'd have to help me work out even more than I do, though, or I'd be a balloon before long and you'd change your mind."

He moved closer and slid a hand beneath her robe, to her waist. "I wouldn't change my mind." He kissed her neck. "And I look forward to when I can be with you every night, if not every day. You may have to start telling me you've worked out enough."

"Think so?" Deanna set her arms over his shoulders and gave him a light kiss. "Try me, Sergeant Dawson."

With a glance down, he untied her robe and moved it away. Deanna closed her eyes and enjoyed his caress, and his finesse, and then took him back to their room.

Daws took the phone out to the front step and closed the door, shutting off as much of the noise as he could. He should have asked about the guy's weekend hobbies before he agreed to move in. Too many visitors. Too much noise. Much of the time, he didn't care. He did get tired of dodging girls. And it made it hard to talk with Deanna. She warned him, teasing, every time, to look the other direction if those girls got too showy. He told her, every time, he had no interest in any other girl, no matter what they showed. And he asked when she was coming to visit. Every time.

Less than a month since he'd been away from her and it felt like six.

Listening through the rings until he heard her voice, he felt himself relax at the sound of it.

"Hey, guess what?" She was in an incredible mood. "Never mind, you'll never guess. So I just heard today. McCallister sent Todd to another branch."

"Farther away?"

"Oh yeah. Much farther. Alabama." She laughed. "As much as he made fun of me for my southern roots, he's going to hate it."

"Good."

She laughed again. "Good that he'll hate it?"

"Maybe that too, but I meant good that he'll be away from there. When?"

"Already left. His wife wouldn't go. Guess he'll have an easier time hiding his marriage that way."

"Her problem since she knows he will."

"I hear she was just as glad, or nearly as glad, as I am, that he's away. Sad, isn't it? And I'm being horrible gossiping. Didn't mean to, just thought you'd be glad to know."

"I am."

A pause came over the line. "What's wrong, Freddy? Something happen?"

"No. All's fine."

"No, it's not. Don't try to lie to me. You know you can't."

He couldn't help a half grin.

"Another party tonight?"

"Yes. And I'm wishing you were here."

More silence.

He shifted and grabbed a deep breath. "So what did you do with your day?"

"Something's wrong."

"No. Just talk to me."

"Nightmares again?"

Daws clenched his jaw, then released it. "Yes. Just talk to me, Anna. I want to hear your voice."

With a light pause, she started in about her day, her current project, her meeting with a client who loved the direction they were heading and offered thoughts of her own. The job was perfect for her. He could hear it in everything she said, in the tone of her voice, the way she was always so much happier.

When he finally let her off the line, he set the phone back in the trailer and went to wander around the park to enjoy the freshness of spring. He thought of sitting out on his balcony with her while they gazed at the stars.

Deanna headed the rental car toward where she hoped she remembered the trailer was. She'd had a time getting them to rent her a car since she was a new driver, and had to put plenty of insurance on it, but she was glad she did. If she'd taken the bus again, Fred would have had to pick her up. She wanted to surprise him the way he had for her when she most needed it.

And she liked the Grand Am. She liked the odd straight back window and she loved the way it felt. Maybe she'd have to get one.

She sighed relief when the park came into view. He said he'd be home. Deanna had told him she'd be out late and would call him instead. Checking the number to be sure she had the right trailer, since they all looked nearly the same, she spotted his car and pulled in beside it. Her own engine revved as she turned off the car's engine.

It seemed much longer than she knew it was until the door opened. A guy in fatigue pants, socks, and Army brown tee gave her a curious look. "Yes?"

"I'm looking for Fred Dawson."

"Really?" He eyed her up and down.

"Is he here?"

"Yeah." He left the door half open as he disappeared. "Hey Daws, not mine. For you. You invited a girl over?"

Deanna grimaced. She should have warned him not to say anything.

But Fred's voice filled the distance. "Funny. And enough already."

"Hey, I'm serious. Some chick is here asking for you."

Silence, except for a rattling pan. *Some chick.* Deanna rolled her eyes.

"Going to come answer it?"

"Carson, if you're pulling something again, I'm moving out."

"Nah, promise. No idea. But she's kinda hot so if you're not interested…"

"Stop there." Fred's voice faded into more clinking metal. "Watch the gravy so it doesn't burn."

Deanna grinned and forced herself not to walk in. When he came to the door, dressed the same as the other guy, an annoyed expression changed to confusion. "Deanna?"

"Thought it was my turn to surprise you." She studied his face as he stared. "Is it okay? Because it is a long drive, especially when…"

"You drove?"

She nodded toward the car.

He stepped out onto the little porch and kissed her, both arms wrapping around, one on her back, one behind her head. A long kiss. Apparently it was okay.

"Hey Daws, careful your girlfriend doesn't find out."

When he released her lips, they both looked across the little gravel road to another doorstep at the grinning soldier.

"This is my girlfriend."

"Yeah, right."

Freddy took her inside, grabbed a BDU shirt off the couch and threw it at his roommate, then shoved a pair of boots out of the way. He introduced them and went to the kitchen.

Sergeant Carson eyed her again. "You're really his girlfriend?"

"For two years now."

"You let the gravy burn." Fred took her side.

Deanna wrapped an arm around him. "Doesn't matter. I'm taking you out. And you might want to pack a bag because I have a hotel booked for the next three nights. I'm going to enjoy the pool and the weight room and get some work done during the day and then keep you to myself all night." She glanced over at the E5. "No offense."

"Hey, no problem. Good to see he wasn't making you up. Some of us were starting to wonder."

Fred gave him a 'knock it off' look and Deanna a kiss on the side of her head, then told her to have a seat while he changed. "Carson, watch your language for a few minutes."

She enjoyed the few minutes of getting to know Fred's roommate but was glad he didn't take long and was glad to let him drive. He held her door, got in behind the wheel, and leaned in for another kiss. "Where are we going for dinner?"

"Anywhere you want. I got a bonus with my last paycheck. Thought I'd spend it on you."

"A bonus already?"

"Landed a nice account." Deanna couldn't keep her excitement hidden after having waited so long to tell him in person. "A new art gallery."

"That's incredible, Anna. Congratulations. The first of many."

"Let's go eat, soldier. Then we're going back to the hotel to relax in the sauna, and then I'm taking you up to our room and helping you unwind enough you'll sleep well tonight."

Daws could hardly make himself release her to drive. He'd been right. Now that her feet were firmly under her, Deanna was showing every ounce of her take-charge spirit. He couldn't be more glad to see it.

He was tired. Tired of being always in charge and responsible for so much. Tired of the desk work they had him on. Tired of being away from home. Tired of always being the one everyone came to with their problems because he knew, usually, how to handle them. Tired of having so much pushed on him because he would get it done. He was tired.

Of the nightmares, also. The more he saw the news about Somalia, the worse they got. He could easily be pulled over there or they could refuse to let him out in October. He'd go, if called on to go. But he was also tired of being away from her.

Daws did not want to be retained just because of some little show-of-force war in which he saw no point. He wanted out. Someone else could be the front line of defense for a change.

And he was more than willing to let Deanna be in charge as she wished.

=== July ===

"I have to run." Deanna packed up her papers and checked the clock. Fred would be home within the hour. She wanted to be there first. Even if it had been only a month since she went up to visit him, she was anxious to see him. And he was only there for the long weekend. They would spend the Fourth together and he'd have to return, although he was stopping in Vermont for a couple of days on his way back. He wanted to check on Ryan in person. Again.

He kept saying they'd go together soon, so Deanna could see the boy play. After he decided to introduce himself, and if the kid didn't tell him to get lost.

"Deanna?"

She turned back toward Libby.

"Don't you want your purse?"

"Oh. Yes, I should probably take it."

Her boss chuckled as she brought it over. "Have a nice weekend and tell your sergeant I said hello."

"I'll do that. Happy Fourth." She pressed out the door and hurried along the sidewalk to the metro. From her new office, the metro was much more convenient than the bus. Libby and Fred had met in April when her boss insisted on joining them for lunch one day. They got along well enough, although she was pretty sure Fred would have preferred to lunch alone.

They would be alone tonight. And she had a nice meal planned, his favorite.

Maybe they would stay in all weekend and watch fireworks together from his balcony.

He had other plans. Deanna greeted Ellis and Holly Andrews, said hello to their kids, and asked if they knew where they were going. The couple looked at each other and then at Freddy and shrugged with a grin.

"So everyone knows but me?"

Fred ran a hand down her back. "A surprise. Something I've always wanted to do."

"Okay, but we are going to watch the fireworks, right? I don't want to miss them."

"You won't miss them." He kissed the side of her head and ushered her to a waiting taxi van.

Deanna listened to the chatter behind her as she looked out at New York at early dusk. She loved dusk. They even had a nice sunset beginning to flair across the sky; nice from what she could see of it behind and between buildings. She hoped the view from wherever they were going would be at least as good as it was from the balcony.

The taxi stopped in front of a tall building she didn't recognize. It wasn't close to the harbor. There was no view. But maybe it was only the first stop.

The children, four and six if she remembered, nearly bounced throughout their unending chatter. They were cute, though, and well-mannered, other than being so talkative. The little girl grabbed Deanna's hand as they went in and headed toward the elevator.

Holly finally drew the girl away and asked her to calm down, and Deanna noticed they were at the tenth floor and still climbing. She couldn't see the control panel. Freddy blocked it. "How far are we going?"

He grinned and ran a hand through her hair. "All the way."

She moved closer. "With the kids around?"

He chuckled at her wink. And the elevator stopped at the twelfth floor. "We use stairs from here."

"Stairs?" She stepped out and saw a sign pointing to the roof. "Are you kidding?"

"I didn't ask if you were afraid of heights."

"No. But..."

"Should be one of the best views in town." He set a hand on her back and told the couple they'd meet up later.

"You're not coming?"

Ellis laughed. "Not with these two little hellions. We have friends here. We'll watch from the window."

Deanna couldn't help be relieved. She'd have him alone for fireworks after all. Stepping out onto the flat roof made her nervous, even without a fear of heights. It was also exhilarating. She walked out far enough to look over the city, the Harbor where the fireworks would be set off soon, with the summer breeze brushing her hair around her face.

Fred came up behind her and kissed the back of her neck. "Come this way."

She followed to where he had a large blanket spread out and held down by a cooler and a couple of folding chairs so far lying flat. And a vase full of Cannas of every color. The wide vase was decorated with red and white stripes and blue stars.

"A thank you for your part in supporting the mission." Reaching into the jacket he carried, he pulled out a long jewelry box and opened it. Slipping a bracelet out of the box, he wrapped it around her wrist. White pearls with ruby and sapphire gems.

"Freddy." Deanna touched the bracelet and met his eyes. "You don't need to keep doing this."

"Don't like it?"

"I love it. It's gorgeous. But…"

He kissed her, allowing the jackets to fall onto the blanket so he could hold her with both arms.

As they waited for the sky to grow dark enough, he pulled a bottle of wine from the cooler, handed her a glass, and teased her with chocolate covered strawberries. He held them for her and let her lick the quickly melting chocolate from his fingers. By the time the fireworks started, they'd abandoned the chairs for the blanket and she returned the teasing, her hands underneath his shirt, her lips nuzzling his neck.

She drew back enough to turn and watch, cuddled in as close to him as she could get.

They began slowly, small pops and then brief bits of flickering lights that fell into the water. And then they rose, high above the Statue of Liberty that stood for everything for which he'd spent so much time protecting. He would continue to do so, if in a smaller way.

It had been such a long time, and yet so little, since he'd enjoyed the sight of night fire, the explosion, the strong flickering glowing light, and the resulting smoke that covered the harbor in a haze. He'd never been close enough to see it before. In a way, it seemed wrong to cover the harbor of freedom in a haze of smoke. But it would clear again. And the memory of the lights and explosions and the resulting peaceful silence was worth the smoke that would clear. It always did. As long as they held onto the thought of what lay behind it, it always would. It would always clear.

========

Settling onto a chair at the back of the dark club, Daws ordered a Jack and Coke, light on the whiskey. The band was still setting up, and Ryan argued with the guitarist about something. Then he changed the speaker arrangement himself and moved mics around. The guitarist shook his head but let it go.

Their manager paced along the front of the stage and spoke to the band. Ryan glanced at the guy and went on tuning his acoustic against the keyboards. As they started their set, girls close to the front yelled Ryan's name and waved at him. He flirted in return, shoved his bangs back from his face, and moved closer to them.

It was a song Daws hadn't heard. He focused on the words, the way the kid worked the strings. It wasn't the acoustic he'd left for him, but something newer, more expensive. A Gibson, he thought. The lyrics reflected a lot of anger, a lot of searching. About a girl. Of course it was about a girl; the kid had girls on his brain far too much. And they seemed to know he did. It attracted them.

"Mind if I sit?"

Daws looked up at a woman roughly his age in a tight low-cut top. "I have a girlfriend."

"Do you? But you're here alone."

"She had to work."

"Well, maybe I'll just sit here and listen with you." She pulled a chair close. "Gonna be a gentleman and offer me a drink?"

He figured it was at least good cover and beckoned to a waitress to get the girl's order. A slow screw. And she looked at Daws as she ordered. He turned his attention back to the stage.

The kid was overall angry tonight. It was all over his expression, his stance. And yet he flirted mercilessly, at times squatting on stage to be eye level with one of them. Through the night he relaxed to an extent. When he took breaks, he had at least one girl at his side, usually more, but they were short breaks. To the obvious chagrin of his band, he didn't stop longer than a few minutes and then jumped right back to work.

He loved what he was doing. No matter how much Mrs. Reynauld tried to convince Daws when they talked that Ryan should find a different path, it wouldn't happen. The kid belonged on stage.

The woman beside him kept trying to move in, so Daws got up and moved closer to the stage, along the edge behind small groups of teens and barely twenties. He'd switched to plain Coke after his first drink. He had to drive at least half way back to Drum when he left. He could skip PT but was expected in the office by o-eight-hundred.

He'd left Deanna again only that afternoon. It was getting harder all the time, even if he did see her more often.

During their next break, Ryan pulled a girl onto his lap when she came over, one who'd been flirting constantly and boldly. A guy yelled over at him to leave his girlfriend alone. The girl got up and tried to interfere as the stocky man moved in on them.

"Come on, kid. Apologize and move away." Daws spoke under his breath and headed that direction.

Of course he didn't. Ryan straightened, pulled his chin up as though he thought he might look threatening that way, and told the man to "F off."

The guy shoved him. "Find your own damn girl, asshole. This one's taken."

"Yeah? Not taken well since she's been hitting on me all night. Not my fault you can't keep her happy."

Daws cringed as the guy decked Ryan in the jaw. Stupid kid. Brave. But stupid.

One of his band mates backed him up. Not well. The others stood by and watched as the large boyfriend blocked a punch and knocked the kid to the floor.

Pushing through the commotion, Daws grabbed the guy's arm just before he threw his fist into Ryan's face again. He shoved him away. "Back off."

"Man, stay the hell out of this. He's hitting on my girlfriend."

"I'd say you made your point. Now back off before I put you on the floor."

The guy sized him up and huffed away, pulling the girl with him to the other side of the bar. She didn't seem unwilling.

Daws offered Ryan a hand. "Can you get up?"

"I'm fine." He tried to do it himself but faltered and accepted.

Daws pushed him into a chair and asked for ice from a couple of the waitresses. The bartender was there, also. "Need a shot of straight gin and a towel."

"He can't have it..."

"It's not to drink." Dismissing the guy, he set a hand alongside the kid's face and studied the damage. "Going to be a hell of a black eye. How many fingers?" He held up two.

"Thirteen."

"Funny. How many?"

"Two. I'm fine. Except for the jackhammer on my brain." Ryan pushed a hand against his head. "Damn, Mom's gonna freak."

The bartender returned. Daws put the towel against the side of Ryan's head. "Lean back."

"What?"

Daws grabbed Ryan's hair to pull his head the direction he wanted it and dumped some of the gin over a gash between his eye and his hairline.

"*Ow! Damn.* What in the hell are you *doing*?" The kid tried to push him away.

Daws handed the glass to someone hovering and held him down. "You don't want that infected."

"*Damn.* How about that cream stuff? *Shit* that hurts."

"I'm not your mom. I use what's handy."

"Who in the hell are you?"

"I'm the guy who just saved your ass."

"Yeah, great, but who are you?"

"Tonight, I'm your bodyguard. Seems you're going to need one if you can't find better common sense than you just showed."

"What?"

He was still dazed. Daws had doubts the kid heard much of what he'd just said. His guitarist asked if he was going to be able to go back on.

Daws threw him a glare. "Could have if you'd all stuck by him as band mates should. Not like this, he can't."

"Hell, why give him more loyalty than he gives us? He wouldn't jump into that if it was any of us."

"Yeah, I would've. No matter how much I don't like you." Ryan tried to turn to him but clenched his eyes and pushed his hands against his head.

"Come on." Daws gripped his arm. "Probably have a concussion. Need to get it checked out."

"Hell. No way. I just need aspirin. A ton of it. Ten minutes, I can play again."

"Not tonight, you're not. Let's go."

"Man, I don't even know you. I'm not going anywhere with you."

Daws had to give him credit for that much. "Fine. Tell me who to call to pick you up."

"No. Hell, they'll freak out."

"Unless you're going to hide out for a couple of weeks until you heal, afraid you'll have to deal with that. Who do I call?"

His shoulders slumped. "Will. My brother. Tell him not to say anything to Mom." He mumbled a phone number Daws didn't catch but he pretended he did. He knew the number. Leaving Ryan in the care of a couple of waitresses, he gave the Reynauld house a quick call. Then he went back to sit with Ryan until they arrived.

The rest of the gin was still in the shot glass and Daws handed it to him. Half a shot wouldn't hurt anything and the kid had a long night ahead. "Here."

Ryan stared at him. "Yeah right, then you get me in trouble for drinking, right? This some kind of set up?"

Daws had to force himself not to laugh. "Since I ordered it, I'd be the one in trouble. Just keep your mouth shut about it and we'll both be safe enough."

He only hesitated a second for accepting and downing it like he had plenty of practice. "Damn. One more thing for Mr. Straight and Narrow to bitch at me about."

"Who?"

"My brother. The good one who does everything right. Never gonna live this one down."

"Be glad you have him."

Ryan finally focused on his face. "Yeah. I am. Most days. Do I know you?"

Did he possibly recognize him from the funeral? Daws figured it was possible, somewhere in the back of his memories. "Big question is, still know your name? Pretty hard hit. How do you feel?"

"Like hell. They're butchering my song." He turned enough to look at the stage. "Cretins."

Again, Daws forced himself to keep a straight face. "Might not say that where they'll hear you."

"Already have."

"No wonder you get along so well."

Ryan made a face and looked back at him. "Didn't answer me. Have we met?"

"Don't think we have." Not technically, anyway. "I've been here now and then. Was enjoying your music."

"Yeah? You don't look the type."

"You don't look the type to be playing that music, either."

He grinned, then winced. "Touché."

"I think you'd do better with straight pop. The rest of it doesn't fit you."

"Yeah, you a music expert or something?"

"No. But I know what sounds good. And you sound all right as you are. Though I think you could do better."

"Not without a better band." He wiped blood from the side of his mouth and onto his jeans.

"I'd agree about that."

Ryan returned his full gaze. "What do you do?"

"Protection. I'm in the security field." Not a lie.

The kid chuckled. "Yeah, not surprised. Mighta guessed a linebacker or something." He tried to feel the gash on his head. Daws pulled his hand away. He didn't argue. Surprisingly. "So when I get big and need an actual bodyguard, gonna look me up? Name's Ryan Reynauld. Someday everyone will know it. Damn, they're destroying my song. Should sound better than this."

The kid was making it too easy. Daws pulled a card from his wallet and handed it to him. "My number. Give me a call."

Ryan studied the white card that had his name and cell number and the phrase *personal security* engraved. "Doesn't have a company name."

"No. Building my own. No name yet."

"You serious with this?"

"Hold onto it." He asked for a gin refill and despite the kid's protest, he poured more over the gash, patting off the extra gin mixed with blood. Ignored the cursing.

When Will arrived, he checked his brother's head, asked if he was hurt anywhere else, and pretended not to know Daws. The connection between them was deep, regardless of what Ryan had said. It was in their expressions as they studied each other.

Will quietly told him his mom was in the car. She didn't want to embarrass him by coming in but they were taking him to the hospital to check his head and Tracy was there to drive Ryan's car home. Ryan refused. He was already becoming more clear headed, his gaze was more focused.

"Ry, we have to check this out."

"No. It's just a scratch. Hell, he's already drowned it in gin. It's gotta be all right after all that. Damn that hurt. *Twice*, mind you."

"It's not the scratch that concerns me. It's your head."

"Hell, not that I use it much anyway, right?"

Daws interrupted. "Can you stand up?"

"Yeah, I can stand up. Hell." Ryan stood, sort of, and Will caught him.

Forcing an arm under Ryan's shoulder on the other side, Daws helped Will walk him outside, where he promptly threw up in the bushes. A definite concussion.

He kept an arm half around the boy and overrode his objections to going to the hospital, insisting he needed to be there. Mrs. Reynauld didn't hide their acquaintance as well as Will did, but Ryan was too absorbed in his nausea and headache to notice. He did mention his guitars and equipment he couldn't leave.

Getting him in the car with Tracy's promise she'd get everything and Will's assurance it was all right to leave her with Daws as an escort, his mom and brother drove him off.

Tracy thanked him for his help in retrieving the equipment, as well as convincing his band they'd have to do without anything that belonged to Ryan for the rest of the night. And she suggested Daws could go ahead and she'd handle getting it home. But she was shaken, worried about her fiancé's brother. And he was not leaving until he made sure the kid was all right.

He followed her to the house, helped drag everything inside – his offer to wait and let her call a friend to join them if she was nervous to let him in was dismissed – and drove her to the hospital with her directions.

By the time they arrived, the doctor had already determined they'd keep Ryan overnight for observation. He'd gotten sick again during the exam. Daws didn't believe he'd hit his head quite that hard. Out of the family's hearing, he told the doctor so. And when the man stalled about giving him information without knowing who he was, he told him that, too.

"Ah. Edward and I were old friends. Nice to meet one of his men."

"Pleasure's mine. Don't let the kid know. His family does."

"Their business, I guess. The nausea is nerves, more than likely. He's had it since losing his dad. Had him on something for it until he decided he didn't need it. My guess is this scared him more than he'll admit. Another reason I want to watch, but he'll be all right. We'll keep him awake for twelve hours or so and watch him. Marianne says you were with him. Was he drinking?"

"Cola, a lot of it. And half a shot of gin to ease some of the pain. Wouldn't have if I'd known about his stomach."

"I imagine that's been washed out by now. I gave him a couple of stitches, too. Nice to see it was clean although I can imagine how he complained about that at the time."

"Not bad. I've seen grown men throw ten times the fit he did." Daws glanced around him into the room. "I have to get going. Okay if I talk to him a minute first?"

"If Marianne doesn't care, it's fine with me." The doctor told his family he'd be back soon and walked away.

Daws eased closer.

Mrs. Reynauld came over to him. "Thank you. I'm not sure if I said that..."

"No need. Glad I was there. Mind if I have a minute with him?"

"Of course not." She turned to Ryan. "We'll be back in a minute, honey."

The kid moved and cringed. "Go on home. It's late."

"You know I'm not. Mr. Dawson wants a word with you. We'll be outside."

As they closed the door behind them, Daws moved up to the bed where the kid was propped up with pillows. "Have a question if you're up to it."

"I'm fine and dandy. Stupid to keep me here for this. If I could, I'd refuse."

He couldn't help a grin and shake of the head. "I knew someone a lot like you once."

"Yeah? Sorry."

"I'm not. Good man, as an adult. Highly respected."

The kid snickered. "Not too much like me, then. Plain you don't know me."

"Maybe. Given we've just met. Never know."

"So what's the question?"

"How hooked are you to your manager?"

"He's an ass."

"Then why are you with him?"

"You're not from here, right? I can tell you're not. So I don't know why you're here, and can't imagine you'll stick around long, but there's no one else. Someday I'll find a real one. For now, he's old enough to get us in places that won't talk to me 'cause I'm not *legal* yet. Another year."

"You plan to keep going in music?"

"Hell, yeah. It's the only thing I'm good at."

"My guess is you'll be good at anything you set your mind to."

Another snicker. "Mom set you up to this, didn't she? Figured I'd need rescuing one of these days and you could talk me out of taking this big time? Not gonna work. Another year and I'm going somewhere I can really do something with it. Nothing you say's gonna matter. Don't get me wrong, I appreciate the save tonight, but it won't change anything."

Daws tried not to look as amused as he was. For a skinny little thing with more attitude than anything to back it up, he was sure as hell sure of himself. And determined. Driven. "Okay." He turned and started to walk out.

"Hey."

After a second, he turned back.

"Dawson? Is that what you said your name is? Don't know where the card went."

"Fred Dawson. Friends and colleagues call me Daws."

"Yeah? So are you gonna make me call you *Mr.* Dawson?"

"As I said, it's Daws."

"Why?" When he didn't get an answer, he pressed. "Why'd you give me your info if you were here trying to talk me out of it?"

"Didn't say I was."

Ryan cringed and pressed a hand against his head. "Yeah? Then why are you here?"

"Call me when you decide to take this farther. We'll talk then. I'll leave my card with your brother." Daws moved to the door and gripped the handle, and turned back. "If you don't mind some advice, take it easy with the girls. Plenty of time for that later when it's not so dangerous. And take care of that head. You will need it."

He paused to talk with the major's family and said he'd call now and then to stay in touch, then he headed out, back to work. A check of his watch told him it was after one. He wouldn't drive more than half way tonight, if that.

A rough road ahead of him. The major's words flashed back into his mind, talking about his youngest son. Yes, he had no doubt. As he closed the car door and started the engine, buckling his belt, he looked out at the stars. "If you're up there paying attention, I sure hope this is what you meant by watching out for him. No way in the world will I change his mind. And you're right. I'm glad to have met your boys. Should have stuck around to introduce me yourself, though." After a minute, he pulled out and headed toward the end of one path that would lead to his next.

Deanna laughed when Fred told her about his encounter with the soon-to-be famous, or maybe infamous, Ryan Reynauld. She wasn't sure he appreciated her laughter, but she had to admire the kid's moxie.

And she bit her tongue when he told her his new major had called him into his office to try to convince Fred to stay in. He was offered the E7 board and Battle Staff School. She knew he was tempted and she considered telling him he should consider it. But he sounded sure.

And he'd had enough. He didn't like the new duty they had him on since he had less contact with his troops and they didn't feel as much like "his" as they used to when he worked beside them. He missed the connection. His leg still bothered him at times, worse on rainy days. His roommate drove him crazy, but he didn't want to move for the three months he had left.

Benefits for new enlistees were being cut and recruiting standards had lowered. That bothered him to no end. Worried him. It made her think about the conversation they had the day they met, about why he was okay with being so hard on his men, to protect them. Deanna heard him worry too often these days, sound down too often. She couldn't possibly encourage him to stay and go farther when his heart wasn't in it.

Or maybe she only imagined it wasn't; maybe she wanted him home and settled with her. Maybe she wanted him to be taken care of for a change.

"They're sending me to California." Deanna's voice was bubbly, in a great mood, which normally raised his spirits.

This time it didn't. Daws lowered onto the edge of his bed and shoved a hand through his hair. He didn't need this now. Not today. She couldn't move. They were too damn close to what they'd planned. And he couldn't deal with it today.

"Still there?"

"Yes." He forced a deep breath. She loved her job. He couldn't stop her. He supposed he could try to convince Ryan to move that way instead of to New York, but he wanted to be in New York. He'd been nearly counting days.

"Is that bothering you? It's only for a week. I'll have a phone. We can still talk."

"A week?"

"Yes. Oh. Is that what's wrong? Did you think I meant I was moving? I wouldn't do that. When you're finally about to come home? Never. I'm down to counting days until I have you, really have you. I'm not going anywhere. Well, not for more than a week."

He listened to her chat about the client who wouldn't fly but wanted to meet in person and how Libby said Deanna could handle it on her own just fine and how excited she was, that she'd never been there and she wished he could go with her.

Finally, she calmed. "You do know I would never leave you, right?"

He stood up and paced around the small room in the trailer. "I know you love your job. Wouldn't hold you back. I said I wouldn't."

"Oh, Freddy. Yes, I love it. It's exactly what I wanted, but I love you more. I'd leave the job for you in a heartbeat, without hesitation. Don't you know that by now? A job can be replaced. You can't."

He was quiet for a moment. "Sorry. It's been a long day. And I know. So this is a promotion of sorts?"

"Yes. It's ... a huge leap of trust. Already. After all those years over at that other place, it's so refreshing.... What is it? What's wrong?"

"I'm happy to hear it. When are you going? They're putting you up somewhere nice, right? Safe? And you're meeting him somewhere safe?"

"Yes. A big hotel with a restaurant and lounge and we'll meet at his office, a high rise, in an open conference room. What's bothering you?"

He sat again. "I want to hear more. What's the project? Can you say?"

Deanna told him what she could, leaving out names, company and client, and rambled a while, giving him time. He knew she'd ask again. When she did, he stopped putting it off. "Lost one of my men today."

"Lost him how? AWOL?"

"No. Wish he'd done that instead." He stood again, pacing. As much as he could in the small run-down space.

"Freddy? What happened?"

"He strung himself up in his barracks."

"What?"

"Hardly knew him. I'm not at work much now. Getting my paperwork and everything in order, turning everything over to the incoming platoon sergeant. He was new to the unit. Had trouble fitting in. I should have..."

"No. Don't do that. It's not your fault if he wasn't stable."

"They shouldn't have let him in in the first place. It was all over his records. Mental evaluations. Trouble at home. Trouble at work. He tried to use this as an escape. They shouldn't have let him in. Standards have gotten too lax."

"Okay. Wait. He was unstable coming in. So ... he's new? Not just to your unit?"

"Buck private, just out of basic. No idea how he got through it. Shouldn't have."

"What happened?"

"Got too smart-mouthed, from what I hear. Called in the rest of his unit today to find out what we could. Said he was cursing them constantly and wouldn't listen to orders, got the whole unit extra duty more than once. They all turned away from him, wouldn't talk, set him up. He went off on his sergeant. The sergeant put him in for dishonorable discharge, said he should go home. Note he left said he couldn't face going home."

"Oh, Freddy. I'm so sorry. But don't put this on yourself..."

"Should have paid more attention. He was one of my men. His sergeant reported trouble. When I talked to him, he listened well enough, or seemed to. And I turned him over to the incoming platoon sergeant. Thought he'd handle it. I shouldn't have..."

"Listen to me. Do you hear yourself? This wasn't you. This was everyone before you who pushed him on through to where he shouldn't have been. His family, for starters. If he couldn't face going home, that was a family issue. Someone there screwed up. Whoever allowed him in screwed up. Lots of people did, not you."

"He was one of my men, Deanna. No matter what anyone did before me, I failed him."

"No. He shouldn't have been there."

"Hardly matters now. It goes on my record. More than that, on my conscience. Nothing I've done up to now matters, after this."

"That's not true."

"Good thing I was already out processing so it doesn't look like I ran from it. Though, I suppose the inference will still be there. I have to go tell his family."

"Oh. I don't even know what to say. But do you have to go?"

"He was one of my men."

"I'm so sorry."

Daws grabbed a deep breath and sat again. He had to change the subject. "Shouldn't have told you today. You should celebrate tonight, Anna. You deserve it. Do something fun. Call a couple of your girlfriends..."

"I can't."

"Why can't you?"

"When I know how much you're hurting? How can I? I'm staying right here, on the phone if you want or by the phone, at least."

He shoved a hand through his hair and dropped his head.

"I wish I could be there to go with you."

"Wouldn't want you there. And I mean because it'll be rough, either because it'll be hard on them to hear or because it won't be. Impossible to tell at this point."

"I'd still be there if I could. Just ... you remember what I'm telling you: no one can screw up a kid like his family can. If they do it bad enough, nothing anyone else does matters much. You know that. And if it wasn't them, it was someone else who mattered to the kid. Someone screwed him up, but it wasn't you. If it didn't happen now, it probably would have later. You focus on those soldiers left behind. They're still here. And they probably feel even more guilty than you do. Focus on them."

He leaned down to start unlacing his boots. He wanted them off. He needed out of the uniform, into civvies. The movement, action of some sort, made him feel slightly better. Although it was more her. "Maybe you're in the wrong line of work, Anna."

"Why?"

"You'd make a great counselor."

"Oh. No. I'm not ... I just don't want you to be too hard on yourself. I love you too much and I don't want you to hurt."

He stopped, sat up, grabbed a deep breath. He couldn't even imagine this ever not hurting. Stupid kid. He would have helped him. If he was that set on staying in, not going home, Daws would have done everything in his power to help him. He'd offered help. Why didn't the stupid kid take him up on it?

"Freddy?"

He grabbed another breath, clenched his eyes. "I'm here."

"Are you okay?"

"Will be. I love you too, and I can't wait to be out of here and in your arms. Just promise me something."

"Of course."

"When Ryan moves to New York, as he will, make sure I don't miss anything with him I shouldn't."

"Oh. No, you won't. You'll do wonders for him."

"The major will never forgive me if I let him down."

"From what you've said of him, I think he would as long as you tried. But you won't let him down. I know. And if we have to move Ryan in here with us to watch him together, we'll do that. He'll be fine."

A deep sigh made him suddenly exhausted, but he couldn't let her go. "So talk to me, Anna. About anything. Anything else."

=======

Deanna paced along the gravel road in front of his trailer. Sergeant Carson invited her in to wait, but she decided it would be best to stay outside until Fred got back. A couple of soldiers said hello, since they recognized her from previous visits. One of them stopped to talk for a while as she sat on the steps. The company was nice. Carson had brought her a plastic glass of iced tea and repeated the offer to come in, begged nearly. He said he'd leave the front door open if she felt better.

She started to wonder if she should take him up on it. The heat was causing moist spots on the back of her blouse and made her jeans stick to her skin. Still, if Fred was so insistent about his men not stepping foot in his place when he wasn't there, Deanna wasn't about to violate the rule.

Fred should have been back.

As horribly depressed as he sounded over the phone the night before and again this morning before he left for Connecticut to talk to the private's family, Fred needed her there. She knew he did. Libby didn't object in the slightest.

Deanna checked her watch again. Nearly two hours now. She'd alternated between sitting on the steps and pacing along the road since she arrived and had to admit she was getting tired. There wasn't that much to see in the little run-down trailer court. They all looked about the same in shades of faded whites, browns, and light mustard yellows. Unkempt patches of grass and weeds broke up the space between one's parking space and the other's living quarters. A couple of them had potted plants on their porches or tucked in front of the bedraggled trim that Deanna supposed was either to hide the fact that the mobile houses sat on cement blocks or to keep critters out from underneath. Maybe both.

At the end of his dead-end road, she turned again and headed back. Maybe she'd go in. Would he mind if she did when he wasn't there? He didn't even know she was there; Deanna hadn't decided until after talking to him earlier that she planned to be.

Reaching his parking area again, she half considered finding a hotel and cleaning up, making herself presentable. But she wanted to be there when he got home.

As she leaned back against her rental car to consider, Deanna looked up at a car's approach. It was automatic by now; she'd watched every vehicle that came close for the past two hours.

This time it was a brown Chevy Malibu. Freddy.

He nearly stopped in the road when he saw her, then inched forward into his space. The engine was barely off when his door opened and he stepped out. In his dress greens, minus jacket and tie. So tired.

Deanna went to meet him and touched his face, sorrowed by what she saw in his eyes.

Fred pulled her against him and held tightly. He didn't even ask why she was there. She gave him a light kiss on the neck after a couple of minutes of simply standing still and letting him hold her. He returned it to the side of her head, then her lips, and in front of her ear, her neck.

Someone whistled and jeered. Carson told the guy to shut the hell up, from the trailer's doorway.

Fred's chest rose and fell heavily, and he held Deanna's gaze for a moment before moving it to his roommate.

"How'd it go?" Carson held out a shot glass half full of a light brown liquid. "Need this?"

Fred shook his head. "Have what I need right here." He brushed fingers along Deanna's face. "You're getting hot. Why aren't you inside?"

"Hey, I tried." Carson shrugged. "Several times. Even said I'd leave the door open, though she had nothing to worry about. She insisted on waiting for you. Nearly two hours. What took so long?"

"Two hours?" Fred caught her eyes. "You've been out here for two hours?" He ran fingers along her bare shoulder, down her arm; his eyes dropped to the front of her skinny tank top. "By yourself? And you didn't burn."

"Sun block. And not exactly by myself..."

"I was keeping an eye out." Carson encroached on their space, leaving the door open behind him. "Though everyone here knows she's your girl. No one's going to bother her."

"Damn well better not or they'd be missing a head." His words were soft, but horribly serious, as he stroked her back.

"Yeah, they know that." Carson focused on Deanna and bent his neck toward the door. "So come on in now. Want another tea, or something stronger?"

Deanna studied Fred's face. She wanted him alone, but she couldn't be quite that rude to his roommate after as much as he'd gone out of his way to try to make her comfortable. She told the guy tea would be fine, just to get him away for a minute. It worked. She pulled Fred's face to hers. "Are you okay?"

He grabbed another deep breath. "You know, as much as I was ready to get away from my parents, I was damned lucky compared to him. We'll talk more later. Need to get out of this uniform and you need to get out of the sun. You could have gone in. He's an okay guy. Wouldn't stay with him otherwise."

"Oh, I figured, but ... well, I guess I wanted to be out here waiting when you pulled in."

"I'm glad you're here. How long can you stay?"

"How long do you need me to stay?"

He raised his eyebrows and touched her chin. "If I could, I'd keep you here until I can leave. Until we can go home together."

"Well." She brushed her lips against his. "Not sure I can do that, and I do have to be in California next week, unless I ask them to send someone else, but I can come back..."

"No. I won't take that from you. If you can spare a few days here, I'll be more than happy with that."

"Oh, you have a few days. Guaranteed." She grasped his hand. "Let's get you changed."

Deanna sat with Carson in the little living room and gave Freddy a few minutes to himself to shower and change into jeans and a T-shirt. He sat close to her and gripped her hand as he told them both about knocking on the door of the private's home of records, along with his captain, and how some woman opened it and slammed it promptly in their faces.

They rang again, waited some time, knocked. Next time it opened to a young man a few years older than the private. He had similar features. They asked for the private's mother. She'd been the one to slam the door. The boy called to her and she screamed back that they already enlisted one of her sons, the only one she could do without so far, so they could just go away and leave her alone; she'd done her duty. Being told it was about the son who joined, the boy at the door let them in, asked if he got in trouble already, that they all told him he'd never make it, that he'd joined out of anger one day after the mother said she was no longer getting paid for him and he was too lazy to help so he was of no use to her.

Fred and the captain waited until the woman returned, throwing a fit about how busy she was and passing a couple of teens pushing and yelling at each other without a word to them.

The captain began to tell her what happened but she cut him off, said it wasn't her responsibility if they had trouble with him, he was legal and not her problem anymore, that none of them were worth much of anything, but him the least worth anything.

Fred cut her off sharply, and told her what happened.

There were a few moments of stunned silence before she told them not to send him back to her to bury, that he'd go to the devil for doing what he did and she didn't want any part of it.

Carson stood and shook his head. "No wonder that kid couldn't face going home. Talk about the devil, that woman would know."

Deanna rubbed Freddy's back. "What did you say?"

"Shouldn't have said anything. But I told her he was likely in a much better place now than he was before he enlisted. She got in my face then and screamed until the captain sent me out. Shouldn't have said it. He'll write me up, my guess. As he should. Wanted to ask her why in the hell she had kids. Did keep from doing that. Barely."

"If he writes you up for that, he's an idiot." Carson took his side. "She needed to be told..."

"Wasn't my place. Just infuriated me that the kid seems to make more difference to me than he does to her."

"Probably does." Deanna touched the hair above his ear. "And you can't get down on yourself for it, for what happened. As you said, they shouldn't have let him in. They should have sent him for help."

"Guess they thought they were. As we were leaving, the one who opened the door came out and said he'd pushed his brother to join, to get him out where someone might help him. They couldn't afford to pay for it and he wasn't dysfunctional enough to admit anywhere. He hoped the change of atmosphere would help." Fred stood and paced.

Carson shook his head. "These parents think they can ignore their job with their kids and then ship them off to someone else to fix. Then it's our fault when something goes wrong. We're not supposed to be a corrective institution." He set a hand on Fred's shoulder. "And Deanna's right. Don't beat yourself up about this. They had him screwed up from the beginning."

"Doesn't change that he was one of my men."

"Daws." Carson moved face-to-face with him. "Don't do it. He was barely yours. You're out-processing, so he was only part yours. And he was new and he shouldn't have gotten through boot camp. You have a hell of a record. You saved several lives out in Saudi. Nearly lost your own doing it. You oughtta be E7 by now and you know it as well as I do, if they weren't so afraid of paying more just because it's deserved. I haven't known you long but I'm damn sure proud to be your roommate, your friend. Don't let this get to you." He stepped back and glanced over at Deanna. "Go take her somewhere nice and then come back here to unwind. I'll find somewhere else to be tonight..."

"You don't need to." Deanna moved over to them. "I didn't come to be in the way."

He gave her a grin. "You're not. And I don't mind." He turned back to Fred. "You've found a real special lady. I envy you. Let her help you feel better tonight." With a nudge to Fred's arm, he moved away. "Actually, think I'll head out in a few minutes. Heard my privates set up a poker tournament. Might drop in and see how many of them I can bust, just for kicks."

Deanna watched him head to the back of the trailer, to his room. "Bust them for playing poker?"

"He's joking. But I imagine they won't know he's joking when he tells them." Fred wandered into the kitchen area. "Want coffee if I make it?"

"Sure." She followed and leaned against the counter as he filled the carafe with water. He had to nearly lean in against her to reach the coffee, as she knew he would; her position was intentional. He caught her eyes when their bodies touched but continued his task to completion. If Fred Dawson was anything, he was a man who carried his tasks to completion. She loved that about him.

Deanna remained where she was and waited for his return. And he did. He moved in front of her, close in front, and pressed in, claiming her mouth. She gripped the back of his neck, slid the other hand up under his shirt, and made sure he understood the invitation.

"Ah, sorry." Carson's voice barely separated them. "Just letting you know I'm heading out. See ya sometime tomorrow. Carry on. I'll lock the door."

She couldn't help but grin at the teasing but Freddy barely glanced over and waited for him to leave before he pulled back and grabbed two mugs.

Deanna let him lead for the moment. They took their coffee out to the living room and discussed whether to make dinner in or go out. She offered a nice restaurant; he didn't want anything fancy. She offered to cook; he mentioned there wasn't much there to cook. She offered to run to the store, alone or together; he didn't answer.

"Indecisive tonight, aren't we?" She brushed fingers along his arm. He stared into his coffee mug. "Okay." Deanna took the mug from him and set both on the table. Then she stood in front, pushed his shoulders until he was against the back of the couch instead of slumped over the edge, and straddled him.

When his eyes questioned her, she took his face in both hands. "I'm in charge tonight, so here's what we're doing. I'm going to go get cleaned up because I was sweating like a pig walking around out there waiting for you, and then we're going out to that little cafe close to the hotel and finding a table in the corner so we can talk. We're both splurging on horribly seductive over-the-top calories dessert. Then we're coming back here to work it off. And I don't mean with your weight set." She ran a finger down his chest. "Got it? So finish your coffee while I run through the shower 'cause you'll need the energy. That's an order."

To drive her point home, Deanna kissed him gently. "Mm, you kiss nice. And I probably smell, so…"

He took her arms when she tried to get up.

"Are you refusing a direct order, soldier?"

"No." He leaned in to kiss her neck. "Adding to it." His mouth lowered to her shoulder, to the top of her breasts where the cleavage almost showed above her tank top.

Deanna arched back to allow access and gripped his arms for support. Freddy slid his hands underneath her thighs, picked her up, and took her back to his room.

Daws bit into the large slice of warm apple pie and watched Deanna dig into her chocolate brownie topped with ice cream and hot fudge. He thought back to the first time she'd ordered the same, her favorite dessert, the week they met. She'd offered him a bite, throwing a victorious smile when he took it from her fork.

"Want a bite?" She caught him staring and grinned.

"Later."

She laughed. A delicious laugh. "Hm. You know how much I love the way you flirt?"

"Was I flirting?"

"Weren't you?"

He eyed her as he grabbed a swallow of coffee. Full of life. She grabbed it with both hands. He loved that about her.

The waitress appeared to refill his coffee and Deanna told her to keep it coming – she wanted him awake tonight. Daws figured it was another test. She still wondered what it would take to embarrass him. The waitress laughed it off; she'd waited on too many soldiers by this time to be easily bothered.

"What are you thinking about?" Deanna reached across the little over-varnished wood table to grasp his free hand.

Daws shook his head. Nothing to talk about; nothing he wanted to talk about.

"Okay. Just to let you know…" She took another bite and made him wait until she enjoyed and swallowed it. "I'm staying until I'm sure you're okay, no matter how long that takes and even if I have to skip California, so I hope your roommate was being honest when he said I wasn't in the way."

He set the mug down and took her hand with both of his. "Anna, relax. I won't break. And you're not skipping California." When she dropped her eyes, he sighed. "You're still worried about those pills."

Her eyes flicked to his. "I know what they are."

He frowned and gave her a light shrug. "I told you what they were."

"Yes, but..."

"But what, Anna? What is it you're so worried about?"

"You."

"Why?"

"Because I know what they are, what they're for."

"Okay."

"It's not okay, Fred. Saying everything's okay doesn't make it okay. I know someone can seem perfectly fine, or at least mostly fine one day, strong and capable and able to handle everything and then one day it isn't. One day they just snap and nothing's fine..."

"Deanna..."

"I know. I saw it. They gave them to her, too. I saw her take them nearly every day for a month and then just stop because they didn't help and she 'didn't need' them. She was *fine*. She was *always* fine. Until the one day we lost my little brother, only for a little while when he decided to wander, but a neighbor found him and accused her of neglect, of being a bad parent, and she was going to report her and..." Her fingers tightened. She lowered her eyes.

Daws got up and moved to the other side of the table beside her.

"You don't need to hear this tonight. I'm here to help you be okay. Just tell me you really are, not only saying you are, because..."

"Tell me." He stroked her hair back from her face. "Anna, I'm bothered, yes. But I won't snap. I guarantee you I won't. So tell me."

"She did. A nervous breakdown, they said." Her hand shook as she sipped her tea. "They took her away. She didn't even know us when we visited. The others wouldn't go back. It scared them. I went every Saturday, on top of becoming the mom and taking care of them all. I went every week, to talk, to tell her it was all right, that she could come home when she was ready and I would be more help. And she never said a word. But I kept going. I needed her, but I wouldn't tell her I needed her. I told her everything was okay."

Daws wrapped her in his arms. "I'm so sorry, Anna. And I'm sorry this brought it back for you, that it worried you. But let me tell you something now." He raised her face to his. "I won't break. I won't do that to you. No matter what happens. They give those out as a general sleep aid. They are no more than that. And my guess is she needed a whole lot more help and her doctor should have paid better attention."

"It runs in the family." Deanna pulled back enough to play with the melting ice cream on her brownie. "They say her mom went nuts. I never met her. But ... maybe it's me I'm worried about more than you."

He pulled her eyes back to his. "They used to tag that label on a lot of women. It didn't mean they were. And you aren't."

"No? Any idea how much I talk to myself?"

He grinned. "Well, at least you know you're talking to yourself. That's not crazy. To be honest, I find it adorable."

"Do you? It's part of why I don't want kids. I'm not sure I can handle it. I think that's most of what got to her, having so many of us. And I had my fill of being a parent when I shouldn't have been."

"And you know it's all right with me that you don't, although I'm sure you could handle it if you wanted." Daws claimed the fork she was playing with, speared a piece of brownie, and offered it. "Without kids, I can keep more attention fully on you. That works for me."

Her eyes closed for a moment, savoring the indulgence. And then he took a bite of it, holding her eyes.

"Still not flirting?"

He ran a finger down along the thin strap of her low-cut blouse. "How about we finish dessert and get out of here?"

"How about we take it with us and leave now?"

Daws turned to find the waitress and asked for the check.

Deanna excused herself from Ellis Andrews, who had been sweet enough to give her a ride to Fort Drum for Freddy's separation ceremony. She wasn't sure, watching him chat with old friends in the post theater, whether he had come more for Fred's sake or for the chance to hang out with his old Army buddies. Either way, it was nice to have his company and to not have to take the bus or rent a car.

With a smile, she made her way to the familiar face she hadn't expected. Mandy Hodgkins gave her a big hug. "Oh it's nice to see you again. You look wonderful."

"So do you." Deanna was reminded of the bright red sports car comment as she studied Mandy's shiny red blouse and black pants. "I'm so glad you came. Are you enjoying Hawaii?"

"Well, yes and no. The place is beautiful, of course, and so much warmer. It'll be nice not to deal with two feet of snow all winter. There's a friendliness issue, though, and I'd heard about it but hoped it wasn't true." Mandy gave a dismissive shrug. "We had to come back for this. Shel was so flattered Daws asked him to present the award, he couldn't refuse." She lowered her voice. "I guess he never got comfortable with his new unit."

"No. But I didn't know he asked your husband. I didn't know he could."

"Well, not just anyone receives an MSM. It's a big deal, more than he's probably admitted to you."

Deanna figured that was true. Freddy didn't say much of anything about the award. If he asked Captain Hodgkins to return from Hawaii, though, it apparently was a big deal to him.

"We found him already. I left Shel with him to take care of business and came to find you. Where are you sitting?"

"I'm not yet. I'm wandering, talking with Andrews and Zakowsky and a few others."

Mandy laughed. "Careful, Deanna. You're starting to sound like him, using their last names."

She chuckled. "I guess it does rub off."

"So what do you think? Will he be happy in his new career? We all expected him to stay in for twenty, at least."

"Yes. So did he, but things have changed too much for him. And I hope he'll be happy. I hope he isn't doing this for me. I didn't ask him to. I told him I'd move anywhere in the world with him, but he knows how I love my new job and ... I just hope I didn't push this when he didn't want it."

"Push Daws?" Mandy laughed. "Now surely you know him better than that by now. Daws doesn't push if he doesn't want to be." She took Deanna's hands. "He found something he wanted more. And I'm glad he did. He might have stayed in if he hadn't found you but he wouldn't have been as happy as he is now. I'm glad he found you. I wasn't sure he'd ever let himself." She gave her a light grin, then reclaimed her normal bouncy demeanor. "So let's find a good seat..."

"Ma'am?"

Deanna turned to the voice at her side. "Charlie. And you still won't call me by my name even though he's out after today?"

"No, ma'am. The sergeant is still the sergeant and he'd still have me against the wall." With a grin, he gave Mandy a friendly greeting and put his attention back on Deanna. "There's someone outside asking to speak with you. She won't come in."

"For me?"

"Yes, ma'am. Won't give me her name. Says you invited her. I heard her ask someone if they knew you."

Deanna's heart thumped. There were only two people she invited, with Fred's permission. One she knew outright would never be there. "Will you take me to her?"

"Of course."

Mandy invited herself and Deanna didn't at all mind. She tried to decide how to greet the woman, what to say, whether to go get Fred...

"Ma'am." Charlie stopped in front of an elegant woman with dark blonde wavy hair, just touching her shoulders. She wore a smart pant suit in grey shades and small splashes of magenta. She looked as though she'd just stepped out of the beauty parlor, a very upscale beauty parlor, but her expression was wary, uncertain.

Charlie introduced Deanna.

The woman offered fingers by way of a handshake. "Sue Ellen Rollins, formerly Sue Ellen Dawson. I have to say I was surprised by the invitation. I accepted out of curiosity, I suppose."

Deanna hugged her. It surprised the woman, she could tell. It also surprised herself. But she'd come. After all the times Fred told her his sister had no interest in being so, she had come all the way from North Carolina.

Sue Ellen raised her eyebrows and straightened her jacket. "Yes. Well, it's nice to meet you, also, although, as I said, I'm unsure why I was invited since he never bothered before. I didn't even know he'd joined."

Realizing Mandy was still at her side and horribly curious, Deanna introduced them quickly. Charlie had slipped away.

Sue Ellen cast her eyes on the bodies moving around them, many in uniform, and seemed at least as uncomfortable as Deanna was her first time on base. "Are you his wife? The note was unclear."

"Oh. Not technically, but practically. I'm his girlfriend. And he never thought you would come, said I was wasting my time, but I'm glad you did. It is so nice to meet you."

"I suppose I appreciate your effort. And I can't say I'm surprised he hasn't bothered to marry you. He may not, you know. Just as a warning. Always said as a kid he wouldn't. As stubborn as he is, I have to think he meant it."

Deanna chuckled. "I can see you're related. You both have that tell-it-straight gene."

"No offense intended."

"I'm not offended, and the ring he gave me is enough. I'm not concerned about the paper." She showed the woman and was a bit too prideful about her reaction. Sue Ellen was indeed impressed.

"So where is Fred? He was a child last time I saw him. I'm not sure I'll recognize him if he's mixed in with all this green beneath hats."

"He's getting ready to cross the stage. Please, come in and we'll find a seat. It should start soon. They do tend to be prompt with their schedules."

Mandy led them to a place close to the front to where Charlie stood. Holding seats, if Deanna wasn't mistaken. She was glad to have her friend at her side when she had Fred's sister on the other. They talked a bit about his military career, in basics, and the woman told her about her husband and three children who were all excelling in school, music, and extracurricular activities. Deanna asked what music they studied and nudged it into the conversation that she and Freddy were both music obsessed and how he'd started the guitar and gave up due to his thick fingers.

That at least got a light curvature of her lips. Yes, she saw plenty of similarities in them. While Fred pulled away from the idea of family due to his upbringing, Sue Ellen had jumped in with both feet and both hands.

She was relieved when the ceremony began so she could regroup. The woman studied her too intensely. Deanna never minded being his girlfriend instead of his wife, but at this moment, she would be far more comfortable talking with his sister and showing such possession of him as his wife.

She shoved the thought aside. Sue Ellen could think as she wished.

A deep breath accompanied her change of position when they stood for the Pledge of Allegiance and were reseated upon request. There were others receiving awards and separation papers and Deanna enjoyed watching it all. For the last time. They would soon no longer be part of it. Something about that, although she barely had been, made her feel a tinge of regret. She could only imagine his, and hoped it wouldn't last.

When he came out on stage, she pointed him out to Sue Ellen. But his sister had recognized him. Deanna wondered if the look on her face was surprise or pride, or maybe regret.

Captain Hodgkins read the description of Fred's Meritorious Service Medal: for putting his own life ahead of others and for saving the lives of several of his troops during Desert Storm, as well as for showing highly proficient skills and exemplary conduct throughout his twelve years of service. Deanna watched her boyfriend. She didn't care if he was husband or boyfriend; he was hers. She was immensely proud of that. And she was terribly glad she was taking him home.

Deanna noticed his sister glance over when she wiped moisture from her eyes, but her attention stayed on Fred. He remained still, no expression, no movement, eyes forward, throughout the presentation, through Captain Hodgkins pinning his new medal on his chest, and through reading of his separation statement. Deanna knew the soldier he'd lost was on his mind more than the accolades were. And it hit her what they'd said: saved the lives of *several* of his men. She only knew about Andrews. He hadn't admitted to more than that. Would he if she asked?

She had to wait through one other soldier's presentation and then the theater resounded with applause and people getting up from their seats and shuffling and talking.

"So he's all yours now." Mandy grinned at her. "How's it feel?"

"I'll let you know when I can get to him." She looked around and judged how long that might take. "A question, though." Deanna leaned in close to her friend. "He saved *several* lives?"

"Oh. He didn't tell you. I'm not surprised." Mandy glanced around. "Catch me later. Outside. Alone. You should know."

Suddenly unsure she should have asked, Deanna turned her attention to her guest, Freddy's guest. "Let's go find him."

"It might be better if I wait out of the way..."

"Of course not. Come with me. He'll be glad to know you're here." Deanna hoped he would be. Either way, she insisted. It took some time to get to him. He was still being congratulated. She nudged Carson until he grinned and made a sweeping gesture to let her through. Fred's eyes found hers and he reached toward her, stepping forward. She nearly threw herself on him.

Fred raised her face to his. "You realize you're stuck with me now on a day-to-day basis."

"I think I'll be okay with that. And I'm sure ready to try."

He kissed the side of her face. "Thank you for hanging in there with me." He turned to now-Sergeant Jenkins and took a bouquet of flowers from him. Cannas. White. With red and blue edges. Interspersed with red roses. So many she could hardly hold them.

"I love you, Anna. Can't wait to show you that every day."

"You already do." She touched his face. "I love you, too. And I suppose with everything else you were brave enough to get through, you'll be able to deal with me full time."

He grinned. "I think I'll be okay."

Movement at Deanna's side made him look over. His expression changed again. Hardened.

"Fred." Sue Ellen stepped forward. "Your ... girlfriend invited me. I do hope that was all right as she said it was."

"Knew she did. Never expected you'd come. You look well."

"Thank you. And you ... I never expected this, either."

"Don't suppose you did." When asked by his roommate, Fred introduced his sister. Deanna noticed surprised exchanges from several of his friends but they all held their tongues and he told Sue Ellen they'd talk more outside.

Daws positioned his hat atop his head as they stepped out into the mild October sunshine, Deanna on his arm and chattering, celebratory bodies all around. He nearly regretted the invitation to Sue Ellen, since, now that she was here, he didn't know what to say to her, but Deanna filled in conversation. She relayed news of three children, his nieces and nephews by all rights, and mentioned they were into music. Trying to grasp for common ground. There wasn't much.

Sue Ellen was a stay-at-home mom who volunteered with a couple of charities and otherwise centered herself around her children. A surprise to Daws since she resented doing the same for him. Of course, Deanna resented having to be responsible for her siblings, also. She didn't mean it against them. His girlfriend had much more in common with his sister than he did. The husband was a business attorney.

At a moment of awkward silence, Deanna excused herself to go talk with Mandy, to confirm group dinner plans, she said.

"Have you been together long?"

Daws grasped the hand of one of his new troops who wished him well as he was leaving and put himself back in the conversation. "With Deanna? Two and a half years."

"She showed me the ring. Very nice. You must be doing well."

"Why did you come?"

Her eyebrows rose. "Why did you never tell me you joined the service?”

“Didn’t see you once you hit eighteen. How would I have?”

“You had our phone number.”

“You had no interest.”

She sighed. “I suppose I was afraid to know. They were trying so hard to turn you into them, I expected they had. I’m glad they didn’t. How’d you get out of it?”

“Joined the service.”

A minimal grin highlighted her rigid face. “Smarter than I thought you were.”

“Always was.”

Now, she stared. Studied him. “I’m sorry, Fred. I was a horrible sister to you. I resented him so badly and it all came out on you. But I’ve changed. I grew up. I have wondered about you at times but I didn’t know how to find you except through that lawyer and I just couldn’t...”

“Could have come by the apartment, sent a note.”

Her eyes widened. “You’re still there?”

“The will asked me not to sell it.”

“Yes, but how can you stand it? Doesn’t it remind you of them?”

“Not anymore. Had Deanna redecorate. She’s an artist. Designer. It’s gorgeous. And it’s ours. Don’t think about the rest anymore.”

“You were always the strong one.”

“Didn’t have much choice. Come and see it if you’d like.”

“Oh, I don’t know if I’m ready for that.”

She asked what he would be doing now, and in between quick chats with stragglers who stopped to congratulate him, Daws filled her in on his budding security career.

Deanna sat on the bench of a picnic table just outside the theater and wondered if she should let Mandy fill her in on the details Fred hadn’t. It had taken time to get away from everyone and she was somewhat surprised Fred was still talking with his sister. A good sign, she supposed.

“So.” Mandy sat close and grasped her hand. “We should make this quick. They’ll want to get going soon.”

“I’m not sure we should. If he doesn’t want me to know...”

“Oh Deanna, I imagine he’s only afraid of what you’ll think. But I’m not. And he shouldn’t be. Because I know you’ll understand and it could help him...”

“Afraid of what I would think? Why would he be?”

“Does he still have nightmares?”

“You know?”

She nodded. “And I know what happened only because Shel was there. He saw it. Daws has never spoken of it.”

“Okay, you have to tell me now.”

Mandy shifted and glanced around to see that no one was close. "Their mission, since they were sent over so late as background support, was more cleanup and retrieval than anything else. They were only supposed to go through secured areas to check for weapon stockpiles and make sure the area was clear and safe for civilians to return to their homes. Many had stayed because they had nowhere to go and the guys would share supplies with them, bandage wounds, leave them food and clean water."

"That I know. He mentioned sharing food with women and children who looked destitute."

"Yes. That would be most of what they found. So sad. The women have no power and are virtually nothing but servants. I can't imagine. It wasn't always like that. Anyway, they were headed back toward Kuwait, near the end of their mission, when they started taking fire. Daws was separated from most of his men, who were just ahead of him. He'd stopped to get orders from Shel. As soon as he realized Shel was hit in the shoulder, he pushed him into an empty house and told him to stay put, he was going after his men. They were holding their own, hidden behind whatever they could get behind, burnt out vehicles and such. Shel didn't stay put, of course. He was trying to work his rifle with his left hand since the shoulder took his right arm out of commission. The enemy was hiding behind civilians, though, their own civilians, holding women and kids in front of them as cover as they moved in. Made it hard to stop them. Our guys wouldn't risk hitting the innocents."

Mandy shook her head. "Then Shel saw, from the side, sneaking toward where Daws's men were grouped, a boy, maybe six or seven, heading toward them. He had a bomb strapped to his chest. An IED actually strapped onto this child. He stopped and the insurgents hidden behind a crumbling wall yelled at him.

"Well, Daws saw him from his position, though his men couldn't yet. He took aim and waited to see if the boy would stop. Shel said the kid looked scared to death and a woman also behind the wall, held by the men, screamed. The kid looked back at her and kept going, toward our guys. Shel tried to take out the men threatening him, but there were a lot of them and he couldn't aim well with the wrong hand and he and Daws would have had to walk out in the open in order to get to them. They never would have made it.

"Daws, bless his heart, he saw the boy about to walk into his men and some from another unit and blow them all to smithereens ... so he took aim, yelled at his men to take cover, and fired at the walking bomb."

"Oh." Deanna felt her eyes moisten, her heart race. "The boy."

"He had to do it. Would have lost them all if that kid had reached his target, and the kid was a goner either way. Shel put it in the report that it was a young man, made it sound ... well, there wouldn't be any point in mentioning his age. The effect would have been the same. Shel didn't even realize until afterward that Daws had been hit the same time he was, in the leg. Didn't stop him. Luckily it wasn't bad, but bad enough to drench the inside of his boot."

Deanna pressed her hands against her face. No wonder he had nightmares. Hit in the leg. The Purple Heart. That's why he tried not to accept. It reminded him of the boy. *Some things are better forgotten.*

Mandy took her hands. "He had to do it. It was only the boy or all of them. All of those boys. And he was okay. Shel said he kept going, wrapped something around the leg and helped clear out the area so it was safe again, held it together fine … until he got home and saw the young wives and little kids running to greet their dads, the ones whose lives he saved that day. He didn't have anyone there, so Shel and I tried to take him home with us that night. He refused, wanted quiet and his own bed."

Deanna hugged her and forced tears back. She wouldn't cry today. Not on the day of his ceremony. "Thank you. For taking care of him until I could find him, and for telling me."

"Well, it was Major Reynauld who really looked after him. Daws refused to spend time with his family as invited. Said it wasn't in regs, but we figure it was the boys he was avoiding. The major stopped by his place now and then, took food over, to discuss some issue that could have waited. And he moved him to flight assistant duty. Figured he needed a change of scenery. Tried to put him in for a Medal of Honor but Daws refused, said he didn't want it and wouldn't accept it. The MSM is partly for that, along with his Purple Heart, but they made it more general so he wouldn't turn it down. The man deserves the Medal of Honor as much as anyone. Shel doesn't know how he got out of there without … well, I can't even say it."

Deanna nodded, but she fully understood why he wouldn't accept it.

"And let me tell you something: those monsters they were fighting – they were monsters, cruel and unfeeling. Except for the kids they forced into service because they needed bodies. Most of them dropped their weapons and surrendered as soon as any of our troops got close. They didn't want to fight us. They had no choice. Their families would have been executed if they'd refused. That's what we were fighting. Don't listen to anything else. They don't know."

"Mandy, I'm not arguing. I know."

She grabbed a deep breath. "I'm sorry. I get carried away. I get so sick of hearing the lies."

Deanna squeezed her fingers. "Guess I had it a lot easier coming in after that. Though I wish I'd been there for him when he came home."

"He did all right. And you're here now."

"Are we interfering?"

They looked up at Fred and Shel's approach. Deanna went to her boyfriend, set her hands alongside his face.

"What's wrong, Anna?"

She shook her head, trying to decide whether she should admit...

"I told her what they meant by the 'several lives' you saved."

Fred stiffened and stared over at Mandy. "You told her what?"

"The truth. She needed to know."

He put his eyes back on Deanna as Shel chastised his wife for butting in. "She shouldn't have." He waited for her reaction. Wary.

Deanna kissed him. "I'm glad you did it. I would have done the same. I would have done it for you alone."

"I wouldn't have wanted you to, to have to live with that."

"I would have. And I would have lived with that just fine, with saving you. Much easier than living with the alternative."

"Is it? I can still hear his mother scream. He was just a child. He didn't volunteer for that."

Deanna held him close. "Freddy, they're the ones who did it. Not you. And that was your past life. That part ends today. Tomorrow we start again. We'll make different memories. Together. Let it go now. You couldn't have helped him."

He moved back to see her face. "I wasn't sure how you'd react. Didn't think I could ever tell you."

"Do you forget that I'm the child who had to put her favorite horse down to keep him from suffering? You thought I wouldn't understand? You did it for love, just like I did, the greater right. Fred Dawson, don't you ever be afraid to tell me anything. I love you, and I am on your side, through everything."

As Daws pulled his car out of the parking lot and toward the front gate, for possibly the last time, he let his gaze fall on the red brick buildings marked with green signs, on organization logos, brown directional signs, BDUs and PT uniforms, perfectly trimmed lawns and shrubs, thick metal railings along cement stairs, and sharp salutes.

He was no longer part of it, and yet it would always be a part of him.

He would miss it. Twelve years. It often seemed much longer. Today it felt as though it had gone by in a flash, like a rare burst of flame from a howitzer at night. A brief, glowing surge of hot, rich light that singed him to the core, hardened him, strengthened him.

With Deanna at his side, he would go to the trailer and change into civvies, then go meet his friends, his family, for the dinner send-off. Sue Ellen had rejoined her own family at the hotel where she left them. Someday, she said, maybe they would all drop by and see what Deanna had done with the apartment. Before she gave him a quick, rather uneasy, hug, she'd said she was proud of the man he'd become. He had no idea why that still mattered to him.

The dinner was at a hotel where he and Anna would stay the night and meet Captain and Mrs. Hodgkins for breakfast. Then he would take Deanna home, to New York City, and carry her across the threshold of their apartment to begin their new path.

PART 4

"We are a nation of communities ... a brilliant diversity
spread like stars, like a thousand points of light
in a broad and peaceful sky."
George H.W. Bush

She supposed it was only fair that since she was privy to his, he should be privy to hers. Her biggest stumbling block.

The night of his Army separation, after the way-too-fun dinner where his men, his friends, shared more stories than he appreciated, Freddy talked to her. About that boy, about the way he'd been lectured that he should have hit the boy himself and not the bomb, so there was enough of him left for his mother to bury. They figured he was too gung-ho, that he hit the bomb instead to be sure it didn't fall back into enemy hands.

Only to Deanna did he admit it wasn't true. He couldn't do it; he'd hesitated nearly too long to save his men because he couldn't make himself put a bullet in the boy's head. He had to hit the target instead. It was the only way he could, by focusing on the bomb, seeing it only as a target.

They'd talked late into the night. She wiped away the few tears he allowed and her own, as well. And she snuggled against him, held him close, and showed him just how much it didn't change how she felt. In fact, she connected with him in a way they hadn't before. His guard was down. Flat. He let her all the way inside and it reflected in the way he made love to her, with her. She felt fully one with him: an amazing, sensual, spiritual experience she had no idea could exist.

Now he wanted to take her home for Thanksgiving, to her family home. She couldn't possibly refuse. Deanna supposed she should get up and shower, get ready to go.

In a few minutes. There was no rush. He'd kept her up late again. Or she'd kept him up. She could do with a few more minutes...

"Anna? Getting up sometime this morning?"

"Mm. Yes." She glanced over at him in the bedroom doorway and closed her eyes. A few more minutes.

He came over and sat on the bed. Chilly fingers brushed across her face.

"You smell like outside." She rolled in closer against him.

"Just came from outside. There's something I want you to see."

"Hm." She slid her hand up his leg, toward his thigh. "Can't see it in here?"

He caught her hand and leaned down to kiss her head. "No. You're going to have to get up."

Holding him back didn't work. She missed his body next to hers as soon as he stood.

"Come on, baby. Long drive ahead." He brushed fingers through her hair. "Your warnings haven't scared me. We're still going."

With a grin, Deanna forced herself up. "No, Fred Dawson, I don't suppose you are scared, but don't say I didn't warn you." She forced her way through a shower and raised her eyebrows at how often he came to check her progress as she got herself together. The fifth time he did, Deanna grabbed his shirt and pulled him in. "Wow you're acting like a ten-year-old on a sugar high. What's up?"

"You're stalling."

"Yeah, maybe, but..."

"Have something to show you."

"Like you have anything I haven't already seen?" She kissed him, expecting it to be light and quick. But he grabbed her around the waist and deepened it.

"Mm, so how about we stall a while longer?" Deanna traced a finger down the middle of his chest, over the taut knit mock turtleneck she'd bought him, deep red with a sensually soft draping material that helped highlight his pecs.

"We'll stall later." Freddy grasped her fingers and kissed them.

"Are you sure? Because you don't seem to be."

"Nearly sure." He kissed her again. "And I do have something you haven't seen. Let me show you and then you can come back and keep playing around in here while I get breakfast for us."

"Thought we were having breakfast out, on the way."

"Thought we were leaving an hour ago."

Deanna chuckled. "Okay, so show me. I'm ready enough. Then we'll go eat." She chuckled again as he grasped her hand and threw her last bag over his shoulder, checked the apartment to be sure everything was off and locked up, and held her coat.

In their parking space, next to the Malibu, was another chocolate brown car, a Monte Carlo, perfect as far as she could see, shining and spotless.

"This is what you've been looking for." Deanna peered inside.

He unlocked and opened the door. The scent of leather from the smooth black seats rushed out.

"It's beautiful. Very classy."

"Rides even better than it looks. Ready to go?"

"I'm so glad you found one, and in time to show it off."

"Well, in time for our first long road trip. Hoping to put a lot of miles on it together. And we'll trade the Malibu for anything you want."

She kissed him, touched his face. "I think I'm happy enough with that for now. A lot of nice memories in that car."

After a quick breakfast stop, they pulled out onto open road and Freddy pushed a cassette in the player: Bob Seger's *Night Moves*.

Near the end of their second day's drive down to Kentucky, Deanna turned off the radio and put in ZZ Top.

He turned it down a couple of decibels. "I have to hear you when you tell me which way. The exit's coming up."

"I know. A distraction. We can still change our minds."

He didn't bother to answer. She turned it louder again with the first beats of *Give It Up* and sang along, throwing directions into the middle of it as needed.

Some distance down a gravel lane, which he took far too slow in order to keep from throwing rocks up onto his paint, Daws began to wonder if she had led him off into the middle of nowhere, miles from her mother's place, or anyone else's.

She lowered the volume and pointed. "Turn right up there, by the mailbox."

He held his thoughts about the little structure atop a post.

"It's our box. Yes, an outhouse. And yes, it's been there for years. The oldest made it. His father thought it was hysterical. Mom thinks it's embarrassing. I tend to think it's a little too appropriate. Sure you don't want to change your mind?"

He glanced over in between dodging holes in the gravel lane. "Still not scared."

"Hm, then you're a better man than I, Fred Dawson."

"Relax, Anna." He braked when the house came into view and a couple of dogs ran up barking in front of the car.

"Keep going. They'll move."

"And if they don't?"

"Fewer mangy flee-ridden nuisances to bother with. If they're too stupid to get out of the way, it's their own fault."

"I take it you don't like dogs."

"Not much. Hope you didn't plan to get one. I'd rather not." She rolled down the window. "*Scram*, you stupid beasts."

They barked louder and circled to her side of the car.

Daws let up on the brake, creeping forward as he considered her hostility toward animals doing what animals did: protect their property. They did move, running alongside, barking all the way.

There was only one house, a peeling white two-story with faded magenta shutters that reminded him of the accents on his sister's outfit, and a long front porch full of folding chairs, old bicycles, a porch swing lacking varnish. Several vehicles dotted the surrounding patchy grass; some looked drivable. An old trailer was propped nearby, also potentially usable. "Where do I park?"

She raised her eyebrows. "How about at the hotel? Seen enough yet?"

He gave her a grin and pulled into an empty space beside one of the usable cars. And he took her hand. "How about at the hotel tonight, we take full advantage of the hot tub and then I'll give you a massage to help you unwind?"

"Hm, it's going to take more than a massage, after this."

"Then it'll be more than a massage." With a kiss, he opened his door. The dogs were right there. Growling now. "Do they bite?"

"If they do, I'll take a baseball bat to their heads. And no, I'm not exaggerating." She opened her door and got out. "*Move*, stupid beasts. And *don't* growl at him."

They took off toward her and Daws jumped out ... they were wagging their tails while barking. She yelled at them again to move and pushed the closest one away with her foot.

A male voice yelled over not to hurt them.

"Then get them out of here."

"Real nice to have you home again." The boy rolled his eyes and called the dogs to his side. And he looked at Daws. "You a dog hater, too?"

"Not if they don't have a problem with me being here."

"Nah, they wouldn't hurt a fly. They're just noisy." He scratched the stained white T-shirt over his concave stomach and came over to offer the same hand. "I'm Zack, brother number three. And jiminy, were you born with that build or you use them them steroid things to look like that?"

"Zack, behave." Deanna came around and introduced him. "And no, he's not that stupid. Think I'd be serious about someone that stupid?"

The boy, probably seventeen-ish, shrugged. "He came home with you."

"Thank you. Move." She pushed him farther from the trunk and shoved one of the dogs as she asked for the keys.

Daws opened it and helped pull out the box she'd brought for her mom. "I got it." He touched her eyes for reassurance and noticed another boy, younger, approach.

She took the box and handed it to the kid during introductions. "Take this in and be careful. Don't drop it. Thank you. Zack, get these stupid dogs away from me before I make them get away."

"Really, Dee, loosen up. They aren't hurtin' nothing." He started jogging toward the house, calling names. The animals gladly ran with him.

Deanna answered his glance. "Don't look at me like that. I spent way too much time cleaning up after all those nasty dirty beasts that ran in and out of the house. Can't tell you how many flea bites I had."

Daws rubbed her back. Before he could answer, a young girl flew out through the screen door calling her name and gave her a tight hug.

Fifteen-year-old Rosie introduced herself and gave Deanna a sly smile. "Y' were right all ways around Sunday, Dee. He's just scrumptious." She giggled as she stared at him. "Is he a good kisser, too?"

Deanna touched his eyes and whispered into her sister's ear, causing more giggles.

Enjoying the interaction, Daws nearly didn't notice the woman on the edge of the porch. Until she moved. Deanna saw her then, also, and took him to meet her mom.

Mrs. Meyers was a petite woman, frail and uncertain. Daws could see within the moment he looked at her why Anna was so intent on protecting her. After Deanna gave her a long, gentle hug, he offered his hand. Her fingers were cold although the day was fairly warm and she wore a long sweater over a house dress.

"It's an honor to meet you, ma'am."

She smiled, a warm and welcome smile. "And you. Our Deanna just couldn't stop talking about you when she came last Christmas. It's so nice to have you visit. Please, come in. I'm afraid it's not much. Time and a dozen kids have done their job on it, although I try."

He looked at Deanna.

"Not a dozen. She always says there are, but there aren't."

"Surely feels like it most days."

Daws followed Deanna into the house and moved out of the way when she grabbed the collar of another dog, a mountainous thing, and booted it outside. He started to understand her feeling about them; the house smelled strongly of animal. It looked clean, though. And neat. If a bit plain and run down.

Mrs. Meyers took them to the kitchen and Deanna told her to sit while she made coffee, arguing it wasn't at all too late in the day or any trouble. Rosie pulled a chair close to him and propped her elbows on the table, her head cocked far enough for her long ponytail to nearly touch her elbows. "Are you going to marry Dee?"

Deanna turned from where she helped her mom. "*Rosie.*"

The girl shrugged. "Well, you're the oldest and Nat and Kim are already hitched and mama says I shouldn't live with a boy until I marry him. But you live with him..." Her mom hushed her.

Conversation swirled away and he answered questions about the Army and about his new plans, without mention of Ryan, and helped push it back to Deanna's job. The two boys went through and paused to hear parts of it. All the older ones wouldn't be around until the next day, Thanksgiving, although the oldest brother and his family lived in the trailer he saw.

Deanna's father would be home from work in an hour or so.

=======

"I don't have to listen to this." Deanna stormed away from Kim and over to where Fred looked up from his card game with Zack. "Let's go. I'm sorry I made you come."

He stood and set a hand on her back. "How about we deal you in?"

"No. I've had enough. I don't know why I thought we could have one decent family Thanksgiving without them doing everything they can to embarrass me."

Her very pregnant sister snickered. "You do that okay by yourself. You always have."

Freddy stroked her skin through her thin sweater, behind her, where they couldn't see. "No point in being embarrassed in front of me. And I can't imagine why you care what anyone else thinks."

She stared at him. He had to know Kim could hear him, as could they all.

He dipped his head closer. "Anna, you are a beautiful, charming, sophisticated, intelligent woman, and caring on top of it. Very rare. Most will never understand how rare you are, how special you are. You can't let it bother you."

"Special. Like in *special ed*."

"That was your area, nit wit."

"Yeah, I seem to recall you getting a private tutor or two or three."

"Not my fault they don't know how to teach no better than that."

"*Any* better, Einstein."

Deanna did her best to ignore the surrounding banter over top of the football game her father and oldest brother pretended to understand once a year.

"Yeah, if she's so special, why haven't you bothered to marry her instead of living with her? Not special enough for that, right? Come on, we know this is just a cover. Trying to make us think she's settled with a great job and boyfriend and it's all just sham, right? She pick you up in a bar or something and offer you money to come make her look good?"

She saw her father chuckle. On top of her mom trying to hush Nat and Rosie mouthing back that she doesn't know anything and should shut up, Deanna saw her father actually chuckle. At her expense. He hadn't said a word to Fred the whole time and now he was laughing.

Fred noticed. He caught her eyes and slipped his fingers down to her waist, half on her hip. "Any of you are welcome to come to New York and visit. We have a spare room. If you come for the Fourth, you can watch the fireworks from our balcony. It's a nice view."

Deanna stared at him. He had to be crazier than she was.

Rosie jumped up. "You can see them from your balcony? You have a balcony? Like Romeo and Juliet."

Fred gave her a grin. "Except too high up to talk to someone on the ground."

"How high? Are you in one of those big buildings we see in pictures?"

"Fifth floor. But be warned. She takes the stairs more than the elevator. Bring walking shoes."

Deanna nudged in against him, allowing his calm to flow into her. "And by the time you come, I'll have it painted dark green and cream, to match the inside." She nearly laughed at Fred's expression. He was balking at the idea. Good thing she hadn't done it.

"Can we go to Central Park? I want to see Strawberry Fields."

"Of course. Again, you need walking shoes, no heels. It's the best way to see the city. I walk in the park a lot. It's down only a couple of blocks from us."

"When? When can I come?"

"As soon as Mom says you can. Maybe this summer during school break?"

"They're making it up, idiot. You're so gullible."

Rosie swirled back to Reese. "They are *not*. She *wouldn't* lie to me."

"Who cares what they think?" Deanna gripped Fred's shirt against the curve of his back. "Come see for yourself. Maybe Mom will come with you. She needs a vacation from this." She knew how pointed it sounded and she didn't care. Her mom's eyes watered and Deanna went to her, hugging her from behind. "You do, you know, and it would be nice. We'd love to have you. No cooking. No cleaning. You can put your feet up and just rest. Come this summer and bring Rosie for your travel companion. Say you'll think about it."

Her mom nodded and wiped her eyes.

"Mama, you know they're making it up." Kim scooped an arm beneath her stomach. "They aren't together. Heck, have you even seen him kiss her, much less hardly touch her? They don't look together. Not like me 'n Jake. Heck, I look like a tub by now and he still has his hands all over me. They're not together. It's a sham."

"Yeah, too much all over you. It's gross. Stop it." Rosie swiveled back to Fred who she still stood beside, as she had been much of the day. "You are too really with her, aren't you? 'Cause I hope you are. You're so nice to her. It's nice to see a real gentleman for a change and I'm going to find one, too. Tell me you are with her."

He gave her a grin, too obviously taken by her charm. "That ring I gave her means forever, or for as long as she'll have me."

"Oh, come on." Kim again. "You're what? A decorated hero? That's what she said. Why would you settle for a nobody from nowhere when you could have, I don't know, a rich businessman's daughter or something?"

"She's not a nobody." Fred moved over to Deanna and ran a hand alongside her face, through the edge of her hair. "It's a shame you don't know her better. The truth is she's a very talented and successful advertising executive, an incredible artist and designer. She's also my partner in every sense of the word. My friend. My love." He kissed the side of her head. "I'm not hanging on her because it would be disrespectful of her to do so in front of her family, her parents in particular. And I would never disrespect the only woman I've ever loved. The hands will have to behave until we're alone tonight."

"The heck they will." Deanna's voice came out as a whisper. She wrapped her arms up around his neck and kissed him. He took her in and nuzzled his head against hers when she ducked her face into his neck and hid there. He let her hide there, caressing her back, down to the hemline of her jeans. She ignored the murmurs around the room. They didn't matter. She'd let him all the way inside her world and he didn't care.

She was ready to go home.

This time, he agreed. And he invited her mom and Rosie to their hotel the next morning for breakfast before they headed back to the city, where she belonged.

She was still tense, despite all he'd done to help her unwind the night before. And in a couple of hours, part of her family would be there for breakfast. "Anna." He slid arms around her as she stared out the hotel window. "What's on your mind?"

"I shouldn't have brought you here. It was … I was just trying to show off with my good job and my incredible boyfriend and I deserve that they don't buy it because it was wrong to try to show off and especially wrong to use you to do it. I'm sorry."

He kissed her neck, nudging hair out of his way to reach her nape, to feel her body press back into his. He moved his lips to her shoulder, his hands down to her waist, up to her rib cage, up farther to cup her breasts. Her head turned toward his mouth. "Freddy. I just told you I was using you…"

He met her lips as his fingers caressed the soft skin beneath the thin pajama top.

"Are you listening to me?"

"Yes." He turned her toward him. "You said I was incredible." He teased her mouth, pulled her body in next to hers.

"And I was using you."

"Mm. Wish it had worked better for you." Daws fulfilled the teasing with a deep kiss.

Deanna's eyes were closed when he released her, stroked her face, her hair. "Maybe you shouldn't have been such a gentleman. *This* might have worked better." Her head tilted back as he smoothed fingertips along her neck. "And you are incredible. Doesn't matter if they know. I do."

He'd only meant to tease her, relax her, but she reacted too well, let him go too far. They had two hours, more than enough time. He swept her into his arms and took her back to bed.

"How about a quick swim?"

Deanna laughed. "Wow you're full of energy these days. Not that you weren't always, but…"

"Haven't done PT in weeks. Need to get back to that."

"Oh, I don't know. I'm enjoying your energy."

"Are you? Come swimming. Still have an hour."

"I need time to get ready before brunch."

"Only enough time to get dry." Daws rolled out of bed and held a hand out. He wasn't letting her refuse, even if she wanted to just sit at the edge and lose track of time. If she wanted to use him to show off, they might as well do it right.

And she did sit at the edge after a few laps and let him continue on his own. The work-out was refreshing. He pushed to his limits. Until he caught sight of the small group approaching. Something had told him it wouldn't be only her mom and little sister. He'd left word at the front desk where he and Deanna could be found.

As they drew closer, he did two more laps, purposely splashing Deanna to keep her attention where he wanted it, then swam up to her, in front of her, and pulled her down for a kiss. No one else was in the pool so early, as he'd hoped, so it looked more private than he knew it was by now.

"Careful, Fred Dawson. Keep that up and we'll definitely be late for brunch." She slid both hands down his shoulders, resting them over his chest.

"That was the plan." With a wink, he pulled her into the water and wrapped her legs up around him. It worked well; she was faced the wrong direction to see them. He pretended he didn't. She kissed him again, her fingers pressed into the bare wet skin on his back.

"Still think it's a sham? My guess is he's a really good kisser like she says he is."

Deanna pulled back at Rosie's voice and lowered to her own feet. "Oh. What time is it?"

He caught her eyes. "Left my watch upstairs."

She nearly commented, but instead, looked over at not only her mom and Rosie, but Zack and the other unmarried girl. Reese.

Her mom blushed. "Your father didn't think it was a good idea for Rosie and me to come alone. I hope it's okay the others are here."

"Of course." Daws pushed himself out of the water and held a hand out to Deanna as she used the stairs. She accepted a towel from him and looked over at her sisters' whispers. "You can stop staring now. He's practically your brother-in-law."

Zack snickered. The older girl blushed. Rosie, however, kept eyeing him until her mom whispered a complaint. It didn't stop her. "How'd you get that scar?"

Deanna grabbed his shirt and handed it to him as they headed toward the lobby. "You're looking too close. Behave yourself before Mom has to lock you in your room until you're thirty."

Rosie shrugged. "I'm fifteen. It's okay to admire a boy at my age."

"If he's close to your age."

"How old is he?"

"Close to my age."

"How close?"

"Thirty next month. Too old for you to stare at."

"He's built really good for an old guy."

Deanna laughed and shoved the girl's shoulder. "Not old. Only a year ahead of me. And you mean built well."

"Really well. How'd he get the scar?"

Daws rested a hand behind Deanna's neck and stopped at where the hallway led up to their room. He spoke to Rosie. "Tell you what. If you're not squeamish, I'll tell you how I got it after we change and meet back here in a few minutes. Can you find a table for six?"

"*Sure.* I'll make 'em push two together if they need to. Hurry, though, I'm starving."

Deanna shook her head as her family headed toward the hotel restaurant. "Remember how you said a while back you wish you'd met me as a child? You just did, except I was the oldest and she's the baby. Otherwise, their complaints that she's just like me are pretty accurate."

"Lucky man who ends up with her."

If there was anything her little sister wasn't, it was squeamish. She asked for too many details about how it looked while Deanna cleaned and took care of it for him. She knew by now the swimming "too long" was intentional and well planned on Freddy's part, but she wasn't sure if letting them see the scar so he could tell them how she'd cared for him was part of it. Either way, it worked. At least three of her siblings believed their relationship, especially when he continued to touch her during brunch: caressing her neck or her arm or shoulder, getting up to refill her coffee from the breakfast buffet, as well as her mom's. And the way he kept catching her eyes in that way that said there was no one on earth he'd rather sit next to and kiss goodnight.

Rosie was full of questions about New York and the apartment and just how much they could see from the balcony.

"So did you decorate your place with all thistle bushes?" Zack laughed between gulps of juice.

"Thank you." Deanna rolled her eyes. "No, I'm represented by Canna lilies these days."

"Thistle bushes?" Fred looked amused.

She shrugged with a careful glance at her mom. "We all had some type of flower painted on the wall over our beds when we were little, to remember to respect nature, Mom said. She painted them herself."

"And we all had our own flower." Zack took over. "Mine was a dandelion because I'm so cheery and yet I suck all the strength from her like a dandelion sucks nutrition from the grass."

"Of course they don't. Who told you that?" Her mom's light scold accompanied an austere gaze at the boy.

"Nat and Kim. They do. That's why Dad keeps trying to get rid of them. He even said it was so, just like me."

"They don't. Just the opposite. They help feed the soil. I used to beg your father to leave them alone but it was pointless. Everyone said they weren't supposed to be there so he wouldn't allow it, whatever I said. They feed the soil, just like your cheerfulness feeds my soul. That's why you got the dandelion."

"No shit? Sorry. I mean, are you serious?"

"I'm very serious. You think I would insult you like that?"

He shrugged. "I don't know. Everyone else's is pretty and useful and such, like Rosie's red and orange rose. But me and Dee got a lot of grief about ours." Zack looked over at Fred. "She had thistles." He laughed and took another gulp of juice. "Because she's so prickly."

"Weeds interfering with the beauty of the garden, so dad said." Deanna wasn't sure she'd said it loud enough for anyone but Fred to hear...

"No." Her mom stared. She apparently heard. "Is that what he told you?"

"It's okay, Mom. I know I was the oddball. I'm okay with that."

"*No.*" Her raised voice seemed to surprise her, also. And she quieted again. "No, Deanna. That's not why I painted you a thistle bush. I gave you the thistle because ... it reminds me of your father. Your real father."

She felt herself stiffen. "The one who left? Why? It's not my fault he did."

"Honey, I love thistles. Have you ever seen them? They're beautiful. They're purple: it stands for creativity you know, and they're the symbol of his heritage. His ancestors fought with Brian Boru; they were fearsome and well respected, Scottish hired warriors who went back home instead of taking offered land because home mattered so much to them. That's where you come from. It's why I knew you would go far and do great things. It's why I told you to go when you talked of leaving for the city. Because I knew you would excel there, and you have. The thistle is a symbol of strength. Perseverance against the odds. It's you."

Deanna stared at her mom through the silence. She'd been told her father was brave and strong but she hadn't believed it. After all, a brave and strong man doesn't desert his child. She always thought him a selfish coward. She still did, whatever his background. He'd left the woman he got pregnant, stuck her and just left. He was a selfish coward. She took a sip of her coffee for the movement. "I don't want to hear about him. I don't care about his ancestors."

"Deanna, you don't mean that."

"I do. He walked away from us. He's a coward. I'm nothing like him, and I don't want to know anything about him."

"No, honey. That's not true, and I should have told you sooner."

"I don't want to know. It doesn't matter."

"It does matter. Deanna, he wasn't the coward. I was."

She felt a shudder through her whole system. "No. You stayed. You were there. Don't try to excuse him."

"I used you to try to keep him home." She twisted a napkin in her fingers, her eyes on the table. "They were making allowances. Men with babies to take care of didn't have to go if they had no other means of support. I didn't want him to go."

Deanna felt Fred's eyes but it didn't help. She didn't want to know.

"He was drafted." Fred rubbed her neck, but he spoke to her mom. "She was born at the beginning of Vietnam."

"Yes. I didn't want him to go, so I got pregnant on purpose, gave him a way out. He was furious. He refused to use it. He said he'd send money as he could to help support you but he would never marry me after I tried to manipulate him. I wasn't trying to manipulate him. I was trying to keep him alive. It was wrong. I know now that it was wrong, but I loved him and I'm still glad I did it because I have you. And part of him is still alive, at least."

"Part of him?" Deanna scorned herself for asking. It didn't matter. It didn't.

"He sent money twice and then it stopped. And nothing. I never heard. He was marked as MIA for a while but I never heard if that changed. I have to expect he didn't come home. He would have helped take care of you, for you, not for me. He was an honorable man, Deanna. Strong. Brave. Through everything. You are like him."

Deanna pushed back from the table and walked away.

Daws asked her family to stay, told the attendant he'd be back as he handed her a credit card for the bill, and followed Deanna. He caught up with her as she shoved out the front doors. "Anna, come back inside. It's cold."

She shook her head and kept walking.

He followed only long enough they were away from anyone who might overhear, and took her arm. "Talk to me."

"What's there to say?"

"What are you thinking?"

"Are you kidding?"

He brushed fingers along her face.

"Don't." She backed up and pulled her arm away.

"Anna..."

"We shouldn't have come. Everything's messed up now."

"Why is it?"

She shivered and wrapped her arms around herself, half turned away.

"Nothing has changed, Anna. You're still who you are..."

"No, I'm not. Fred, I was nothing more than a pawn for a protestor. I'm a protest baby. It goes against everything you stand for. She didn't want me. I was a tool. All those years I told myself it didn't matter if my coward father was too chicken to stay around because my mom wanted me and she married a man she didn't want and had more children than she wanted because *he* didn't believe in birth control and I told myself it was for me, because she wanted me that badly. And she didn't even want me. She got stuck with me.

"I built myself up to be the opposite of my coward father, to be stronger than he was, to fill in and help her the way he wouldn't, to protect her. And it was all a lie. He wasn't a coward. She was. I felt sorry for her. I defended her because she wouldn't defend herself. And it was all her doing. That thistle over my bed? She can say what she wants now but it's so obvious. I was a thistle to her, a thorn in her side because her plan didn't work. All these years, I've been degrading a father who did his duty despite her little trick and I've been defending and protecting a coward. What does that make me? Other than naive and gullible and ... and used. I thought it was bad to have men use me, but my own mother did worse than anyone."

She shivered again and he went to her, wrapped his arms around her shaking body. "I think you're looking at it wrong."

Deanna pushed away. "Of course I am. I'm the moron I accuse everyone else of being. I don't know anything."

"Anna, you're not..."

"I am." She backed away, her whole stance a warning for him not to move in again. "And I ... I need time to myself. I can't ... I don't know how to deal with this." She turned and headed down the sidewalk.

"Where are you going?"

She kept walking as she spoke barely loud enough to hear. "I don't know. I just..." She shook her head and kept going.

"Let me know."

She didn't answer and didn't stop.

Maybe he shouldn't have, but he repeated what she said to her mom as they sat in the lobby. He didn't regret making the woman cry. So often, he wanted to tell someone those words, tell them what their own lack of responsibility put onto someone around them. He figured it was fair to do it this once, through Deanna's words.

He couldn't, at this moment with Deanna so upset, feel any empathy for the woman beside him. He'd seen it too often, felt the effects too often. Paid for it too often.

She didn't argue. Daws had to wonder if she'd ever bothered to argue with anyone in her life, to ever stand up for herself. He wanted to tell her to give it a try. Just once.

As the woman talked, about her mistakes, about her daughter who might never forgive her, never come home again, Daws kept an eye on the front door. It had been an hour. He'd hoped she would have calmed by now and come back.

A twinge in his stomach took him to his feet. Maybe she wouldn't. Maybe he'd have to go reel her back in, if he could find her.

He dialed her cell phone. Unavailable. She had it off.

"Let's go." He offered a hand to Mrs. Meyers to help her up.

"Where?"

"To get dessert." He could see she at least considered arguing, but she didn't. Rosie, Zack, and Reese trailed along from where they'd been standing just inside the doors. He took them to his car and held the door, then drove over to the shopping center across the street. "Where's the best place to find something over-the-top in calories?"

With Rosie's suggestion, he parked as close as possible and grabbed his jacket from the back seat.

At his suggestion, Deanna's siblings headed the opposite direction to search for her and he told them to meet back at the Baskin Robbins/A&W. As he scanned the seating area, he felt himself relax and got her mom's attention, pointing out the table all the way in the back.

"How did you know?"

"Go talk to her."

She looked at him wide-eyed. "She won't want to talk to me now. You should..."

"I'll wait here. It's not my place to fix this."

Mrs. Meyers hesitated. But again, she didn't argue.

Daws found a bench nearby where he'd see Deanna if she came out, but where she wouldn't see him, and sat down to wait.

He paced now and then, looking into shop windows, watching

shoppers, keeping an eye out for her siblings so they wouldn't interrupt. He sat a while again, then got restless and went in to browse the jewelry store behind him. He could still see her from the open store layout if she left the area. The clerk asked to help and he shook his head. He wasn't looking for anything.

As happened with Deanna, he found what he didn't know he'd been looking for, and didn't bother to ask the price. Then he went back to the bench. Thirty-five minutes. He hoped the conversation was going well.

"Hey." Rosie flopped down beside him. "We've looked *everywhere*. Why are you just *sitting* here? I thought you were really *cool*. I thought you *loved* her. Why did you let her leave and *why* aren't you looking?"

"She knows how to take care of herself." He couldn't help being amused by the girl.

"But she's upset and I don't blame her. Come on." She stood and grabbed his hand as though she could pull him off the bench. "Come help us look. She has to know you even bothered to *try*. I would want my boyfriend to try to find me when I needed him."

"She's fine."

Zack put an arm around his sister. "Where's Mom?"

"Having dessert." He nodded toward the Baskin Robbins.

After a quick glance at her brother, Rosie took off, ignoring his attempt to stop her. The other two followed. Daws stayed where he was.

He took the necklace out of its box and rubbed a thumb over the charm, let the chain slide down through his fingers. Until he felt someone approach and hid the thing in one hand.

Deanna stepped in front of him, her legs nearly between his. "You've been waiting out here the whole time?"

"You've waited for me often enough."

Her chest rose and fell. Her eyes were red. Her family behind her. People moved around the group, some with a curious glance, others oblivious.

Moving even closer, her legs brushed his thighs and she ran a hand through his hair. It was now long enough her fingers could actually slip underneath. "Let's go home, soldier."

He stood, his body pressing hers as she barely moved back to allow him space to stand. "We have the room another night if you want it, if you need to stay."

"No. I want you to take me home."

He nodded and slid the necklace up around her neck, clasping it and straightening it in front of her chest. "You know blue stands for loyalty. Found this and thought you needed it."

She took the charm in her fingers. "I can't see it."

Rosie pulled a little mirror from her bag and handed it to her sister. "It's beautiful, Dee, and you better keep him 'cause he is really cool."

Deanna studied the heart made of sapphires and met his eyes. "Yes, he is really cool. I do think I'll keep him if he's crazy enough to put up with me."

"I think I'll be all right."

On their way out, he put his jacket on Deanna and handed the hotel room key to Rosie. "It's paid already. Go enjoy the pool and treat your mom to a night off." When no one else noticed, he slipped a fifty into Zack's hand.

She didn't volunteer information about her talk with her mom and he didn't ask. It was between the two of them and Deanna was doing her best to understand. She supposed she never would entirely, any more than her mom understood how Deanna had been happier alone waiting for Freddy to come home than she'd ever been with someone who was home every night.

But now he was home with her every night and it was glorious to cuddle up and sleep beside him and not have to plan for the next departure date. Once things kicked in with Ryan, if the kid would agree, it would change again, to an extent. But she could go visit when she wished, or needed. And touring wasn't year-round.

And it wouldn't start for a couple of years or so. Fred said she'd be more than willing, by that time, to have him out of her hair now and then. She doubted it, but she could deal with it.

He set his book aside when she crawled into bed beside him. Their bed. Deanna was glad to be home.

"What should we do tomorrow?" He kissed her head.

"Nothing."

He chuckled. "Nothing?"

"I have to go back to work Monday. Until then, I want to do nothing, with you."

He held her in close. "Do you want me to find out?"

"Find out what?"

"What happened to him. Your father."

"Oh." She met his gaze. "How would you do that?"

"Not sure, but I'll do my best. If you want to know."

She felt herself frown. "I don't know if I do. Is that horrible? What if he did come back and didn't bother to find me? Not sure I'd want to know."

"His loss if he did. If you ever decide you want to know, I'll do what I can."

"Thank you." She touched her lips to his, teasing. "Rosie's right. You are pretty cool. Think I'll keep you."

He grinned and moved in against her, propping himself half over top. "Think you're going to have to. I already depend on you being here."

Deanna accepted his kiss, his caresses, but her mind wandered. Unusual, since he normally drove everything else out of her head when he was so close. An amazing feat. Normally, her brain was way too overactive.

"What is it, Anna?"

"Sorry."

"What's still bothering you?"

"No, nothing. Doesn't matter." She tried to convince him to continue.

He drew back. "Talk to me."

She sighed and he sat up, propped by pillows, and encouraged her to join him. Tucked under his arm, her head against his shoulder, she caressed his bare chest, traced the scar on his side with a finger. "I don't understand people who won't stand up for what they want, or don't want. Mom didn't want all those kids, you know. She does now that she has them, most days, but she didn't and yet she wouldn't drive into town to talk to the doctor and prevent it. I don't get it. And she couldn't even answer as to why she wouldn't. It's like she didn't know why. How could you not at least know why you wouldn't?"

"She doesn't want to admit it to herself, I suppose."

"I don't know. It just irks me to no end to see people refuse to stand up for themselves. Maybe because I got so sick of doing it when she wouldn't, and when a couple of my sisters wouldn't. How hard is it to say, no, I don't want that? Why do they have to leave it to someone else?"

He ran fingers through her hair. "I don't know, Anna. I've had the same thought. I've seen it plenty. They get too used to someone taking care of things for them and forget how to do for themselves. Easy to blame the parents but then the parents learned it from someone…"

"Or they're just lazy."

"Hm. Don't know, but I can tell you I'd rather be the one jumping in to help than the one who won't do for himself. Couldn't live like that. Just thankful I'm not one of them."

"Yeah, I guess. But then you always get stuck with that." She traced the scar on his side with a finger. "How do you not get mad that you do?"

"I have. But it's my choice. Wouldn't have to. Neither would you."

"And then what? Let the pieces crash where they may? Then I'd get crushed under the rubble, too."

"And you won't let that happen if you can avoid it."

"No. But I'm tired. I'm just so tired I don't always know if I can stand one more fight."

Freddy shifted and tilted her face to his. "I understand that feeling well. But you can, and you will. After you recharge. And that's what we're going to do for a while. Recharge. Ignore the rest of the world. Do our own things. We'll jump back in the game when we're ready."

"Sounds incredible. Recharging with you." Deanna let all of the wandering thoughts dissipate as she let her fingers wander along his skin. "There is something I want to do first, though."

"Yeah? Involve me in any way?"

She laughed. "Oh. In all kinds of ways." Teasing, making him wait, Deanna caressed the most tender areas of his skin, the softest parts of him, and bit his lip lightly.

"Mm, if this is what you meant, I figure we'll do it first, last, and plenty in between. Part of the recharging."

"You are bad, Fred Dawson." She nipped the bottom of his ear, kissed his neck. "I meant I want to meet your up and coming pop star."

Fred pulled back. "That's your one thing?"

"Hm, well, I figure he's going to be a big part of the future..."

"If he agrees, and if it lasts."

"I'm betting he will. And I want to see what's coming."

"Do you?" He rolled her onto her back. "He's doing a New Year's Eve show. Want to go up for it?"

"Yes."

"Hoped you might. Already planned it."

Daws spotted the Reynaulds at a table near the front of the stage, but he didn't want to be obvious, so he led Deanna to a small one close to the back. She was transfixed already. He had to nudge her to see he was holding her chair. She grinned and let him push it in for her.

The place was nearly packed and it was still early. He scanned the crowd. Some were yelling conversation over the music. A good percent, though, were tuned in to the young singer. His sound had changed, mellowed, less mixed, less angry. Getting where he needed to be.

Deanna ordered a fuzzy navel, her schnapps experience with Virginia Gray having expanded her horizons in more ways than one. Daws opted for a gin and tonic. The car was at the hotel. A taxi had brought them and would pick them up again. They were celebrating tonight.

"Wow, he is good." Deanna leaned in against him. "Thought you said he wasn't good with the electric."

Daws watched the kid's technique, a nice solo, before he answered. "Obviously been practicing. Good to see."

She gave him another grin and turned back to Ryan.

The kid had made several changes, in fact. Different bassist, a better one. Different set-up, the others were more background. Less attention to any specific girl. More focus on the room in general. He learned fast. And he listened. Good qualities.

Before long, Ryan spotted him with a quick moment of surprise and gave him a nod. Two song endings later, he announced a break. He paused at his family's table only long enough to grab a swallow of his cola, then made his way over. "Hey, expect to have to save my neck again? Family's here. Have to mind my manners." He scanned Deanna. "Damn, she's hot. She's yours?"

"So much for manners." Daws sipped his drink, his eyes on the kid.

Deanna laughed. "Yes, I'm his. And I'm too old for you so you can stop leering."

"Oh, I don't know. I could make an exception." He took an exaggerated step back from Daws. "Kidding. Don't kill me."

"I wouldn't have to. She would if she needed. Don't think she can't." He set a hand on his girlfriend's shoulder, his rather amused girlfriend. Amused by Ryan. Definitely a charmer. "Deanna Meyers, Ryan Reynauld."

The kid bowed and claimed her hand with a kiss to the fingers. "Soon to be known world-wide." He winked.

"You know, I believe that could actually be true." She reclaimed her hand and took a sip of her drink.

"I'm flattered and that's not easy to do. Hey." He put his attention back on Daws with a brief reply to someone who said hello in passing. "Come on over and sit with my family. There's space."

"Not necessary..."

"Sure it is. You're too far back. Come on. They won't mind. They're still grateful you saved my ass. Or so they say. I was doing fine on my own." He tilted his head and started away as though he didn't expect an argument.

Deanna accepted. She wanted to be closer. Daws couldn't refuse her.

Ryan re-introduced him to Mrs. Reynauld, Will, and Tracy, and held a chair for Deanna as he added the new introduction. He had manners. Even if he did flirt with her as he held the chair.

Daws kept an ear on the conversation around him as he could hear it, enough to be polite to the Reynaulds, but he kept attention on the major's youngest son. In a couple of years, he would be ready. Possibly, he was ready enough by now, music-wise, with the right direction. His mom would never have it, and the kid needed time to finish being a kid.

He'd wait. And Daws wanted that time to establish himself. He wanted Ryan to see him as entrenched inside, as someone with enough experience to guide him. The kid wouldn't be fooled. He had too much of his dad in him.

When Ryan started taking requests, Daws paid even more attention. He rarely turned one down, even if he knew only part of it and had to apologize for not knowing the rest. The audience was impressed. So was Daws. Knowledge of that many songs, in a wide variety, meant the kid was studying his predecessors well. Also a good quality.

"Okay, so one more, then I get back to what I know." Ryan paused to listen to the yelled song titles. But he looked over at Deanna. "Newcomer's choice tonight. Have a suggestion for something really sexy? I can do pretty much whatever you ask." He gave her a mischievous grin.

Daws had a suggestion for him, but he kept that thought to himself.

"Sure." Deanna wrapped an arm around his and gave him a teasing glance before she turned back to Ryan. "Bet you don't know how to do it, though. It's kind of old for someone of your experience level."

The kid laughed. "Try me. You could be surprised." He winked.

A firecracker. Will Reynauld was right on target with that one. His wits would be well matched with Deanna, though.

"Ever hear of a song called *Hey Stoopid*?"

Ryan laughed again. "Hell yeah, but you don't listen to Alice Cooper."

Deanna shrugged. "Just say so if you don't know it and I'll come up with something easier for you."

With a quick raise of the eyebrows, Ryan said something to his band and started messing with a tune. And he worked into the song.

Deanna shook her head in surprise, kept rapt attention on the kid, and leaned in to Daws. "Think I have a new favorite version of this song. You need to grab hold of him if you can. I'll tell Ginny she better, too."

Daws didn't answer. Something inside cringed at the thought of making money off Ryan's talent, as he would if the kid wanted to hire him. But someone would. His guess was a lot of people would. And he would earn anything he got from it, by helping to screen out as many leeches as possible, by steering Ryan in directions better for him, not better for the label or someone else who stood to gain, but better for Ryan. And by stepping in front of him if ever necessary.

He would do it without hesitation.

At the end of the show, Ryan came over to the table, turned a chair backward, and straddled it, facing them. "So." He gulped soda and sopped his moist forehead with his T-shirt sleeve. "Any ideas about people I can start contacting in the business?"

Daws took a swallow of his drink. "You're not ready."

The boy straightened his shoulders. "Ready enough to start checking into it. Might take a while, right? I've been trying but nobody'll talk to me because of my age."

"Ryan, he's right. It's too soon." Mrs. Reynauld threw Daws a warning glance.

"Just want to start checking. Don't worry, I'll finish school fine. Don't want them to look back and find I didn't, need it or not."

"Assuming anyone cares enough to check." Daws swirled his glass and waited for the reaction.

"Oh, they will."

"Seriously, Ry. Don't let the ego get ahead of the talent."

He shrugged at his brother. "Not ego. Determination. Not the same." He looked back at Daws. "So? You know people, right? Gonna put in a word here and there?"

"What's in it for me?"

Ryan laughed. "Money, of course. Bigger I get, better I'll be able to pay. Kept your card. Have a name yet?"

"Yes. My own."

The kid shrugged. "Works for me." He nodded toward Daws, talking to his mom. "Hope you were nice to him. This guy's gonna be the one in charge of saving my ass if I need it."

"Am I?" Daws took another swallow.

"Don't tell me that's gin?" He laughed when Daws didn't answer. "Healed well, anyway." He shoved hair from his forehead to show him where the small gash used to be. Hardly a sign of it left. "So what'll it take to convince you to take me as a client when I need you and can afford to pay you?"

"How do you know you want that?"

"Easy. Three things. First, you got good taste in girls. I like her." He threw Deanna a grin. "Second, you're here again and you're not from around here. Means you're more interested in my music than I know why but I suspect there's a reason. You know how to pick the right horse to back. Shows good music sense. Third." Ryan dropped his eyes for a moment and quieted. "You jumped in to help me for no good reason but that I needed it. My dad was like that. I saw him do it. I respect it. Not many would. My band mates didn't, even. That's good enough for me."

Daws watched for signs that his family had let on who he was. Instead, Mrs. Reynauld explained that she'd lost her husband a couple of years before. She was helping him cover. Supporting his efforts.

He met Ryan's serious gaze. The kid wanted him to agree. It was all over his face. He wasn't nearly as cocky as he pretended to be. He was looking for a safety net before he flew too far out on a limb. "Call me when you need me. I'll be available. But I have guidelines. I don't support self-destructive behavior. You get into the wrong kind of scene and I walk. Won't be part of that. As long as you keep your head in the job, we'll do fine."

"Hey man, no problem. My name matters to me."

"Daws. Don't call me *man*."

He snickered. "Yeah, okay. Daws." He stuck a hand out. "We have a deal?"

"Don't know what you're getting yourself into, Reynauld."

"'Course I don't. But that's half the fun of it. Right? Gotta go out and seize life while you can."

The major's son. At this moment, full of animated, optimistic life spirit, Ryan was nearly a mirror of his father. A good man. Well respected. Honorable and memorable. Something worth being part of.

He accepted the firm handshake. "Look forward to it."

============
============

The Gettysburg Address
President Abraham Lincoln

Four score and seven years ago, our fathers brought forth on this continent a new nation: conceived in liberty, and dedicated to the proposition that all men are created equal.

Now we are engaged in a great civil war ... testing whether that nation, or any nation so conceived and so dedicated ... can long endure. We are met on a great battlefield of that war.

We have come to dedicate a portion of that field as a final resting place for those who here gave their lives that that nation might live. It is altogether fitting and proper that we should do this.

But, in a larger sense, we cannot dedicate ... we cannot consecrate ... we cannot hallow this ground. The brave men, living and dead, who struggled here have consecrated it, far above our poor power to add or detract. The world will little note, nor long remember, what we say here, but it can never forget what they did here. It is for us the living, rather, to be dedicated here to the unfinished work which they who fought here have thus far so nobly advanced.

It is rather for us to be here dedicated to the great task remaining before us ... that from these honored dead we take increased devotion to that cause for which they gave the last full measure of devotion ... that we here highly resolve that these dead shall not have died in vain ... that this nation, under God, shall have a new birth of freedom ... and that government of the people ... by the people ... for the people ... shall not perish from the earth.

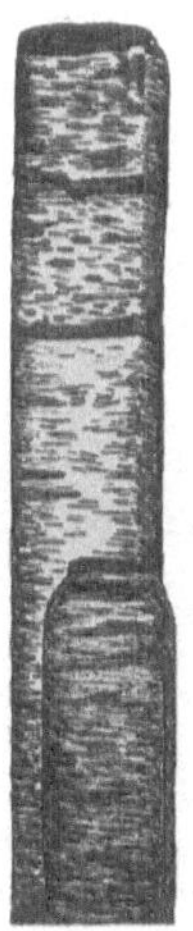

"And like the old soldier in that ballad, I now close my military career
and just fade away, an old soldier who tried to do his duty
as God gave him the sight to see that duty."
General Douglas MacArthur

Author's Note:

This story is a work of fiction. Although real events and personal experiences
provided framework, and it follows a historical timeline as well as remembered
and researched military procedure and protocol, small changes were made to
accommodate the story, which is fully the author's imagination.

Excerpt from...

Off The Moon
LK Hunsaker

Elucidate Publishing 2009

~ ~ 1 ~

"C'mon Reynauld, you're already in fryin' water. Where're ya going?"

Ryan veered around his bodyguard, dodged an ugly silver car doing a bad job of parallel parking, and jogged across the street. Daws would stay on his heels even if he was late, and Mac could wait. What choice did he have? Ryan paid for his time.

He stopped in the middle of the sidewalk to peer up at the office building. The height made him cringe. It wasn't even one of Manhattan's taller buildings. Seven stories. Tall enough.

"What is up with you today?" Daws stopped at his side. "You're edgy as hell and you've seen this building a thousand times. What is so fascinating?"

"Not sure. Maybe nothing." He strode a wide angle around a couple of girls heading his way as they eyed him, pushed through the glass doors, and slid between a crowd of business suits and briefcases. It reminded him of a mud-covered pig rooting through tight-assed penguins. Grinning at the thought, he decided to hold it in his mind to use later.

Daws cut him off. "The paycheck is *that* way."

"And what are you going to do? Throw me over your shoulder and make me go? Come on, lighten up. I'll only be a minute." He feigned anger at the body blockade. "Either get out of my way or come with me. There's something I gotta do."

"Something you can't do across the street where you're supposed to be?"

With an eye on where the girls he'd avoided were descending and joining forces with a few more, Ryan shifted out of their vision as much as possible. "Not unless you can pick this building up and move it over there. Might get kinda messy, though."

Daws crossed his arms in front of his chest. "I'm not one of your flattering fans who thinks you're hysterical. You're holding everyone up and no matter who you are, their time matters..."

Ryan ignored the rant and ducked around to sprint toward the elevator. He called for someone to hold it when it started to close. Stares answered and relief showed on a suit's face just before the door clenched tight. "Great. Guess we do the stairs."

"Let it go, Reynauld. I promise if you're good and play nice, I'll bring you back after work."

"Funny. We're getting a crowd, you know. The more we delay, the more there'll be and I'm not giving in." Ryan noted the glower and did his best not to smile while near-sprinting toward the stairwell. He took the first couple of flights two steps at a time as he called to Daws he'd meet him at the top, and slowed part way up the third. What was he doing? Why did he have to check it out when he was already late? But then, when wasn't he late? Why today? He shrugged. Why not today? It woke him up the night before. There was no sense letting it nag him instead of walking up and looking.

At the seventh floor, he pushed aside the yellow no trespassing tape and turned the door handle. It worked. The hallway he crept into looked like any other hallway, except no one was in it. A deserted office building floor after nine in the morning was a strange thing, but no stranger than the building owner marking the floor off with no explanation. It had gone unused for months. No code violations. No events Ryan ever heard about. It was simply closed. His writer's brain couldn't accept there wasn't a reason. No one else seemed to care, remarking only that the owner was eccentric and did such things from time to time. It wasn't good enough. There was a reason.

Ryan walked down the hallway and peered through open doors. There was nothing in the offices but a few scattered desks and chairs. A good place to write. Quiet. Non-distracting. Maybe that was why he'd been drawn to it. He could find the owner, or have someone find the owner for him, and ask about using it. Not using it exactly, but *not* using it, since the guy wanted it *not* used. Writing music, sitting by himself, wasn't using it – only occupying a bit of its space. There was plenty.

Nearly at the end of the hallway, he turned at a door slam.

"Are you happy yet, moron?" Daws gestured with his phone. "Enrico says there's not only a couple or three girls down there, but a whole damn army of them descending. Can we escape out of here before I have to call in the crew?"

"So we'll wait 'em out." He ran his fingers along the white wall trim. No dust. And no dusty smell. The silvery blue carpet looked new but without the new carpet scent.

"You're shittin' me, right? Wait 'em out? And that's worked real well in the past."

"Yeah, okay." With a deep breath and a thought that Daws would've been more occupied if Ryan had arranged an actual army of girls, he headed back.

And he stopped.

"This way. Let's go."

Taking three steps back, Ryan looked into the empty office he'd just passed. Nothing. He thought he'd seen something, but there was nothing. At his guard's taunt, he continued forward. But the window was open. Why? At the next open door, he peered inside. The window was closed. So was the next one.

"Hang on a second." He returned to the room. The window was open. There were no bars, nothing. And no one there.

"What are you doing now?"

"Something's out there." Ryan drifted closer. The seventh floor. He could see people in the windows across the road, shadows floating around in the building where he was supposed to be.

"Reynauld, if you saw something out that window, it damn well better have been a bird or I'm calling the nuthouse like I should have umpteen times before."

"Maybe it was a bird." Of course. He *was* a moron. What else would he have seen? Too many shots. It was nothing but way too many damn shots the night before. Still, he wasn't sure. And he couldn't look. "Do something for me. Look out the window." He frowned at Daws crossing his arms in front of his chest. "I'll go, no hassle, no stalling ... just look out the window for me."

"Not interested. I've seen pigeons and I'm not a big fan of the dirty creatures."

Ryan gave up. Seven floors were too much to look out over. His stomach twinged already from standing halfway across the room from the open window.

At the door, he paused. He had to know.

With a knot in his throat, he hurried over before Daws could stop him and before he lost his nerve, and touched the frame. A cool breeze slapped at his face. Spring air. Normally he loved it, but this time it made him shiver. Or it was nerves. Daws muttered in the background about leaving his ass there. Ryan knew he wouldn't, not for long. He would be back.

Gritting his teeth, he stepped closer, prepared for the flapping of pigeons. There were no birds. But there were shoes. To his right, on the wide window ledge, a pair of old tennis shoes was perched, their heels against the window and toes pointed forward ... out. His stomach turned while his eyes followed the shoes up to baggy jeans, a faded sweatshirt covering most of the fingers underneath, and a diminutive face with long straight hair sweeping across it with the breeze. Startled eyes caught his: round greenish-brown eyes. A girl. Young, emaciated. Afraid.

What did he do now? Yell for Daws to get the police? It would scare her more and that was probably the last thing that would help. If anything would help. Maybe nothing would. Maybe this would be the life-changing event his brother told him would eventually happen to make him be an adult. Maybe he was destined to live forever with watching a young girl end her life. But not if he could stop it. No amount of venting through songs would ever help him deal with that.

He forced his voice not to shake as he had practiced a bazillion times at the start of his career. "Is the view nice up here? Myself, I prefer the ocean view. You know, 'cause if I fall in the ocean, I can swim. I've yet to learn how to fly, though. But hey, to each his own, right?" He got nothing but a stare. "I bet it's cool to watch everyone down there scurry like ants. I don't have the nerve to look myself. Heights aren't my thing. But hey, describe it for me. I'm visual. I'll get it from what you say."

Her eyes remained on his, wary. She said nothing.

"How about if you come this way more so I can hear you better? I haven't heard a word yet."

When he reached a hand toward her, she slid farther from him. He pulled it down. "Hey, it's okay. I'll listen harder. I'm Ryan. I'm supposed to be at work across the street but decided to check out your place first. Glad I did. I don't often get to meet anyone who goes to extremes to be alone as much as I do. It's quiet out here, huh? Well, not so much since I'm annoying you and you can tell me to go away if you want. I know how it is." Complaining to himself about sounding so stupid, Ryan heard Daws return and tried to wave him away.

"Had enough air yet? I should leave you to deal with that crowd alone. It'd serve you right. What in the hell are you looking at?" Daws stuck his head out.

The girl pulled away more.

"No, it's okay. He'll leave. One of us is bad enough, right?" Ryan shoved the guard back and found her leaning to try to see inside. "Come in. It's okay."

She leaned back against the dirty brick wall. Hair blew into her face and out again.

Ryan studied her features and decided she had to still be in her teens, although it was hard to tell as thin as she was, much too thin to be healthy, and pale. Where were her parents? Other family? Friends? Someone. There had to be someone who wondered where she was, someone who was supposed to be caring for her. He had to gain her trust, at least somewhat. How?

His mind drifted to his favorite thing other than music. "Do you like boats?" She held the stare. "I love boats, and I can tell you the view from a boat drifting out on a quiet lake is like nothing else. Isn't it? Especially when the sun begins to set and even better when it begins to rise. It's been forever since I saw it. How about we go check it out? Weatherman says it's supposed to be gorgeous the next few days. Want to get up before dawn and watch the sun rise over the river? I know a great spot where we won't be bothered."

Her face relaxed.

"I can pick you up from wherever you want and you can bring a friend or two along. I know it would be crazy to accept a blind date from some idiot who just happened to show up on your window ledge, but if you invite someone, it's cool, right? Daws'll be there. He's nearly everywhere I am, although I can ditch him if you'd rather. He's not as grouchy as he looks. Well, he is grouchy, but he's a sweet grouchy. Don't tell him I said that." He waited while she stared. "What do you think? I can try to arrange a boat. Do you like boats?"

"I've never been on one." The voice was nearly a whisper – soft, shy, and still afraid.

"No? Wow, then you're missing something. I bet you'll love it. Can I take you? Not just you, but you and whoever you want to bring. A brother or something is fine, too. Whoever."

As she watched him, the fear drained but something else filled her eyes. Sadness. Longing. She was entirely too desperate. Stupid thought. Of course she was desperate. Why else would she be up there? He wasn't letting her go. She was coming back in. Whatever he had to do, she was coming back in.

To continue Ryan's story, find Off The Moon *at*
ElucidatePublishing.net
or request it from your local independent bookstore.
Also available in ebook.

About The Author

LK Hunsaker is the author of a string of intertwined novels centered around the arts and societal issues, combined with strong romantic elements. Spouse of a decorated career soldier, she has traveled widely, moved several times, raised two children, and earned degrees in psychology and art. Her short stories, poems, articles, and book reviews have been published in literary ezines and print magazines. She is now settled in western Pennsylvania.

LKHunsaker.com
ElucidatePublishing.net